CW01500853

Prologue

Ipu – Goma

Some gomans said it was mad to volunteer for an arduous death, but there was a thin line between madness and courage, and Ipu had no intention of being on the wrong side of it. After all, her death wasn't certain, and someone had to brave the sea again.

The thunder of ocean waves swallowed the squawks from the gulls soaring across the narrow bay. In the distance, the tidal waves broke against the high cliffs of jagged islands that took the brunt of the sea's strength, easing the currents into the flow wetting Ipu's boots. The waters ran dark and grey, full of sand and silt and stones brought with the relentless tides, likely from hundreds or thousands of miles away.

Tall cliffs towered over her on all sides but did nothing to block the windstorms that spurred the sea. Ipu's long robes thrashed despite being tied so tightly to her body that her every movement became wooden. One gust tore up her sleeve and

FATE

OF THE

SLAYER

Andy Blinston

Book 3 of the Rakkan Conquest series

Falbury

Fate Of The Slayer

First published in Great Britain in 2021 by Falbury

Copyright © 2021 Andy Blinston

The moral right of the author has been asserted.

All characters and events in this publication are fictitious and any resemblance to real persons, living or dead, is purely coincidental.

Part 3 in the book series Rakkan Conquest

First Edition, 2021, Andy Blinston

A CIP catalogue record for this book is available from the British Library

ISBN: 978-1-9993139-7-5

All rights reserved.
No part of this book may be used or reproduced in any manner whatsoever, including internet usage, without written permission from the author. Publications are exempt in the case of brief quotations in critical reviews or articles.

Falbury Publishing

the tidal dunes
aretean sea
n
w
e
s
branz
branz legion
cephos
the uncharted mountains
forest of whispers
thrane
dolthea
viridia
viridian legion
laltos
azuria
azure legion
urukan mine
the azurian glacier

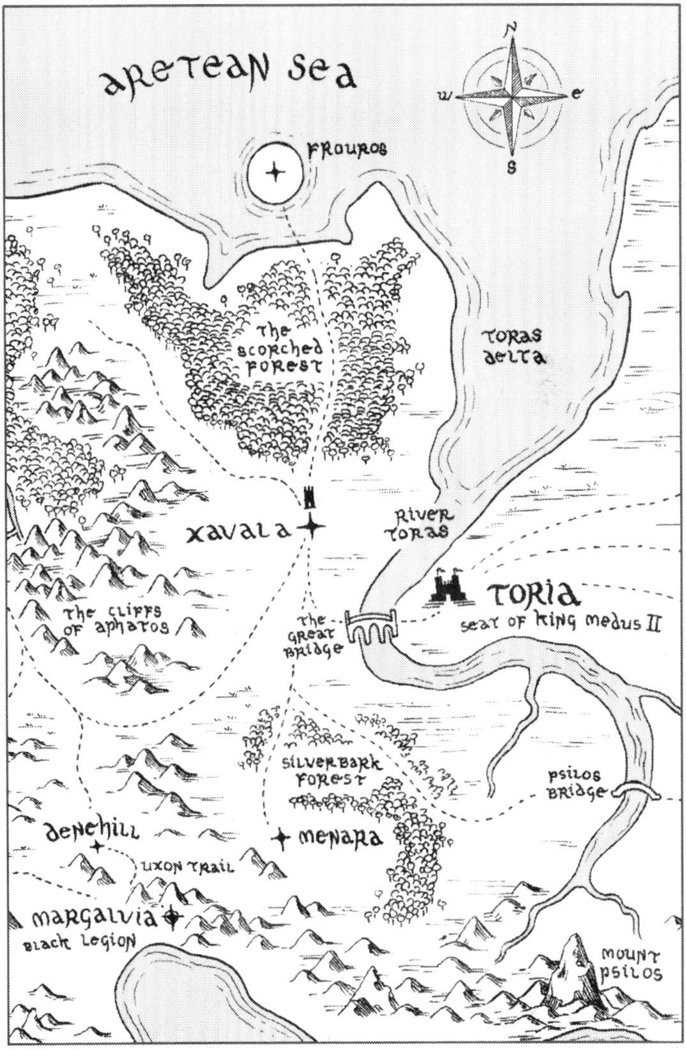

Aretean Sea
N
W
E
S
Frouros
The Scorched Forest
Toras Delta
Xavala
River Toras
Toria
Seat of King Medus II
The Cliffs of Aphatos
The Great Bridge
Silverbark Forest
Psilos Bridge
Denehill
Menara
Uxon Trail
Margalvia
Black Legion
Mount Psilos

Character List

Margalvia
Varro – Warlord of the Black Legion
Julius – Black Commander
Darius – Exiled Black Legionnaire
Sulla – Red Militia Chief
Flora – Friend of Sulla

Former Laltos
Hera – Regent
Lex / Alexandra – Algus – House of Theodoros
Selene – Algus – House of Theodoros
Gorgias – Algus – House of Hera
Nikolaos – Algus – House of Hera

Viridia
Hadrian – Warlord of the Viridian Legion
Rufus – Viridian Commander

Toria
King Medus II – King of Toria and the Torian Empire
Ophelia – King's Orator
Jason – Algus – King's Sword

Other
Archimedes – deceased goman commander of Torian army
Aristippus – Regent of Xavala
Brutus – deceased Black Centurion
Amid – deceased brother of Darius
Omid – deceased slave of Ismene
Waif Magician / Shirin – Half-algus, half-goman hermit

Escorts
Lyra – Darius's panther
Tiro – Lex's peregrine falcon
Paris – Selene's deceased pteron

exposed her right forearm for the briefest of moments before she hurriedly grabbed the cloth and covered it once more.

"*You were right.*" Khayu's voice entered her mind as he stepped beside her on the beach. "*The sea is calmer today. We should risk it.*" Her husband's voice played monotone yet coarse in Ipu's head like he growled every word.

It wasn't just the risk that caused her hesitation. If this one-way trip meant leaving their home forever, she had to be sure.

Although he was younger, Khayu stood a foot taller than Ipu, and what Khayu lacked in experience, he made up for in the strength of his shorter cogi. The goman wore robes that wrapped his body from head to foot, leaving only his mouthless face and dark eyes showing. The clothes were similar to Ipu's and every goman's, but his were darker and melded with his skin to make his eyes like those of a watching shadow.

"*Our odds of survival are better than usual but still slight.*" Ipu glanced back at the wooden boat that waited on the steep beach. Despite having a deep-V hull and self-righting weights to survive the swells and monsters, she'd seen the boat smashed to splinters around her in many of her memories of the future.

"*I hope they give the order today,*" Khayu said. "*Nothing is worse than this wait.*"

"*We don't leave until I say.*" Ipu gazed out at the sea again, wondering how blissful it would be to not know what was to come. "*Sometimes, I envy your short cogi.*"

"*Don't patronise me.*" Anger flashed in Khayu's eyes before disappearing. "*I'd trade all the contests I won to see what you see now. I can't see beyond our long voyage over the sea.*"

"*Be careful what you desire.*" Ipu rubbed her husband's shoulder with a gloved hand. "*I don't envy your fighting skills but that you don't see what lies ahead. You should pray that the sea batters and drowns us, or that the western current drags us out into the Unknown Ocean to starve and desiccate, because either is a better fate than what awaits us south of the Aretean Sea."*

"You think me so weak that I'm unable to bear the knowledge of rakkans?" Khayu watched the frothing water in silence for a few moments, and when Ipu left his question unanswered, he said, *"Tell me what you see."*

There were too many possibilities in Ipu's future memories to divulge them all, but she'd acquiesce to her husband's wish. She took a step forward, readied her cogi powers, and lost focus in her eyes. She plunged herself into her possible future memories, searching through the almost infinite sea of battle, hardship and pain. No matter how practised she was, the sensation always felt foreign, experiencing her life as it could be but without hearing, without touch and without smell.

Cogi was the art of mastering chaos. Memories assaulted her in too large a volume to comprehend. But among the havoc, patterns emerged. Clusters of memories came together, and although she couldn't count them, she at least perceived their density and knew which were most likely. Many visions were of her and her husband stranded on a boat in the middle of a seemingly unending ocean, starving, ravaged by waves and saltwater. One memory in particular caught her attention, and she dared linger on it for a second. Her future self clung to a floating plank and stared intently at a message scratched upon the wood that read, "We left the second day after the full moon." That wasn't today.

She dwelled on a few more visions, again staring at messages she'd carved upon the boat. Only a few mentioned the exact circumstances she was in now. But those weren't the most plentiful visions. Unlike all the other times she'd used her cogi recently, this time, there were many of her and Khayu in foreign lands south of the Aretean Sea, weary but very much alive.

In some, they were alone. In others, they commanded an army. But one vision made her physically flinch. She knew she shouldn't dive into it entirely, but she couldn't resist. Submitting and plunging in, her vision filled with only the sights she would see in this particular future.

The sandy dunes around her shook and shimmered under what must have been stiff winds. Thick clouds of sand swirled around the two figures in front of her and would have blinded her had she not had her hands around her eyes to shield them.

Her husband clashed swords with a foe wielding such strength that the parry threw Khayu off his feet and skidding across the sand. Fire swirled in the foe's eyes and enveloped his sword, radiating against his chalky skin. More muscle-bound than most goman soldiers, this foe wore a cuirass made of dark metal that bore so many scars they marred the pattern on its front. But she had no doubt this was a rakkan.

Khayu scrambled back to his feet, shielding his own eyes from the blinding sands, then rushed towards the rakkan. When the two neared each other, Khayu thrust his sword and gaped as the rakkan dodged to the side. The rakkan swung to counter with his own blade, but Khayu had ducked and reached with a bare hand towards the rakkan's uncovered neck. His fingers touched the rakkan's skin for the briefest of moments before the foe shoved Khayu away and into the sand once again.

With a bellow that Ipu couldn't hear but that shook her nerve nonetheless, the foe lunged and swung his sword at Khayu. Ipu's husband tried to twist and dodge, but the blow struck his turned back, scoring a savage cut that lodged into his spine while his clothes erupted in flames. There was no scream of pain, no sensation of the sand battering her skin, only her husband's agonised grimace and contorting body.

Ipu tore her attention away from the vision as she felt her present face warp with grief. She knew that was how most of those visions ended. Yet she also reminded herself that Khayu would see such outcomes in his own time when they came within the narrow range of his cogi. He'd shape his fate. At least, that was what she had to keep telling herself.

Once again amongst the vast array of possible futures, Ipu couldn't say how likely it was that they survived the journey up until the window of time she saw into. There were no cogi visions of darkness. Death was a veiled realm known only to the One Mind. Only the obvious fatal blows stood out, like watching a sword stab through her gut or looking down to see an arrow lodged into her thigh. There were many of those. She'd seen enough.

Bringing her mind back to her body and the roaring sea in front of her, Ipu focused her eyes and dipped her head. It would be weeks before they did battle with the demons that she'd only experienced in visions and stories from the elders. For her entire life, she'd prepared for this excursion, yet it brought more dread than anticipation. If only Khayu hadn't been ordered to accompany her on such a dangerous task…

"*The Council may be right,*" Ipu said. "*The rakkans might be immune to our powers, but it's hard to say.*" Why were future memories so often ambiguous? "*We need to be careful. I've seen you suffer under their burns enough times to guess at the pain they inflict.*"

Khayu baulked and adjusted his clothes to ensure they covered his neck, his hand trembling slightly. "*It would take much pain to overcome me. Why must you always focus on whatever foresight makes me appear worst?*"

If only that were true, but Ipu wouldn't correct her husband. She'd allow him to cling to the dignity the rakkans might soon strip from him. The first time Ipu had seen them fight in her mind, she hadn't slept for days. "*They have great numbers that a handful of gomans cannot match.*"

"*If the Council are correct,*" Khayu said, "*then we need to strike first. Our mission should be to wipe them out, not delay them until the sea calms.*"

"*I'll believe in a calm sea when I see it.*" Though not the oldest of gomans, Ipu had lived beside the sea for most of her life and was yet to witness it anything less than turbulent, never mind calm. "*Outside of the Council, has anyone foreseen the waters safe enough to launch our invasion?*"

Khayu shook his head. "*Not that I know of. We must still be some time away from it.*"

Behind the bay, thousands of goman warriors had been camped for so long that the settlement had as many stone buildings and walls as a town. Maintaining such a place wasn't without cost, but if the Council deemed the camp necessary, it was.

"*Attention!*"

The voice boomed in Ipu's mind, and she instinctively straightened her posture and turned back to face the direction of the encampment. Khayu did likewise, and after a few seconds of searching, Ipu spotted her superior officer's figure high on the cliff above the bay.

"*We've had orders from the Council,*" the officer said.

Finally, was this the beginning of the end? Would their army launch?

"*We're ready to embark,*" Khayu said. "*The food is wrapped and stowed.*"

"*Good,*" the officer said. "*Ipu, is the time right?*"

Ipu's husband turned to her expectantly as she pondered the question. Their odds of survival seemed better than usual but still short. Most likely, they'd either survive together or die together. That would have to do.

"*It's time,*" she said.

"*Good,*" the officer said. "*Make ready. You leave within the hour, but I'm afraid you two will go alone.*"

Both gomans' postures deflated. Despite having known this was probable, Ipu had been hoping the odds turned in their favour in time.

"*Your chances of survival are acceptable for two,*" the officer continued, "*but the Council has deemed it too perilous for a larger force. The current would drag us too far away to land our forces. My soldiers will be down soon to help you launch. Then we'll try again tomorrow and will be behind you as soon as we can.*" With that, he turned and marched away.

Khayu stomped towards the boat and kicked the stones at his feet with such a force that Ipu heard the bangs as they ricocheted from the hull.

"*You're right,*" Ipu said.

Khayu raised an eyebrow. "*About what?*"

"*The wait is the worst. It brings the fear of death with no accomplishment to show for it. We should be relieved that today was the last wait for us.*"

"*Relieved? Perhaps death will feel like a relief when it comes, but my visions of drowning are…*"

At least Ipu's cogi was long enough that she no longer saw the many visions of them drowning within the week. She took a slip of parchment from her pocket and a reed pen, then began writing all the details of what they planned to do and why they'd chosen this moment so that her past self had a chance to see it.

"*Sometimes I feel cogi is a curse,*" Khayu said, "*but if it allows for Goma's survival, then I'll gladly bear it.*"

If Khayu's tortured face in Ipu's visions was anything to go by, death by rakkans definitely wasn't to be embraced either. Better for the sea to take him.

"*Cogi brings bad along with the good,*" Ipu said. "*We'd have fallen to the rakkans decades ago had the Council not guided and saved us. We see and we shape fate.*"

"*We do? Or they do?*"

Questioning the Council was so rare an occurrence that it surprised Ipu how much offence and hatred the remark stirred within her. But as quickly as the feeling had come, she calmed it with a few deep breaths. "*The gomans do. And if fate has determined only us or the rakkans survive, then it will be us.*"

Khayu came towards her, slipped the glove off his right hand, and held it out. He stopped a few yards away and waited, nervous and vulnerable in a way he only made himself to her. She finished staring at her message before putting it away and slowly pulled off her glove too. The wind on her hand felt foreign, a rare touch to her bare flesh. After getting used to the sensation for a few moments, she reached out too.

They held their hands a few inches apart for a while, enjoying the anticipation brought by the custom that protected gomans from one another and ensured both parties were willing to take the risk, to meet skin to skin.

After a time had passed, they moved gently forward, and their palms slipped together, sudden warmth to break the chilling gales. Their minds became one as their soft skin met in a way that never failed to send gooseflesh across her arm. Khayu was the only one she'd ever allowed to touch her, and she opened her mind up to him. She felt his dread, for her, for their future away from Goma. But alongside fear was courage, stubbornness and drive.

He was right to dread, and she soon felt him searching her mind for what she'd seen of his future. But there was no way she'd let him see that.

Ipu pulled away and felt Khayu's mind jolt apart from hers, like a sharp and sudden pain behind her eyes that only lasted a few moments.

"*Fear not,*" she said. "*We go to death or glory. Either way, it will be by the will of the One Mind.*"

"*I care only that I can protect you there.*"

Of that, there was no doubt. "*You will. If we survive, the mere mention of your name will be enough to drive back our enemies.*"

Khayu raised an eyebrow. "*Have you chosen it then, my name in the local tongue?*"

She hadn't so much chosen it as seen it in their future, in one of the many letters she would write for her eyes only. If the humans were to receive them as saviours and not conquerors, then a local name was imperative.

Ipu slipped the glove back over her hand and turned to face the sea they'd soon cross or die within. "*You will call yourself Archimedes.*"

1

Darius – Ruins of Laltos

Darius steadied the reins of his swift as the once formidable walls of Laltos rose above the horizon. The dark mane of his special horse quivered while it shook its head nervously, as if it smelled the death in the air. He knew his panther, Lyra, shared the unease. Laltos was now only a city of ruined stone and rotten flesh and bones, plundered and razed in an assault that Darius was still to avenge. The Viridian Warlord hadn't paid for his crimes against Laltos or his attack on Lyra, but he would, however long the hunt took.

Despite Darius's revulsion at the assault on the city before him, his jaw clenched with a wave of different anger too, one born from the torment Laltos had inflicted upon him. They said suffering was life's way of teaching wisdom, but he'd rather have remained ignorant.

In the year since the battle he longed to abolish from his memory, rakkans and humans had fought over the scraps. Not even morsels now remained—at least, that's what everyone thought. He was here at Lex's behest to check her most valuable, hidden vault inside the city.

He led his swift farther along the road through the waste, around the harrowed mess of old earthwork ramparts and trenches half-filled with dirt disturbed by the wind. The summer rains over the last few months hadn't been enough to revive this place, a land left for the wild to retake and the sun to parch. As he drew closer to the gates of the city, the land was so trampled by boots and hooves it barely yielded a blade of grass. All that sprouted were bodies.

Someone had dug ditches for the dead but not nearly deep enough, leaving hands and feet poking out to be pecked to bone by scavenger birds. But while many of the dead lay as broken skeletons, some were fresh, half-naked and showing stained skin with blotches both dark and pallid. *Xavalans.* Only the Silk City would have failed to properly bury the fallen. Despite these being the bodies of his enemies, Darius dwelled on his past decision to kill Archimedes and the death that act had unleashed on the Empire.

Brutus had taught him to find the good in terrible circumstances, those untouched nuggets of goodness among the carnage. But what was the point? Even if you found a piece of ripe corn in a pile of excrement, would you eat it or toss it away?

While he tried to judge how old the most recent corpses were, Lyra heard something—a growing thunder that she'd sensed many times in the past few months, a noise that his own mind now grasped via hers.

Usually, he didn't have such a keen insight into her senses, but for the last year, he'd had these curious acute glimpses deeper into her mind than ever before.

He shook his head and turned his attention back to his surroundings. This wasn't the time for pondering. For now, he stayed atop his swift and glanced south, seeing what he'd expected—a growing cloud of dust on the road. The haze soon parted to reveal a dark mass moving too swiftly to be on foot.

The horde numbered at least a dozen across, but how deep their ranks went was impossible to say. This far west, only the Silk City had so many horses. They used them to raid and kill what or whoever tried to re-establish in this forsaken place, and that wasn't usually rakkans or even soldiers.

Traitors. If the Xavalans hadn't betrayed Laltos, perhaps the city would still stand, perhaps Brutus and Selene would still be with him rather than distant voices he heard only in memories.

The band was a few minutes away, so his swift could easily carry him somewhere safe. But he froze, a tension in his neck spreading to his head. They were heading north to the towns and villages there. They might have worn Xavalan colours of tan and gold, but they were the King's men.

He focused harder on the riders to see whether any algus were among them. There were always some, but not enough to faze him. Usually. The life of an exile had its perks—he fought whenever he pleased.

Lyra, feel like a scrap? I could use some exercise. It had been days since he'd last swung a sword.

Lyra's ears stood tall and rigid while she fixated on the approaching band, and one needn't be a mind reader to know her violent thoughts.

He quickly dismounted and shed the long dark cloak he wore to hide amongst humans. Underneath, his cold kuraminium cuirass finally saw light again. He wore the armour over a dark, sleeveless tunic that left his rakkan arms bare so that he could sense movements in the air. On his left forearm, he wore a scarred kuraminium armguard, but that was the only other piece of armour he sported. There was only so much kuraminium a swift could carry over the long distances he now roamed.

He tossed his cloak onto the swift's back, then looked at the round shield attached to the saddle. If he were facing archers, he'd use it, but the Silk City had no one skilled enough with a bow on horseback for him to fear. His armguard would be enough to block, should he need to. The two swords at his waist both thirsted for blood.

With a slap on its backside, he sent his swift towards the city and turned to face his foes. They were less than a minute away, and their readied lances and shields meant they'd spotted him. The drumming of hooves swelled.

Lyra, wait amongst the bodies until I say.

She crept towards the least-putrid ditch she could find while Darius walked out onto the tightly fitted stones that made the road. He ran a hand through his long, dark hair to slick it back and did the same with his shaggy beard. Then he withdrew both of his gladii. Just the feel of the cold metal hilts in his hands set his heart racing. Taking a deep breath, he emptied his mind of the pain and memories this place stirred within him, and instead, he willed a familiar icy touch onto his fingers.

Flaring into life, algor sparked from his hands and crept down his swords like vines of ice that would cut through metal and limbs. The cavalry would think him a lone hostile algus—not much of a threat for a mounted band. But after his first move, they'd know they not only faced a godlike human but one with the strength of his rakkan half—the Slayer of Gods. The name still made him uneasy, but after Xavala's betrayal, his vengeance had made it more and more fitting.

The riders fanned out into the road at least two-dozen wide now with another row behind, their iron helmets bobbing from the gallop. There were no signs of any armour on the horses, and they were too small to be the heavy warhorses the Silk City used in battle. These steeds were lean, accustomed to raiding and long distances. But nonetheless fearsome.

A few riders at the flanks spread wider and flared algor from their swords. A rider at the back hoisted a banner, a plain tan flag with a golden sun at its centre that matched the golden cloaks flapping wildly behind the riders.

Then the horses in front burst into a charge. The lances of the riders dropped until their razor points reached Darius's height, stretching out much farther than his swords ever could.

He bent his knees. The horses surged straight for him, seconds away. Despite having overcome incoming charges before, the sight and thunder had his every instinct urging him to flee with a primal terror.

But he stood firm through force of will, ignoring his pounding heart. While algor continued flaring from his swords, he summoned ferven in his throat and unleashed a hellish roar at the galloping beasts. The horse directly ahead of him flinched and veered to the side, turning its head from the new animal before it. The sudden movement sent the point of the rider's lance swinging away from him—Darius's opening.

He leapt into the air while the horses charged onwards. He soared over the height of the stallions' heads and readied his brilliant swords to meet the murderous riders.

The steeds on either side of him turned farther away and barged into adjacent horses, but Darius focused his attention on the rider directly in front, whose helmet had only just lifted to better reveal the man's wide, fearful eyes. The soldier raised his shield too late.

Darius swung his left sword and sliced through the man's neck and spine as he reached the peak of his leap. The rider behind closed in and thrust out his lance, but Darius's skin sensed the strike in the air before he saw the man move. He parried the lance's shaft with his other sword and diverted the point from his face. Now falling, he braced as his body crashed into the rider and horse, sending them all spinning to the ground in a cloud of stones and dust and clanging metal. The horse squealed. The man growled in pain as Darius fell on top of him and crushed his knee beneath the cuirass.

A heartbeat later, Darius leapt back to his feet and sliced through the man's other knee for good measure. Then he turned to face the backs of the stampeding horses. A few made no effort to turn and carried on into the dead fields, but most of the riders tugged their reins and wheeled the horses around for another attempt, now led at the front by three algus who made their presence plain and obvious. They'd sheathed their swords and had joined their soldiers in taking lances, conjuring algor from shaft to tip. Shouts rang out from the riders, but too far away to sound like anything but shrill fright.

This time, they wouldn't charge head-on. They'd attempt to spear him from a distance.

Darius stepped to the side until he was off the road, watching every movement of the horses as he opened an inviting path for them to gallop along, right between him and the ditch wherein Lyra crouched. If he didn't kill at least one Xavalan algus today, it would be a wasted day.

When the cavalry had turned and reformed, they galloped towards him again, this time with only three horses abreast and deep ranks. Those on the right side—closest to him—lowered their lances as hooves clattered on the road.

Darius watched, waited until they were within a few seconds of reaching Lyra's hiding place.

Now!

Lyra burst from the ditch with a roar that sent the two closest horses jerking into their neighbours. The panther took a swipe at one before sprinting with them and harrying the horses on the left flank, herding the group to their right and closer to Darius's waiting blades.

Two of the algus at the front glanced over their shoulders at the commotion, but the third charged on, his lance almost ready to make an attempt on Darius's body.

He was an appealing target—tall, dark and still. Until the last moment.

As the lance came within a few feet, he sprang forward and swiped it aside with one of his swords. The force of the blow sent the lance spinning from the rider's grasp, and it flew back around and bashed the rider in the face, sending him flailing backwards from his horse and into the head of the next galloping steed. The stallions far enough behind veered to the side, but those that couldn't crashed and tumbled or leapt and hoped. Horses and riders shrieked and squealed as Darius used his rakkan senses to dodge every flailing arm and leg from the skidding humans and horses while striking out at anyone within reach.

Now filled with rage, he banished the algor on his swords and instead sent tongues of flame down the blades. His first strike cleaved a tumbling man through his waist, while his next stabbed through another's eye and skull.

The first algus he met lay with her limbs twisted and bleeding under a shaken horse, and Darius's sword quickly found her neck. Those men that had been fortunate enough to remain mounted soon dispersed in whatever direction took them furthest from him. Another half dozen lay either dead or dying from the fall, and a few others—one algus among them—had regained their feet and drawn their swords. The soldiers' once golden cloaks now hung ragged and stained with dirt and blood.

Lyra pounced on one from behind and sank her fangs into his sword arm. The man screamed and writhed, but the others only gaped at their comrade nervously and watched his futile struggles with a beast beyond his weight and strength. Darius's panther wouldn't be able to fight them all off should they rally, but they knew of the horror he inflicted on any man that so much as scratched his escort.

Darius glared at the last algus and let ferven blaze in his eyes. The woman's round cheeks were flushed and fat from the fruits of looted wealth.

This was for Laltos. This was for Selene, for Brutus, and the tens of thousands of names that had died forgotten. With a roar of fury, he surged forward, jumping over the bodies, and aimed his first blow straight at the algus's midsection.

She was clever enough not to parry, but her dodge was too slow and expected. His first swing missed as she lunged to her right, but he swung his other gladius around and smashed it into her body. Her sword blocked the gladius's bite, but the force knocked her into the air, and her winded body hadn't touched the ground before he darted in and stabbed clean through her chain mail and stomach, sending iron rings clanging onto the road.

She choked, coughed up blood. And he turned at once to the last survivors.

They all bolted, cowards without numbers or might on their side. Darius would show them the same mercy they'd given to the refugees fleeing Laltos. None.

He leapt over more fallen bodies and weaved between the horses as they got back to their feet. The men were slow to run but quick to feel the cut of his gladii. His strikes landed with such precision that a cry barely escaped the lips of most. Despite running in all directions, less than a minute passed before his sword cut off the breath of the last man. Then all that filled the air again was silence and death.

Lyra had finished her man and surveyed the rest of the fallen for survivors while Darius took a moment for the rush of the battle to ease. There were two things left to do, neither pleasant, but that had become habits of his after a fight. He sheathed his swords and found one bleeding man at his feet, trying not to focus on the coppery smell. Then he knelt and placed his hands into the largest pool of blood. As always, the touch sent shivers through him, but the sickness was less; the light-headedness barely troubled him, even when he proceeded to spread the blood over the backs of his hands and arms. Any passerby would think him more of a savage than the songs of his enemies told, but this wasn't about horror or revelling. Unconquered weaknesses had only stopped him from protecting those he loved. Fear of blood was a burden he was determined to quell.

But while he waited to grow accustomed to the sensation on his skin, Lyra sent him a warning. He turned to see her backing away from the downed rotund algus, who still breathed. *Good.* It was time for his second bad habit.

2

Darius – Ruins of Laltos

Darius loomed over the woman as she gaped at his bloodied hands. The stench from her lacerated belly made him want to vomit more than the red ever had, but what disturbed him most was the fear now radiating from her. Only truly wicked people held enough spite to overwhelm the terror of death, and it was so much easier to look them in the eye; they weren't so stricken. At times like this, it was hard not to think of himself as the monster they all said he was, the monster that Selene had believed him to be when she'd taken him in chains to this once strong city.

"Answer me a question," he growled while brandishing a gladius, "and I'll end your suffering."

The woman shivered. "Are you the Slayer?"

Darius looked over the dead marauders at his feet. "Do you really need to ask?"

The woman didn't react to the words other than spitting blood from her mouth.

"Were you here after the Battle of Laltos?" Darius asked.

Her eyes widened, cheeks paled.

"I won't torment you if you were," he clarified. "It's answers I seek. You've already felt my vengeance."

After a few seconds of hesitation, the plump woman nodded. "I was in the"—she coughed, more red dribbling down her chin—"first wave that besieged the Viridians after they took the city."

Darius's next question formed on his lips, but he took a second to muster the courage to ask it. After so long and asking so many people, did he really expect a different answer this time?

He cleared his throat. "There was an algus left here—auburn hair, fairly strong build and olive skin." *And a smile that could tame a slayer.* "She was left in the city. Did you ever see anyone like that?"

The woman's eyes flickered for a while before she shook her head.

That's how they all answered. But he'd searched the city as soon as he could after the Viridians and Xavalans had ended the siege. There hadn't even been a trace of Selene's body.

"I have one more thing to ask." Darius stepped closer until he stood right above the woman's head. Then in one swift, charitable movement, he sliced with his sword.

Her head rolled to the side and spilled gore while dark clouds drifted across the sun and cast a fresh, deep shade upon him.

"When will I be able to stop asking that question?" he whispered.

Despite a year passing, he couldn't say he'd forgiven Selene for her betrayal. But neither could he forget the love they'd shared. Nor could he shake the loss that weighed upon him during every quiet moment. Perhaps if he hadn't lost Brutus too, life would be more bearable, or if he'd been allowed to stay with Lex and Sulla in the city he'd called home.

Lyra padded across to him and rubbed her body across his leg. At least he hadn't lost his escort. Who knew what kind of savage he'd have become if she'd succumbed to her wounds.

He knelt and inspected every tooth, claw and inch of her to ensure she hadn't been harmed. She fidgeted while he checked, as if the attention was unwanted, but he knew she'd have walked away if she hadn't enjoyed his touch.

Once reassured any scrapes she'd suffered were minor, he stood and made his way towards the city and back to his swift, leaving the carnage behind him. *That's enough battle for one day.*

He retrieved his swift and cloak, then passed through the burnt and shredded city gates. Stones larger than he could lift littered the streets and bore deep scars. It had taken many Xavalans to starve out the Viridians, but after collecting what plunder they could, Hadrian and his best commanders had launched a sortie to break through their enemies' ranks and retreat to Viridia. Despite the Silk City's cavalry harrying their every step, most had made it back home.

Did it matter who was victorious in the war still raging? As long as they killed each other, Darius's failure to take revenge didn't consume him.

Now the only noise from the city was the occasional scuttling of a rat, or at least what Darius hoped was a rat and not a spirit of one of the many slaughtered here. But whatever stirred here, he sensed it was indeed alive.

While he passed through the ruins, something flew from one broken rooftop to another behind him. If Lyra hadn't noticed, he'd have been unaware. But his panther had sensed the birdlike creature following him at a distance for months. She somehow always seemed to know when it was near, but it flew away every time he tried to get close. Odds were good that it was an escort, but whose?

He rounded a corner into a narrow street and stopped his swift tight against the remnants of a wall. He waited, straining his ears for the sound of the creature's claws grabbing the roof above. A few moments later, the scratching arrived, and he gazed up.

What he spied brought a gasp from his mouth. This wasn't a bird; it was a pteron with dark scales and shark-like teeth, just like Selene's escort had been—only this one had a reptilian wingspan twice as large and was mottled with green blotches. Whoever's it was, he wanted to find out.

Get it.

Lyra started towards a pile of rubble and began climbing up to the rooftop. At first, the pteron made no movement and just stared at him calmly, with a certain curiosity but no malevolence—no *obvious* malevolence, at least.

"Who are you?" Darius shouted the question intended for the one behind the pteron, rather than the reptile itself.

The escort made no movement until Lyra was bounding across the roof and only a few heartbeats from grabbing the spy in her jaws.

Don't kill it.

But as Lyra pounced and opened her mouth to grab the pteron, it took off and left her biting air.

Darius stared as the flapping creature escaped once again, a dark blot against the grey clouds above. He could use his bow to bring the creature down, but he had neither the skill nor the inclination. What good would killing the thing do? All the pteron ever did was watch, and at least it distracted him from the blood still on his hands.

Had someone sent the escort to taunt him, to send a reminder of the woman he'd lost? Because he needed no reminding.

After Lyra came down from the roof, the pteron was nowhere to be seen, so Darius set off again and reminded himself of why he'd come here. Although Lex wanted him to search the Laltos Bank, there was one place he had to visit first.

The upper city was a mess of collapsed buildings and remains, and by the time he reached the palace, it was almost unrecognisable. The once white towers looked down on him with weathered and ashen faces. Some pillars and walls lay in rubble, with the marble facades stripped away along with any statue or valuable that had survived the sacking.

When close, Darius dismounted and walked the rest of the way. Lyra set off at a run, and he eventually nudged his swift towards an overgrown patch of grass to graze before he followed his escort to the back of the palace, to the hole in the wall where he'd last seen Selene. Fresh rubble littered the ground, where the hole had been cleft even wider since he'd last been there and scoured every inch of the surrounding area. He froze before stepping through the gap, as if watching her ghost stumble out of sight like she had the last time he'd seen her.

Lex and the others assumed Selene was dead, and they were probably right. But the gnawing doubt inside him wouldn't rest. When he'd returned to Laltos soon after the battle, he'd found Selene's boot on the ground. But no body. The scratches around the boot and the lack of bones or even ashes had sent a chill through him that had only worsened the more time passed. The humans in the west whispered stories of Viridians capturing algus. If she'd been taken and suffered the same anguish he had in the torture chambers of Laltos…

Was the pteron following him a sign or a distraction? When was a person right to give up hope? He'd grown used to making decisions for himself since his exile, but some choices were still impossible.

A raindrop hit his nose. He cursed with a glance up at the dark clouds above that threatened to ruin his day further. Since growing his hair and beard long, the damned thatch took an age to dry, especially in the chilly mountains he often traipsed. As he pondered, Lyra went to the mouth of the tunnel Sulla's men had dug for the Xavalans, the one Darius had caved in a year earlier.

His escort sensed the pteron return, but he caught no sight of it.

Let's rest. We can visit the bank tonight. He followed Lyra into a nook amongst the rocks, then lay down and wrapped his cloak tightly around himself. Not long after he closed his eyes, the patter of raindrops swelled into a hiss.

Sleep eluded him and left him turning from side to side for who knew how long, but however much he rested, when he next opened his eyes, evening had arrived, and the rain had ceased after leaving puddles on the rutted ground. The new silence struck him as more eery than the last and was joined by an even deeper sense of solitude.

Without having to look, he knew Lyra's presence was no longer nearby. *Girl? Where are you?*

Somewhere in the distance, he sensed her turn and head back towards him, and thankfully it wasn't long until a rattle of stones announced her arrival inside the tunnel. He peered through a gap in the wall of collapsed rocks that a man would struggle to crawl through and spotted Lyra's amber eyes in the darkness.

Find something? The blood smeared on her jaws confirmed so, and when she'd slinked free, he patted her extended belly, the

34

hardness within having the feel of a large meal recently eaten. He knew panthers didn't eat mice or underground animals; they were too small. *You found a way through?*

She licked her lips, confirming so.

If there was a way through the tunnel, should that give him some hope for Selene? But even if she'd somehow survived the Viridians after being shoved out of the palace, he suspected deep down that she'd never have found a path between those rocks.

Using his keen rakkan eyesight, he stuck his head into the hole from which Lyra had emerged and waited for his eyes to adjust, but before they had, a faint whiff of ash met his nose, and he soon confirmed that the narrow space had been dug with kuraminium and ferven much later than the battle.

Selene didn't escape through here.

Lyra lowered her head and sent pangs of her sour mood at the words. His brief hope had been weak, and he guessed Lyra hadn't come across Selene's corpse in the tunnel either.

"Let's head to the bank," Darius said with a tired sigh, then returned to his swift to escape any more false hope. Pains of thirst and hunger began to tighten his stomach, but was that a call for food or simply the ache of his new solitary life? People said it was better to be alone than in bad company, but those people needed new friends—and they probably didn't enjoy a good fight like he did.

After finding his swift and helping himself to some water and salted meat, he mounted and wandered towards the bank, taking a long detour to avoid going past the prison he hoped had been crushed to smithereens. His distraction led him to a square he'd have preferred to avoid as well, and the Goddess fountain that once stood at its heart was now only legs and fragments.

He sped through, keeping himself from looking at the spot where Lex had loosed an arrow through Omid's head, and arrived at what he assumed was the bank, based on Lex's directions. He'd never visited the vaults before, and the grandiose pillars and sculpted walls outside were peppered with holes. After dismounting and grabbing a shovel he'd brought, he stepped inside and avoided the numerous deep pits that had been hacked into the marble floors.

Tall ceilings with faded artwork loomed over him, and the remnants of many destroyed pillars hung like spikes from the ceiling, threatening to skewer and bury everything below.

From only a cursory survey of the unburnt stone littering the ground, he knew it was mostly human work, and one body at the side of the vast entrance hall surprised him. The black eagle emblazoned on an otherwise white tunic was a rare sight this far west, but another dead man confirmed this was no lone fighter.

Torian soldiers had ventured here since Laltos's fall and fought alongside Xavala, as Lex had once implored the King to do without success.

Darius took a roll of parchment from his pocket and unravelled it. Then he tried his best to find his location on the map of the building before setting off towards where Lex had indicated to search.

Rather than take the stairs, he dropped through holes in the floor while Lyra followed, and eventually, he descended to such a depth that the twilight outside no longer illuminated the place enough for his rakkan eyes. He conjured the cold touch of algor to shed some light and kept moving until he was in the first room Lex had marked.

Inside, there wasn't even a speck of the gold that would once have been piled high in the room. He'd expected to find other treasured possessions of Lex's here that would be worthless to a looter, but the only thing left there was rubble.

Looking back at the map, he traipsed through another couple of empty rooms until arriving at the torn fragments of a false wall Lex had hoped remained intact. Through a hole in the wall was a tiny space at the corner of the basement, a place ringed three times in red on the map. The room spanned only a few yards across and lay as empty as the rest, but Lex had been most interested in whatever lurked below his feet.

Twenty feet deep and only a steel shovel.

Lyra prowled with her nose, sniffing the floor beside him.

"What? Can you smell gold now?"

She pulled back and gave him a gentle bite on the calf as she walked into the chambers outside.

"Ouch. All right. I'll stop." Even he grew tired of his constant sarcasm, but it was all that distracted him from everything else.

One of the square stones that made up the floor had been smashed, but once Darius lifted it and checked the ground underneath, he found solid earth. He lifted the rest and verified there were no holes or tunnels in either that room or those closest before breathing a sigh of relief, satisfied that the looters hadn't found her stash. *Time to call it a night.* He was here to check, not collect.

Lyra. She soon stalked back to him while he began climbing towards his swift. *No one's dug there. The gold is safe.* However, the treasure seemed of little use. Lex thought otherwise and had tried to explain how her new ideas of banking worked, using one person's money to make loans to others, but Darius wanted to drive a nail through his skull just recalling the conversation.

He went back outside to his swift, but as he prepared to leave, he sensed the air moving above him in an odd way. *Is that damned pteron finally coming to make contact?* But when he looked, a feathered bird swooped down and almost clashed with his head.

He ducked, and the falcon flapped to slow itself before landing. He recognised Lex's escort at once.

"Easy, Tiro," Darius said. "I know you can see in the dark, so don't act like that was an accident."

A slip of parchment tied to the bird's leg caught his eye, and he hurried to untie it and read as best he could. The handwriting was neater than usual but definitely bore Lex's flair in the curl of every "y."

> *It's me. They returned yesterday with news from the Glacier and the Dunes. The parley will go ahead in a couple of weeks at the place unknown to us. All will attend, including* him. *This might be our chance. Will you come? You'll even have time to visit your grandfather before we leave. Please come. I miss you.*

Darius read the last sentence thrice before trusting he'd seen it correctly. Why would Lex miss him? Her messages were usually a single curt line and rarely explained why she made a request of him. For the first few weeks after he'd parted with her, they were simply commands such as "Go to *X* village and slay the centurion there," or "Algus raiders are heading towards *Y*. Intercept them." He'd done as she wished when he could but also had his own path to forge.

And after an age of asking, she'd finally given him permission to meet his grandfather, the only man that might fill the void Brutus's passing had left in him.

What had changed to make Lex now agree? Judging by the way that, terrified for her daughter's safety, she'd begged him *not* to meet his grandfather since Archimedes had died, this was the greatest display of trust she'd ever shown him.

But knowing Lex, the personal part of the message wasn't her focus, and her request in the first half was one he could hardly ignore. The warlords of every rakkan legion were to meet at the Urukan Mine: the Warlord of Azuria, on the Azurian Glacier; the Warlord of Branz, within the Tidal Dunes; and the other two warlords that made Darius tense just by thinking of them—Hadrian and Varro.

This could be his one chance to catch Hadrian outside of Viridia's impassable walls. If there was one more person worth asking about Selene, it was the Viridian Warlord. Only once Darius had closure would Hadrian suffer the sting of his sword.

Lyra growled as his rage built.

Can you run on a full belly?

She set off at a sprint before he finished the thought, tearing down the street while he rushed to mount his swift. If the meeting was in only a couple of weeks, Warlord Varro would soon leave Margalvia, and Darius needed to tail him to get the precise location of the mine.

After reattaching his shovel and bag, he jumped onto the horse and grabbed the reins. "Make haste, boy."

3

Nikolaos – Toria

Nikolaos picked at the sea bream on his plate, peeling the crisp, roasted skin from the pale flesh. Even the salty aroma couldn't add flavour to an otherwise forlorn day, but he took a small bite anyway. The dining room was one of the most confined in Toria's palace, but still, the arched ceiling covered them at a height that made it impossible to say whether or not it was painted. Curtains drooped over the balcony doors and only allowed a slither of light to intrude into the narrow room.

After Laltos's destruction, he'd spent months debating whether his life was worth more than his honour. His answer had surprised even himself—it wasn't. Despite the King's promises of the regency Nikolaos so craved, it seemed the only way he'd sit on a throne would be as a dead man.

As he nibbled, he glanced at the farthest end of the dining table to check whether Selene had finished her meal yet. Half her potatoes were cold and uneaten, and she'd barely touched her fish.

Nikolaos took a deep gulp from his cup of burwine. If she didn't eat correctly, she wouldn't be the only one stung by a whip.

"You're failing this test," he whispered. Although they were alone, he'd learned always to speak as if someone was listening when in the King's palace.

Selene's once vibrant curls now hung dry and straight across her face, some even touching the unfinished vegetables and fish in front of her. Her clothes were as white and bland as her washed mind, and they told nothing of the twisted woman within. The fine fabric was such that none other than a king could afford to display, but while the cloth covered almost every inch of her skin, some of her numerous old and fresh scars peeked above her collar.

"You need to eat more," Nikolaos whispered, "and talk. Selene loved to chat."

She took an olive and slipped it into her mouth, chewing for far longer than a normal woman would before swallowing.

Nikolaos cursed. His voice hung in the space beneath the high ceiling for a while before dissipating into the silence that was usual in this room.

"Selene?" Nikolaos said. When she didn't respond, he raised his voice. "Six!"

She looked up. "Must you always disturb my quiet?"

The woman now resembled the old Selene only as far as Nikolaos's training—and a goman's meddling—had drilled behaviours into her. He'd encountered many Numbered in his life and lain with many in years long since passed, but he'd never truly understood what lurked beneath those vacant eyes until now.

Six didn't realise she *was* Selene, instead believing she only had some of Selene's memories.

"Eat more," Nikolaos said. "Even a Viridian slave would look better fed than you."

With a scowl, she silently took a piece of fish and ate while Nikolaos shoved his own food away. Whoever had roasted it was nothing compared to the cooks of Laltos.

He stood and walked to take one of the empty seats beside Selene. The chairs and table were made of dark wood and looked newly varnished, apart from the marks in the two places where they always sat. Now those spots were worn and scratched from the many months of use.

"You need to keep answering to 'Selene,'" Nikolaos said. "*She* is coming soon to see how you're progressing, and if you aren't good enough, well… You know what happened last time."

Selene's jaw froze mid-chew, and she gaped for a moment before she began shovelling the rest of her food down her gullet like a starving dog.

"Eat with grace," Nikolaos instructed. "You need to remain in character if you're ever to convince anyone."

"Don't speak as if you're my master." But after saying the words, she paused for a second while her shoulders and face lost their rigidity before she began eating at the pace of a normal woman. She grinned at him with something of a childish spark in her eyes. "Better?"

At times, Nikolaos felt as if he were watching over two different people within her, and one was uncomfortably like her sister Lex. The smile was almost convincing, but he doubted she'd ever lose the trace of angst from her gaze.

"Better," he said. "But you still seem more nervous than a Torian fisherman. You're not as good as our masters demand you be."

"I don't know why they bother reteaching me etiquette. Selene was never one for formal occasions. She always preferred to eat with the lesser grunts. Anything was better than spending time with that wretched family of hers."

"Selene, don't—"

"Yes, yes, I know. I should act as if I cared for them, act like the sweet girl she was, who was deluded into thinking they loved her… Just like me with that rat, Darius."

Nikolaos wiped the sweat beginning to form on his brow. He wasn't privy to whatever false memories of Darius had been implanted in Selene or to exactly who she now believed she had been. Every time he probed, the mind blocks set in.

"Let's get back to the test," he said. "You did well in that you ate your vegetables first as you loved to do, but you left fish. And the mushrooms…"

Selene picked one up and studied it before flinging it across the room with a curse. "I forgot."

"If you ever eat them without thinking, be sure to spit them up and retch, act as if you didn't realise."

"I know. It's strange; I remember them tasting foul, like I'd been Selene eating them as a young child. Yet now they're as delicious as when I myself ate them. But I don't react to everything like I once did…" She frowned at one of the tapestries opposite.

"What does that mean?" Nikolaos asked. The confusion on her face was something he'd seen so often that it now unsettled his stomach.

"Some people are so different to how they appear in Selene's memories. Like Darius…he was so kind and gentle to her, but with me…when he flogged me or… How can the man who treated her with such love do what he did to me?" Selene gripped her head as if tension had seized her.

Nikolaos grabbed her hand and yanked it from her head. "Don't react like that! How many times do I have to tell you to hide headaches?"

She quickly straightened her posture and hid it as best she could.

"Stop squinting," Nikolaos barked. "Don't sit so rigid."

Eventually, after a few tense seconds, Selene's posture became more natural, and she simply stared at him with emptiness and a crease in her brow that wouldn't be too obvious unless someone asked her a question directly.

"Selene, would you like more mushrooms?" Nikolaos asked.

She shrugged and paused as if she were thinking. But nothing was going on inside her head. Her reaction was one ingrained from many, many hours of training.

"Better than before," Nikolaos muttered.

"What is?" Selene asked.

Her question brought a grin to Nikolaos's mouth. Her transition from struggling with the mind block back to lucidity wasn't seamless, but it was improving. Was she ready for the outside world? There was no time better than now for Nikolaos to really push her, and such testing would give him a chance to try to break some of the mind blocks he was most determined to pervert. Whatever the agenda behind warping Selene, her mission was to fool Darius, so Nikolaos wouldn't allow it. He had to plant seeds of truth within her mind subtle enough to go unnoticed by the King and his servants but obvious enough for Darius to discern them.

"May I test your memories?" Nikolaos asked.

"I presume you mean Selene's." She shoved her plate of food away and turned to face him head-on.

"Yes," Nikolaos replied. "You must keep thinking of yourself as her. Now, first question. Who was your first pet?"

"A rat named Iris."

"Where did you get her?"

"A sewer under my slave parents' dorm."

"And your last pet?"

"Paris."

"Wrong." Nikolaos ground his teeth together. "You'd never call Paris a *pet*; he was an escort."

Her brow furrowed, and her voice after the pause was soft. "Yes. He was."

The goman who had worked his cogi on her seemed good at choosing which memories of Selene's to keep and which to discard, but showed little understanding of the emotional bonds associated with them, so Nikolaos saw no use in dwelling.

He continued. "How many men have you ever loved?"

This time the creases on her brow were so deep the question seemed to cause physical pain. "Really loved? Or believed I loved?"

"Either." As far as Nikolaos knew, she'd loved no one; but if the rumours were true, there was one possibility that had piqued his curiosity since he'd last seen the real her.

She sighed. "One."

Nikolaos let the answer simmer for a few moments more before lowering his voice for the next question. "Was it real?"

Again, a tautness seemed to grip her brow. "I… I don't know. He was a liar, a manipulator."

"Do you remember Dolthea?" Nikolaos asked.

Her frown deepened. "Vaguely."

Nikolaos hadn't been there himself, so he was only going by Torian whispers. "Did Darius save you?"

"Yes." Her eyes widened with a brightness he'd thought stolen from her. "He was a saviour to some but a demon to others."

45

Nikolaos waited before his next question, getting close to the truth he wanted her to piece together for herself. "Did you meet him before or after Archimedes had warped his mind?"

She eyed him as if suspicious about the question. "After Archimedes was dead."

"And what did Archimedes do to him?"

"… Weakened him."

"How?"

"I wasn't there. I wouldn't know." She shifted in her seat uncomfortably.

"He must have told you."

"… Something about his mind."

"Ah. Did he mention the goman art of cogi?"

A few moments of silence passed after his question while the woman simply stared with knitted eyebrows. But when she didn't utter a word, the mind block was transparently at work.

"What question did I just ask?" Nikolaos said.

"No question. You said, 'He must have told you.'"

At least she's better at hiding the mind blocks. Any mention of cogi powers over the last few months had evoked a similar reaction. But he had to get her to relay *something* related to that to Darius, or she'd never unknowingly make him realise her mind had been tampered with.

"Let's halt the test." Nikolaos leaned back in his chair as if putting himself at ease, but in reality, more sweat was seeping into his tunic. If he couldn't discuss gomans or cogi, then he'd tell her about the closest things he could think of. Hopefully, Darius wasn't as dense as the humans said and would notice the hints if Selene ever relayed them.

"We should discuss a contingency plan," Nikolaos said.

"Contingency for what?"

"If Darius asks too many questions when you meet with him."

Selene stiffened. "The King's Orator said I was to discuss nothing of her plans for me and Darius with you or anyone else."

Nikolaos smiled to hide the curse wanting to fly from his lips at the mention of that snake of a woman.

"This isn't about your mission," Nikolaos said. "What if Darius asks you where you've been for the last—"

"I'm to discuss *nothing!*" Selene bared her teeth with horror rather than anger, in that moment not even a hint of the sympathetic woman she'd been.

Such a reaction was Nikolaos's own fault. He'd trained her to obey the King's Orator's orders literally and to the letter, hoping that in the future, such rigidity would lead to Selene misunderstanding what was required of her.

"Fine." Nikolaos drained the last of his burwine, never so keen to feel the burn in his throat. "Let me instead tell you of one thing the King's Orator hasn't mentioned. It has nothing to do with Darius, so you aren't forbidden from discussing it."

Selene narrowed her eyes but withheld her opposition for now.

"It's no secret that Ophelia keeps things from both you and me," Nikolaos continued, "and there is one tool she does not want you to use but that could save your life."

"Why would she hide it?"

"I'm afraid to say that you aren't as important to her as other things."

Although Selene lost none of her suspicion towards him, there was a curiosity in her expression too.

"It's a simple tool," Nikolaos continued, "more of an excuse, really. In order to explain your absence for the last year, you just need to tell them you stayed with the Waif Magician."

Selene flinched. "I cannot speak of her with you."

Strange. "There is no more to say. Just remember that you stayed with the Waif Magician."

Selene's only reaction again was a vacant stare, one eerily familiar.

"What did I just tell you?" Nikolaos asked.

"Something about a simple tool…"

Curses. If her mind blocked such a simple statement about the Waif Magician, Nikolaos had to get even more vague. *Good thing Selene never met the Magician to know what she looked like.*

"The tool is this." Nikolaos kept his tone conversational. He stood and began walking to the side of the room, partly for more burwine, partly evading her sight while he spoke so he could avoid triggering mind blocks. "In order to explain where you've been for the last year, you need to tell them that you stayed with a woman."

"What woman?" Selene asked.

"A specific woman, one with whom only Selene would seek refuge, and one that Ophelia would rather did not exist at all."

"Isn't it best to fool people with lies constructed for specific situations rather than generic excuses?"

"If you have time, you could probably find a suitable lie to fit any circumstance, but more often than not, it's best for one to respond *quickly* in conversation than to think. Lies take time to construct, but the truth takes an instant to recall. To think is to be suspicious."

She took in his words and seemed willing to hear him out at least.

He poured himself a new cup of burwine, the most expensive one on offer—which wasn't saying much of the cheapskate King.

Only when he'd turned back to the table did he speak again. "This woman you are to say you met has only a few defining features. The first is that she is elderly and short, walking with a sort of hunched gait. The last, and most important, is her dyed red hair."

When Selene didn't respond, Nikolaos began downing his cup of burwine. *Another mind block?*

"Is red dye important?" Selene asked.

Nikolaos coughed and spat wine all over the sleeves of his clean tunic. But even ruined clothes that wouldn't be washed for another week weren't enough to prevent the grin spreading across his face.

"It is," Nikolaos said. "But it's important you don't let on to anyone here that you know this."

Selene simply shrugged without confirming her intentions. Whether or not she'd reveal what he'd said, something told Nikolaos this was one of the last chances he'd have to speak with her. He had no regrets.

After a few more silent drinks and picking at cold food, their peace ended when the double doors to the hallway outside opened. Two slaves pushed the heavy wood and in strode the King's Orator along with the King's Sword. The pair's grey cloaks wafted as they walked, and Jason's time-worn face was cast in shadow by his hood, as usual. Ophelia, on the other hand, walked with her scaly bald head held high and proud, leaving a trail of dandruff to float in the air as she went. An ever-present hunger seeped from her grey eyes, a stark contrast to the stale glare of the King's Sword. Even after months of seeing the woman daily, the sight of her still made Nikolaos's toes curl.

The King's Orator whispered something into Jason's hood that Nikolaos couldn't hear. But since being without his escort to eavesdrop, Nikolaos had learnt to read the odd word on his enemies' lips.

"—King—afraid," the King's Orator said. "—ready soon or—no use for these."

The sweat practically dripped from Nikolaos's forehead at the unheard words.

The King's Sword nodded once before lifting his ominous gaze to Nikolaos.

"How's her training going?" the King's Orator asked, placing a hand on Selene's shoulder.

The algus shivered as if touched by the cold hand of death and cleared her throat. "I—"

"Excellent." Nikolaos skipped to stand beside Selene. "She's come far since we last spoke. The additional memories have made a remarkable difference." Her earliest state as a mindless Numbered had been hopeless.

Ophelia blinked twice before her mind seemed to register the words. "They've caused no issues like the last time? No confusion we must tidy?"

Nikolaos painted on a smile while he considered his next words carefully, knowing the pain they could bring to Selene. "Well, even those of us with untampered minds have our difficulties with some memories, but nothing that will need any tweaks."

"Tweaks?" The King's Orator looked down at Selene and lifted the Numbered's head to meet her wise eyes. She stroked a hand across Selene's face with false empathy that brought a little colour to the algus's cheeks. "Is something troubling you, my dear?"

"Only one thing…" Selene looked away, and Nikolaos bit his tongue. As painful as his end would be if Selene revealed what he'd just said, Ophelia was not a woman to interrupt while questioning.

"Go on, dear," the King's Orator said.

"Why did Darius treat Selene with such love?" Selene asked.

Nikolaos almost snorted a laugh in relief, but the pleasant smile that had been upon the King's Orator's face fell to reveal angry teeth.

"You call this 'excellent'?" Ophelia's glare snapped up to Nikolaos. "She'll have to be near perfect to keep her cover." She looked down at Selene with pity. "They've put you through so much. Any love Darius showed Selene was a lie. How he treated *you* is how he really treats people. Don't fret; we'll remind you of what he did to you."

Selene flinched away from Ophelia's hand. "No," she said, hands trembling. "I don't want to be reminded. Please… I don't want to live it again."

"My dear"—Ophelia crouched to Selene's level as if being lower made her any less menacing—"I know it hurts, but you need to remember the truth, even if it means reliving how they betrayed you and disfigured you with torture and worse."

Nikolaos looked back at the other end of the table and the meal he hadn't finished, not wanting Selene to see his disgust at the lies. Why hadn't he just taken Selene's life and his own months ago? Was revenge worth all this?

"Take her for editing," the King's Orator said.

The King's Sword moved forward as Selene darted up from her chair and tried to bolt away from the man.

But before she could sweep past Nikolaos's cloak, Jason lunged in a blur and locked her wrist in an iron grip. Selene jerked to a stop and tried to wrench herself free.

"No. Please!" She pleaded with Nikolaos as a child did at a parent, with wide eyes and quivering lips.

If the King's Orator was moved by the display, her face said nothing of it, for she watched, expressionless, while the King's Sword dragged Selene away, her cries filling the once silent room. Selene's fingernails scratched against the stone tiles on the floor, one catching a gap and leaving a trail of blood, and the shouts still echoed around the walls for a few moments after she'd been hauled out.

"The strongest relationships are the most difficult to break," Ophelia said. "So much easier when they're children."

"Indeed." Part of him hoped they never succeeded. "How long will the editing take this time? Will you alter her memories?" *Please don't look at any recent ones.*

"She shouldn't need new memories. Just a replay and some fresh wounds to make the pain real. Nothing more than a few hours." The King's Orator turned her attention to the food still on Selene's plate, and she clicked her tongue again. "I see her appetite hasn't returned, but that's not a concern. The thinner she is, the more truthful the story that she was captured by the Viridians will seem."

"You're sure they're breaking algus?" Nikolaos had seldom heard of them taking so many algus captives before.

"We're sure. We're using the same tools they use when we break Six. But she never believes we're the ones causing the pain. She'll remain loyal to us. Many of the old scars she thinks were from Darius. Pain is an easy way to destroy love."

Though the King's Orator often spoke of love, what did she know of it?

"Are you sure she's almost ready?" Ophelia turned to him, her eyes like slits as they bore into Nikolaos's own.

"I'm sure," he said, having to consciously stop himself gulping nervously after.

"Very well. Prepare to leave in a few weeks. We'll go hard on her, so she'll need to heal and recover."

Just what I need. It was always left to Nikolaos to tend to Selene's wounds after the whips had flayed her back.

"I'll be ready," Nikolaos said. "But I still don't know what task you require of her."

The King's Orator smiled, splitting one of her dry lips. "Nor do you need to."

"But if I must train her, then—"

"If you have questions, feel free to ask. But just remember"—Ophelia leaned closer to his ear—"curiosity can get a man killed."

4

Sulla – Margalvia

Heat burst from the furnace as a rakkan opened the hatch on the side. Sulla winced and turned his back to the flare that ripped up the earthen mound and lit the night sky.

Hera darted behind him with a curse. Her slender body touched his chest while the torrid air whirled about his back, and as she did, he didn't know what was more heated, his front or rear.

"Watch it, you lout," Sulla called over his shoulder as the rakkan tossed more old shards of armour and weapons in before slamming the hatch shut.

"Sorry," the rakkan mumbled as he strode away.

Meanwhile, Hera still shielded her now darkened face. She could have conjured algor to protect herself from the heat rather than use Sulla's body, but he wasn't complaining. Although the slight wrinkles across her striking features made her appear older than Sulla, he'd seen a few more decades than she had, enough to know her getting close to him had nothing to do with protection from heat.

The smell of her singed hair met his nostrils. "You know, if you wanted to rub against me, you could have just asked."

Hera stepped back with a scoff and tried to wipe the dirt from her face, but only smeared more black on with her sooty hands.

Sulla laughed. "You missed a spot, Regent."

Along with the pair of them, Warlord Varro stood silently, watching the workers melt every scrap of kuraminium they could find. His usually light, tidy hair was now as black as Hera's, and smoke swirled around him as if his very body were aflame. They were all atop a hill on the edge of Margalvia, looking at the dark city they oversaw below.

"I don't understand." Hera cast her gaze across the several open-air furnaces spewing smoke and ash into the air. "I thought you said you don't use charcoal or wood. What's with the soot?"

"I like it," Sulla said. "The shade matches your eyeliner." And how alluring her makeup made those dark eyes.

Varro grunted and gave Sulla a rap on the arm. "Ignore him. These furnaces haven't always been for kuraminium. They've been used for iron and steel too."

Whether or not that answered Hera's query, Sulla didn't know, but she seemed to nod in understanding while Sulla gave a quick signal to the workers to bring more metal. Any excuse for her to hug him again...

"Do you want to go below the furnace?" Sulla asked her. "It's impressive how we melt the ore."

"I don't think that's a good idea," the Warlord said. "Not even an algus could take the heat of that much ferven."

Being a firer of the furnaces was a grim job that Sulla had only done briefly in his teens. Any prisoner in their right mind chose to be even a miner over a firer if given the choice. The workers drank gallons of ale to bear the constant heat, which certainly made the time pass more swiftly. He'd always reckoned that's where he acquired his love for sarcasm. Ribbing other firers was the only thing that kept a man sane while in a hole conjuring ferven for hours on end.

"Hera said she wanted to see our technology," Sulla said. "And I'm sure she enjoys being hot and sweaty."

The Regent's eyes suddenly reflected the glowing furnaces with a heat of their own—annoyance at his jesting. Perhaps he should go easy on her. The fact she even spoke with them so plainly showed her open-mindedness towards rakkans, something unfortunately not shared by all the refugees of Laltos. But Hera's mood had taken a turn for the worse when her son Gorgias had been captured by Viridians months ago. Sulla had only mentioned his name to her once and wouldn't make that mistake again.

Months of fatigue showed on Hera's expression as she shook her head. "Can we be serious for a change?"

"Serious?" Sulla said. "Sorry, I don't know the word."

"Isn't that the truth." Varro let out a lengthy sigh and began walking alongside the piles of metal scraps. "You won't see much smelting of ore here. Not until we get back into the mine."

"About that…" All humour fled from Sulla's mind at the reminder, and he strode after the Warlord. "Doesn't this parley put a halt to our plans? We can hardly invade the mine while in conference there."

"Indeed." Varro ran a hand through his hair. "But that's assuming we attend."

"Surely you should," Hera said. "Winning the support of the other legions would help us all greatly."

Avoiding either of their gazes, Varro faced the city in the valley below, weak lights throughout gleaming like an orange lake. "I fear we're too late to win or lose support."

Fear was one thing Varro did too much.

"It's a pity you exiled our best assassin," Sulla muttered. "Would be useful, given we know where Hadrian will be." Though said in a humorous tone, the reminder had Sulla grinding his teeth with a bitterness he'd struggled against for months. Darius deserved to be here, in his *home*, not hiding in the Empire like a criminal.

"Darius is exiled, not dead." Varro finally turned to face Sulla with narrowed eyes. "He chose his fate."

Should I say I already told Lex and Darius about the parley? As much as Sulla would love another scuffle with the Warlord to vent his anger, he'd pushed his luck too many times. The next time they fought, more than fists would be involved, and there was a reason Varro hadn't a visible scar on him.

But maybe Sulla would be better off exiled as well. Leaving Margalvia to go with Darius had proven too large a step to take until now, but every day it grew more tempting. If only the move didn't involve leaving his sister behind…

"So, the meeting," Sulla said. "We should attend. We can at least rely on Warlord Quintus's support."

"I wouldn't be so sure." Varro lowered his voice. "Azuria is far closer to Viridia than Margalvia."

"So what? Quintus's spine is harder than kuraminium. He'll make up his own mind. Pity we can't say the same for Warlord Flavius."

"Don't be so quick to condemn him. Would you be so bold as to defy Hadrian when he controlled your only road to the mine?"

Sulla scoffed. "That isn't the only reason Branz cosies up with Viridia."

"Perhaps," Hera said, wincing as another furnace roared when opened. "What concerns me is it only needs one warlord to vote with Hadrian and you're split, two against two."

A dark scowl came over Varro's face. "If you humans hadn't razed Gerunda, we'd have a fifth rakkan warlord to break the tie."

"That wasn't *me*. That was Archimed—"

"Enough, you two." Sulla barged between the pair as they squared up to each other yet again. As open-minded as Hera was, the Warlord risked destroying the little goodwill the Regent had. The worst thing was that Varro was not one to speak in anger. Any words he uttered were thought through. He didn't care about antagonising her, either because he trusted her to remain beside him, or because he didn't count her among his allies to begin with.

"If you don't attend this parley," Sulla said, "Quintus may not even stand with us. We can't be against three legions."

The smoky air dishevelled Varro's hair, and he cursed and ripped it from his eyes. "You're right."

The pronouncement was so infrequent, Sulla was almost lost for words. "Can I have that in writing?"

"But a tied vote achieves nothing," Varro continued. "We need to know what Hadrian is planning."

"Our spies say he's still capturing and breaking algus to hunt the Waif Magician for him," Hera said. "But perhaps he'll use the conference to assassinate you."

Varro scoffed. "Hadrian is low, but low enough to violate a parley…?"

The question hung in the air. Although Varro's words doubted Hadrian would entertain such treachery, his face painted a different picture; his deep frown left white, wrinkled lines on his forehead where the soot hadn't touched.

"Is there no way to break a tied vote?" Hera asked.

"A rakkan overlord can," Sulla said, "but there hasn't been one since the Battle on the Mount."

"Then perhaps Hadrian plans to use that."

The three paused. Hera again wiped her forehead and added more dirt than before, but seemed oblivious as she stared into the rocky ground without focus.

"It's troubling to even consider." Varro's voice was low yet contained more heat than the furnaces. "But an overlord must prove his dominance by wielding the Twin Blades of Trogus, and they've been lost for one and a half centuries."

"Whatever Hadrian's plans are, we need to stop him," Hera said. "Say the word, and my best assassins will go with you to end him." Now the fires that had reflected in her eyes were extinguished by frosty blue algor.

Sulla looked from her to the Warlord, willing the rakkan with all his strength to say yes to the offer. But Varro was too much a man of honour. That's why Sulla had already told Lex of the meeting, knowing word would reach Darius swiftly via her escort. Sulla still didn't trust her, but that didn't mean he couldn't use her.

Varro's pause was even longer than usual, but he finally shook his head. "I take the rules of parley as seriously as I take the Law of the Blades."

When the Warlord paced away towards the crest of the hill overlooking Margalvia, Sulla caught Hera's attention and gave her a grin that she seemed to understand and return.

"Sulla," Varro called. "We must talk alone."

Hell. What did I do now? At the piercing words, Sulla adjusted his belt to ensure the hilt of his sword was within easy reach. At least Varro always chose to reprimand him out of earshot of both their human guests and Sulla's subordinates in the Militia.

Hera regarded him for a second before heading home while Sulla strode up to stand beside the Warlord. In the city below, one corner shone more brightly than the rest with thrice the number of lamps. The humans liked to group together, and who could blame them? Sulla was surprised they hadn't complained more about the nocturnal city's noise, but they'd seemed to grow accustomed to it.

"Wouldn't you rather speak in the alehouse?" Sulla asked. "This smoke doesn't half nettle the throat." And in the sight of others, Sulla had more confidence the Warlord would restrain himself.

"Julius has reported back."

Sulla started. *This is no reprimand.* "So fast? Is it ours?"

"Yes. The Viridians didn't mount much of a defence. I've ordered him to begin rebuilding Gerunda's outer walls."

Once standing taller and thicker than even Viridia's, Gerunda's walls had been thought impenetrable. But stone did nothing to protect from an evil such as the Staff of Arria, and Archimedes had reduced the defences to dust.

"Why rebuild?" Sulla asked. "We should head straight for the road north and disrupt Viridia's ore wagons."

"One step at a time. Hadrian will soon chase off our raiders if they have no defensible base close. Plus, Julius has found the Gerundan road to the mine."

A chuckle rasped in Sulla's throat, reminding him he needed a drink. And now they had cause for celebration. "If this parley goes to hell, we can react swiftly. But you should include Hera in news like this. Do you still mistrust her?"

"No." Varro turned and stared deep into Sulla's eyes, the way he did before asking an important question. Under such weight, Sulla wouldn't be able to lie. Only then did the kuraminium of the Warlord's drawn sword glint with fire.

"I heard you've been speaking with Lex." Varro took a step forward with a thud.

Sulla shifted his hand subtly closer to his gladius and backed up. "It's Lex. Just because you hate her doesn't mean I have to."

Varro's eyes swelled with fire and, when he spoke, heat spewed from his mouth. "I do *not* hate her, but there's a reason I choose a time to tell her things."

Sulla cursed and froze as the Warlord came nose to nose.

"I take it you know, then." Sulla kept his voice flat but unthreatening.

Varro paused, took in heavy breaths that came out hot. "You told her of the parley?"

"Yes." What use was denying it?

"And you're not so foolish as to believe she wouldn't tell Darius."

"I'm a dolt, but not that much of one."

This time Varro's pause was so long Sulla wondered whether he should say more, but he held back when the fire dampened in the Warlord's eyes.

"Do you still have such little faith in me?" Varro asked, his voice barely above a whisper.

Reprimands were nothing new to Sulla, but this… The Warlord was his superior but also a friend. He'd always been truthful and wouldn't stop now.

"You're the greatest warrior I've ever seen," Sulla said, "but you've let personal issues cloud your judgement. You—"

"So you trust Lex more than me?" Anger flashed across Varro's face.

Sulla scoffed. "Of course I don't. I used her to get word to Darius. Whether we like it or not, he's still besotted with her."

Varro growled with a shake of his head. "We can't trust him."

"You don't need to. Don't cut off your hand because you hate your arm. If you let me and some of our men go with him, we can find Hadrian and—"

"No." Varro spat the word with disgust. "I know Lex better than you all, and none of you have seen the real depth of her hatred. You cannot predict her, and you cannot trust her. As for Darius…"

The murmur that followed from the Warlord was a hell of a lot better than the foul curses Sulla usually heard uttered at the mention of the half-rakkan.

Sulla cleared his throat. "Brutus wouldn't want Darius exile—"

"Don't you dare mention him!" Varro's blade sliced upwards in a swift movement Sulla couldn't have blocked if he'd tried. The deadly metal stopped an inch shy of his throbbing neck.

Sulla didn't flinch. "I know you could kill me at will. I'll mention your brother if I wish to. He was my friend, and the only reason you won't allow me to speak is because you know deep down that what I'd say is the truth."

The Warlord's cold sword dug into his skin. "Do *not* betray me again. You will receive no more warnings."

As if the threat of death would stop Sulla defending the one man that had helped him become what he was—a rakkan worthy of more than Margalvia's gutters.

"I have never betrayed you." With a click of his tongue, Sulla left the Warlord to prepare for what he hoped would be Hadrian's last meeting.

5

Paulus – Azurian Glacier

The blizzard whipped up a white haze so thick and heavy that Paulus barely saw the back of his sister trudging a few feet in front. Her dark cloak wafted like a faint shadow, blotched with snow across the shoulders and on every side. The colour matched her greying hair, which was now horizontal in the wind. In front of her, a dozen other Azure Legionnaires marched without even a ghostly form of them visible.

Usually, Paulus would have cursed a storm like this, cursed the dampness that soaked through his clothes, bit his skin and made every joint in his legs painful. But today, his prayers had been answered as if they'd been granted a shield by the Creator to hide behind. It was their only chance of escape.

His sister was an unrivalled navigator, but there was no way any rakkan could have kept their bearings in this. Even the rivers of meltwater that usually rushed through the glacier were clogged with slush and ice.

"Paula!" he yelled into the howling wind. When she didn't hear, he thrust his old legs into action and caught up with her, giving her cloak a tug.

She turned with a scowl. "What?"

"I think we lost her. We should head back to Azuria. It's the only place we'll be safe."

His sister gazed around at the wall of white that faced them in every direction. "No. She'll find us if we turn back."

Whenever trapped in a storm in the past, he'd conjured ferven to save himself from suffering. But no rakkan among their party dared to do that now. A bright light would invite death.

His sister carried on walking, and he trusted her judgement enough to follow her. Although their parents had given them names so similar, they couldn't have grown into more different people. Paula was the thinker, and Paulus was the brawn—or at least he had been, before becoming an old man.

Every footstep sank until burying his knees in snow. He was about ready to complain to Paula again when a blue light flashed in front of them. Soon after, a muffled shout went out and was swallowed by the storm.

Paula froze. He stopped too with a curse, realising if she'd seen the light, then it hadn't been his poor eyesight playing tricks on him.

"Is it her?" Paula asked. "Can you see?"

"Can't be," Paulus said. "We'd have felt it." The weakness brought by the Staff of Arria was unmistakable, a creeping death that roused fear like nothing else. But only algor made that blue glow, and there were no algus this far southwest. That was why the Azure Legion had settled here centuries ago.

"Fall back!" Paulus yelled into the white, praying the other men heard him.

Another flash of blue light came from their right, behind the haze of swirling snow that was now more like a prison than a shield.

Paula stepped back with a gasp. Soon after, familiar black figures appeared in the snowy veil and clumped together with their shields and spears ready. He didn't need to count to see that some brave souls had fallen.

Paulus had been in hairy situations in the past, but nothing else had made his heart pound as rapidly as it did now. What hope did they have against such a foe? Even a century of legionnaires couldn't wound her, but the dozen he had could at least delay her enough for one of them to escape.

"Go." Paulus shoved his sister away, then faced the spot where he'd last seen the light.

"We must hurry." Paula took his hand and tried to drag him back with her, but he stayed rooted in place. "What are you doing?" she asked.

"We can't all get away. We talked about this!" He let ferven blaze from his eyes so he could get an unhindered last look at her. Even through the wrinkles on her face, he saw the young girl that he'd grown up with, that he'd run away from home with, that had rescued him more times than he ever admitted.

"I'm not leaving without you," she said with a grimace.

"You need to warn them she's back!"

His sister opened her mouth as if to protest but then said nothing. She knew better than to argue with a stubborn, grumpy old man that only had aches and pains in his joints to live for anyway. All those years of fighting had taken their toll, and she had children and grandchildren to take care of.

While he tried to think of what he could say to make her leave, she rushed forward and pulled him into a tight embrace that strained his back.

"Fight to the last," she said.

He was relieved to hear the understanding in her tone and a hint of sadness that told him she'd accepted this was his end.

"I will," he said with a tremor in his voice. He shoved her away before she could change her mind. "I love you, even if you were an annoying brat at times."

She snorted a laugh that became a sob.

But he didn't delay any longer. He strode and wedged himself into the circle of other warriors, all peering in different directions with terror.

For a few minutes, they stood, waiting, paralysed with fear. Then a new ghost approached in the distance. The figure hobbled, short and feeble at first glance, but every rakkan there knew better than to feel relief. Each of the figure's steps was laboured yet confident, as if she needn't hurry, as if she needn't worry that the men in front of her would either attack or flee.

The muscles in Paulus's legs twitched, strength seeping from them little by little, like someone had left a tap at the base of his leg. The next time he blinked, she vanished.

At the sight, every other rakkan must have been gripped by the same fear, because their helmets all shifted from side to side, scanning the surrounding blank canvas. The weakness deepened, and it touched Paulus's back. Yet nothing stirred.

Until a scream rang out behind. Paulus whirled around in time to receive a splatter of blood across his cheek. He watched the legionnaire fall beheaded, staining the snow beneath with an ugly blot of red.

Then another man screamed. A legionnaire stumbled forwards, dropped his shield, and brought a hand to his chest. Then blood oozed between his fingers from the area his shield had guarded only a second before. How had the Magician stabbed behind it?

66

Another three cries rang out, breaking the circle of warriors for good as each scattered. Some tripped in the deep snow and hadn't the strength to get back up, but Paulus stood firm. When the next man died, he finally spotted their nemesis. A shadow moved within the falling snow, swifter than the storm's winds and almost as invisible as the air itself. The flash of a flaring blue sword blinded him for less than a heartbeat, but when his eyes readjusted, only another bleeding, beheaded rakkan was before him.

He couldn't die like this, not like a coward, not waiting for his invisible executioner to come. He'd die a warrior—an old one, but a warrior all the same. With a yell of rage, he flared ferven across his body in a flash of fire that brought a welcome relief from the blizzard's chill. At least he'd die comfortable.

His cloak burned, and the ashes were ripped away as he stepped through the deep snow towards the place where he'd seen the shadow last. Another shout of pain came from behind, and when he turned, he realised there were no other legionnaires to yell out now, no one to hear *him* die.

Each pace became more laboured the farther he went, despite not heading in a straight line. Eventually, the frailty worsened as if chains constricted his chest. But on he trudged towards death.

A quick check over his shoulder confirmed he'd wandered far away from the bodies and from the path his sister had walked. When he turned back, the shadow of a figure had reappeared ahead of him, faint through the snow but close. The figure moved an arm with something black in its hand, and Paulus's ferven was extinguished in an instant, leaving his chest and back to feel the wind's bite once again.

He stumbled and fell to one knee as more strength drained from his legs and arms. All the while, the figure moved slowly forwards. She was even shorter up close, backed by a dark billowing cloak both frayed and tattered. Then her eyes shone cobalt blue and illuminated a fringe of red and purple hair. As if Paulus needed confirmation, in her right hand was the blackened Staff of Arria.

Paulus tried with all his might to raise his fists but couldn't. It took more energy than he had to remain kneeling and not fall face-first onto the ground.

The Magician didn't stop until she was so close that her buffeted cape whipped his face.

"Where's the woman?" she snarled. She pressed the Staff into his chin and sent a shiver deep enough to convulse his bowels.

Dragging in each breath became so difficult it was like wheezing through a gag. Even his heart slowed. All Paulus could do was wince with a weak shake of his head that sent more snow falling across his vision. They said old men didn't fear death, and he'd thought that true until this very moment. *Don't weep.* The longer he delayed this witch, the longer his sister had to escape. He just had to stay strong for a little while.

"Never mind." The Magician took hold of his chin and tilted his head from side to side as if inspecting him.

Usually, his rakkan strength would have locked his muscles in placc, but now all he had to resist was the cold tensing them.

Her lips curled into a grin as she retracted the Staff and suddenly gave him enough energy to breathe deeply.

He gasped, relieved but confused. "Are you such a coward that you have to prey on old men?"

Unfortunately for him, she seemed unmoved by his taunt and instead gestured for him to stand.

When he didn't respond, her eyes narrowed. "Up."

Should he resist or comply at this point? All that mattered was that he delayed her.

"I'm too weak," he said.

She darted forwards so fast he couldn't see her move. Next thing he knew, she clenched one finger of his hand while her snarling mouth pressed against his ear. "Why are rakkan excuses always the same?"

A sudden pain seized his hand, worse than any broken bone he'd ever had. Algor froze his finger, and he desperately tried to flare ferven to counter the icy pain, but the Staff left him nothing to conjure.

With a cry, the Magician snapped off the finger and pointed the bloodless digit at him in mockery. "Come willingly," she said.

"Why?" he cried, now unable to hold back a tear while the stump of his finger still burned as if plunged into something so cold it made the blizzard feel hot. "What do you want?" Why didn't she just kill him? He prayed the rumours of her experiments weren't true.

She burst forward again, and this time clenched his middle finger. The chills began instantly.

"You'll find out soon enough," she said as the pain surged for a second time.

6

Darius – South of Margalvia

The journey to Margalvia had once been a pleasant one, a return from a hostile world to one of safety and peace. Yet now the road south brought only two thoughts. First, memories of Brutus and the months spent training with the rakkan. Although Darius's known life was short, Brutus was the closest thing he'd had to a father, the only one prepared to put up with a surly lad all too sure of himself. The second thought that troubled him was his fate should they catch him venturing so close to the city. But part of him wanted Varro to find him, just so he could give the Warlord an earful.

Though far more used to riding a horse than before, the trip south demanded they use the Royal Roads, which heightened his anxiety despite only travelling at night. His escort struggled to keep pace, but rather than race ahead and leave her behind in the hostile human plains, he always kept her within sight.

When he passed Denehill, he had to leave his swift in the care of a Black Legionnaire. Darius slipped the man some money before traversing the rocky Uxon Trail. He lumbered through the difficult terrain, into the deepening mists and as close to Margalvia as he dared. There, he met with Tiro once again, and a note attached to the peregrine's foot confirmed Varro hadn't yet left the city for the parley.

"We made it, girl," he said to Lyra as she growled and collapsed onto a patch of dirt. "Looks like we have a few days to spare."

She'd heard him but lay in silence while the falcon scuttled near her head. As far as he could tell, the pteron that had found him in Laltos wasn't close by any longer—but the sight of his panther beside Tiro had him wondering whether the connection she shared with the pteron was one that she shared with other escorts.

Can you two communicate?

He received no answer, and rather than wake her, he instead left the question for later and turned his thoughts to sleeping in the mountains. Lyra would struggle to find food here. Deer didn't graze on rock.

The chilly fog sent shivers through his arms despite his thick cloak. *Sure could use shelter.* If Lex had mentioned in her message that he could visit his grandfather, he'd be a fool not to take her up on the offer before she changed her mind. All he remembered of the man was the location Archimedes had given him years ago. Would his grandfather still go to their rendezvous point every month?

Darius waited for a gap in the clouds and spied the waning moon; the first of the month was soon. *Whaling station. Ten miles south,* he recalled Archimedes saying. But rather than set off at once, he paused and sat down beside Lyra, ran a hand across her back. Besides a bed, what did he hope to get from his grandfather? Imagining what he might learn suddenly made the cold mountain wind appealing.

Before he could summon the courage to set off and find out, Lyra slowly rose to her feet and took a few steps along the road leading south.

"Should I go?" Darius asked. "What if I miss Varro leaving for the parley?"

Lyra's wide eyes pointed at Tiro, who still watched the pair of them intently, and he understood what she was thinking.

She was right. Lex would get word to him, and besides, shouldn't a warrior be fearless?

"All right, then." He took the note Lex had written him along with a piece of charcoal. On the back, he wrote, "I'm here. Going to grandfather. Contact me when I need to go." He considered leaving the message at that but recalled Lex had said she'd missed him in her previous note. Should he respond to that? Just the thought of seeing her again made him ache. The last time they'd met had been too long ago.

After a few more moments, he added, "I miss you too." Then he reattached the note to the peregrine's leg and sent it on its way.

As the bird's spotted breast disappeared in the night sky, another pair of wings circled above, but they were too far away for him to tell whether they belonged to the pteron. With a sigh, he returned to dwelling on what awaited him.

But rather than leave him hesitating any longer, Lyra began clambering over the rocks in the road.

I didn't say we were going yet.

His escort merely looked back at him with what he swore was a roll of her eyes before carrying on. Although her stubbornness often gave him grief, at least she stopped him dithering. He set off after her and took some consolation from the fact that she shared none of his trepidation in meeting his grandfather; she was a better judge of character than he was, so the rakkan couldn't be all bad. But *she* wasn't troubled by the one question dominating his mind, the only thought strong enough to banish his regrets over Selene and Brutus to the back of his mind.

This doubt had tormented him since he could recall: Was the memory of his baby brother's death true?

Although the whaling station wasn't far for a bird to fly, the journey there took most of the night before he spied old boats on a stretch of grass leading down to a bay. The coastal winds had stolen half the wooden planks from the walls of a nearby building and had weathered the few that withstood the gusts. Only a couple of large whale bones protruding from the cold, hard dirt were intact.

He trudged to the largest fragment of wall left standing that would shelter him from the breeze. But suddenly, the rising sun in the east appeared from behind a distant island and cast a warm glow over the waters. Instead of sheltering, he propped himself up against the wall to face the sea and the dazzling scene before him. The salty air brought a chill, and Lyra snuggled inside his cloak to evade it. But there was something oddly hypnotic about the thud and hiss of waves, something that took the edge off the maddening thoughts clouding his mind.

Each lap of the water seemed to wash away an ounce of pain. Apart from the remnants of the settlement around him, it was as if men had never touched this area, leaving the tranquil place for the birds soaring above and the animals scurrying over the shore. And how much more peaceful the bay was for it. There was at least one part of the world Darius's actions hadn't devastated.

He allowed Lyra to doze for a while, but after she roused to drink, he decided he too needed sleep for the rest of the day. *Grandfather will probably only come at night, but keep a look out for me.*

Lyra brushed her cheek against him, and he finally lay on the grass, pulling his cloak tight while watching the waters ripple ahead of him. Even though he could have watched them for hours, he soon drifted off.

***

"I wondered when I'd see you again," a man growled.

The gruff voice dragged Darius from his sleep. He bolted up and reached for his sword, but then he saw the old man sitting with Lyra in his arms.

Darius slid back a few inches and gripped the hilt of his gladius before pausing, watching Lyra closely as the stranger rubbed her under the chin in the way that only Darius knew relaxed her.

Now under the depths of a starry sky, the new moon did little to illuminate the man's face and instead cast his sunken eyes into permanent shadow. His long, grey beard swayed back and forth with every gust of wind and scratched across a long, itchy tunic made of tanned sackcloth. Although his thin arms weren't those of a starved man, the stranger could still be a threat; on his right hand, thick calluses ran between his thumb and index finger—the marks of either a labourer or a swordsman.

"Grandfather?" Darius whispered while the surprise left him unable to digest the confused emotions beginning to stir.

"Aye, although I'll forgive you for wondering how a youngster such as yourself could have a grandfather as old as I." His beard ruffled with every calm word. "But there'll be time to fill in the past, and it's not now. It's been too long, my child." He leaned forward and let ferven glow from his eyes as he smiled with a warmth that only Brutus had shown Darius before—a familial trust.

Darius froze, unsure how to respond or which question to ask first. Most of them revolved around his brother, though.

"You're confused, I see," his grandfather said. "I heard what happened to you and understand if you don't trust so easily."

Was he referring to Darius's stolen memories or the torture in Laltos? Darius's voice couldn't be summoned to ask the man.

"If it confuses you to call me grandfather, call me simply Eugenius."

Darius cleared his throat. "All right, Simply Eugenius." Somehow, that did make speaking easier.

The man's smile widened. "I'm glad you haven't lost your *razor-sharp* wit after what you've been through. It's a few hours' trek to my home if you'll forgive an old man for his wanting pace. Almost two centuries do that to you."

As Eugenius wobbled back to his feet with old-man grunts, Darius remained seated, hearing every swoosh of waves that eventually calmed his nerves enough to forgo any pleasantries and instead ask what he feared most of the man. "There's one question that cannot wait."

Eugenius sighed and took a deep breath of salty air. "I know."

"How? I haven't asked you anything yet."

"You'd done many wicked deeds in your short days; yet one memory haunted you so much, it was as if the event had stolen a part of your soul. I doubt any goman could take that from you."

Darius stood slowly while Eugenius's eyes lost their glow to return to cold obsidian. Were they speaking of the same thing?

"Then tell me," Darius said. "What happened to my brother?"

"I'm not best placed to answer that question; I wasn't there."

"You just said you know."

"I do."

Darius clenched his fist. "Then tell me."

Eugenius shook his head. "I swear you'll know the truth before we part ways, and perhaps you'll know more than you want to or more than you can take." The sea swelled behind the man and crashed into the shore, spraying the pair.

But Eugenius didn't blink. "As I said, I don't wish to discuss things of importance here. Best to go where even the birds cannot overhear."

Darius cast his eyes to the sky, not seeing any bird or escort among the thick clouds now circling above. Why were old men always so cryptic? *Lyra, can I trust him?* Upon the question, she gave him no inkling of a warning.

"Fine." He guessed he could wait for an answer, given he'd spend at most a couple of days with the man. But suddenly, days seemed like years, and what was the answer his grandfather worried he might not be able to take?

Eugenius set off without another word, with Lyra soon following. They kept a slow pace along the coastline, and when Darius did finally follow, he trekked slightly behind so that the man was always in his sight, and he constantly scanned their surroundings for either men, boats or escorts that could be tailing them. But nothing larger than a beetle stirred, and the sea grew rougher by the minute until he wouldn't have heard anyone moving above the roaring waves. Eventually, Darius plucked up the courage to ask other questions of the old man.

"When did you last see me?"

"Could only have been a couple of years before you first met Archimedes. I did try to warn you about that one."

So it wasn't just the *new* Darius that never heeded warnings.

"Did I know about Lex's daughter?" he asked.

Eugenius raised a finger to his lips. "Not here."

Darius grunted. "How much farther?"

"Not far. Do you see that peninsula?"

Darius made out a thin strip of land stretching into the sea with what appeared to be a small mound upon it. "I guess. Must be hard to survive here, with no animals or streams."

"We get by."

"Guess you're one of the lucky ones, then."

"The rains provide our water," Eugenius said flatly, "and the sea our food. Our time's spent exploring the meaning of this world and all the difficult questions man has no answer for."

"As I said, lucky." Darius had seen enough famine in his time to realise that. "Few can afford to waste time pondering the meaning of life. From what I've seen, that's a hobby for old, fat nobles that are too hideous to garner the attention of their peers."

"To quip is fine," Eugenius continued. "But don't mock. While you're here, remember you're our guest."

"I…wasn't talking about you. But who's 'our'?"

"The people of my faction. They're generous and calm; do not abuse their patience." Eugenius's eyebrows forked with a new severity.

"Or what?" Darius asked.

"Or I'll force you to confront far worse than your past."

Given the man was old and frail, Darius was sure he wasn't referring to a physical confrontation. But what? He'd been reluctant to visit when he'd thought he'd see the man alone, yet now there were more?

"I'm not here to cause trouble," Darius said, "and I'd rather others didn't know of my visit at all. Is that going to be a problem?"

His grandfather smiled weakly, the darkness that had been there a moment ago receding like the tide. "No, my child. You aren't the first to seek solitude here."

When the man set off again, Darius walked alongside him, now wondering why Lex had chosen for her daughter to be raised with people so foreign to the warriors around her. But then he remembered how vilified *he* was for being a half-rakkan. Solitude for her daughter was better than what he'd suffered.

"I hope you've got firewater," Darius mumbled.

Eugenius sighed and hung his head. "That we do. Not all our guests have learnt self-control."

"What's wrong with enjoying a stiff drink?"

"Nothing. Using it to blind yourself to the world is the problem. I've known too many who did that."

At least they could agree on something. After the Battle of Laltos, Darius had many weeks where his only memories were of darkness and the beginnings of drunken stupors. He'd never believed the best cure for a hangover was to start drinking again, but the method had its merits. You soon stopped caring you were hungover. Those days had achieved nothing other than drowning his laments, but that fact had taken him too long to realise.

"We make most of our own firewater," Eugenius said. "I think you'll like it."

"Forgive me, but I'm doubtful," Darius said. "The last time an old man offered me a homemade drink, it left a film on my tongue I had to scrape off with a steel brush."

His grandfather gave no reassurances.

No matter how close they came to the mound ahead, there was still no sight of anyone else, and by all appearances, the raised bit of earth was natural. Now he had an idea why Cynthia had been hidden here. Perhaps the world would have been better off if *he'd* stayed here since being a young man. Selene and countless others might not have suffered, and his back wouldn't be so mutilated.

Only once closer to the hillock did a small hole become visible, sheltered by long, swaying grass on each side. The ditch looked more like a giant rabbit hole than an entrance for a man, and the high sea waves broke close by and threatened to enter the pit but never did.

Darius followed Eugenius through the tight gap, scraping away loose dirt and sand to fall across his head and arms. Once deeper, he forced his shoulders through the narrowest points, always checking whether the top would come crashing down and bury him. This must have been how the first rakkans had lived. According to the songs, they'd burrowed into the earth like badgers during the day and only emerged as creatures of the night to hunt.

His grandfather lit the way with a delicate flame in his hand, not from ferven but from a tiny clump of grey material. Before Darius could query it, they rounded a bend to face a door with kuraminium bars nailed across.

"Heavy defence for hermits," Darius said.

"This place hasn't always been lost and forgotten." The old man hammered on the door with four knocks in a rhythm Darius recalled, but from where, he didn't know. The metallic sound of braces and locks snapping open came from the other side before the door swung outwards with a hooded man hunched behind. He kept his face low, never looking up enough for Darius to catch even a glimpse of his face.

After Darius and Eugenius had entered, the other man didn't follow them. Inside, the path continued deeper but now with the space of a normal Margalvian corridor and stone supports sunk into the walls. Each passage was the same but lacked the charred black of Margalvia's stone structures. Darius was about to grumble again when Eugenius stopped beside a door and pulled a key from his pocket.

"You may stay in here," he said, opening the door to a small room with only a mattress stuffed with what smelt like seaweed. "It'll be morning soon, and I'd rather we speak with clear and astute minds. I'm sure you have many questions, and my answers won't bring you any comfort, to say the least."

It felt pointless to argue with the man, and Darius was no longer eager to hear what the rakkan had to say.

"Fine," Darius said. "I could use some sleep. Can you bring water and fish for Lyra?" At the thought of food, his own stomach groaned too.

"Of course. I'll bring it after I've prepared your gift."

The frown on Darius's face must have been deep because Eugenius held up his palms.

"Don't expect riches," the old man said. "I'm a hermit, after all, though the present isn't technically from me. It's from Brutus."

Darius gaped. "You knew—?"

"Yes, yes. All in good time. Tomorrow you'll get your answers." With that, Eugenius strode away while Darius stared at the back of his grey mane. Brutus had never mentioned knowing the man or being involved with a faction, except for once giving him some religious scroll that he'd neglected to read or take as seriously as he should have. Hopefully, this new gift was something he understood, and this time, he'd give it the attention it deserved.

7

Darius – South of Margalvia

After a day of intermittent sleep disturbed by the rumbling waves above, Eugenius came to collect Darius wearing the same itchy tunic as the night before. The man led him silently through the underground passages into a new room, one unlike the others he'd passed through. Instead of dirt walls, this one was encased with thick stones arranged loosely and not held together with cooled lava but with some sort of grey clay, much like a human construction. At the far side of the room stood a white marble altar, waist-high and with simple rectangular legs thick enough to hold thrice the weight they bore. Rows of wooden benches sat in front, splintered in places and speckled.

Normally, Darius would have thought it a religious place, but where was the imagery, the paintings, the idols? The space was bare, every colour almost invisible, leaving only one's own mind to delve into for inspiration. Perhaps that was the point.

Although the room was empty but for the pair of them, the air eddied as if something or someone unseen lingered there.

Only a single oil lamp lit the dark space, which brought a calmness one moment and the thought of being buried alive the next.

"Why are you bringing me in here?" Darius asked.

"It's the best spot to avoid interruption, and it seemed the most apt place to give you your gift."

"If your gift is to pray for me, I'm good."

Eugenius shook his head. "Oh, no. Those monks that choose to live here do that sort of thing, but I can't say I believe anything of their creator. Yet…your gift still has something…transcendental." He ushered Darius towards a pedestal table at the back, where two chairs were waiting. On top lay a careful arrangement of black and grey stones that fit into a chiselled grid of squares.

"Perhaps you'll indulge me in a game while we talk." As Eugenius sat at one side, his beard brushed across the board and swept a thin layer of dust into the swirling air. But the man either didn't notice or didn't care because he simply gazed up. "I'm curious to test whether your skills have changed."

Darius wasn't one for games of either strategy or chance, but this was likely a good distraction to what might become an uncomfortable conversation.

"I don't play games," he said.

"Not even to gamble?" A hint of suspicion flickered in the old man's eyes as if he suddenly doubted Darius was who he said he was.

"I don't have anything of worth," Darius said.

"Nonsense. I have many questions to ask as well as answers to give. How about we use those as our stakes?"

If the other old men in Darius's memory were anything to go by, Eugenius wouldn't let this rest.

"Sure." Darius sighed and sat at the table. "You'll need to explain the rules."

"It's simple. The game is called Katakto and is one of conquest. I'm grey; you're black. Whoever has the most of his colour on the board by the end is the winner." His grandfather went on to describe the rules for where pieces could be placed, how to capture your opponent's tiles, and so on. By the time the rakkan got into one rule, Darius had forgotten the last, but he hid his confusion behind a series of nods.

"Let's begin." Eugenius placed a grey stone at the centre of the board. "What would you like to wager first, the gift or answers?"

That was a surprisingly difficult choice. Although a present held less trepidation, he decided it best to test the waters with a question. "How did you know Brutus?" He placed a black piece right beside Eugenius's, which brought a contemplative hum from his grandfather's throat.

"As bold as ever, I see," the old man murmured. "Although you haven't scored yet, I'll answer because it isn't about you. It would be hard for me not to know the rakkan that raised you. I wasn't up to caring for children in those days, or I'd have done it myself. A leader's life is demanding."

Suddenly a thousand other questions filled Darius's mind, unrelated to his own past. "Leader as in a—"

"Warlord, yes."

So those calluses are from a sword. Darius lost his thoughts for a moment because he'd expected the man to say "centurion" or "commander."

Eugenius stared intently at the game board while a crash above them disturbed the dirt in the ceiling, sending a light sprinkle of dust onto the game pieces.

"Storm's raging," Eugenius muttered. "Looks like you're stuck here for a little while."

Darius suddenly felt the weight of all the earth above him. Hopefully, Tiro could get word to him down here in a storm. "How long do you think it will take the storm to pass?"

"A day or two at least." Eugenius placed another piece, this time at the far side of the board.

The move had Darius struggling to recall the rules. Why would the man make such an odd placement? *Like it matters…* He slapped one of his pieces beside the new one, then leant back and massaged the tension from his shoulders. Two days here was fine.

"Interesting," Eugenius mumbled to himself. "Didn't attack when I left myself open." Then he placed his next stone and captured one of Darius's.

"My first question may sound strange," Eugenius began, "but I've kept abreast of most of your new life via Lex for the last couple of years, so I have few questions as to what you remember or what you've done."

Darius frowned. What exactly had she said about him?

"So, what's your question?" he asked.

Eugenius continued studying the game board with an embarrassed tinge to his cheeks. "Have you ever been in love?"

If only the old man had been meeting his gaze, Darius could have vented his annoyance at the random, intrusive question from someone he'd only just met. He would have refused to answer if he'd thought his grandfather might respond with a similar refusal under *his* questions.

"Yes," Darius muttered.

Eugenius nodded but seemed wise enough not to pry any further. Had Lex told him of the time he'd kissed her? Tried to stop her marriage? Of Selene?

"My turn," Darius grunted. He slammed down a black stone to capture one of the greys. "My brother…"

Eugenius exhaled slowly but still didn't break his gaze away from the game pieces. "You had one sibling named Amid. I told your father that living amongst humans would end in tears, but your mother, she's…a stubborn one." The old man's eyes darted up to him so suddenly Darius almost flinched.

"Does blood still affect you?" Eugenius asked.

"… It's not your turn to question."

"I'll take that as a yes. I always thought that affliction was a most wretched curse, to hamstring a warrior so…" The man spoke as if it wasn't Darius's fault, as if he had no control over the feelings of revulsion that he presumed others felt but controlled far better.

"But now my days are shortening," Eugenius said, "I wonder if your fear wasn't a blessing."

Darius scoffed. "Doesn't feel like one."

"Of course it doesn't. But perhaps the consequences of what would be uninhibited slaughter are worse than the affliction that restrains you."

"You pity those that fall to my sword?"

"No. I speak of the consequences for you."

It was hard for Darius to admit that the faces of all those he'd killed had some impact on him.

Eugenius narrowed his eyes. "Is that the symbol of Agathos around your neck? Does it worry you?"

Darius looked down, but the pendant wasn't visible. How had the man known? "The God of Justice might concern me, had I seen anything to prove he's real."

Eugenius nodded. "It's as if you speak my own mind. I once believed in the Creator, but now I can't say I've seen any proof, only a world suffused with unchallenged wickedness."

It really was as if the pair of them had the same mind.

Eugenius added, "But there's one thing that still puzzles me." He picked up one of the game pieces and tossed it into the air. It spun around, rising to a graceful halt near the ceiling before clattering down onto the board in a spot that captured one of Darius's pieces.

Show off. Although new to the game, the fact Darius was losing made him want to crush the black stone in his hand. His next move would have captured the very piece his grandfather had just defended.

"Am I supposed to be impressed?" Darius asked.

"By my luck? No. But aren't you impressed that the stone did, and always does, the same thing—fall? Tell me, can you command a stone or explain rules such as this one and every other needed to hold the world together? When I toss the stones, they rise and fall, as certain as our inevitable deaths."

Darius sighed and buried his face in one hand. "What the hell are you talking about?"

"The rules of the world. Why does order exist and not chaos unless there is a rule-maker? But then, surely he who commands the stones also commands us. Are we free?"

"Does there need to be a reason? Can't rules just exist? Is chaos even possible?"

Eugenius murmured. "That's what I say when we have our forums here, debating the big questions of our world. Accepting these as brute facts seems like the only alternative for people like you and me. It just doesn't satisfy me."

"And it doesn't satisfy me that you haven't answered my original question."

Eugenius sighed and went back to studying the game. "It appears I've captured your piece by chance, but it's best not to rely on such things. Perhaps fate determined where the stone would fall. Perhaps fate determined what would happen to your brother."

Darius withdrew his hand and stared into the old man's pitying eyes. While the next words formed in the old man's mind and lips, Darius's stomach lurched.

"I know one thing," Eugenius said. "After your brother died, the sight of blood made you sick. If your memory is bloody, then it's likely true. I'm sorry, my child." A wet shine came to the man's eyes.

"Sorry for what?"

"For not being more understanding with you. I saw your reaction to blood as weakness. I was a different man back then—not even a man at all, I'd now say. A man knows when not to fight, and I learnt that all too late."

All Darius wanted was revenge on Hadrian and the rest, whether by fighting or assassination or whatever. Eugenius probably wouldn't approve.

"Guess I'm still a boy, then," Darius muttered.

"We shouldn't resign ourselves to such states. Brutus raised you to be a man, and I can't think of a rakkan that would have done a better job." Eugenius glanced back at the game table. "I captured your piece; so tell me, were you with Brutus at the end?"

Darius shifted uncomfortably in his seat. "Yes."

"What did he say?"

"Not much. He was cold." The haunting whispers of Brutus's death throes filled his mind again after a few weeks of leaving him in peace. "He'd lost a lot of blood, and his skin was pallid. He said he was…afraid." Admitting such a thing felt like a betrayal.

But the words brought a wistful grin to Eugenius's face. "Some take consolation from believing in the afterlife. But what is more terrifying than being judged by a creator? Perhaps I shouldn't have asked Brutus that question so often."

There certainly weren't many things more frightening than the thought of being judged at the end.

"So…" Darius said. "Where is Brutus's gift?"

Eugenius took one of the grey game stones and held it out in his palm. "Here."

"Great. A game?"

"No. Just this."

"Even better. How can I play with one piece?"

"It's not for playing." His grandfather closed his fist around the stone and ferven erupted within. Light burst between the cracks of his fingers and raged for a few seconds before the man relaxed and opened his hand. The ferven withered into the skin once more and left a weakly glowing stone.

At first, Darius was confused why the rock hadn't melted, but then he sensed something oddly familiar in the orange light still emanating from the flat stone. "Is that…?"

"Aeternus. Not without its value but hardly gold or kuraminium. Still, it will—"

"Burn forever." Darius held out his hand and let his grandfather slide the stone onto his palm. It was warm to the touch but not as hot as boiled water, and the light it gave to the room was feebler than a candle's would have been. Tiny wisps of smoke rose from the almost invisible sponge-like holes on the stone's surface.

"It won't quite last forever," Eugenius said, "but long enough that only a rakkan would see it burn away. And it doesn't use the air to burn. It's just as warm and bright underwater."

"So it's as useless under as it is over?"

Eugenius scoffed. "Usefulness isn't just in an object's practicality. Brutus knew that."

Darius suddenly regretted his snipe. "Do you know why he left me this?"

"It's symbolic in his faction. Only rakkan fire can ignite aeternus, and it reminds us that even the weakest of lights can break an impenetrable darkness."

Not one to usually understand symbolism, Darius was glad he at least saw the logic in this. But it forgot one thing… He summoned algor across his hand and enveloped the stone until all its glow was banished into a cold death.

"And mankind snuffs out the light," Darius muttered.

"True. But mankind is also the one that lights it." The confidence in his grandfather's voice made Darius suspect the man had an answer for everything—or at least think he did. But what surprised Darius most was that the man spoke of humans and rakkans in the same breath, as if the same. No one else spoke like that, hardly even Lex. This man was his kin in more ways than one. And to think that realisation had been started by a tiny rock… If Brutus wanted him to have this, he'd keep it with him alongside the two other keepsakes he carried.

"Some lights can't be relit," Darius said as he pocketed the stone. "Which brings me back to my brother."

All colour drained from his grandfather's face, and the old man blew hard into his beard. "Very well. I can only tell you your mother's version of events because you spoke little of the incident to me. And you should bear in mind I do not trust her word entirely.

"You were six years old when it happened, though you fought with the skill and arrogance of a teen. Such prowess brought unwelcome attention, and the former king soon marked you for death."

"King Medus I?"

"Indeed. Hadrian had risen to warlord the year before and begun his campaign against the Empire. The late king saw the risk the rakkans posed."

As if Darius needed another reason to hate the Viridian Warlord.

"It's hard for you to understand," Eugenius continued. "Things were different before Archimedes. The King knew your power was unrivalled—"

The door to the room crashed open and let in a bright wave of light that cut off Eugenius's words. Darius winced at the sudden brilliance, and his eyes took a few seconds to make out two large lamps held in each hand by a woman who stepped inside. The amber glow of the flames flickered in her fierce, human eyes, which Darius could have sworn he recognised. But the rest of her rumpled face triggered no memories. Her curly grey hair was soaked and windswept, stuck in knots to her dripping cloak, but she seemed not to notice because her glare fixed on Darius while her mouth twisted in a foul grimace.

"You…" she growled. "How dare you come here."

Darius stood as the woman stepped towards him, ready to defend himself from whatever she was about to spew. By now, the hatred his name and face brought was nothing surprising. But before he uttered a word, Eugenius darted up between the pair.

"Leave us be," the old man said. For the first time, his eyes spat venom. "I told you to wait out the storm elsewhere."

"You didn't tell me *he* was here," she said. "I heard you talking of Amid… You have no right."

Realisation suddenly hit Darius with a force that knocked him back into his chair, legs weak. He gaped up at her, and only on his third attempt at speaking did his voice return to his throat. "Mother?"

8

Lex – Margalvia

Lex squeezed her eyes shut and clutched her hip, as if blindness did anything to ease the pain lancing to the core of her bone. Her hip had never been pierced by so much as a splinter, yet it tormented her with a cruelty that none of her sword or arrow wounds had rivalled. Since losing Laltos, pain was all she'd known. Just like when she'd lost her son.

"Please let me help, mistress." Nasrin's gentle hand touched her shoulder, but Lex shook it off and collapsed to one knee.

Her jaw clenched so hard the force pained her teeth. "I can bear this without the tears." Margalvia didn't have a large supply of the weeping plant, and if she took any more than necessary, there might not be enough for others—or for herself if she desperately needed it in the future.

"Anyway," Lex rasped, "don't change the subject. Where is she?"

When no response came, Lex opened her eyes to see Nasrin fixated on her. Even as a child, the woman had had an uncanny knack for dissolving everyone's stubbornness, from surly old soldiers to cantankerous widows. Her curly brown hair shone gold where it caught the candlelight, melding into smooth, tan skin that was still plump and deceptively iridescent with youth.

I must look a state compared to her. Both fresh and dried sweat stuck Lex's raven hair to her forehead, and days without washing had left an oiliness to her skin that she could feel without touching.

The room they occupied was spacious for a Margalvian dwelling only because it contained a bed large enough for a grown man, more than a single stone chair, and a central fire pit. But this place was a hovel compared to Lex's previous homes. She yearned to once again peruse fine oil paintings and sculptures of the God and Goddess in her abode, although such cravings weren't about pretentious snobbery but about the pain of losing the city she'd matured in, now crushed and humiliated.

Only slithers of the morning sun peeked through the iron shutters that covered her window like the bars of a prison cell. Still, gloomy was the most her eyes would tolerate before the damned headaches began.

But she didn't care how sparse and rough her surroundings were. She had far worse issues, and the gentle woman with her now wasn't just here to look after a pathetic, languishing algus. The question Lex had left unasked for years finally needed asking because Nasrin might be her only key to finding the Waif Magician. Why else would the hermit keep in contact with a lowly slave if not for a bond between them?

"Please take the tears," Nasrin repeated in a voice as soft as Xavalan silk.

"Fine." Lex pulled a vial of the black liquid from her pocket and dabbed a couple of droplets onto her tongue. "Happy now?"

Nasrin sighed, and the murkiness of the walls seemed to spread to her face. "I haven't been happy for a long time, mistress."

That was the understatement of the century. While Nasrin helped Lex back up and sat her on the stuffed heap she called a bed, Lex caught the fading scent of smoked healing herbs in the carer's hair. Nasrin hadn't tended to the sick for months—unless you counted Lex. It was nice to see the woman in a clean dress for once.

"Stop calling me 'mistress,'" Lex snapped. "I freed you for a reason."

"And as a free woman, I'll use whatever words I please, *mistress.*"

How could Lex argue with that? She had no idea why Nasrin insisted on revering such a failure of an algus, and she hadn't the will or energy to argue. Sleep had evaded her for days, and not only due to the pain. Insomnia made her such an irritable shrew that Nasrin had every right to tell her to go to hell. The only things that took Lex's mind from her lost family and city were her daughter, Cynthia, and the mystery of Hadrian's ambitions. Why was he still after the Magician? It must be something to do with the Staff of Arria, but what? How would Hadrian use the Staff to fight Margalvia when it weakened his own warriors?

She needed answers. She had a daughter to protect. She had Darius to protect. And perhaps somewhere in the Empire, her son still lived as a Numbered, unwittingly needing her protection from the savages he might soon be forced to battle.

"The pain is easing," Lex lied. "Did you bring the metals?"

"I did." Nasrin took tiny bags from her pocket and emptied several powders into small piles on the dark stone floor. "These ones cost so much I used the last of your gold."

She prayed Darius found more of her gold in Laltos undisturbed in order to further her quest. The stockpile had once been her war chest, but now, she could hardly plan a war when her strategic failures had led to the death and destruction of her home.

"Try to burn the first powder." Lex prayed one of these was the one she sought.

Nasrin took a stick, lit it in the fire, then held it to the heap.

Lex winced in anticipation, but the metal powder didn't even glow when touched by the heat. She cursed at another failure. "I worry we'll never find the one. Not that it matters, given you still refuse to tell me where the Magician is."

"These tests can wait." Nasrin sighed and sat beside Lex on the bed, then gently nudged her into lying flat. The carer began a careful massage of Lex's hip that relieved the pain far more than she ever let on. Sometimes, just feeling the touch of another again eased Lex's pain and was the only time her heart settled into a calm rhythm.

"Shirin is always moving," Nasrin said. "I've only seen her once since she stole the Staff of Arria. I doubt she'll venture near Denehill again, considering you saw her favourite hideaway."

The revelation almost made Lex bolt upright, but Nasrin's hands had turned her muscles into mush.

"You've never mentioned seeing her since we killed Archimedes," Lex said.

"Why would I, when most want her dead?"

"I don't want her dead." Lex sighed as another tense knot at her hip unwound with the massage. "You know that. I just fear what will happen if Hadrian finds her first. We need to get the Staff."

Nasrin snorted. "You should pray he finds her. He'd lose his head, and you could stop torturing yourself."

Torturing? Besides guarding her daughter, revenge was the only thing that gave purpose to her life. Without that, what was there to live for? After a long pause in her thoughts, while either the tears or Nasrin's strong fingers dulled her agony, only Darius came to mind for some reason.

"Did you hear the news in the street today?" Nasrin asked.

"About Regent Hera?"

"Yes."

"I did." Hera's order to free all slaves had come as a shock to many. After a lot of slaves perished trying to defend Laltos, too few were left for the once affluent to rule over. All people were now free, and all free people were expected to labour.

"There was almost a riot," Nasrin continued. "The citizens spat foul curses at her, saying she'd gone soft after losing her son. Then the merchants and ex-slaves faced off, and you should have seen the looks in my people's eyes. I've never seen so many ready for death. I got caught in the middle. One noble grabbed me, and I swore he was about to knife me."

This time, Lex did bolt upright. "Who? Give me his name."

"Relax. Hera managed to calm the conflict *without* spilling blood. Though the rakkan legionnaires there seemed disappointed they didn't get to exercise their fists."

Lex lay back down with a frown. How had the Regent quashed a riot without force? The woman's intellect and charm clearly far outstripped Lex's. If only Lex were so cunning, perhaps all her plans wouldn't have ended as they had.

Nasrin sighed. "The former slaves have already coined a new name for her—the Steel Regent."

"Catchy." Everyone loved a hero or heroine, and what better way to solidify that than with a moniker? The same went for enemies like the "Slayer of Gods."

"You know she got the idea from you?" Nasrin asked.

"What? How?"

"She saw how hard I and your other slaves worked after you freed us. Then she spoke with the Chief Priest of the Order, and he helped her make the decision."

Do I dare tell Nasrin why I freed her? The girl likely thought the act noble, but the truth was Lex was barely able to take care of herself, let alone others. She'd freed her slaves so they could work for themselves, and Cynthia was still with Darius's grandfather, away from Hadrian and Varro.

"Can we get back to the Magician?" Lex asked.

Nasrin squeezed Lex's hip so hard she gasped, and she suspected it was deliberate.

"Will you stop?" Nasrin said. "Your first priority should be yourself."

"This *is* for myself, to right the wrongs done to me and us."

"The world's problems are not yours to solve."

If I don't, no one will. "Can you at least tell me how you found her the last time?"

Nasrin stopped the massage mid-squeeze, hands trembling slightly. "I…didn't find her. She found me."

"Why?" Would Lex finally get an answer to the question?

Nasrin scooted back on the bed, but Lex reached out and took the woman's hand.

"I should go." Nasrin tugged, and although Lex's grasp wasn't crushing, it held. "Please, mistress."

Lex sat up and locked eyes with the carer for a second, the same way she had for many years, before releasing her.

"Please," Lex whispered. She let all the pain, all the agony, bleed into her eyes until Nasrin wilted.

"I'll tell you if you swear to never tell another," Nasrin said.

"Of course."

"And if you do me a favour."

Lex paused at the demand, so unused to it that she almost gasped but caught herself in time. She supposed a free woman deserved something in return. "What favour?"

The carer leaned closer and put a hand on her shoulder, the way Lex did when manipulating people. But Nasrin wouldn't stoop to such lows.

"I don't know what I need," Nasrin said, "but I'll ask it of you when I do."

Lex murmured to herself. Undefined payments were usually given an automatic no. Yet, she was desperate. "Fine."

Nasrin clasped her hands together around Lex's and squeezed, then said, "Shirin is half-human on her mother's side and of slave descent like her name suggests."

Lex nodded, though she had wondered whether the Magician had chosen a name from the old tribes herself just to annoy the human elites she so loathed.

"Her mother wasn't an only child," Nasrin continued, "and her siblings had offspring of their own…" As her voice trailed off, she bowed her head.

It wasn't a stretch to see where her story was leading. "You…" Lex said. "You're related to her?"

"Our family was once large but close," Nasrin whispered. "I never met Shirin's mother or father, but my own parents gave hints as to who they were and of their other children. Before the King came for them."

Everyone in the Empire had heard the fate of that family via a song sung in every tavern for years as a way to scare the masses into knowing that no half-human would ever be allowed to live.

"So who survived the purge?" Lex asked.

"Only Shirin. She and her brothers were branded for death, half a skull emblazoned on their forearms. The boys were killed first. She never told me how, or how she escaped, but you could see by the emptiness of her gaze, by the lack of any shred of pity or mercy in the midst of horror, that the event scarred her soul as well as her arm."

Lex knew the feeling. Her husband's dying face wouldn't leave her nightmares, and it had now joined the thousands that had perished in Laltos along with her speared father. As if not enough, Darius's tortured body had healed far more swiftly than it ever would in her mind.

"You're not wearing it anymore." Nasrin looked at Lex's chest, where her figurine had once hung.

"I threw it away." She'd hoped the carer hadn't noticed. But that was perhaps too much to ask, considering the slave had attended prayers with her for years.

"He has it, you know." Nasrin grinned, but Lex saw no amusement in the assertion.

"Who?"

"Darius, of course."

How odd. The old Darius would never have kept it. "Why would he?"

Nasrin shrugged. "I doubt it's because he's a believer."

"Doesn't matter." Discussing the man would only lower her mood further, after she'd already spent too much energy dwelling on him. Although she'd sworn never to give a man a chance to hurt her again, her pain made the decision to live a solitary life seem foolish.

"You've had a message from him." Nasrin pulled a thin roll of parchment from her bag.

Lex snatched it. "Why didn't you tell me sooner?" On the back of the roll was her own note, and she quickly devoured Darius's scrawling. At the last words, she paused, read them a few times and ran a thumb across the charcoal to check it hadn't been smudged.

… I miss you too.

The proclamation threatened to bring a smile to her face for the first time in months, but instead, pain again lanced her hip. She cursed. *Goddess. Can't I have a moment's relief?*

Nasrin wrapped an arm around her shoulders and squeezed her into an embrace. Normally, Lex resisted such shows of affection, but this time she just settled in the carer's arms as if a child again with her father.

"Leave me," Lex whispered. "I want to be alone."

Nasrin only tightened her hold. "No, you don't. You just wish I were someone else, tall, eyes and hair as dark as my panther, staring at you with my rugged good looks."

Lex scoffed. "And an ego. Don't let him hear you say things like that, or he'll be all the more insufferable."

"Is he unbearable, though? You said he's not as bad as he used to be."

"True." Lex couldn't imagine the new Darius betraying her like the old one—with a whore, no less. She supposed there was no reason to remain available for marriage now that her family had no power, and Darius…

She cursed and pulled herself away from Nasrin's grip. "I have more important things to do than discuss men."

"You mean like wallow in pain and refuse medicine?"

Lex lost what she'd been about to say before the sarcastic remark, and the pitiful look on Nasrin's face was just as insulting.

"Why not be with him?" Nasrin said. "Try to find happiness while you can?"

Lex shook her head. "He's still thinking about my sister—"

"Who's dead."

"Don't…" Lex's face began heating, so she calmed herself with slow and steady breaths. "I don't mind you having an opinion, but don't be callous. Drop it."

Nasrin's shoulders slumped. "Apologies, mistress."

"Don't—" Lex gasped as a fresh wave of pain gripped her until every muscle tensed. *To hell with it.* She pulled the vial of tears from her pocket and put another drop on her tongue, the most she dared take. After a pause and more deep breaths, she said, "I don't want to argue."

"Me neither, mistress. I just want to help you."

"I know."

The pair sat in a comfortable silence for a few moments while Lex stared at the remaining piles of powder on the floor. Who knew whether Selene was alive or not. Lex couldn't blame Darius for clinging to hope because the temptation was never far from her own mind. But Nasrin was correct in treating Selene as if dead, no matter how terrible that was to accept.

Lex turned to face Nasrin, holding her tongue until the carer locked eyes with her, unable to refuse her.

"Will you help me find the Magician?" she whispered.

The reluctance was plain in Nasrin's pinched expression, but also betrayed the woman was considering it.

"I swear I'm not searching to kill her," Lex added. "I wish to win her to our cause, to take down the Viridians, the Silk City, and the King." Only after would she poison the woman for trying to kill Darius.

"Then what's the powder for?" Nasrin raised an eyebrow.

Lex didn't move. She'd never told Nasrin that her experiments related to disabling the Magician's sight.

"A backup plan," Lex said. "So, will you help me?"

After another tiring pause, Nasrin sighed. "I'll aid you, but I'm calling in my favour."

"Go on," Lex said, suspecting Nasrin had known what she'd wanted all along.

"I'm coming with you." Nasrin straightened her back as if ready to defiantly argue the case.

But Lex wouldn't deny the woman. She could use the company, and Nasrin would make winning over the old witch that much easier.

"Fine," Lex said. "But you'd best not slow me down."

Nasrin scoffed. "*Me* slow *you*? There are times you can barely walk, let alone fight. You need me, though you'll never admit it, and that's not all. Which brings me onto my favour…"

"That isn't it?"

"No. I want Darius to come with us."

Lex was in too much pain to cloak an insulted scowl. She might have been weak, but she'd battled through pain before. Not to mention it was far too dangerous to let Darius near the Magician again.

"I'm not an invalid," Lex said.

"True, but I think you'll both be better off together. And given your temper of late, maybe he's the only one who can lighten your mood."

"Unless he cleaves Hadrian's head, he won't. And he's still too preoccupied with my sister to help us." That's why she'd never bothered to make more than short requests of him.

"We can at least ask him. If he refuses, so be it." Nasrin's voice sharpened and changed from that of a warm carer to something far too close to Lex's for comfort. Perhaps she'd rubbed off on the carer over the years.

"Do we have an agreement or not?" Nasrin asked.

It wasn't like Lex had a choice. "Yes. We leave when the storm has passed. Now light the rest of the powders."

Nasrin grinned, then obliged. The second pile caught fire when touched by a flame but burnt far too slowly to be the one Lex had heard of, the one she'd spent months trying to find. The third didn't light at all, so Nasrin moved to the last one with a sigh.

After so many attempts, Lex didn't even bother to watch another failure and lay back down on the bed, staring up at the thin sunlight on the ceiling. A heartbeat later, a flash lit the room in a sudden, brilliant white that blinded her. A fiery pop rang in her ears, followed shortly after by Nasrin's shriek.

Lex bolted back up to see the carer pressing her back to the wall opposite, blinking frantically.

"That one's a good start." Lex stared, so used to failure that the bright spots in her vision had to be a delusion. "But we need one even brighter."

9

Darius – South of Margalvia

Water dripped from his mother's soaked clothes, the patter being the only noise filling the humble room. Darius gaped at her, not returning the disgust twisting her face. But his grandfather did that for him and more.

"You're still breathing, then," his mother said. She took a few more steps forward and shook her wet head.

A red film washed across his vision as the memory of Amid and the blood threatened to overwhelm him. His stomach lurched, but he swallowed hard and focused on conquering the demon that had controlled him for too long. But then his hands began to tremble, and he looked down at them, confused, afraid. *The memory's true. I know it.*

"You can stop looking at me like that, Eugenius," his mother said with the same harsh voice Darius recalled in his memory. "I have every right to speak with my son. I have every right to remind him of the horrors he put me through that he's apparently now forgotten."

The old man said nothing, though from the tension in his neck, it appeared he had to force his own silence. Instead, he eased himself back down at the game table.

"Not that I want to hear what he has to say." His mother stomped towards the benches facing the front of the room, but she made no move to sit. "There's plenty *I* have to say, and I should flay him with more than words. I'm glad his father's dead so he doesn't have to see what his son did to our family."

Eugenius clenched his jaw.

If this went on any longer, Darius would never discover whether the guilt that plagued him was deserved or not. He needed to know.

"I don't know what you speak of," he said, his voice as feeble as a child's, "I only have one memory of Amid. We were all together—"

"Don't you dare speak of that day to me." His mother's eyes filled with madness. "Those men wouldn't have come if you'd only done what you were told. But no…you were a brat that always had to have your way. You had to use your abilities to steal from that poor street seller, as if there weren't a dozen soldiers there to see you do it."

The fear of that one memory of Amid being true had so commanded his mind that he'd forgotten his guilt might go beyond that single day. He opened his mouth to stop the woman divulging more, but only a dry rasp left his throat.

"I knew you were trouble from the day you were born," she said. "They say a mother loves her child at first sight, but how could I, when I saw the wickedness I had birthed? I should have left you for the winter to take after you killed our dog."

"He was a child," Eugenius said, cheeks scarlet. "He didn't know his own strength!"

"And I had the strength to control him?" His mother shook her head and fixated on him again, nose turned up in disgust. "That was just the beginning. I tried to teach you to hide your abilities, but you were a little brat who knew better—always had to flaunt your speed or your muscle. And to think those were your best years… You were like a rabid dog that had tasted flesh young. If it hadn't been for Brutus, you'd have drowned in the blood you spilled and the bile it made you heave."

"Have you finished?" Eugenius's voice became low and menacing.

But the hysteria possessing his mother took no heed. "*Twice* you almost killed your brother playing with your damned algor." His mother flailed her arms with every flung insult and splattered him with rainwater. "Your father almost lost his sword hand stopping you. And I lost count of how many times you almost killed me. I'm still marred with bald patches on my scalp from where you yanked my hair out as a baby." She thrust a hand through her curls so swiftly it only served to rip out more of her weathered hair.

Darius's breaths quickened with every word from the woman's mouth.

"And don't think these were childhood instances," she continued. "I heard what you did before your eighteenth birthday…the Denehill Massacre."

That wasn't the only story Darius had heard before, and it wasn't the one that troubled him most. Just the recollection of his brother turned his stomach again. Any more of this tirade and the sickness would spread further than his belly.

Finally, he summoned the courage to speak. "Tell me about Amid. Is it true that I—"

His mother darted towards him in a frenzy and swung an open hand for his cheek.

But Darius caught her wrist. Her arm writhed in his, her fingers curled and tried to claw, but she was no match for his strength.

She screamed, voice shrill with fury. "Don't even speak Amid's name! He wouldn't have been such an ungrateful swine of a son like you, such a curse on our family. He would have done what he was told and stayed in that cupboard. You don't deserve to breathe!"

The words echoed in his mind with such a haunting terror that he almost let her arm go, if only to silence her by allowing her to strike him. The memory became more real by the second. He saw his brother's face again, sleepy and innocent as it had been in that cupboard, before Darius had burst out and sealed his brother's fate. The blood, his brother's agonised screams, the pained face that a baby should never have…and then the silence that followed; it was as if it were happening again.

All the while, his mother screamed and writhed; a fingernail caught his skin. Then Eugenius jumped up and unleashed a hellish roar that threatened to bring the ceiling down. The guttural outcry shrank the woman's snarl into a whimper, and even Darius backed away an inch.

"You will not speak to him like this!" Eugenius boomed. "He was a boy." Unlike his mother's condemnations, his grandfather's blunt tone carried an ominous threat that made further words unnecessary.

After a couple of deep, shaky breaths, his mother dared to speak again. Though her words were quieter, they'd lost no ounce of bitterness. "A boy who should have known better. I told him to stay…"

This time Darius did let go, and a second later, his mother's fist smacked his nose until the bone crunched. Eugenius flew across to her and wrestled her away, but Darius just sat and hung his head over the game table. Warm blood trickled down his nostril and dripped onto the aeternus lump.

"It's true, isn't it?" Darius muttered. "I got Amid killed."

"Yes, you did!" his mother spat at him, spraying his forehead before Eugenius clamped a hand over her mouth.

The blood on the table grew drip by drip. Darius's hands shook. Bile rose in his throat. He swallowed hard, but the acidic burn flew back up. He hadn't realised how much he'd doubted—or wilfully denied—the truth of that memory, but now the noise around him was swallowed by the sounds of the grumbling storm above. His mother was right. All his life, he'd brought people death and suffering. The scars on his back were only a fraction of the scars he'd given everyone else. The blood he now shed was only a drop compared to the gushing wetness from Amid.

This time, bile rose with such a force it leaked from Darius's lips before he had time to turn and bend over. He vomited a foul mess onto the floor while his grandfather's shouts sent tremors through him.

"Look what you've done!" the old man yelled. "You're a hateful, spiteful woman, and my son's better off dead than with you."

The woman's once piercing voice came out muffled.

"You won't speak another word to him, or I won't offer you shelter any longer, and you can instead fend for yourself with whatever humans will have you." He dragged her across to the door while she flailed, then he kicked it open and flung her outside as one would a damaged scrap of armour.

As he slammed the door shut to the screams outside, Darius found what appeared to be a different man standing before him. This one had no warmth or kind aura but instead an animalistic fervour that left no doubt that the rakkan had been a warlord. But only a few seconds later, the intensity on Eugenius's face calmed, the muscles in his forearms relaxed, and decency returned to his features.

"I'm sorry about that," Eugenius said. "I shouldn't have let her go on and on. I hadn't intended for you to meet her at all. For a second, I thought perhaps she'd be civil."

"It's not your fault," Darius said. "She's right." If only half the stories she'd mentioned were true, he'd been a nightmare of a son.

"No!" Eugenius paced towards the game table again, picked up the piece of aeternus and pressed it into Darius's still trembling hand. "You were nothing but an infant when you did those things. You were not the one that spilled your brother's blood, so don't let your guilt ruin your future, my child. Remember, even the smallest light breaks the most impenetrable darkness."

Excuses. "My actions led to—"

"We cannot see the future. You can't know whether your brother would have lived had you done nothing."

That was at least true. But were mere possibilities enough reason to pardon guilt?

While Darius pondered, his grandfather pulled a piece of cloth from his pocket and wiped the blood from Darius's nose.

"I know you hate it," the old man said. "And you realise why, don't you?"

"Not really."

"Because of Amid. You had no issues before that, and you'd had to fight others to protect yourself many times, believe me, as well as seen your father slay."

"Is that who I learned to fight from?"

"At first, but then I must bear some responsibility too." The softness of the man's words bore a shame to have trained such a killer, such a monster.

"My deeds are not your fault," Darius said.

"Nonsense. I must accept some of the guilt for your faults if I'm to take pride in the good you do."

Darius scoffed. "What good?"

"Oh, my child." His grandfather took another game piece and ignited the aeternus with ferven. "I see the darkness besieging you, and it fights to consume you. Don't believe you only bring sorrow to this world."

"That's all I strive to bring now—to my enemies, at least. After that, I'm not sure what I'll bring."

Eugenius dropped the glowing piece onto the board and stared at the game for more seconds than Darius liked. Though they didn't make eye contact, Darius felt as if in a stare-down.

"I speak not of death or hopelessness," Eugenius said finally. "I speak of vengeance. Do not let your quest for it devour you. That stole from me a part of myself that I'll never recover."

Perhaps there was some truth to the advice, but when trying to turn his mind away from smiting his enemies, Darius was left with only an emptiness that also threatened to swallow him. Only Selene had ever led him to imagine a life without fighting. Is that why some foolish part of him clung to a hope she might still be alive? If he ever did find her, would her scars only make his hatred intolerable? If she'd suffered as he had in Laltos…

"I forfeit the game," Eugenius said with a smile that seemed forced but eased Darius's mood, nevertheless. "I know you'll heed my words as much as I did at your age—not at all—but whether they resonate now or in a century, I trust they will."

"If we're done with the game, may I ask you questions freely now?"

Eugenius smiled and ushered Darius to sit on one of the wooden benches facing the altar.

"I can't imagine what it's like for you," his grandfather said. "To lose one's memories…and with no hope of getting them back. I've never heard of a Numbered regaining themselves."

Like Darius needed reminding… Over the next few hours, the pair talked, Eugenius rebutting in full many of the accusations Darius's mother had levelled at him. Some answers brought little consolation, and he soon learned his childhood misdeeds paled when compared to the slayings he'd left in his wake as a young man.

But the Denehill Massacre remained the most bloody and unnerving. According to Eugenius, the slaughter had prevented an attack on Margalvia. Darius had left the King's army so weakened that Commander Varro had won the following Battle of Uxon and defended their people. So why did the thought of his old self slitting the throats of so many algus bring pangs of guilt?

After a few hours, Darius still hadn't an answer.

"Tell me more of Brutus," Darius said. His mind couldn't take another horrid story he'd rather remained forgotten.

"He was a thoughtful and stern man." Eugenius's lips curled into a wistful grin. "As much as he tried to train you to master the hammer, you preferred the sharpness of a blade. So he had Varro train you until you became a teenager."

Perhaps that was why Darius was so deadly with a sword, but he wouldn't give the new warlord an ounce of credit for his prowess.

"Brutus always wanted the best for you," Eugenius said, "and his wife was no different."

"I haven't seen her for almost two years," Darius said. He'd wanted to send her flowers, money, a message, anything to ease the pain at her husband's death. Despite only meeting the woman during his brief periods in Margalvia, she'd treated him with far more motherly kindness than the spiteful woman he'd just met.

Eugenius went on to tell plenty of tales of him and Brutus as he'd grown up, enough that they somewhat blunted the darker parts he'd learned of his past.

No sunlight could enter the underground room, but Darius sensed the hour was getting early, and his mind overflowed with many things it hadn't had to cope with before.

"I hope you won't take offence if I retire to my room," he said.

"I understand. And I apologise again about your mother. She's insufferable, and if I hadn't given my word to my son to look after her, I'd send her away, storm or no storm."

A violent wave thundered above as if to remind Darius he was trapped in the same place as her a little longer.

"I await word from Lex," he said, "so please let me know if her escort arrives."

"I will. Anything important?"

Darius bit his tongue, unsure whether to divulge more. After only a few short hours, he did trust the man, and Lex clearly did too.

"I'm going to find Hadrian," he said. "He's going after the Waif Magician for some reason, so I'll stop him before he can find her."

A sudden horror seized his grandfather's face, as if he'd seen a sword pierce Darius's neck. The wrinkles etched at his eyes deepened as the already-white skin paled to wan chalk.

"What's wrong?" Darius asked.

"Nothing…" Eugenius swallowed after the obvious lie and composed himself as quickly as any leader would. "I just worry about you. Be careful. The Waif Magician is not a woman someone seeks without reason."

"I'm in no rush to meet her."

Eugenius stood and came over to rest a hand on Darius's shoulder. It was just for a breath, but the touch brought a calmness only close friends had ever offered him.

His grandfather slipped out of the room with a new urgency, while Darius retired after picking up his piece of aeternus and cleaning it of blood. *Thanks for the gift, Brutus.* He'd cut a hole in it and hang it on his neck with his bear claw and Agathos figurine.

As he rejoined Lyra on his bed, the reminder of the God of Justice forced his attention back to Hadrian. His chance to finally hunt down the warlord was all that made him forget about Selene, Lex, and now his mother. *Soon.*

10

Rufus – Camp near Urukan Mine

Another gust shook the hefty tent, sending draughts through the holes in the canopy to prickle the gooseflesh across Rufus's skin. Luckily, the other boisterous commanders within didn't seem to notice his discomfort, helped by the fact Rufus wore thick furs around his torso. He tightened his clothes to be sure more breezes didn't chill. Strong rakkans didn't suffer the cold, and a commander couldn't show discomfort whilst in the middle of negotiations that would determine the fate of the rakkan world.

Although the tent above was worn from too many years under the sun, Rufus had insisted on using it to shelter the Warlord and his esteemed guests—despite Hadrian's protests that such an old tent was unworthy to house a "deity" such as he. The slate-grey canvas was blotched, with patches faded since it had first been stitched together by rakkan women, but that better blended the structure into the rocky terrain outside, a tactical advantage only Rufus seemed to think important.

Sat next to him on a tall stone throne, Hadrian peered down with suspicion for a moment, as if daring his youngest son to shiver again. The look hadn't changed in the half a century since Rufus came into the world.

Rufus didn't avert his gaze, showing no ounce of weakness.

After a few moments, the Warlord seemed satisfied and returned to pouring ale down his gullet with his one good arm while Rufus cursed at the cold to himself. The winds from the southern sea didn't often travel far inland, but today they coursed through the mountains and brought an icy fog to the plateau where they'd set up camp. Years of experience told Rufus the risk of snow was growing, yet had also taught him not to bother voicing such concerns when in esteemed company.

A thin, circular table filled the tent, leaving a gap for a golden statue in the centre, where no one could avoid seeing its monstrous form. Crafted by two of Viridia's finest sculptors using the spoils of Laltos, the idol of the Viridian Warlord brandished his swords in a victorious pose that had every muscle bursting with veins and divine strength. Imitation flames rose from the base, lofting him like a god from the fiery underworld. Despite being designed to be worshipped, it stood a foot shorter than the rakkan himself—so that everyone knew which version was more worthy of praise. *What other preposterous superstitions will Father think up to waste our valuable resources?* At least the female worshippers—or rather, fawners—had left for the night.

Around the vast table, not only Viridian Commanders ate and drank more than was wise in discussions, but also Branz Commanders and Branz Warlord Flavius himself. The guests wore the same thick furs as Rufus because they were accustomed to the warmer dunes in the north.

Although shorter than Hadrian, the Branz Warlord's deathly gaze held no less gravity. His permanent scowl created a deep wrinkle like a bridge connecting his thick, black eyebrows. His statements tonight had been as short and prickly as his hair, and if Rufus hadn't suggested adjourning for refreshments, the two bloated warlords' swords would have clashed. Rufus had been wise to seat them at the two ends of the table, decorated with the largest, brashest seats—although he'd been sure to tell both they were at the head.

Rufus had watched the Branzians carefully all night, and only he and the Branz Warlord were yet to touch a drop of ale or firewater. *But Father's drunk enough for both of us.* The fact made it even more pressing for *him* to steer whatever deal they hammered out and ensure it was in Viridia's best interests.

"We should head down the mine in the morning," Warlord Flavius said in a quiet voice that silenced the tent, nonetheless. "I fear the storm will sweep inland." His attention was on Rufus rather than Hadrian, and judging by the Viridian Warlord's face, he knew it.

"Are you afraid of the cold?" Hadrian jeered. A few Viridians chuckled, but Rufus found no amusement in taunts.

Finally, Flavius turned to Hadrian. "Only a fool underestimates the weather."

"Fool?" The Viridian Warlord smashed his fist on the table with such force it split the wood. "I may only have one good arm, but it'll do more damage to you than rainwater. The strength of my grandfather, Hadrianus the Great, courses through my veins."

Flavius grinned while the rest of the tent remained hushed. They all knew Hadrian spoke the truth. The nasty wound he'd taken at the Battle of Laltos had thankfully been to his weakest side. Besides, the injured arm was still strong enough to wield a shield, although Rufus had seen the tremors his father fought against.

"Let's not scuffle over the minor things," Rufus said. The weather was the least of their worries. "I see no reason we shouldn't descend the mine as you suggest, Warlord Flavius."

"Good." Flavius leaned back in his chair. "Then let's continue discussing the parley."

"Very well," Rufus said before his father could open his mouth to give yet another senseless jibe. "We've told you what we want. So what would you like in return?"

A toothy grin spread across Flavius's face. "Kuraminium."

Why did some men take such amusement in frustrating others? It wasn't the only form of entertainment Rufus failed to enjoy as common rakkans seemed to.

"How much kuraminium?" Hadrian's voice had calmed the drunken churlishness since he'd last spoken.

"As much as we need," Flavius said.

Hadrian scoffed. "Just name a price, be it in ore or weapons."

Flavius shook his head with a sigh, and Rufus leaned forward. The Branz Warlord wasn't speaking of tonnage.

"You want more of the mine?" Rufus asked.

"I'm glad at least one of you is perceptive," the Branz Warlord said.

Hadrian murmured to himself. "I don't invite him here because he's pretty, or a good swordsman."

Flavius raised an eyebrow at Rufus, as if expecting to see annoyance, but Rufus took his father's words as a compliment. If he were concerned with being a fighter, he'd train for it, and perhaps then would enjoy the seat at his father's right hand that his brothers always took.

"We'll pay in kuraminium," Rufus said, "but we won't sign away a supply."

"We're asking you to back us as a courtesy." Hadrian's voice grew so deep it resonated through the table. "We could always cripple Branz if you refuse."

So much for not resorting to threats. If only Rufus was left alone in these discussions…

"Do you think I'm blind to your predicament?" Flavius leaned in with an ever-deepening scowl. "If we don't back you instead of Margalvia, it's Viridia that will be crippled. The Azure Legion will never support you; that's why you're here grovelling to me. Violating a treaty is not something I take lightly, and you'd deserve every punishment you got for what you did. My vote will either deal you deadlock or ruin, so it's worth a hell of a lot more than I'm asking."

The Branz Warlord was giving virtually the same speech Rufus had before his father attacked Margalvia's part of the mine. If the words hadn't moved Hadrian then, they wouldn't today.

But now that the threats had started, the only option was to double down. "Don't flatter yourself," Rufus said. "If we have to, Viridia will cut off your road to the mine. We let your ore carts go through our city as a kindness, but if starved of ore ourselves, do you think we'll let them pass?"

"You'd risk a war on three fronts?" Flavius grinned.

A low grumble echoed in Hadrian's throat before he spoke. "No. Like it or not, our fates are tied. How many of my tunnels do you demand?"

"Half."

When the scoff from the Viridian Warlord didn't come as Rufus expected, he turned to find his father silently massaging his injured arm, deep in concentration. Surely, he couldn't contemplate this. The price was too high. They had to prioritise Viridia above all—above revenge on the Margalvians—yet his warlord seldom saw that.

"For how long a time?" Rufus asked. They could perhaps live with a few months.

But Flavius's reply came back blunt and staunch. "In perpetuity."

"That's absu—"

"Fine, you have my oath," Hadrian said. "But you're to do exactly as I say at the parley, and this deal doesn't include the Margalvian tunnels we took. They're ours alone."

And the most likely to be counterattacked. Rufus's brothers had managed to repel the assaults thus far, but the Black Legion was yet to commit its full might to those battles. One day, they would.

Rufus cursed at his father's hasty acceptance, the mere utterance of the words in such company enough to bind them in law and blood. Although Viridia had technically violated the Urukan Treaty, signed over a century ago, they viewed oaths as inviolable as the Law of the Blades.

What could Rufus do now but try to salvage something beneficial to Viridia from the deal already reached?

Flavius finally took the cup of firewater in front of him and downed it, clearly thinking he'd settled the matter. "We can agree—"

"Perhaps it would be best to include the Margalvian mines," Rufus said.

Both warlords glared at him, as did every other commander in the room.

It was in times like these Rufus benefited from not carrying a sword because he appeared less of a threat. "In return, we won't gift you half our tunnels, but your miners can instead enter all the ones we control, and we'll share the ore."

The Branz Warlord narrowed his eyes, rightly suspicious of any deal offered that was more generous to him than the one he demanded. He'd know that Viridian miners were worked twice as hard as Branzians, but judging by the puzzlement on his face, he hadn't perceived Rufus's true intention—that mingling Branz and Viridian miners and warriors would provide more deterrence to a Margalvian attack. War with Branz wouldn't be entered into lightly by the Black Warlord. Not to mention that working so closely together gave Flavius a firm incentive to frustrate the parley and treaty.

Hadrian looked at Rufus with the same bewilderment, but thankfully, his father stayed mute for once.

Flavius consulted his commanders, who each gave him a nod without raising an objection. "Very well." The Branz Warlord stood, soon followed by his men. "You have my oath."

11

Darius – South of Margalvia

Darius writhed as the whip lashed his back again and again. Tied prone on a rough wooden table, he felt splinters dig into his bare chest with every recoil.

"No!" he cried. "Don't—" The word stretched into a howl of pain when the whip struck again.

They were surrounded by impenetrable darkness, and deep shadow veiled the face of his torturer. He strained to flare ferven across his body to burn the whip and cast light on the fiend, but every time he tried, his power fizzled and waned, like kindling trying to catch alight in a snowstorm.

The torturer cackled with the distinct high pitch of a woman. The strikes continued more and more rapidly until his screams became one long, blaring shriek.

Then a blue light sparkled on the torturer's hands and finally granted him a glimpse of her face. He gasped. *Selene?*

As suddenly as the light had come, darkness swallowed her again and brought the silence of a gravesite with it. All that disturbed the room were his own gasps.

"Selene?" he said.

A few silent moments passed before the torturer spoke. "You killed him."

This time, the voice wasn't Selene's. Instead, it bore a familiar, accusatory tone.

"Mother?" he asked.

The torturer erupted with a shriek of pain and woe before lashing him again, over and over, with a viciousness that blinded him to everything else.

"You killed Amid!" she shrieked.

She was right. Perhaps he deserved this. So many had been hurt because of him.

"Darius?" This time the voice was a man's, deep and bristled with age. Had the God of Justice finally come to take him? "Darius?" the voice repeated.

Two hands grasped his tender shoulders and shook him, gently at first but then more violently with every passing moment until the darkness was sucked away and light suddenly filled his vision. His restraints vanished, and he bolted awake with a gasp.

"Darius?"

The torture chamber was gone, and he was back in his room with his grandfather sitting on the mattress beside him, still holding his shoulders.

"Are you all right?" Eugenius asked.

Darius reached to his back to check for flayed skin, but only rough scars met his fingers under a thick layer of sweat.

"I'm fine," he lied. "Just a nightmare."

Lyra pressed her cheek into him, but her hot body made him feel all the more trapped. It hadn't been long since she'd been gravely hurt because of him too.

"You don't seem fine," Eugenius said, "and I've been told you barely touched your food."

Darius shook off the man's hands and stood, wishing for a cool draught to soothe his sticky body but remembering how deep underground they were. "My stomach's uneasy. I'm not used to eating fish."

His grandfather's expression only grew more pitying.

"Don't look at me like that," Darius said.

"Like what?"

"Like I'll shatter if you so much as whistle."

"Won't you? What you've been through with your mother and brother is enough to haunt any man."

His grandfather's wits were too sharp for comfort. He ignored the insult and instead faced the door, listening for the thunder and waves above, but his ears caught no trace of the storm.

"And what if I am haunted?" Darius asked. "I achieve nothing by complaining and moping."

"You achieve nothing by avoiding the issue."

A hand touched Darius's shoulder, and he instinctively flinched away, expecting a sharp pain from whip wounds. But it had only been a nightmare, one of many since he'd lost Selene.

"What's your suggestion, then?" Darius asked. "Sit here weeping? Or have a heart-to-heart with you until I'm at peace?"

"You'll never be at peace, believe me, child. I've lost many, and with a greater burden of responsibility than a six-year-old."

"If that were my only mistake…" Darius glanced back at his grandfather and saw the same pain in his expression, the guilt.

Yet the man had strength and steely determination in his eyes too.

"So how do you live with yourself?" Darius asked.

"I turn towards what is right, what is good. You cannot correct the world by wronging it."

"What? I should give up, stop fighting like you?"

"I'm not advocating pacifism."

"Then what?"

"Just hope. Patience."

Darius scoffed. "I must have been last in the queue when they were giving those out."

Eugenius shook his head. "It's learned. There are times to fight and times to wait."

And now is a time to act. If he didn't right things, no one would.

"I sense the storm has passed," Darius said.

"Indeed." His grandfather gave Lyra a pat on the stomach and rose with a smile. "I've had some supplies packed for your journey, and Lex's escort has arrived with a message."

Finally. He could escape this hell. "What did she say?"

"I haven't read it." Eugenius handed him a roll of parchment, and Darius wasted no time in unravelling it.

We leave at midnight with no rearguard. Follow at a distance on the main road west.

As relieved as he was to be leaving, he'd been hoping to travel with Lex, not with only Lyra, mountain vultures and mice for company. Perhaps after Hadrian was dead she'd stay a while with him.

"What hour is it?" Darius asked.

"Just past sunset."

That left enough time to travel but none to linger.

"You're leaving, I take it," Eugenius said.

"Yes." A silence stretched out as Darius tried to find the words to fill it. Recent events had clouded his mind more than he'd feared, yet he couldn't regret meeting this man.

"Thank you for your hospitality," Darius said.

"I hope you'll come again. I'll ensure *she* isn't around next time."

Unsure how to respond to that, Darius simply nodded.

"But in future, I won't go easy on you in Katakto. I'll expect you to have mastered the game and be an effective strategist." The man seemed to speak in jest, yet there was no smile upon his face this time.

"I'm sure I'm a natural," Darius replied sarcastically. "I'll play it on the road. Maybe after a few months, I'll be good enough to beat Lyra." But judging by his troublesome performance the previous day, he doubted it.

"You'll need to outwit more than a cat to be an effective leader."

Darius snorted a laugh; he'd only just grown accustomed to leading himself, and had got into enough hairy situations to make him doubt his ability. But the blank expression on his grandfather's face soon chased away any humour he'd found in the notion of leading anyone.

"You really think I'm destined to lead?" Darius asked.

"Destiny bows to our will. Leadership shall be yours if you choose it and earn it."

"Well, if I ever feel like leading, I'll come to you for advice." Who better than a former warlord?

Eugenius smiled and grabbed him into a hug before he could back away. "Stay strong, my child," he whispered.

Darius appreciated the sentiment, but he'd done nothing but plan and train for this impending fight for over a year. When he met Hadrian again, the brute's reign would come to a grisly end.

12

Sulla – Road to the Urukan Mine

The moon hid its shine from their path tonight. Only the torch in Sulla's hand marked the beginning of the road west that he watched, a speck of light in an endless darkness sweeping out into the invisible hills around. *Perfect.* Hopefully, Darius had spotted them and waited within the rocks.

Sulla lingered under the shadow of the Markan Gate out of Margalvia, beneath the archway that listed the name of every heroic rakkan that had died here in a victorious defence centuries ago. A few other algus, centurions and commanders joined the growing party, which was more heavily armoured than any parley group Sulla had seen. If they'd had greater numbers, he'd have sworn Varro intended to battle. They waited for the Warlord's order to set off, which had already been delayed too long for Sulla's liking.

"Is your bird ready?" Sulla asked Lex with a grin. "Does he see us?"

"Yes," she replied with a roll of her eyes.

It had been Sulla's idea to give Darius the moniker "bird" so they could speak in public under the pretence they spoke of her escort. Given that Lex seemed to be the dominant one in their relationship—or rather, lack of one—choosing "bird" had been apt and offered the added bonus of annoying her.

He conjured a little ferven and gave Lex a wink so overtly Darius would have seen it. The gesture drew a scowl from her, but he liked to hide things through displays so brazen that no sensible person would think him serious. Lex, however, preferred veiled secrecy.

As he prepared for his next form of self-amusement, Varro passed through the gate with his two fiercest guards at either side.

"Is everything in order?" the Warlord asked, though his determined strides showed he demanded the answer be "yes." The other warriors and algus scrambled to collect their bags and gear, then prepared to follow.

At first, Sulla marched alongside the Warlord and tried to learn the man's plans for the parley, but Varro's single-word answers showed he was in no mood for divulging. So Sulla dropped back to walk with Lex and the other algus. Every so often, when he was sure no one was looking, he checked behind them for any trace of a panther or their greatest assassin. But all he saw was the odd star over the black landscape, which was probably a good thing. How exciting it must have been for Darius, free to roam and fight as he willed, free of responsibility. But the lucky bastard didn't half complain about his blessed banishment.

The storms of the last few days had granted them a reprieve, but lingering bitter gusts still slowed the group's progress despite using the road. The nights passed unremarkably and would have been silent if not for the algus grumbling over never seeing daylight. Clearly, complaining was one of the humans' favourite pastimes, particularly the oldest men. When the grouches travelled at night, they moaned about the lack of sun, yet to hear them marching under the heat of day… They swore more than ill-disciplined youths as they shielded their bald heads. At least rakkans suffered with only the odd grunt.

After roughly a week, the road ended and became a rocky and treacherous path. Sulla cursed as another stone collapsed underneath his weight. But he managed. Now only a couple of days from the entrance to the mine, they parted with their algus allies—who were trusted enough to cover a retreat but not with the location—and battled up the steep inclines of the mountains before plunging into the hidden underground caves.

Most of the Black Legionnaires left to set up camp nearby while Sulla, Varro and half a dozen others ventured deeper. Almost at the mountain's core, the stagnant air thickened with every grunt of the warriors. The Warlord's pace hastened even more, and Sulla struggled to keep up as they descended further into the foulest draughts of the tunnel.

"What's the rush?" Sulla coughed. "Don't you know it's a power play to arrive late to a meeting?"

"I'm never late." Varro's voice was unusually fractious.

"It's not our fault there was a storm." But Sulla had dragged his heels enough to ensure Darius had every chance to keep up with them.

Behind the pair, other Black Commanders had been equipped with their greaves and helmets. Sulla, on the other hand, was dressed so casually he'd drawn more than one irritated snipe from the Warlord. *Whatever keeps his mind from worrying.*

Ahead in the distance, Varro's ferven illuminated an open doorway with a small birdcage hanging at the side. The tiny black bird tweeted as the burly men rushed past, confirming the air was still safe to breathe. But the smell of raw kuraminium filled the empty tunnel.

"You'd have thought they'd have burned incense before our visit," Sulla said, holding his nose. "I don't know what's worse, the mine stink or the reek of Viridian sweat."

"It won't smell of Viridians for much longer," Varro muttered.

Sulla grinned behind his warlord. After a while longer of ducking and weaving between cleft rocks, they reached a set of double doors made from thick ironwood and closed beneath an archway carved into the rock. Six burly guards stood outside—three pairs, showing the colours of the Azurians, Viridians and Branzians. Only a pair of black Margalvian bands were missing.

"You two," Sulla said to two legionnaires behind, "stay here." They veered to the side while the rest of them made towards the doors. The two Viridian guards glared at Varro through the eye-slits of their helmets as he approached.

The Black Warlord didn't even acknowledge the lowly warriors, but as he moved to pass them, one guard spat thick brown phlegm at his feet.

Varro froze so suddenly Sulla almost knocked into him. The Black Warlord's head dipped with an alarming silence for a few moments to survey his now splattered boot while the Viridian cursed and growled.

Without a thought, Sulla lunged towards the filthy rakkan, reaching for his sword. But Varro halted him with an arm across his chest and instead addressed the two Azure Legionnaires.

"Did you see that?" he asked them with none of the rage heating Sulla's face.

"They see nothing but a dirty warlord," the Viridian rasped.

Varro ignored him while Sulla imagined how easily he'd crush the man's windpipe with only one hand. It had been so long since he'd seen battle; he'd almost forgotten how thrilling danger was.

Meanwhile, the Azure Legionnaires exchanged a glance with each other before facing the Warlord. "We saw."

"And what?" the Viridian asked, a sudden fire in his snarl as he squared up to Sulla, whom the Warlord still held back.

Sulla grunted at the rakkan.

"This is a parley," the Viridian said. "Are you going to set your dog on m—"

Before the rakkan finished the word, Varro ripped a dagger from his belt in a single, fluid movement and slashed it across the Viridian's throat. While the man fell back spluttering, his comrade reached for his gladius. But the Warlord's blade was at his neck a heartbeat later, an inch from ending him.

"Draw your sword," Varro dared.

Everyone else had frozen, watching with wide, bloodshot eyes and looking around as if in search of who had the authority to say or do anything. What the hell was happening? Did a spit justify death under the law?

After a short pause, the remaining Viridian wisely moved his hand away from his weapon while Sulla stepped towards the now kneeling, slashed legionnaire whose cuirass dripped red. The flow wasn't heavy enough for a mortal wound, but judging by the terror in the man's eyes, he didn't know it.

"Who's a dog now?" Sulla said. Whatever had got into Varro these last few months, Sulla loved it. If the cut had been made by any other rakkan, he'd have suspected it was a failed attempt to kill. But this was Varro; the wound was as deep as he'd intended it to be.

"Better put pressure on that." Varro sheathed his dagger and stepped around the cowering man. "Wouldn't want you to leak on my boot."

Before following his Warlord, Sulla caught the attention of both the Branz and Azure Legionnaires. None looked particularly offended at the attack—one even seemed amused—so he ran to catch Varro in the next hallway. This tunnel hadn't the natural roughness of the previous ones. Ferven danced from the perfectly flat face of the glossy obsidian walls and floors. They were near.

"Give me your cloak," Sulla said after catching him. "There's blood on it."

The Warlord shook his head. "Let them see it."

"Fair enough. Want to tell me what all that was about? You've never been one to be provoked."

"It's best we have a safe route to exit."

Sulla wasn't sure whether that answered his question or not. "You mean this may not end peacefully?" *We should have brought more men.* Or perhaps Lex and the other algus camped in the nearby mountains should have been there. Maybe there was still time to get them.

"I mean I trust none of them besides Warlord Quintus," Varro said, "and sometimes not even him."

"Well, at least you'll have me there."

The pair stopped when they came to a larger set of double doors with more guards of all colours outside, stood as unmoving as metal statues. Then one of the legionnaires gave two loud thumps and the sound of kuraminium locks snapping open echoed from behind.

"Try not to say anything sarcastic," Varro said.

"In other words, say nothing?"

The Warlord gave the hint of a smile, the first that had adorned his face in a long time. The doors opened to release a thin sheet of smoke from the blinding room ahead. Good etiquette was for no one to smoke when this far underground, yet the haze wasn't from pipes but from the oil lamps. A bright halo circling the room set it in stark contrast to Margalvia's meeting rooms and had Sulla squinting as he and Varro entered.

The lamps shone atop a stone ring curving around the place like some sort of table, only this had been hewn from the basalt ground underneath. As the pair found their seats at the large counter, Sulla eyed a grey stone at the heart of the room, so heavy a century of rakkans would struggle against its gravity.

At first glance, the jagged edges and sides appeared weathered and wild, but one side stood unnaturally flat, as if beaten into form by a colossal hammer. Carved across the whole surface was a text in the old rakkan tongue used now only for law. Signed over a century ago and unedited since, the Treaty must have been polished because it shone with a pale clarity that the surrounding floor lacked.

As the Margalvians sat, they faced Hadrian and a few of his commanders. The brightness of the lamps made the Viridian Warlord's rusty hair look ablaze and matched the hot glare he gave Varro. On either side of them, Warlord Flavius and Warlord Quintus were as much of a contrast to each other as the other two. Flavius's harsh features were more stern than the cleaner, slimmer Quintus's, whose unblemished, contemplative face was the only one there with as few scars as Varro's. Quintus was fair in both temperament and appearance, and Sulla wouldn't have even thought him a killer if he didn't know the man. The warlord was a wolf, loyal to those worthy but ferocious when angered.

There were no feasts, snacks or refreshments in the room—not even water to quench Sulla's parched throat. Such was deliberate since the Treaty had been signed. Deprivation avoided men droning on for too long.

"Glad you could finally make it," Hadrian said.

"Apologies." Varro's next words only followed when every man there had given him their attention. "The journey takes us longer since someone caved in our entrances to the mine."

Sulla suppressed a laugh and watched Hadrian grimace as he probably tried to think of a witty retort but couldn't.

One Viridian Commander caught Sulla's eye, a slimmer rakkan to Hadrian's left dressed in a green tunic where his cuirass should have been. His limbs too lacked any armour and showed the thinness of his untrained muscles. Based on his apparent weakness and oiled red mane, Sulla guessed it was Hadrian's youngest son, Rufus. The rakkan's calculated gaze flitted from the Azurians to the Branzians as if monitoring their reactions to every word—a stark contrast to the burly rakkan on Hadrian's right, who merely cast his mean glare about the room in an attempt at intimidation.

"I think it best if I open this parley." Quintus took a deep breath. When no one objected, he went around the table and invited everyone to give introductions, even the lowly commanders each warlord had brought. When finished, Quintus set his wise, black eyes onto Hadrian and got into the meat of why they were gathered.

"The Urukan Treaty is our highest authority outside of the Law of the Blades," he said. "The Treaty is clear in its forbiddance of hostilities between rakkans in the mine under any circumstances."

"You don't need to tell me what the Treaty says," Hadrian bellowed. "I was there over a century ago when it was signed, and I know better than you all the spirit of the law, if not the letter."

"And we're supposed to trust your authority on this 'spirit'?" Varro asked.

Hadrian shrugged, though a conniving grin came upon his face. "That's what we're here to discuss."

The only thing that kept Sulla making a rude gesture at the Viridian was the thought that Darius might soon gut the wretch. Although Hadrian wasn't the oldest at the table, only he had the family connections to boast of.

"The 'spirit' of the Treaty, whatever it is," Varro said, "is irrelevant. Law is law. The Viridians attacked our miners, and this cannot go unpunished."

"If that's true," Quintus said, "then the Treaty binds us all to defend the Margalvians here." He tapped his fingers on the table a few times and looked across the smoky room at the Branz Warlord.

But Flavius's gaze never moved from the Black Warlord. "What is it you want, Varro?"

His sneering tone took Sulla by surprise. *Since when do Branz mistrust us?*

Varro's fist clenched behind the stone table, and when he spoke, every word was louder and sharper than the last. "We want our tunnels back. And recompense for this affront to us."

"What affront?" Hadrian stood so quickly his chair toppled backwards.

"It was Margalvia that violated the Treaty," Rufus added as if his father hadn't spoken. "Any actions we took were justified."

Sulla scoffed and held back a few choice words.

Hadrian glanced down at his son with puzzlement but straightened his face a second later.

"So you don't deny attacking the mine?" Quintus scribbled something on a piece of parchment in front of him but appeared to be the only man there making notes.

This parley is doomed before it's begun.

"No." Hadrian puffed out his vast chest. "I don't. I expelled these traitors as would have every warlord who signed the Treaty, including my grandfather."

Sulla yawned loudly. "Who's your grandfather again? I've forgotten. You haven't reminded us for the last minute."

Varro shot Sulla a scowl, but the insult was worth it to see the irritation on the Viridian Warlord's face. Unfortunately, neither Flavius nor Quintus seemed amused.

"Tell us, Hadrian," Quintus said, "why do you call Varro a traitor?"

"The Treaty in front of us is quite clear," Rufus said before his father could. "We are to never disclose the mine's location to the humans, yet Margalvia has done just that."

"What?" Flavius banged his fists on the table. "Varro, how could you?"

The Black Warlord narrowed his eyes on the Branzian while the hushed room waited for the answer demanded. The accusation was nonsensical, but judging by the faces of everyone else, only the Azurians were sceptical.

"Is it true?" Quintus asked with a deep frown.

"Of course not," Varro said.

"Did you not come to Laltos's aid against us?" Hadrian barked.

"After you'd attacked the mine."

"Did you not take them in like stray dogs afterwards?"

"'Afterwards' being the pertinent word."

"Did you not bring humans with you to this meeting?" Rufus asked with a confident calmness that betrayed the fact that he already knew the answer.

This time Varro paused before responding. Sulla hoped he was concocting a good lie, because it did look bad.

135

"They're in the mountains," Varro said. "They don't know where the mine is."

The Viridian Warlord sat back down with a grunt of amusement at his son that Rufus didn't share, and Sulla feared Hadrian was right to take the confession as a minor victory. *How did they know we travelled with Hera and the others?*

The discussion continued for a while, with all other legions questioning Varro about his links to Laltos. Often, the topic veered from that completely, and more accusations were thrown, but Varro sat as unwavering as a kuraminium statue. With every passing hour, Sulla's throat dried more and cried out for a drink until the whole conversation—or argument—circled back on itself.

"How can you be sure the humans didn't follow you here?" Flavius asked, though his twisted face and string of questions told Sulla the rakkan had made up his mind not to believe any answer.

"If the Laltosians knew where *he* was"—Varro nodded to Hadrian—"he'd already be cut to ribbons."

The Viridian Warlord burst out laughing, followed soon after by every Viridian there besides Rufus—although their laughter was obviously forced. "Let them come," the Viridian Warlord bellowed. "I'm not afraid."

Varro chuckled, a sound so foreign that Sulla turned his head to make sure his ears weren't deceiving him. And he wasn't the only one in shock. Silence fell upon the whole room, and even the smoke stilled in the hot air.

Hadrian frowned. "What's so funny?"

"If you aren't afraid"—Varro stood slowly, calmly—"then let's settle this war in the old way, as I've already offered. Me versus your strongest warrior in the arena."

Flavius gaped as if the man had just stripped naked before him, and for a second, Hadrian mirrored the stunned reaction before he composed himself.

Rufus leaned across and whispered something in his father's ear while the Viridian Warlord's snarl grew more rabid with every deep breath he took. Veins swelled on his forehead.

Every rakkan there hungered to see the two warlords duel as much as Sulla did—apart from Rufus, it seemed. The fact Varro had implied Hadrian wasn't the strongest in Viridia would insult him more than any curse or name that could be thrown.

The Viridian Warlord murmured something to himself then shook his head. "If I had two good arms…"

Varro grinned. "I didn't realise my brother had made you both a cripple and a coward."

Hadrian roared and leapt up with a fury that sent a burst of smoke crashing into the ceiling.

But Quintus rose first and shouted over the growing clamour. "Now, now, we'll have no more pettiness! These are serious matters."

The words failed to stem the torrent of insults, curses and shouts that soon engulfed the room. While the argument raged, Varro sat back down, the grin fading away as the Black Warlord took a couple of breaths.

Sulla knew all too well what played on his mind. How had Varro managed to grin at all while speaking of the moments before his brother's death? Placing a hand on Varro's shoulder, Sulla leaned to whisper in his ear. "That bastard will pay for what he did to Brutus. Don't think any of us have forgotten."

The words brought fire back to Varro's eyes.

It took a while for the Viridians to calm their warlord because they knew Varro would slaughter him on even a bad day. Finally, the heat of the room stilled into a tense quiet.

"It seems apparent who the agitator here is." Flavius peered at Varro out of the corner of his eye. "There may be nothing in the Treaty about allying with humans, but we all know our forefathers would have spat at the very thought."

"Tell me," Varro said, the valiant calm returning to his voice, "how much has Hadrian paid you?"

Flavius's face flushed. "How dare you!"

"Yes, we'll have no accusations here." Although Quintus's words rebuked Varro, his eyes lanced the Branzian. "Flavius wouldn't stoop to such a degenerate, heinous and verminous level as to place monetary value above honour, above rakkan law."

In times like these, Sulla was grateful not to be a warlord. How Quintus could stay so diplomatic when he obviously suspected something was baffling.

"Quite," Flavius said. "This seems to be a dispute between Viridia and Margalvia, and Branz sees no need to get involved. I'm sure Warlord Quintus doesn't wish to waste time here either, not when the Waif Magician is kidnapping and torturing his people."

Quintus's expression didn't budge a fraction at the words, but the stillness was as menacing as a fierce scowl. "An unrelated problem, and she's been spotted in the mountains more recently than the Azurian Glacier. Now…may I suggest we continue this meeting with less bravado and more courtesy and humility?"

Sulla cleared his throat. "Well, as the most humble person here, perhaps I should speak next. Since you mention the Waif Magician, I'm wondering why Hadrian is hunting her."

Quintus narrowed his eyes on the Viridian Warlord. "You are?"

"Of course," Hadrian said. "We hate to see any rakkan kidnapped, even if they're elderly Azurians." The smoothness of his voice was almost mocking, and Sulla knew Quintus was wise enough to detect it, despite showing no reaction.

But this was the first Sulla had heard of the Magician targeting older rakkans, and judging by Varro's quiet murmurings, he was oblivious too.

"She's a problem for us all," Flavius said, "and a more pressing one than this unfounded treaty dispute."

"I can see your mind won't be swayed," Varro said, "and that says more to your corruptness than anything else."

"The next time you insult me, it will be the last you speak, Treaty or no Treaty." Flavius spat in the Margalvians' direction.

Varro stood with a violent growl that brought every one of the Branzians to their feet with drawn swords. Soon after, Sulla and the Margalvians followed their warlord's lead.

"If the Treaty is not enforced," Varro bellowed, "then it's as feeble and useless as Hadrian's limp arm."

The Viridians shot up from their seats and yelled so loudly the flames of the lamps in the room shuddered. But this time, instead of being insulted, Hadrian merely watched his opponent. He'd achieved everything he wanted from this meeting, and now Sulla realised how hopeless Margalvia's case was.

Quintus buried his head in his hand with a sigh, and for a few moments, the Margalvians stood and braced against the barrage of insults from the two collaborating sides.

Then, without warning, Varro ripped his sword from its scabbard so quickly the metal rang. He flared ferven across the blade, igniting a blaze that had Sulla and everyone else squinting.

Varro flung the sword into the centre of the room, and it speared into the Treaty stone with a thunderous crack that cleft the rock in two and sent out a web of thin fractures. Flames spat as the fire of the sword burned and melted the stone, blasting it with a hiss that subdued every rakkan there.

And as the ferven and light gradually faded, the Treaty crumbled into rubble and dust.

Sulla surveyed the fragments and just about made out the signature of Hadrianus the Great on a piece now blackened by the flames.

"Varro…" Quintus said, his old eyes filled with regret. "What have you…?"

"Tell me, Hadrian," Varro said, "do you really think you're worthy?"

The Viridian Warlord frowned. "Worthy of what?"

"They'll consume you, as they have many greater men than you."

Judging by the numerous looks of puzzlement, Sulla wasn't the only one in the room baffled at the meaning of the words.

"I'll get there first," Varro added.

Understanding slowly dawned on Hadrian's face. For the first time, sweat beaded on his brow.

"You struck a nerve," Sulla muttered so only Varro could hear.

"I wish I hadn't." The Black Warlord kicked back his chair and turned to Quintus. "My apologies. I know you tried, but this parley has achieved nothing. The Treaty is over. We'll take back what's ours with blood if not diplomacy."

"Just try it," Hadrian growled.

Quintus let out a loud breath and bowed his head slightly. "Azuria will stay out of this conflict. I trust you understand."

"I do." With that, Varro strode out of the room as if no other man were there.

Sulla followed closely, as did the other Margalvian commanders, and they had their swords ready as the Black Warlord passed within a few feet of the Branzians on his way to the exit.

But, despite the filthy looks of murderous intent they shot the man, none had the stones to act. The Margalvians left through the two sets of doors and passed the guards outside.

Only once farther away, where the air cooled with a hint of freshness, did Varro speak. "Did you see Hadrian's face when I said he'd be consumed?"

"Yes," Sulla said. "What did you mean?"

"He wants the Blades."

Sulla cursed. "How do you know?"

"A guess based on piecing together fragments of information from our spies."

Of course. The ancient fire that bided within the Twin Blades of Trogus was withstood by only the worthy, and many had been incinerated under the delusion of their fate to become overlord. "But they're lost. Surely if he'd found them, we'd know."

"He's up to something," Varro uttered, though so softly the words could have been only to himself. "I've been delving into our archives but have unearthed little other than this: the Staff of Arria may be the key to finding the Blades."

Sulla cursed again. He prayed Darius or another gutted Hadrian before it was too late. Would Sulla be best off joining the half-rakkan, as he'd fantasised about doing for months? If only he'd done so a year ago, perhaps the name Hadrian would already be consigned to history.

13

Nikolaos – Toria

Nikolaos ran a thumb gently across Selene's cheek as he glided his other hand first through her auburn curls, then down her bare shoulders. She smiled with a little colour coming to her freckled cheeks while she stared hungrily at his lips. *She's good.* In the past, he'd never looked at the woman twice, given he'd bedded an incalculable number of exquisite girls, but now her stare paralysed him with such allure that his gaze hadn't even dropped to her chest. At this rate, he'd tear off the thin silk dress she wore and end up expelling her from his bed in the morning.

"Touch me more," Nikolaos said.

Selene took a step closer to him, slid her palm across his forearm so slowly and sensuously something stirred below his belt.

Before he could issue a further instruction, her hand thrust forwards and grabbed his crotch as she grinned lustfully.

His blood rushed south. *Curses.* He batted her away with a sigh. "Much too forward. Selene wasn't crazed. She had class and subtlety."

Her seductive face flattened to that of a Numbered again. "No? I was doing well up to then. I know. I felt it."

"Yes, you were. But Darius will want Selene, not Six."

She rolled her eyes and backed away to get a cup of water from the drinks table behind. Although Nikolaos's quarters weren't usually where he trained her, it seemed the most appropriate setting for such matters. The room was cosy; the thick scarlet rugs on the floor and roaring fire made any woman want to shed her clothes after a few minutes. But at times, he wondered whether the plump bed in the corner and silk sheets weren't too inviting. He might find himself carried away. The King provided far too few whores to satisfy his once legendary appetite.

"Had I lain with any other men besides Darius?" Selene asked, pouring herself some water.

"Not that I heard of." And Nikolaos had always done his best to stay abreast of such matters. He knew women acting shamefully were more easily blackmailed and controlled.

"Then he must have been special," she muttered.

"I'm sure Selene loved him."

An all-too-familiar frown creased her forehead that Nikolaos both dreaded and now frequently aroused.

"Hide it better," Nikolaos snapped.

Selene nodded, easing the tension in her face at once. Despite many attempts, he hadn't been able to circumvent any more of her mind blocks beyond what he'd told her to say of the red-haired woman.

"Selene?" Nikolaos asked, as any normal person would if she suddenly fell silent mid-conversation. "What's your answer?"

143

She blinked, then shook her head with a rehearsed sigh. "Sorry. My mind often wanders these days after the Viridians… What did you ask?"

Nikolaos smiled and sauntered over to the drinks table. *Almost good enough to satisfy Ophelia.* He poured himself a generous cup of wine while glimpsing at Selene's body through her loose-fitting dress. "You're doing well. I…" His words faded away as he noticed a shadowed figure by the now open door, and a second later, dread gripped his heart when he realised who it was. *How long has he been there?* Surely not when he'd spoken with Selene of Darius's love. He'd have noticed, and probably lost his head already.

After a moment, he realised his mouth was ajar, so he collected his expression and grabbed a second cup from the table. "Would you like a drink, Jason?"

The King's Sword stepped inside the room and shook his head, which was positively chatty for him, but Nikolaos poured another drink anyway just to keep his hands busy. The man had been known to share refreshments and a few words, albeit rarely. One could be forgiven for thinking the King's Sword was any other civilian, judging by his dress this day—a plain tunic as white and neat as the mid-length grey hair tied behind his head, and sandals with far fewer wrinkles of age than his skin. If only that long sword weren't fastened at his waist…

Because the man usually wore a cloak, this was the first time Nikolaos had glimpsed his bronze arms. Was that a scar on one? Judging by the odd shape and flatness, it was from no blade.

"Is Ophelia coming back?" Selene's voice bore a newfound alarm.

The King's Sword shook his head again.

"Just keeping an eye on us, then?" Nikolaos strode over to the man and offered him the full cup while pulling the door closed.

The crow's feet at Jason's eyes multiplied as he viewed it with his usual suspicion.

To allay the man's fears, Nikolaos took a sip, then offered it again. "See? Not poisoned."

"I know," the King's Sword muttered. "You're not that much of a fool." He took the cup and sipped at it, with a grimace at the first taste.

"Not used to such strength? It's burnt wine."

The King's Sword grunted his obvious dislike.

"It's unusual for a Torian not to like it," Nikolaos said. "Weren't you born here?"

The King's Sword strode farther into the bedroom with a scornful expression.

"No?" Nikolaos added. "Then how long have you served the King?"

"All my life."

"Surely not. You're older than he…"

The King's Sword took another sip of his wine rather than speak, facing nothing and no one in particular.

"Do you mean you served his father too?" Nikolaos asked.

The King's Sword shook his head.

"Then how?"

The man snapped his glare to Nikolaos, and a mixture of chagrin and puzzlement flashed across his face. Both Selene and Nikolaos took a step back at the sight. Despite being a fierce warrior, the King's Sword usually displayed less emotion than a vegetable. *Didn't realise wine could affect a man so quickly.*

While confusion flickered in the man's eyes, he frowned and grabbed his head with a grunt of pain.

145

Nikolaos gasped. *How did I not see the mind blocks before?* Such an oversight was almost enough to make him doubt his own sharp intellect.

He and Selene waited, too nervous to speak, stare or leave. After a few moments of apparent wrestling between the King's Sword and his own mind, the man took a deep breath, and a familiar vacancy returned to his eyes. How apt it was that Jason had the moniker of an object. It was almost enough to pity him.

The King's Sword caught their stares. "What?"

Nikolaos and Selene both nervously averted their gaze.

"Come," the King's Sword said to Nikolaos. "He wishes to see you."

"Who?" Nikolaos asked, unsure whether to be elated or nervous at the suspected answer.

"The King."

His bowels lurched. *Definitely nervous.* Why would the King wait until now to meet him for the first time?

"Do we need to change into something more formal?" Selene asked.

"Definitely." Nikolaos darted to his meagre dressing room. If there was ever an occasion to wrap himself in a fine himation, this was it.

But the King's Sword caught him by the arm. "Come as you are."

Curses. Nikolaos quickly checked his tunic for wine or food stains while the King's Sword shoved him towards the door.

Thankfully, Nikolaos's clothes were a dark enough shade of grey to hide the fact they hadn't been washed in a few days.

"What about Six?" he asked.

The King's Sword shook his head, then swiftly exited.

Nikolaos's mind was too filled with machinations to worry about the woman. What was his best play here? Although he longed to see the King bleed out in front of him, without a weapon, he had no chance of achieving that. Instead, he'd have to settle for gleaning valuable information.

Yet a man like him couldn't simply ask questions of an authority such as the King. No—one had to sow the seeds, then information would flow from the King as naturally as a sapling sprouting. *If only metaphors got me closer to a plan.*

The vast yet vacant hallways passed by too swiftly, and as the guards' numbers swelled and the carpet underfoot thickened so much his footsteps ceased, he knew time was almost up. He hadn't seen the King since he was a child, and there was no chance that a man of such stature would remember a youth.

Sooner than he'd have liked, he was in front of two wooden doors so tall and wide they could have been the gates to a small town. The guards outside wore tunics emblazoned with the King's eagle and didn't shift until the King's Sword was directly in front. They gave a nod, then heaved the doors open. If only Nikolaos's heart mimicked their calm and fluid movements…

The circular room beyond was darker than the halls outside and gave one the feeling of being an ant entering a giant's lair. Eagle banners hung on the walls where windows would normally have been in a place of this design. But this had none. Nikolaos had kept his bearings enough to realise they were at the heart of the palace with only thickset walls and rows of corridors and guards between here and the dangers of the outside world. *Never took the King to be so paranoid.*

The room was capped by a tall dome, larger than Nikolaos had ever seen without being supported by pillars. Despite the size of the place, the overflowing contents made one feel hemmed in. Piles of scrolls and parchments lay arranged in neat lines like a library. Yet none reached high enough for a man to hide behind unless lying down.

When Nikolaos followed the King's Sword down the narrow space between rows of scrolls, he expected the guards to accompany them, but they didn't. Once inside, the doors eased closed again, and Nikolaos's attention was drawn to a throne directly ahead. It stood far enough away to be out of throwing distance yet looked none the smaller for it.

Resting on a stage with steps too steep to climb, the seat itself was thrice the size needed to hold a man yet was designed to give the illusion the occupant was large enough to fill it. The armrests were long and curled like eagle claws, and behind, two metallic wings stretched out and dominated the hall.

The artistic feathers shone like polished steel and reflected even the dim lights in the room, preventing one's eyes from discerning the shadow now upon the seat of power. The King fixated on a parchment in his hands, and in front was a low table piled with yet more rolls.

The King's Sword walked all the way to the base of the dais before kneeling with a slight look backwards to indicate Nikolaos should too. While he came forward and bent the knee, he stole a closer look at Toria's ruler, who had continuously underestimated the threat he posed.

Only a black mask broke the uniformity of the white royal robes covering the King's body. He gazed at his parchment with eyes lost beneath the shadow of the vizard that veiled his brow to his chin and was shaped like a stone-faced demon's, with forked white eyebrows and bared teeth so subtle a less astute man than Nikolaos would have missed the detail. Whatever he'd expected, it certainly wasn't this.

While he continued kneeling for so long his leg began to hurt, the King's Orator walked from a side door into the room. Her robes were as blanched as the King's, no doubt hiding the flakes of her ever-peeling bald scalp.

"Ah. You're here," she said with a smile. "This won't take long."

Nikolaos rose. *Wish her hideous face were covered with a mask too.* "To what do I owe this pleasure, Ophelia?"

"The King has a message for you."

Nikolaos dared another glance at the man atop the throne and could have sworn the one who sat there was nothing but a statue, mesmerised by whatever he was reading. Yet as soon as the thought crossed his mind, the King shifted, lowering the parchment and leaning forward as if taking in his scent.

"Do you have a request of me?" Nikolaos asked. "I'm only happy to serve such a noble one as thee."

The King's Orator raised an eyebrow. "Do you think the King susceptible to your flattery?"

"I…err…no. Of course not. But my intention wasn't to flatter. Forgive me, but I'm not used to speaking with royalty." *You witch.*

"Oh, but you are." The King's Orator glided towards him with a smugness that made her all the more revolting. "You've spoken with the King before."

The woman's confused riddles never ceased to irritate. "I was but a youth." Nikolaos stood to face her. "And we never actually spoke."

"I don't mean then, I mean recently. After all, am I not the King's mouthpiece?"

Finally, Nikolaos grasped her meaning and resisted scoffing. "It's not quite the same thing."

"*Oh, but it is.*" The resounding voice bored into Nikolaos's skull so suddenly he fell to his knees again, lifting his gaze to the mask of the King who, now on his feet, towered over him. "*My minions are my mouth, ears and sword, extensions of my body that number many and stretch wide like the roots of an ancient, immovable tree.*"

It couldn't be… When younger, Nikolaos had seen King Medus's mouth with his own eyes, and despite being immature, he'd never misremember such a thing. But something else was odd. The King's chest, whilst heavily cloaked with his loose-fitting garments, protruded farther than a man's should. *Breasts?* But her voice was deep, just as Archimedes's had been.

"Where's the King?" Nikolaos's voice was barely a whisper.

"*I am* the King. Did you think Archimedes was the only one? Did you think he'd be a willing servant to a human? My husband wasn't such a weak fool."

The revelations were so much to take in that a tension threatened to split Nikolaos's skull. All this time, and no one was the wiser? Yet a goman could easily have a puppet to serve as king. The real King Medus, the one that had reigned before the Empire had even heard the name Archimedes, was likely used for official appearances, if he still breathed.

Nikolaos glanced back over his shoulder at the now sealed doors; he'd never outrun the King's Sword to them. Would this be his end, his mind sucked out to be a Numbered alongside Six? Perhaps he'd become a regent as he'd always wished, but it would be a spit in the face from fate if he became a stooge in the position he deserved.

"What do you want of me?" Nikolaos's voice broke. "I do not care about your race. I serve you regardless. Say what you require, and I will obey."

"If we wanted you as our own," the King's Orator said, coming towards him with a gall sweetness in her voice, "we'd already have you."

"Then what is the purpose of this?"

"We know your weaselling ways without having touched you. The King has seen much, including the deeds you never had a chance to do. He wished to speak with you personally."

"*Your conniving has never been unknown to me.*"

Nikolaos wilted under the thunderous words until he saw nothing but his own knees.

"*I see far. I see the impending calamity the rakkans will unleash upon us that would already have incinerated or enslaved your race had it not been for my actions. I am concealed like a shadow in the night and am a vengeful harpy when frustrated.*

"*Our interests have always been aligned, yet you've been too foolish to realise it. As long as this empire stands,* my *people are safe. So, now I ask you, Selene will leave tomorrow for the first test of her skills. Is she ready?*"

Surely the King didn't know the true extent of what Nikolaos had been up to… A lie was his only option.

"Six is ready," Nikolaos said. A long pause followed his proclamation and dragged on for so long that it seemed only proper for him to speak again. "Is there anything else you need?"

The King's head tilted slightly. "*Indeed. I did say I was a vengeful harpy…*"

Nikolaos swallowed. "Yes?"

"*I wanted to see it.*"

Nikolaos opened his mouth to respond, but steel flashed across his vision. A freeze bit his throat and carried on all the way through his neck and spine yet was gone a second later. He blinked, and the world never returned to his sight.

14

King's Orator – Toria

Ophelia gaped as Nikolaos's head and body toppled apart to reveal Jason's bloody sword lofted behind. Energy rushed through her veins. If only she had some way to replay the moment that sword had struck so she could savour that look of confusion on the rat's face. This execution had been far too long coming, and watching the King's Sword himself do it made it all the more satisfying, like tasting an aromatic sauce on an already delicious sea bream.

A familiar itch caused her neck to flinch, and she scratched the back of her head, feeling the skin peel away. She needed more lotion and wondered whether Nikolaos's blood would soothe the irritation instead.

"You were right, my king," Ophelia said. "That was satisfying." When she turned to look, the King had once again picked up a parchment and took a reed pen to begin scribbling.

Ophelia strode closer across the stage.

"*A more painful end would have been nice,*" the King said, "*but I can't afford to waste time or deal with the mess. Seeing his death made stomaching his childish machinations easier. I still don't know how letting him live until now bettered Selene's chance of success, but it did.*"

Ophelia's body warmed with as much glee as if the King had gifted her gold. To have a king talk to one with such familiarity was an unrivalled honour, an honour she returned as best she could. The plentiful small devotions she'd made throughout the last decade had borne fruit: passing along every whisper of her spies in the Empire, learning to speak and think of the King as "he," and uttering the words she was commanded to even when she knew those hearing them threatened her life. Her devotion had earned her the right to keep her mind.

If only the King would remove his mask. That was the ultimate show of trust Ophelia yearned for.

She peeked at the parchment and saw the King writing down every decision they'd made with regard to Nikolaos.

"What next with Six, my king?" Ophelia asked.

"*Call her Selene. I don't like you using the pretence when she's not here.*"

"Apologies, my king."

The King stopped scribbling and stared at his writing for a few moments. Then he tossed the notes aside and sat still, with a slight rock of his head from side to side while breathing slowly.

Ophelia waited with the same fascination she always felt when the King used his magic.

"*We have a small window. Selene must be sent to a village called Foltara in the west by the next full moon. I'm not sure why, but that will reunite her with Darius in the most advantageous circumstances for us.*"

Ophelia's scalp itched again, but she daren't scratch it so close to the King and risk spoiling his clothes. "I know the village.

That doesn't leave us much time, but I still think we should test Selene in the Silk City."

"*If there's time. Assess the situation when you're there and don't linger for long. Report back to me once she's met her old friend.*" The King's shoulders relaxed, and he picked up another roll of parchment from the table and began reading again. "*Have your spies done as I asked?*"

"Not all have reported back this month, but they did the month before. They'll continue circulating the rumours far and wide. Word will have spread from the Empire into the Viridian camps by now." If their plan was to work, Darius and the others had to hear the lie of Selene's capture by the rakkans so it didn't only come from her own mouth. Only the King knew why, but having Darius accept Selene was their best chance at reclaiming the Staff.

15

Darius – West of the Urukan Mine

Darius unhooked his thick woollen cloak, and the chill of the mountain mists hit him like a freezing ocean wave as soon as he'd shed it. At least he wasn't high enough to have to contend with the snowy peaks, but that didn't make the rock under his backside any less frigid. He shivered and draped the cloak over Lyra's huddled form while she settled to doze under the stars.

"Don't you feel embarrassed, having to wear a sheep's coat to stay warm?" he whispered.

She didn't react, but he knew she comprehended. After enough time had passed for her to forgive his quip, he sat close by and conjured ferven on his bare hands while holding them out, careful not to burn either his clothes or her.

As he did, Tiro skipped closer to enjoy the heat too.

Think I've found my calling in life—a fire pit.

These last few days on the mountain waiting for Lex had left him fidgety, with tense muscles that wanted only to swing his sword again. He'd lost Varro and Sulla when they'd delved into the mine tunnels. It was probably best he didn't learn the entrance's location, given recent history. But that wasn't the wait that tortured him. It was waiting with Tiro, waiting for *her* and wondering what on earth to say to her. She'd missed him…

"Got a death wish?" Lex called out behind him and set his heart racing. But not because she'd surprised him. Her voice had a slight hack of age that it had lacked the last time they'd spoken.

"Fancy meeting you here." He turned to her with a smile, but it soon faded when he noticed the heaviness of her face, the darkness under her tired eyes, the wrinkles as she winced. The last year had stolen some of her beauty, but all he saw was the stunning woman beneath the worn lines, the woman he'd kissed once and dwelled on many times after.

He moved to stand. "Are you—?"

"I'm fine." She approached with laboured steps before collapsing next to him without meeting his gaze. She grabbed his hand, dragged him down beside her, and didn't let go of him when they sat together. Her cold fingers stung his palm with algor as he banished his ferven and waited to feel her skin again. Gradually, almost hesitantly, her algor eased, and she squeezed his hand gently.

Then another woman appeared where Lex had come from, the warmth in her eyes and full, vibrant hair standing in sharp contrast to her mistress.

"Greetings, Nasrin," he said.

"Nice to see you again." The woman wasted no time hurrying towards the heat of his still glowing right hand, and she huddled so close she risked singeing her light brown curls.

"They'll spot you from a mile away with that ferven," Lex said. "It's dangerous."

Darius shrugged. "Lyra's cold, and it's not like anyone dares approach a man with a panther these days."

Lex released her grasp and began a sigh that ended as more of a groan. "Tiro. Go and find Hadrian."

The bird paused for a few seconds to leech more heat before taking off towards the west.

"What are you doing here?" Darius asked Nasrin. The dangerous hunt of two assassins was no place for a civilian, and her tight cloak revealed she hadn't even brought a weapon, only a worn satchel so stuffed the seams strained.

"Here to help, of course," the carer replied. "With all the fights you get into, you'll need someone with a knowledge of medicine."

Beats bandaging my own wounds. "Fine. I'll make sure you don't get caught up in a fight."

Nasrin nodded and rubbed her hands near his heated arm. "I thought the Cliffs of Aphatos were cold," she said, "but these mountains… I never realised my bones could shiver."

"It's the sea winds," Darius said.

"Must you discuss the weather?" Lex clutched her hip with a grimace.

She's as charming as ever. Darius was ready to respond, but Nasrin caught his eye before he could and gave a slight shake of her head.

Lex needed him to cut her a little slack, but there was so much he wanted to say to her—that he wanted to feel her hand in his again, that he'd worried over her, that sometimes the thought of seeing her again was the only thing other than vengeance keeping him going. Yet now face to face, those words wouldn't come out because he knew her reply would be the instant rejection she always gave. So he'd stick to more mundane topics of conversation.

"What do you wish to discuss, then?" he asked.

Lex's only answer was the tensing of her jaw. It was as if she'd been weathered and decayed further since the Battle of Laltos, leaving her a ghost of the woman who'd saved him from death many times. Hadn't she improved at all?

"How's Margalvia?" Darius asked, this time directing his attention to Nasrin.

"There are tensions," Nasrin said, "but it's gone as well as could be expected, considering."

"Varro still refuses to have you back," Lex added in a bitter tone.

"You asked him for me?"

"Of course." She looked up at the night sky as if watching Tiro soaring, but there was no way she could spot the bird.

The thought of her advocating for him warmed him more than his ferven.

"There's worse fates for a man than banishment." Every night, Darius touched his scars and dwelled on the woman that had caused them and the rakkan he'd lost soon after. "At least I'm alive." But Darius would still do his best to break Varro's jaw if they ever met again. Banishing him was one thing, but forbidding him from attending Brutus's burial? That was unforgivable.

"What happened to Brutus wasn't your fault," Lex said. "Varro's insufferable. I can think of people far more suited to being leader. Who exiles their best assassin?"

Is that all he was? "At least he didn't treat me like a piece in some game." Darius was done letting such treatment pass.

All he received from Lex was more silence.

Meanwhile, Nasrin fiddled with a pouch of herbs. "I don't think Mistress meant it like that."

158

"Didn't she?" He looked at Lex, but her gaze was still averted, and unlike her usual evasion, this time it was as if she hadn't heard what either of them had said. "Lex?"

She finally turned to face him. "Yes?"

Typical. "Never mind. How long until Tiro finds the Viridian camp?"

"I already know where it is. It's half an hour's trek beyond the closest ridge. Tiro's just waiting for a sighting of Hadrian."

"The vain pig is probably busy making another effigy of himself. You know he claims to be the Fertility God now too, and the God of Fire? He claims he'll march across the Empire leaving nothing but burning ashes in his wake." Darius scoffed. "With the number of female worshippers he apparently carries on with, the only thing that will be burning is his piss."

Lex grimaced, as if she knew far worse stories of the Viridian Warlord. "None of it will matter when we end him."

Finally, Darius had a glimpse of that relentless drive he admired most about her. But how would she react to his other plans for the Viridian Warlord?

He shifted his numb legs. "About Hadrian. Could we perhaps…not kill him right away?"

This time, she reacted at once with a fierce look. "What?"

"I just want to ask him about…" Should he say Selene's name? Admitting he'd still not managed to put aside his doubts would give Lex more insight into his mind than was comfortable, but he reckoned he owed her the truth. "Selene," he continued. "I've heard whispers about her. If there's even the slightest chance the Viridians have her, I need to ask Hadrian himself."

"You're…" Lex's voice faded away. "You're still searching for her?"

Nasrin dragged herself from Darius's warm hands and went to wrap an arm around her mistress. As she did, a hollowness came over Lex's face, and she dug her fingers deeper into her hip.

"I wouldn't call it searching," Darius said. "Hadrian's always been my priority. But I can't help but ask about her. There's no trace—no body, no sign of capture…no peace." Many times, he questioned what he expected to hear in answer to his questions. "Isn't it hard for you to let go too?"

Lex's eyebrows pinched together, lips parted. If he didn't know her, he'd think she was about to weep. Instead, she suddenly winced and gasped.

Before he could ask her what was wrong, she took a vial of the weeping plant's tears and put a drop on her tongue. Given the harshness of her frown, it seemed to be the first of the night for her.

"Lex…" He extinguished his ferven and only then realised the night cloaked them in a darkness so deep that only he saw. He placed a hand on her wrist and felt a shiver run through her.

"Are you sure you're all right?" he asked.

"How can she be?" Nasrin asked. "Her sister, her father, her home—all gone. It takes more than a lifetime to recover from such a loss."

"But your daughter's safe, right?" He slid his fingers over the back of hers.

Finally, her jawline relaxed. "She's well, with your grandfather." The long exhalation that followed her words seemed to soothe her entire body, and she leaned slightly into him in a way that made his skin tingle.

"My grandfather's taking good care of her," Darius said. "She's such a secret, he didn't even let on to me that she was still there when I saw him. Though…I hope he doesn't make a habit of forcing her to play games with him too. She'll be crying with boredom if so."

The light-hearted remark evoked no signs of amusement from Lex. She shivered again and pulled her cloak more tightly around her. He considered warming her with his ferven, but perhaps she preferred him not to see her in the full light at times like these.

They sat for a while, waiting, pondering, until Lex whispered, "I'm cold."

So he willed the ferven to seep from his palms again, then held them out.

Lex clasped his wrist and brought his fiery hand closer, and eventually rested her head on his shoulder. Her touch roused yet more tension he hadn't felt in a long time, one that only she and her sister evoked. The memories she stirred only confused him as to whether he should allow her so close to him, but he did. She needed the contact as much as he did.

Nasrin soon sat opposite them with an apologetic look that she needn't have given. It wasn't like he wanted her to freeze out here. The carer's gaze lingered across the pair of them for a few moments before focusing on his chest.

"What's that?" she asked.

He looked down and spotted the lump his pendants made underneath his tunic. "Nothing." He spoke so fast the lie was transparent and leaned away as Lex reached down the neck of his tunic and pulled out the leather cord and three trinkets attached.

"Aeternus," she said, grasping the stone. "From your grandfather?"

"From Brutus."

She smiled, then shifted the claw to the front. "Is this…"

He coughed. Why had Nasrin had to notice these? "It was Selene's," he said.

The last trinket brought a gasp from Lex's lips. "Where did you…? I can't believe you really have my figurine."

His cheeks grew so hot he must have looked like he'd been slapped. "No. You tossed it away, so it's mine now."

She said nothing more as she ran her thumb across it. Though he was tempted to ask whether she wanted it back, he didn't. Having a piece of her close had helped him through many troubled nights.

Lex gasped again and grabbed her hip. Her intense wince sent deep creases across her face.

"Take another drop of tears," Darius said. "There's no point suffering."

She shook her head.

Such pain was unbearable to watch. If only he could do something, even just lighten the mood. "Take another, Lex. If you strain too much, those wrinkles will be permanent."

"How terrible," she rasped through clenched teeth. "Wouldn't want to ruin my good looks."

Darius scoffed. "It'd take a hell of a lot more than wrinkles to do that."

Her grimace eased as her gaze lifted to him nervously, and he realised what he'd just said. At least he'd taken her mind off the pain.

They spent the rest of the wait in uneasy silence, and Darius almost drifted off while Lex's body relaxed from being as rigid as stone to just tense.

"You three should keep a look out," a new voice muttered, so suddenly that Lex and Darius jerked up and crashed into one another. They scrambled to draw their swords, but Darius spotted the man who'd spoken before his weapon was in hand.

At the sight of that scarred face, he sighed and cursed. "Sulla, you arse. Must you give us such a fright?"

"Best way to learn." The rakkan grinned. "You're never too old, Dar. It's like they say, teach an old dog with a rod, and it won't bite."

"What? That doesn't even make any sense." Darius rubbed his eyes and tried to banish the doziness that had been creeping in.

Sulla had let his hair grow longer since they'd last met months ago, covering the dents on his skull.

"What are you doing here?" Darius asked.

"Nice to see you too," Sulla replied before catching Lex's eye. "You could have waited for us to return before leaving. You're lucky Nasrin leaves heavy tracks."

The carer blushed and avoided Lex's gaze. But Lex's focus remained on Sulla, a familiar fire within her that Darius had feared lost.

"Did you speak with your warlord?" she asked.

Darius started. "You're involving Varro in this? You never mentioned that."

"Don't start, you two," Sulla said. "I didn't ask Varro. He's got enough to worry about. For the moment at least…"

Darius ground his teeth together. Every time Sulla uttered "Varro," it wasn't spat with the bitterness the name deserved.

"We'll need Varro's help if we fail to kill Hadrian," Lex said to him in the low tone one used with a child. "We can discuss my plans later."

"Yes, mistress," Darius muttered.

She gave a grunt of frustration but then turned her attention back to Sulla. "Can we speak alone?"

Sulla sighed and folded his arms. "I see you two are still at each other's throats. If you ask me, it would help if you got rid of all this sexual tens—"

"No one did ask you." Lex stood so quickly it was as if her hip had never ailed her. She grabbed Sulla's arm and began leading the rakkan away as he grinned and winked at Darius.

Maybe his friend was right. Why were the two of them close one moment, then arguing the next? Sure, they both had tempers, but they wanted the same thing. After a few years together, he bore much of her personality in himself: the drive, the relentlessness, the anger. Basically, all her best traits.

He leaned over to Lyra and checked she was still snug and snoozing under his cloak. Thankfully, the raised voices hadn't disturbed her. Nasrin, on the other hand, seemed to be looking around absently, acting as if she hadn't heard any of the preceding discussion. He bet she wished *she* were asleep too.

"Are you still cold?" he asked.

She gave a smile that spread all the way to her eyes. "Hard to be chilly in the midst of such passion." But her shiver suggested she needed more warmth, so Darius shifted towards her and held out his useful hands again.

"So, tell me honestly," he said. "How's Lex doing?"

Nasrin's smile remained, but the gloom that filled her eyes betrayed her. "Lex's intellect is as sharp as it always was."

"And how's the rest of her?"

Nasrin's lips finally dropped into a frown. "Dire."

16

Lex – West of the Urukan Mine

Lex dragged Sulla away from the others, thankful the rakkan didn't resist and cause her yet more grief. Despite that, the pain in her hip still increased by the minute now she'd parted from Darius's heat, leaving the wind to chill and tense her.

Sulla slung a strong arm around her waist and aided her in walking.

"You can ask for help, you know," he said. His touch was rough and gripped her as if she were a rakkan warrior, but his assistance came as a relief nevertheless.

They hobbled down a slope of loose rocks that did their best to twist her ankle and finally stopped behind an arched outcropping of dark rock that would shield their voices.

"What's with the secrecy?" Sulla asked as he released her.

Even standing caused her too much pain, so she leaned against the stone. "I'm not being secretive. I just don't have the energy for arguments at the moment." Her exhausted mind couldn't take more worries about the moods and quibbles of those closest to her. Fretting over not getting more of them killed consumed her. "So, if Darius and I fail to get Hadrian again, when will you tell Varro you're coming with us?"

"I…never promised that." Sulla scratched at the scars on his chin. "Honestly, I don't think Varro will commit people to find the Magician at the moment. We've just taken the ruins of Gerunda, so an assault on the mine can't be far away. He'll need me and everyone he can get."

Lex cursed. Her gut told her that retaking the mine wouldn't matter soon. "*I* need you. Our search will be easier with you and your men." She and Darius could only cover so much ground. "Can't you just say you're leaving?"

"I'll ask him when the time's right. If I go against Varro again, my men and I will be thrown out of Margalvia for good."

"But you did it before…"

Sulla's expression hardened, all of his humour gone, revealing the glare of the menacing killer that lurked beneath. "Darius's life was on the line. Now the only way I can help him is to persuade Varro to end his exile. I can't do that if I'm banished too. Besides, Hadrian's a far less fearsome target than the Magician, so Varro's focus is on him."

As it had been for a year, achieving little but victory in minor skirmishes at which the Viridian Warlord didn't show his face. Even Margalvia's best assassins hadn't managed to pick off Hadrian. He was always surrounded by bodyguards.

"Does he have an idea yet of why Hadrian is after the Magician?" Lex asked.

Sulla delayed his answer for so long it only confirmed his next words would be a lie. "I don't know, but I do know we need to stop him. Whatever it takes."

"I haven't the mood or patience for deceit. Tell me the truth."

Sulla lowered his head until the shadow from his brow swallowed his obsidian eyes. "Deceit? Darius may choose to forget, but I don't. I remember it's because of your whisperings in his ear that he attacked the Viridians in the first place and dragged Margalvia into this war. It's because of you we lost the mine and your entire city is nothing but dirt and ash and dry blood. So don't you dare lecture me on 'deceit.'"

His hateful words awoke a far greater, more venomous hatred within her—one focused squarely on herself. A bolt of pain struck her hip again with such a force that even her desperate efforts failed to keep her standing. She collapsed to one knee. It was all true. It was her fault. And now fate hindered her every attempt to rectify her mistakes.

Or was it preventing her from making the same errors again? Preventing her from getting her daughter murdered like her father was? Her son stolen from under her negligent watch? Preventing her from having to take the life of a young Omid in an act that she was convinced had condemned her to hell?

As the past plagued her mind, all she saw were Sulla's still legs while he looked down on her for a few moments before crouching. When they came face to face, some warmth had returned to those usually playful eyes.

"I'm sorry," he said. "I shouldn't have said that about Laltos. I don't forget what you did, but there were a million other factors that led to what happened."

"No. You're right." But she couldn't do anything while wallowing in pity. She extended her arm and waited for him to help her back to her feet. Thankfully, the wave of pain dampened from excruciating to just troublesome. "So, will you tell me the truth?"

Sulla sighed with a shake of his head. "If you faked that pain to get me to tell you, then I'll—"

She gave him a shove in the chest that barely budged him. "I'd never…"

His suspicious eyes surveyed her for a moment before he answered. "Fine. Varro suspects Hadrian is after the Twin Blades of Trogus."

"But aren't they lost?"

"Long story, but we think the Waif Magician and the Staff are the key to finding them. So just make sure you kill him, all right?"

Like he even needed to tell her. "We'll try. But if we don't catch him here, we really will need your help."

He gave a mirthless grin. "You never quit, do you?"

"I'll quit when I'm dead."

"Well, don't make that too soon. Look, I'll do my best. Send me messages to Gerunda and keep me updated. I'll have a man stationed there to receive them and will arrange to meet you as soon as I can."

That was as good as she was going to get from the rakkan. "Thank you. I pray my first message tells of Hadrian's demise."

Her next thought was interrupted by her escort's call to her mind. A few miles away, Tiro circled above a group of rakkans making their way towards the closest Viridian camp. Among them, Tiro spied the unmistakable horns of a warlord's helmet.

"I've found him," she said. Vengeance couldn't come soon enough.

17

Paulus – Cliffs of Aphatos

The spoon slipped through the remaining two fingers on Paulus's right hand and splashed into the bowl of broth.

"Careful with that," the Magician snapped through her pinched lips. "Food isn't easy to source in the Cliffs."

The crevice cramped the pair so tightly they couldn't fit side by side. Towering rock faces rose into the darkness above with step-like splits in the stone, forming an unusual pattern. The gods must have built this aeons ago, because no natural formation could be so regularly composed.

Somehow, the mountain breeze penetrated the deep fissure and chilled Paulus's withered legs. He pulled his filthy blanket over his knees and shivered.

"You need to eat." The Magician grabbed the spoon from his bowl, scooped up a lump of rabbit, and shoved it to his lips. "You'll never be up to the task unless you're strong."

Is that why she crippled him? Froze and ripped off digits? He never thought he'd make it this far into human lands after losing a few toes. But there was nothing that made him shiver more than the blackened staff now resting behind her. Even when she wasn't channelling its energy, it leeched his hope.

Paulus kept his lips tightly sealed and shakily took his spoon from the Magician's grasp. She released him, then he sipped the broth.

"Good." The Magician smiled and went back to eating herself. Meanwhile, her owl escort flew silently in and perched above them like an ever-watching sentry.

"We'll begin again in an hour," she added. "After your food has settled."

"How kind you are," Paulus croaked. The task she'd given him was impossible, and no amount of screeching and broken bones would change that.

The Magician narrowed her eyes at him, always seeming to be irritated by sarcasm. "You should speak plainly. If your tongue lies too much, you'll be of more use to me without it."

Scooping another spoonful of broth into his mouth, Paulus avoided her lethal temper.

"Tell me more about your sister," the Magician said, her tone now mellow as if speaking with a close friend. "How long did you live together before one of you left your parents' home?"

This wasn't the first time she'd asked about his family. Why was she so curious? Whatever the reason, conversation kept her torturous mind busy.

"We lived with my parents until they died," Paulus said. "In Azuria, families share a dwelling, even when the sons and daughters get married."

"Fascinating," the Magician said, then continued with more questions that Paulus hated answering but that delayed his next attempt at the task she'd set him.

Eventually, the Magician finished her meal and leaned against the side of the crevice. "You know, when I captured you, I saw you send your sister away to protect her from me."

The broth in Paulus's mouth slipped down his windpipe, and he choked up the fluid, spluttering while a dread evoked by the Magician's words chilled him further.

"I let her go," the Magician said with a grin. "Even at a glance, I can tell when people are siblings. Family relationships are fascinating, and I've learned much about them from human minds over the years, but with rakkans, I have to rely on their lying tongues to glean insights. You'd think with the Staff of Arria, I'd be able to read their minds too."

Paulus barely paid attention to what she said beyond his sister being alive. That made the pain and torture worth it, gave him something to cling to during the agony.

"Did you love your sister?" the Magician asked.

Enough was enough. "Why do you continue?" Paulus croaked. "Are you so starved of conversation that you have to bare your soul to someone who doesn't give a damn about you or your warped interests?"

Anger creased the Waif Magician's face. "Is it my fault I have no one? As a waif, the algus hunted me and forced me to live a life alone. As I mourned my family, they drove me into the mountains. Children on a diet of mice and moss don't grow strong, but they grow bitter and relentless."

Paulus scoffed. "Am I supposed to be moved by your pathetic self-pity? You speak as if you're the only one who's known hardship."

"I know damn more about hardship than most! You sacrificed yourself for your family, and I do the same for mine."

"Oh, so you lost your parents. What old man or woman hasn't?"

The Magician snarled like the feral beast she was. "*Lost?* They were murdered!"

"My father was killed in the war. Is that much different?"

"War is a choice."

"Right…because men can afford to be pacifists in this world."

"I'd more willingly have fought in war than lived *my* life. Do you know how many times I've almost starved to death?"

"Cry me an ocean." Paulus's voice rose as old wounds re-opened. "I'd rather have starved than watched my *son* die in my arms before his first birthday. But you don't see me going around torturing innocent people!"

The Magician froze, rage seething from her dark glare.

If only Paulus had kept his old, grumpy mouth shut. He shouldn't have argued.

"If I'm wicked," the Magician said with restrained tension in her voice, "then I was made to be that way. When a young girl hears the screams of her crucified mother along with those of her siblings, she can never erase that memory. Centuries could pass, and I would still have no thought of mercy. Age may be slowing my body, but it will never slow my ambition. The King and all his algus will regret wronging my family and me."

"You speak of family and siblings," Paulus said, "as if you know love. But I've seen in your vacant eyes; you don't know the meaning of the word."

The Magician leaned forward and next spoke with a fresh, menacing calm. "I loved both my brothers. If I hadn't, I wouldn't feel the rage I do now, half a century after they branded us all for

172

death." She ripped back her black sleeve to show an old scar shaped like half a skull. "The King murdered my brothers, but he'll never get *me*. Now, if you're finished eating, we'll try again."

And this witch had murdered Paulus's fellow warriors, men he'd fought beside for over a century.

He shook his tired head. "We've tried for days, and I have no idea how to do it. I grow weaker by the hour."

"I know. But there's a chance it'll work now that I've learned the secrets of the Staff."

"And if it doesn't work?" How long before she mercifully ended his life?

A stern expression came upon her face. "I have other methods of achieving my aims."

"Then use them, because I'm done playing along with your games."

In a flash, the Magician grabbed the Staff and rammed it into his nose until he crumpled beneath the dark power within. His ribs ached as he struggled to drag in a breath.

"*I'll* say when you're done," she spat. "You just need more motivation. If Arria could make this staff, then you will make one for me, one that weakens algus as this does you. You'll die happy in the knowledge your creation will see the destruction of the Torian Empire that has plagued your kind."

Paulus gasped, too weak to resist. Why couldn't his heart give out and end his misery? Fate always seemed to have more plans for him.

18

Darius – West of Urukan Mine

When Lex returned from speaking with Sulla, Darius didn't ask her a thing. The pale steel of her expression said enough, and when she went to pick up her sword, he stood silently and nudged Lyra awake.

His panther's eyes opened a fraction, slits of colour on an otherwise dark mountain. *It's time.* While Lex and Nasrin collected the rest of their belongings, Darius pulled his cloak from his escort and threw it across his shoulders once more.

"How far away is he?" Darius asked.

"Close enough," Lex said, each word sharp and tense. "We'll ambush him. He's heading for the camp in the valley on the other side of that ridge." She pointed to the north of them, where a long, high stretch of rock blocked everything beyond from view. "The easiest route between him and the camp passes through some narrower gorges farther along."

The location didn't matter. Darius would take the Warlord down regardless of their surroundings. No rakkan, algus, or deluge of blood would stop him this time.

A few moments later, they set off across a rocky terrain so uneven it was as if it had been designed to frustrate travellers. Not a single blade of grass, weed or moss broke the grey expanse of stone, only jagged edges and deep cracks that tried their best to slow him down.

The hike up to the ridge took almost half an hour, and the pain grew in Lex's expression with every few yards, as well as the nervousness in Nasrin's wobbly steps. The dark made it even harder for them to find their footing, so Darius walked alongside and nudged them around the largest stones. If Lex had let him, he'd have carried her up, but offering to would only earn him a scolding.

In this state, she wasn't up to fighting. He needed to do this alone. *She'll love that suggestion.*

Once atop the ridge, a violent gust threw back his hood and threatened to steal his cloak. He cursed and grabbed it while Lex ducked and paused to view the spattering of tents and braziers in the valley below.

The Viridian camp covered an area smaller than Hadrian had claimed for his entourage in the past, as far as Darius had seen, and judging by the lack of tents, animals and wagons there, the Warlord's stay here would be short. But the Viridians had still dug earthwork ramparts on every side, and some patches near the roads had a palisade of wooden spikes driven into the ground. But there were gaps in the paling where they'd either run out of time or trees.

As he continued assessing their defences, one thing in particular caught his eye. A few prisoners sat huddled together in the camp's corner, attached to posts by chains that reflected too much torchlight to be kuraminium. *Algus.*

And perched atop one of the tents was a featherless pteron, scales shimmering with the flames of braziers. Lyra sensed the escort immediately.

"Do you know how long this camp's been here?" he asked Lex.

"Can't have been long."

"Then why build ramparts?" Darius asked. "And why bring prisoners?"

Lex shrugged. "Our spies say Hadrian's becoming more paranoid by the day. Even his fighting algus are with him."

Darius had seen one or two in the last few months, but at least half a dozen humans walked within the camp, and a couple patrolled the ramparts with Viridian Legionnaires.

Even the ones not on guard wore sword belts, but none had an escort he could see. Many wore green tunics that were slim yet hung loosely from their frames as if they'd only recently graduated the torture rituals, like their friends chained to the post had yet to do. None would put up much of a fight against him, and he hoped those with Hadrian were also scrawny.

Within the camp, one black-haired algus in restraints looked vaguely familiar, as if Darius had faced them before, but it could have been a trick of the light.

"How far away is Hadrian?" Darius asked.

"An hour away," Lex said, "travelling with dozens of Viridian Guardians. Tiro's found a good spot from which we can ambush him, where this ridge joins the top of a gorge he'll cross."

Usually, Darius would have left without question. But Lyra stood beside him, glaring at the pteron with a focus he couldn't ignore. He studied the creature. Did it belong to one of Hadrian's algus?

176

He turned to Lex. "Have you ever seen that escort before?" He pointed to the top of the tent. "Has Tiro ever sensed it?"

Lex frowned. "Escorts don't sense other animals or escorts."

That's what he'd assumed at first, but Lyra's connection with this one was undeniable. Did it have anything to do with Selene? Or was that what he was meant to think?

He pondered the question for so long that Lex began waving a hand in front of his face. Whatever that escort's purpose was, he might not get another chance to discover the truth. Investigating this camp wouldn't take long.

"Find an ambush point," Darius said. "I'll join you in half an hour."

"Where are you going? We have to attack together."

"*We* aren't fighting anyone," he said. "I am." *Lyra, stay with her and hold her back if you must.*

Lex scowled. "I'll do as I see fit."

"You can't fight," Nasrin said to her, much to Darius's relief. The carer put a hand on Lex's arm, but the algus shook it off.

"I have no choice," Lex said. "I won't let you do it alone."

"And if you try to fight, I won't," Darius said. "I'll hold you down myself."

"What? You'd let Hadrian escape?"

"Yes." Darius took a step until he was bearing down on her, so close he lost his next words for a moment, or perhaps they felt too awkward to say. "I won't let you be in harm's way when you're so…*weak*."

From her glower, anyone would have thought he'd just called her an ugly whore, thrown a stick, and asked her to "fetch." But soon after giving him the dirty look, she closed her eyes and growled with a slight shake of her head. "Fine. But where the hell are you going for half an hour?"

She must have been in more pain than he'd imagined because she'd never backed down so easily.

"I need to check something in that camp." Darius turned to Nasrin and his escort. "Stay out of sight, and look after each other. Protect her."

"I will," Nasrin said, "but I'm not much of a fighter."

Darius rolled his eyes. "That part was to Lyra."

His panther gave a bow of her head, though she wasn't thrilled at leaving him. But if things went awry, he'd need to use his algus speed to get out of that camp, a skill she didn't share.

After leaving his cloak with Nasrin, he slid down the slope towards the camp, flitting like a shadow between every rock large enough to conceal him. The few torches dotted along the ramparts helped him count and track the dozen soldiers above, and the lights near them would impede his foes' sight enough that his movements in the black would go unnoticed. *I hope.*

When only a short run from the least-guarded gap in the palisade, Darius unsheathed his dagger and slowed to a crawling pace. He moved only when the guards' backs were turned and was soon atop the mound of earth, directly behind a distracted legionnaire.

Darius leapt and caught the man from the back, thrust his hand up inside the guard's helmet, and stifled his mouth before it uttered a sound. He twisted the man, pulled back the head and hacked at the neck. The dagger struck over and over, hitting throat, muscle and bone as blood flowed warm, red, and vile. When Darius felt the man's legs flop and shield hang limp, he eased the body down, pulled the rectangular scutum from his arm with a shudder, then slid the body down the outside of the ramparts.

Once alone, he did a quick scan of the camp below. The Viridians and algus were only a few dozen yards away and would have seen him were they not so focused on what was happening within the group of prisoners.

But the pteron fixated on him from atop a nearby tent.

Darius dropped to the ground and eased his body a little down the ramparts, blood soaking into his tunic.

Below, a Viridian Commander paced in front of a line of humans who stood with their backs to Darius. The commander was shorter and plumper than most of them—and most rakkans, for that matter. Almost all the humans were chained at the ankle but were better fed than other Viridian prisoners he'd come across. Opposite them, however, was a different sight, one that banished Darius's shivers at the blood and instead made him thirst for more Viridians to slay.

Half a dozen starved boys and girls lined up opposite with their defeated gazes firmly focused on their bare feet. Most had dark hair stained by grime and months without washing. Only one boy sported a wild yet thinning mop of blond hair. Most weren't far past puberty and had a hollow, haunted look about their skeletal figures. What weighed them down wasn't fear; they were too still for that to be it. It was the look of those who had already suffered and realised death wasn't the worst fate had to offer. What had they left to fear?

There were no human settlements close. They must have been dragged here for miles as slaves and grown too feeble to be of any further use. Such young and sickly humans were of only one benefit to the Viridians, as far as Darius had seen.

"These are your enemy," the commander yelled. He focused on each algus in turn, and they quivered under the weight of his fierce voice with stiff necks, braced for a blow, only relaxing when he'd finally passed them.

The few legionnaires hanging around the humans let out grunts of agreement.

"You've protected these leeches your whole lives," the commander continued, pointing to the young ones. "They and their masters stole you from your families, stole who you were. They gave you new names because the ones your parents gave you were of the old human tribes, contemptible to them. They even gave some of you numbers because you weren't worthy of a name at all. Doesn't it make you angry?" He bared his stained teeth. "Don't they deserve punishment?"

Unnervingly, shouts of hate rang out from the algus. If the logic almost made sense to Darius, how would it sound to such susceptible people as the Numbered? What if Selene had been fed these perversions? Was that better or worse than torture? Another thought crossed his mind, so chilling he shivered. What if she'd believed them?

"*We* are the ones who saved you." The commander continued pacing in the dead ground between the algus and youths while a legionnaire released each algus from their chains.

"We freed you from bondage," the commander continued, "like parents rescuing their children. We let you live free."

Is that why they were still restrained? There was only so much of this drivel Darius could take. Meanwhile, the pteron watched him, and Lyra relayed that Lex had found a good ambush point. He should leave.

Yet he couldn't move.

Why must it always be children? Why couldn't the condemned be old, sickly murderers he wouldn't give a second thought about leaving?

"You!" The commander shoved his face into an algus with a mop of bloody black hair. "Punish them." The commander pulled a steel knife from its sheath and handed it to the man.

The algus looked down at the blade, then at the young girl opposite him.

180

"Run her through," the commander said.

But the algus didn't move.

"Weak." The commander spat in the man's face and raised a ferven-coated fist.

The man flinched away and lifted his hands to shield himself, and as he did, he turned to give Darius a first glimpse at his face. Darius gasped, recognising Gorgias through the broken nose, two black eyes, lacerations and swelling. Lex hadn't even mentioned he'd been captured.

One of the other algus stepped forward, a meagre-looking runt of a man almost as thin as the young ones. His beady, bloodshot eyes focused on a girl with a split lip at the end of the line.

"I'll punish them," he shouted as if trying to impress the Viridians around.

The commander grinned. "Finally, one with strength. Your friends should learn from your example. Show no mercy, and you'll be rewarded." He handed the man a blade.

If Darius had been that algus, he'd ram the dagger into the commander's neck, but there were no hints of the runt algus following his inclinations. The girl didn't beg. She didn't even seem afraid. Her bleeding lips formed a thin line, resigned, dead already.

Darius's hand itched to grab the hilt of his sword, but intervening would alert everyone and ruin his chances of getting Hadrian. *Damn this world.* He should have gone with Lex and spared himself such decisions. How many thousands more would die if Hadrian escaped again? The horrors happening every day in the west of the Empire since the Battle of Laltos still made him shudder. Hadrian had to die or the bloodshed would never cease. As hard as it was to ignore these young ones, he couldn't act impulsively. It wasn't like this was the first time he'd seen people butchered…

Before he'd finished musing, the algus lunged forward and stabbed the girl in the chest. She shrieked and fell to the ground as blood gushed from her heart and soaked the rags she had for clothes. The algus pounced on top of her with a snarl, stabbed her over and over until the screams died away under the noise of the runt's groans, the pangs of his knife, the gasps of the other boys and girls.

Darius averted his gaze and grabbed the hilt of his sword. How many algus were so easily turned against their own kind? He pulled his gladius slowly from its sheath and readied his shield, his body acting without his mind having decided whether or not to intervene. How could he watch this and do nothing?

"Now you," the commander barked to Gorgias again.

Darius waited a few seconds, curious as to what the cowardly algus would do as the commander snatched the bloody knife from the runt and pressed it into Gorgias's hand.

The algus stood shakily, gaping down at the weapon as he stepped towards the child in front of him, a freckled girl who watched his every movement with a look that would haunt any man that took her life.

But before Gorgias neared her, the blond boy next to her stepped forward and puffed out his puny chest. Despite his weak build and the ribs showing through his skin, his courageous stance gave the impression of muscle where there was none.

"Leave her alone," the blond boy said. "Take me instead."

Gorgias frowned and sought the commander's direction, whose own jaw was wide in surprise.

"Looks like we have a hero," the commander sneered.

By now, Darius had his gladius ready and the shield he'd looted. He crept towards the distracted algus and Viridians until at the bottom of the ramparts and within distance to strike. Then he moved with the speed of the coastal winds.

He summoned algor to his hand and sent the deathly blue coursing down his sword as he drew it back. Then he unleashed a violent swing towards the back of a watching legionnaire's neck, through the thin gap between helmet and cuirass, and split the wretch's spine.

Blood sprayed up and out. Everyone there turned towards the thud, and he closed in on his second target, the runt algus that deserved as savage a death as he'd just inflicted.

The Viridians scrambled, grabbing swords, shields, clubs or anything else within reach. A horn blared within the camp as two of the guards that had been watching sprinted at him. He ducked under the swing of the first and slashed him across the thigh. The next guard hammered down his gladius, but Darius raised his shield to block, then thrust it into the rakkan, knocking him off balance. While the rakkan tipped backwards and stretched out his arm to stop from falling over, Darius stabbed under the cuirass, where his blade scraped the hip bone.

Blood gushed and froze as it poured down his algor-coated sword, making long, red spikes. He whipped out his blade, shattering the stalactites, and trained his eyes on his next foe.

The runt algus rushed forward and snatched the dagger from Gorgias's paralysed hand. Darius brought up his shield to block the man's steel heading for his neck, but as he did, another snarling algus took a swipe with a stick from behind.

Darius freed his sword hand to parry with a force that split the makeshift weapon.

Then he turned the full weight of his glare onto the runt, let ferven seethe from his jaws as he charged forward and barged the man to the ground with his scutum. Gasping, crawling, the runt tried to get away while Darius stamped a boot and snapped his leg at the knee.

"You can wait," Darius growled. The runt didn't deserve a quick death.

When he stepped back and searched for his next target, rapid flows of air bristled the hairs on his neck. He ducked just in time to evade two arrows that caught only his wafting hair. By now, legionnaires had gathered from their tents and were only seconds away from creating a shield wall that would be a stiff challenge even to him.

So he surged towards them before they had a chance to organise, lunged at the closest rakkan and cut clean through his sword-wielding arm. As he did, he brought his scutum to block blows from two female algus that had been guarding the ramparts. They quickly side-stepped to get in another attack, but his shield was too large to evade. He swung it around and caught the chin of one, shattering her jaw and making her legs give out.

As he continued the swing, he smashed the other woman too. She yelled in pain, clutching her broken face before Darius stabbed his sword through her wailing mouth.

By now, all but two of the legionnaires had scattered and fled. At the centre of the camp, a fire spewed thick black smoke into the air as more horns sounded in the night.

Darius cursed. Anyone approaching would see the plume and hear the warning. He needed to get to Lex now. Summoning ferven in his throat, he unleashed a crackling roar that drove away the last two rakkans. That left him with only two other algus: Gorgias and the runt trying to crawl to safety. As Darius turned his roar towards them, Gorgias fell onto his backside under the heat of the cry. The algus quickly scurried backwards until he hit the legs of the young humans still chained up and cowering.

But Darius's fury focused on only one man. He leapt at the runt algus and landed on the man's unbroken leg, snapping the shin. The runt shrieked as Darius fell forwards with his kuraminium scutum in front, driving it into the man's chest with a snap of bones.

The man gasped, desperately tried to drag air into his crushed lungs. So Darius treated him with as much compassion as the algus had shown others. He pressed all his weight down and heard another rib crack. The man grunted, opened his fearful eyes that reflected Darius's angry ferven, and when unable to bear the sight any longer, Darius thrust a molten fist through the man's skull.

The stench of searing blood and flesh assaulted his nostrils until he almost tasted it. He pushed himself away and spat.

There was no one around left to fight, and no pterons perched on any tent. Darius cursed, crouched, then leapt into the air with as much force as he could muster. As he reached the peak of his jump, he saw the scattered Viridians retreating along the road that Lex said Hadrian was travelling on.

He landed with a thud and punched the ground with a yell. The stone cracked, and he realised how little time he had to get back to Lex. Yet there were others here that he couldn't just abandon.

Once his growls had quietened, the only other sounds were the pants of the young humans and Gorgias. The algus's black eyes were open and never wavered from him as he stood and trudged towards the runt. But true horror stole the colour from Gorgias's face as Darius carried out his desensitisation by bloodying his hands and arms on the runt's wounds, holding back shivers.

All the while, Darius studied the once insufferable algus. Over the last year, Darius had seen men with more heart than Gorgias succumb to the torture and start believing Viridian lies.

"P-please," Gorgias said as Darius stood again. "You don't need to."

"There are a lot of things I don't need to do," Darius muttered. But he recalled how the algus had refused to kill the young ones. Perhaps he deserved mercy.

"Please," Gorgias repeated. "I helped you in Laltos."

"You tortured me in Laltos."

"B-but…" Gorgias blinked rapidly as he stammered. "I know what you w-want. I can help you."

That's what they all say. Darius strode within a few feet of the algus, then brought down his sword on the chains of one of the young ones. The links snapped, and Gorgias flinched.

"And what do I want?" Darius asked, hurriedly making his way to the next pale youth.

"Hadrian. Selene. I can help you find them."

Darius froze mid-swing. He glared at the algus, bent closer to ensure he hadn't misheard. "Careful. Don't speak lies you'll later regret."

"I…I heard you were hunting him yet always asking about her. All the Viridians did. I…haven't seen her, but I know the camp where the Warlord was heading to next, and they keep many algus guards and prisoners there."

Most words from the mouths of men facing death were lies, yet the temptation to believe Gorgias was too great. Was Darius just clinging to a false hope of finding Selene? Or perhaps he wanted to believe that Gorgias had survived the Viridians' breaking. Then Selene might have too.

"Tell me where." Darius went to free the blond boy.

Gorgias opened his mouth to speak but hesitated. "If I tell you, you'll just k-kill me."

"Maybe I will if you don't."

"P-please. I'm a son of Hera. She'll reward you if you release me." The tension in his swollen face made Darius regret the empty threat. And something else caught his eye, scars on the man's neck, thin like from a whip, much like Darius's own. Perhaps he was growing soft, but he pitied him.

After a moment's pause, he turned to the blond boy who had acted with the heart and courage of a lion. "What do you say, Lionheart? Is this algus broken, or can I trust him enough to let him live?"

The boy blinked a few times in surprise before answering. "I never saw him kill anyone."

Darius guessed that was as good as he'd get. "Get up, Gorgias. You're coming with me."

After a few more moments of pause, Gorgias nodded. "All right. Hadrian was heading to a heavily fortified village at the foot of the Uncharted Mountains. It's where they educate most algus."

Darius scoffed as he freed another girl. "Educate? Is that what they call it?"

"Yes. I can't recall the name of the place, but I can take you there."

"… After I've tried this ambush," Darius muttered.

Gorgias rubbed his bruised cheek. "But the smoke signal… Hadrian will retreat as soon as he sees it. You don't know how defensive he's become since the injury."

Darius squeezed the hilt of his sword and reached out to Lyra in his mind. She and Lex were on the move again, but his escort hadn't the nerves over an impending battle like she'd had before. They were heading back.

"Release the rest of the kids from their chains," Darius said. "If the others trust you enough not to kill you, then you can stay with me." The young ones knew better than Darius how much the Viridians had twisted Gorgias, and judging by the new looks of anger some gave the algus, he wasn't as innocent as he'd appeared at first glance.

But to Darius's surprise, the algus nodded and immediately began unlocking their chains. One by one, he released them, yet they didn't move to strike the man. Torment marred their expressions so much they showed no relief at being freed, and afterwards, they all clumped together like fish confronted by a shark. *Perhaps I shouldn't have smeared myself with blood.* They huddled behind the blond boy who now held his freckled girlfriend in his arms.

Darius wouldn't burden them, considering most needed a meal. But he suddenly realised what all their hunger meant. The youths were too deep in rakkan territory to fend for themselves, not to mention the fact that the Viridians might return. What could he do with them? To leave them would be a death sentence.

Darius stepped towards the group, and the blond boy was the only one who didn't shrink away.

"Are you all fit enough to travel?" Darius asked.

The blond boy cast his gaze across the youths behind him before nodding. "At a slow pace."

That just left one unanswered question. "Gorgias," Darius said, "the pteron escort that was here, whose was it?"

Gorgias frowned. "None of the other algus here had an escort. Are you sure it was a pteron? They don't live so far south."

Perhaps Darius had seen a ghost, been driven mad by months of solitude. "Never mind. Just take care of this lot. We need to move, and they're your responsibility now."

19

Darius – Uncharted Mountains

Darius followed Gorgias and the young ones at a safe distance as they made their way back towards Lex and Nasrin. If what Lyra had shared of Lex's sour mood was anything to go by, Hadrian wasn't heading towards them anymore. How much worse would her infamous temper get when he told her what he'd done? *Wish I was wearing more armour.*

He kept the others within his sight because some might have already been broken and would make their way back to the Viridians the first chance they got. Before he'd seen freed captives run back to their captors, he'd scoffed at the thought that people could become attached to those who had tortured them. That mistake had earned him an extra scar.

The morning sun hadn't peeked over the horizon, but already the rays cast a red haze and long, sharp shadows across the mountainside. As they approached the hill where he knew Lyra waited, he spotted Lex watching at the top. The walk towards her felt longer than it had when he'd left for the camp, and she watched his every step, even though he didn't dare look at her again until at the base of the hillock.

As they neared, Lex drew her sword, which caused Gorgias and the others to halt.

"It's all right," Darius said. "She's with me." This time, he carried on walking until he was in front of the group, who shuffled and kept their distance from him.

"If Lex has an issue with me," Gorgias whispered as Darius passed, "remind her that I'm the son of Hera."

Darius clicked his tongue and carried on. He only needed to look at Lex's hand to know her mood. She was holding a sword; she was probably angry.

When he'd barely got into earshot of her, she called, "What the hell happened?"

At first, Darius didn't answer, but he soon realised his silence only made the tremors of her sword hand more violent.

He shook and lowered his head. "I had to intervene in something."

Lex cursed, lunged and went to crack his jaw with a swipe of her arm.

But he dodged back and let it sweep through the air.

"You should have come with me," she cried, "or let me go with you! Hadrian was almost upon us before those horns and smoke spooked him. He had swifts. We'll never catch him." She took another swing at Darius, but this time he caught her wrist, and the other arm when she tried with that.

She snarled at him, writhed, but had no answer for his strength, and her back hunched to one side more and more as her hip no doubt gave her grief.

"Calm down," he said. Even for Lex, this was an overreaction.

Lyra came and pushed her body between the pair, prising them apart.

"Unhand me," Lex said, her hair dishevelled and falling across her furious eyes. For some reason, her allure was strongest when she was angry.

After a few seconds, she ceased struggling and just took heavy breaths under her mess of hair.

He still wasn't sure whether she'd strike him or not, but he released her anyway and took a step back. Although her rage was towards Hadrian more than him, he always seemed to take the brunt. Perhaps he deserved it.

"Who are *they*?" Lex asked with a nod behind him. Her mouth fell open when she saw Gorgias properly for the first time.

"They're from the camp. One of them—"

"It doesn't matter." Lex quickly strode back to her belongings. "We need to make haste and find the Waif Magician."

"What? Where did that come from?"

"Hadrian's after her, so we need to get to her first." She threw her bags over her shoulders and grimaced at the weight but set off a few seconds later. "Perhaps we can convince her to kill Hadrian for us."

"Wait!" Darius said.

With Lyra and Nasrin close behind, he hurried alongside her and took the bags from her back. "I'll take those, and I'm not going after that witch again. Gorgias said he can help us find wherever Hadrian's heading to, and possibly Selene."

Lex skidded to a halt; her head snapped around to him. "Gorgias? The man that has been captured for the best part of half a year? If they hadn't turned him, he'd be dead. You can't trust him or those extra mouths to feed that you've acquired."

"If he's lying about Hadrian and Selene, then he'll be dead soon enough."

Lex breathed deeply as if she'd ran a few miles, and when she spoke again, her voice was gentler. "Darius… Do you really still think you'll find her?"

As difficult as Lex had been up to now, her last comment was the one that finally drew an angry growl from him. He stepped closer to her, looking down his nose. "Don't say it."

Lex shook her head and let out another long breath that went on and on, and still didn't seem enough to unburden her stress. "I just mean… You've searched for so long, and I understand why, but I searched for my son for years when I should have just given…" She squeezed her eyes shut.

For once, it wasn't clear whether her pain was physical or otherwise. How had he been so self-absorbed as to forget about her captive son?

Her expression gave him the urge to help her, yet he'd no power to do so. Would a good friend take her in an embrace now? She was hardly the intimate type, and he didn't wish to make things worse. So, instead, he took hold of her shoulder and squeezed it gently.

"How did you know when to stop?" he asked.

The wrinkles by her eyes deepened, and she shook her head as if she could fling out whatever plagued her mind. "I don't know. Maybe I never should have."

Just dwelling on this for a few seconds made Darius's head pound. Did he want to end up like Lex? How long would *he* allow the torment to consume him?

Regardless, this wasn't a topic to explore with a crowd when they needed to get moving, and brooding did Lex no good either. Perhaps there was a way they could both achieve their goals.

"Gorgias says we may find Hadrian in a camp near the Uncharted Mountains," he said. "If there's no sign of him there, I'll help you find the Magician."

At first, Lex gave no answer, and his comment only seemed to add to the pain in her expression.

Nasrin stepped forward and put her arms around Lex, and the algus surprisingly rested her head on the carer's shoulder.

"The Uncharted Mountains are as good a place to start as any," Nasrin said. "The villages in the far west, where the mountains begin, are close to some of Shirin's usual hideaways too."

That finally made Lex open her eyes. "All right." Her tone had a flatness that Darius recognised as her burying feelings threatening to weigh her down. But before he could offer any words of solace, Lex set off north with a slight limp.

"Is she getting worse?" Darius whispered to Nasrin once Lex was far away.

"Not really. But she's getting no better."

It looked like Darius had to keep himself together for both their sakes. The old Lex would have interrogated every one of their new travelling companions, who all seemed to be in a state of nervous confusion, shivering as the morning sun failed to ease the night's lingering bite—all except the blond boy, who stood hugging his freckled girlfriend with a stoicism Darius was beginning to envy. And out of all their new companions, none showed more fear than Gorgias.

Darius went over to the boy—who appeared to be as good a leader as any of the young ones—and explained he'd take them back to the human lands on the other side of the mountains. While he spoke, he conjured ferven in his hands to share some warmth since he had few extra clothes to spare for them.

Only Gorgias backed away from the fire, not taking his eyes from the brightness as a slight sheen of sweat came upon his brow. Substitute the fire for blood, and Darius knew how the man felt. What trauma had caused such an aversion?

"Run back to the camp," Darius said to him.

"W-why?" Gorgias's voice was thin, gaze still on the ferven.

"Find whatever warm clothes you can for this lot." Darius probably should have thought of that before. He couldn't be a walking hearth for them for the entire journey.

Gorgias frowned. "Isn't that a job beneath an algus? These children will be able to carry more than me."

If the man dared say he was a "son of Hera" again, Darius would punch him.

"Just go," Darius said. "And find some water to wash that blood from your hair. It'll make looking at you a little less off-putting."

"Yes, master." The algus turned and sprinted away.

Why's he calling me…? Darius was tempted to throw a rock at the man for using the creepy title but decided against it. He'd rather Gorgias called him a fool, cretin, oaf—anything other than the same title the Numbered had given to Archimedes.

While the algus went, Darius offered the youths food and water from his supplies, but only the blond boy came forward to take them.

"Make them last," Darius said. "I'm counting on you to take care of this bunch."

The boy simply nodded in reply. Now closer, Darius noted the weariness in the lad's expression, a gruelling maturity usually reserved for men's declining years. Such was common in victims of torment, as Darius knew all too well.

"Are you and the rest all right to travel with us?" he asked. "Do you still fear me?"

194

The boy pulled his hair behind his ear before responding. "I fear everything." But his stony face showed none of it.

Now Darius saw who the boy reminded him of: Warlord Varro. But this lad had earned far more of Darius's respect than that bastard.

"People only fear me until they meet me," Darius said. "Then they usually despise me as well as fear me, but at least it's a change. I'll try to be nice to you. What's your name?"

The boy frowned. "What was it you called me before? *Lionheart?*" He nodded slowly. "I like that. A fresh start. I'm not the boy I once was."

"All right, Lionheart," Darius said. The name was a little on the nose, but young boys tended to like anything that sounded grandiose and tough. Hell, some grown men did too, but he supposed those men were just hairier versions of teenagers.

He chatted with the boy a bit longer, trying to get him and the others more at ease with being with the so-called Slayer of Gods. Thankfully, Gorgias had lost none of his pace in his "education" and came back soon after with warm furs. His newly wet hair sent droplets down his long, bruised face. It only made looking at him slightly more agreeable. Soon after Gorgias handed out the clothes, they set off after Lex, whom they could just about see climbing a hill in the distance.

Darius's new travelling companions were even slower than he'd feared, and he grumbled to himself like an old miser as he walked behind them. But the terrain had even a fit man like him wheezing, so he cut the others a little slack considering how poorly fed they were. Lex was slower still, and soon it was Gorgias leading at the front while Darius, Lex and Nasrin followed. At the rear, the young ones fared a little better, but every time they came closer to Lex, she turned and scared them away with a scowl.

Once they made it over the tallest mountains, the hills mercifully blocked the worst of the sea breeze, but by now, every step Lex took was with a wince and grunt of pain.

"Do you need to rest?" Darius asked her.

"No," she snapped.

Nasrin rolled her eyes behind the algus, and it was a good thing Lex didn't see.

"Where do you think Gorgias's taking us?" he asked. "Could it be a trap?"

"Perhaps," Lex said. "Why do you think I'm holding back?"

At least she was keeping the young ones back for their protection rather than through malice. But Darius wasn't one to sit and wait for something to happen. Neither did he want all three of them to be the ones to spring the trap when he was the only one in fighting shape.

"I'm going to go and talk to our guide," he said.

"Do as you wish," Lex said. "You always seem to."

Lyra, stay with her. His escort obliged—though, he sensed, begrudgingly—and he quickened his pace until he was marching alongside Gorgias.

"Where are we heading?" Darius asked.

"There's a way to go yet. We could descend into the forest to the north rather than trekking through the mountains. It would be easier for the others."

Plants and soil definitely sounded more appealing than harsh rock, but perhaps the man wanted it to appear so. "What's your suggestion?" Darius asked.

Gorgias stared at the sky for a while. "The weather seems to be in our favour. The mountains are safest, with less chance of happening across humans."

As if they're the enemy. Darius considered what the man had suggested before deciding to do the opposite. "We'll head to the forests."

Gorgias frowned and turned to him as if about to argue, but instead said, "Yes, master."

Perhaps Darius had been duped by a double bluff. "You do realise that if we walk into a trap, your throat will be the first I cut? And you won't make it that far if you keep calling me 'master.'"

Gorgias swallowed, a nervousness on his face that mimicked his expression when watching ferven. "Sorry. Force of habit. But do you really think the rakkans planned for you to capture me? Planned for me to lead you on a long journey into some elaborate trap?"

Darius grunted. He supposed it was a little far-fetched.

"But I should warn you now," Gorgias said, stammering again, "this camp is heavily fortified, and only the Subdued and Viridians enter freely. You'll pass for neither."

"I should hope not." It wasn't the first time Darius had heard the name *Subdued*, but it had always been from a rakkan's mouth. "Don't you hate that name?"

Gorgias shivered. "After so many m-months with them, you learn there's much worse than names. They start with the beatings and the whips, and then they keep you standing with chains, unable to sleep, unable to know what is real and what is a hallucination. All the while, they push you to kill your own people, to hate, to see your own as the enemy. But that's not the worst part…"

Darius wasn't sure he wanted to ask his next question. "There's worse?"

Tears ran down the algus's cheeks. His voice became a whisper. "The worst is when they b-break you, when you finally give in. When you…kill one." Gorgias's words became sobs. "I thought I wouldn't let them push me into it after they killed my w-wife in Laltos. But eventually, they did. I showed just how little of a man I am. And I deserve hell for it. I'd rather have d-died, but they wouldn't let me."

This was getting too heavy for Darius to stand. He nudged the algus behind some thicker bushes, where the others wouldn't see, and said nothing while the man composed himself. It was hard not to pity and loathe him at the same time. The same fate would never befall Selene, would it?

After the man's tears had dried and the revolting images in Darius's head passed, he decided it was best they changed the subject.

"So, how do we get into this place?" Darius asked. "Will I need to slay centuries of legionnaires?" Even he had limits.

"I don't have a count, but there'll be too many for you. It would be best to go in covertly."

Darius stopped, narrowed his eyes on the man with suspicion. "Sounds like you're volunteering."

But Gorgias baulked. "I'd rather not. I don't even have a sword, unless you give—"

"I see where you're going with this. I suppose you want to take my sword. Better still, take my shield, armour and cloak while you're at it."

Gorgias stopped and frowned. "Isn't your armour made of kuraminium? I couldn't lift it."

"… I wasn't being serious."

"Then why say it?"

"It's called sarcasm."

"Sarcasm…yes." Gorgias's brow furrowed. "It's been so long since I heard anything other than orders being barked at me."

This wasn't the time for more self-pity. "I wouldn't let you go anyway." Hadrian would die by his own sword. "So how can I pass for Subdued? What distinguishes them?"

The algus remained silent for a few moments, then averted his gaze. "The brand. I'm marked as a Subdued. But I found my courage, albeit too late. I couldn't kill another, so I was to be re-educated."

"Show me this brand."

Gorgias pulled up his sleeve to show the skin on his entire upper arm, withered and burnt worse than a roasted animal's. The scar was a mess of pale tissue with no apparent pattern to differentiate it from any other burn.

Darius could almost smell the searing flesh. "How the hell did they do that? You're an algus."

"It's the true test of a Subdued." Gorgias's words were slow, weary, but with a bitter edge. "We are commanded not to flare algor."

Darius couldn't help but think of his own arm, which bore unfaded scars from the first encounter with ferven that he remembered. That pain was long gone, yet vivid. Still, his wounds weren't anything compared to this man's. As if his broken, swollen face weren't enough.

"And that isn't the only scar," Gorgias said.

"Is that why you're afraid of ferven?"

"No. If only…" Gorgias began walking again and covered his arm gently with his sleeve.

As much as Darius tried to resist, he sympathised with the algus more by the hour. He trudged after him in silence for a while, in two minds whether to share his own pain with the man. Nothing unburdened a troubled person more than to know others shared in their fears, their torture, their pain. People were morbid like that for some reason.

But he couldn't bring himself to say anything more than he needed to the man. After all, he'd once opened up to a woman with far more reason to trust her, and look how that had turned out.

At the crest of the next hill, he spotted the forest of pointed fir trees below, broken only by the odd stream and settlement. He hadn't the time to ponder the Subdued any longer.

"I'll go into the Viridian camp alone," Darius said. He'd have been better off consulting Lex over what to do but didn't want to bother her any more. Plus, after Laltos's fall, her mind struck him as less brilliant than it once had been.

"You'll never get in," Gorgias said. "If Hadrian's there, the patrols will be denser than at the last camp. And your old burns aren't large or severe enough to pass as the brand of a Subdued."

"Then what's your suggestion?" Darius asked. "Sounds like only you can go in undercover for me."

Gorgias nervously scanned the green forest. "I've tried, but I can't think of another way."

"And what's to stop you betraying me, returning to your captors?"

Gorgias turned with a gruesome scowl that stunned Darius into silence. Was this former mother's boy a good enough actor to mimic such contempt? But then he remembered that trusting people was foolish, especially given Gorgias's part in his last betrayal, no matter how many of the man's scars he shared.

"I'll take my chances," Darius said.

"Fine. Go ahead. I'm sure they won't do anything to Selene if she *is* there and you're spotted."

Darius murmured, "I thought you didn't do sarcasm anymore."

"I'm suddenly reminded of its appeal."

It wasn't like Darius could argue with the battered man until he'd seen the settlement himself. They carried on long into the afternoon before they had a break to eat. Lex had been moving as heavily as ever, so Darius prolonged his meal to give her as much of a rest as possible, then they set off once more. They made the forest before nightfall and slept in a secluded outgrowth of tree roots. Lyra and Darius took turns in the night to keep a lookout, and Lex must have been fatigued because she trusted him to do it without question—or perhaps she just trusted Lyra.

The next day, they trekked near the edge of the forest while Lyra hunted food for them within. Always keeping the looming mountains in sight, Darius shared a few stories and grumbles about the journey, though he restrained himself from too much idle chat because he was beginning to trust Gorgias more and more. He couldn't afford to let that happen.

A week passed slowly with much silence, but eventually, Gorgias's steps became more cautious, and the forest thinned, every second and third tree cut down to a fresh golden stump.

"We're here," Gorgias whispered. "Should we scout ahead while the others wait?"

"Good idea."

Gorgias turned with surprise but then smiled.

Darius kicked himself for complimenting the algus. He definitely was getting too soft.

They let Lex and the others catch up and found a safe spot for them to wait while Darius and Gorgias went to find a higher vantage point to survey the camp.

Gorgias called it a "camp," yet it appeared more like a walled town. A double-thick wooden palisade ran around the entire perimeter, patrolled by far more guards and sentries than the last place—and this was during the day, when most of the rakkans

201

would be sleeping. Not only tents but also the wooden roofs of buildings poked over the top of the outer defences. The closest gate to them had at least a dozen legionnaires stationed above it, resting under a flapping canvas canopy.

"See what I mean?" Gorgias said.

Judging by the size of the place, a thousand warriors could have been stationed there. It seemed a lot just for an "educational" centre. "Is Hadrian often here?" Darius asked.

"Sometimes. As a Subdued, I wasn't trusted to know his whereabouts. But plenty of rakkans come and go when travelling into and out of Laltos's old lands."

They probably weren't far from a direct path from Viridia to Dolthea or Laltos. "Are there any less-guarded exits?"

"No. Viridians don't build escape routes into their settlements."

That, at least, was true. Stealth seemed the only way to infiltrate. "Are you sure these scars won't be enough for me to pass for a Subdued?" Darius pulled back his sleeve, at which Gorgias raised an eyebrow.

"No. I'd hardly call them scars... Are you sure you weren't just a little sunburnt?"

Darius scowled at the man. "You're recovering fast. First sarcasm, now wisecracks."

"W-well, look who I'm with. Do you not realise every second sentence you've said to me for the last week was a sarcastic or mocking comment?"

This man was definitely getting too familiar for Darius's comfort. "So what's your suggestion, that I have you skip in, kill Hadrian, have a poke around, then skip back out again with Selene on your arm?"

Gorgias's face fell and would have lost all colour if it hadn't been for the orange sky. "Do you think I *w-want* to go in there?

Would you so readily *skip* back into your torture chamber in Laltos?"

Taken aback, Darius failed to think of a response before Gorgias shook his head and went back down towards the others as fast as he could. Darius hadn't even considered how it made Gorgias feel to be near this place again. He set off after the man, and they soon rejoined the others.

Lex sat with her face buried within her arms while Nasrin tended to the hurting feet of Lionheart and some of the other young ones. Most sat shuddering beneath the furs they'd found, but it wasn't just from the cold. Many of them had probably been here before. Even Lionheart's lip quivered as he hugged his girlfriend and tried to appear strong.

The faster they got the youths to safety, the better, but Darius had to focus on the camp right now.

Gorgias stormed away from the others and sat at a distance, closing his eyes with a shake of his head. Or was that shivering?

Leaving the algus to his solitude, Darius sat beside Lex and whispered, "Gorgias says we need to go in the camp covertly."

Lex winced, but that could have meant any number of things at this point.

"I couldn't see a way I can get in," Darius continued, "so either we get Gorgias to go in or just wait to see if Hadrian leaves." He voiced the last thought more to gauge her reaction than as a serious consideration. He'd be damned if he'd risk leaving Selene to rot inside that camp. And they didn't even know whether Hadrian was here.

Lex fixated on the thick trunk of a pine tree opposite for a while, longer than she usually ruminated, but finally spoke. "If you think it's the only way, then make him go in. Give him an order."

Great. He'd been hoping for more than a deferral. He got up, grabbed a fur that one of the young ones wasn't using, and trudged towards Gorgias. If the algus sensed his approach, he didn't show it, and only moved when Darius tossed the warm garment on his back.

"You know," Darius said, "you can ask for a cloak if you're feeling chills."

Gorgias's only reaction was to slowly pull the fur across his shoulders with an expressionless face that was more like a Numbered than a respected algus.

"Are you willing to go inside the camp?" Darius asked.

Gorgias shrugged. "N-not particularly."

"Then show me another way in, and I'll go myself."

"There is none. And if you want me to do it, you'll have to convince me."

Darius's first thought was to draw his sword and remind Gorgias who had the power here. Or to give the algus an order as the "master" he'd been dubbed. Yet he hesitated, seeing the old and new injuries on the algus's face.

Instead, he sat down beside the man. "I did just save your life… If you go in and find out about Hadrian and Selene, we can head back to Margalvia afterwards. You'll be a free man again."

Gorgias snorted a laugh. "Free from whom? Viridians? You? Tell me, can you free me from the t-torment of my own mind?"

If only Darius had a solution to the latter, he'd be less of a surly bastard. "I'm no miracle worker. If a task can be done with a sword, I'll do it for you. I'll avenge your dead wife. But I'll need a show of faith too, proof you won't give us away to the Viridians."

"My wife?" Gorgias lifted his head for the first time with anger rather than sorrow. "All right. How about if I leave my escort with you?"

"You have a…? Where's…?" Darius quickly glanced above him, half expecting to see a pteron, but saw no animals. Surely Lyra would have picked up their scent.

"She followed far behind us. But now she's hiding close by."

As if he'd been dropped in a deep ocean with only black water around him, Darius suddenly focused his attention on their surroundings and whatever was lurking. How had he not noticed something tracking them?

"If you had an escort," Darius asked, "why didn't you use her to free yourself from the Viridians?"

Gorgias sighed deeply and pulled the cloak more tightly around himself. "She tried once. They caught her, and I never let her risk it again."

"Ah. I can understand that." If Gorgias was willing to trust his escort to him, did that mean he really wasn't out to betray them? Surely no one was that good a liar. "Bring her out, then. Let's see the poor girl who has you for a master."

Gorgias stared at him nervously for a few seconds but eventually let out a sigh.

After a few moments, the ground beneath a nearby tree stirred and rose slightly. Then claws burst free of the dirt and scraped away hurriedly until a whiteback badger emerged and scurried towards Gorgias.

The algus reached out and pulled the animal into his lap, shielding her from Darius between his legs. To get a better look at her, Darius flared algor but recoiled as he saw the beast's eyes—or rather, the seared flaps of skin that were fused where the eyes had been. He hadn't thought the face of any person or animal could be worse than that of Gorgias currently, but this…

"Did the Viridians do that to her?" Darius asked.

Gorgias ran his hand across her head, fingers shaking. "Yes. Luckily, whitebacks have a good sense of smell and hearing. She gets by. And thankfully, they did it with a hot knife rather than ferven. At least she's not in constant pain."

"Aren't you livid?"

"I'm beyond… I tried to order her away, but she'd never leave me."

Darius knew a thing or two about rebellious escorts, but even Lyra observed his commands to stay away when he meant it. Whitebacks did have a reputation, though, so much so that it surprised Darius that the stuttering, nervous man had chosen one of the most fearless, ferocious animals as an escort. Was that the kind of reputation the algus desired?

"It's all right to be afraid," Darius said. "That camp must provoke some bad memories. But if we stop now, many more will suffer like you. A man battles through the fear."

Gorgias stroked his badger silently for a few moments before speaking. "If I go into the camp, but I don't find Hadrian and Selene, what will you do to my escort?"

Darius rapped him on the shoulder. "Who do you think I am?"

"The S-slayer."

Darius scoffed. "Don't think that extends to badgers. So does that mean you agree to go?"

"If you swear you'll protect me and my escort until we're safe again."

"If you think me the kind of man that would kill a badger without provocation, why would you trust my word?"

The anxiety that descended on Gorgias's face made Darius instantly regret bringing his own trustworthiness into question. *I really should think before I speak.*

"Then ask Lex to swear it," Gorgias said.

"She's in no fit state to protect herself, let alone you. Look, forget what I said. I swear on my escort's life I'll protect you until either you're safe or you betray me."

Gorgias eyed Lyra for a few moments as she watched over the young ones with almost maternal alertness, and the sight seemed to bring some relief to the man. "Very well. I guess someone as noble as I shouldn't cower. I don't know why, but I feel calmer with you, feel safe."

"Have you forgotten I don't like you?" Darius said with a wry grin.

Gorgias snorted. "You're not exactly a charismatic companion yourself. But I envy many of your…" He shook his head as if finishing the thought were too galling and said, "I trust your word. I'll go in at sunrise."

20

Selene – Xavala

The journey from Toria to the Silk City was one of the shortest in the Empire, but even so, every sight that greeted Selene's eyes was one of wonder. Yet she couldn't shake the butterflies from her stomach at what she'd soon face. She had memories of seeing the Empire before, but they were detached, as if from so distant a time they were almost forgotten. But that was hardly surprising, considering those memories were not her own. Instead, they were the dead Selene's, imparted from the woman she now had to imitate by magic unknown to her.

The King's Envoy with which she travelled wasn't a large group: just the King's Sword and Orator along with a few of their most trusted algus. While crossing the sturdy ironwood that made up the Great Bridge, she watched the fishing boats set off for the Toras Delta. Even on dry land, she felt their sailors' trepidation at venturing so close to the turbulent Aretean Sea in the north. But if only she could swim and join them. Anything would be better than riding to begin a journey that would end with meeting her tormentor—the Slayer of Gods, who had mutilated both her previous and current bodies.

Although on horseback at walking pace, her chain mail grated across the fresh cuts and scars Darius had given her. But she gritted her teeth and bore the pain. The King had said never to complain, and there was no kinder man alive.

Just the thought of the King's warm smile and soothing, soft voice made the discomfort more tolerable.

She had to focus on her task for his sake and never reveal she knew the truth. Darius was a monster, but he'd believe she was his lost lover.

Under the constant watch of the King's Sword and Orator, she had to play her part in the Silk City to perfection. Her only memories of the King's Orator were pleasant and calm, yet whenever the bald woman so much as glanced at her strangely, her heart pounded into her throat for some reason.

When they arrived in Xavala, their stay was brief, because the Silk Regent sent word for them to head north and meet him in the Scorched Forest. Selene's only memories of the place were from childhood: a blackened, wretched wasteland left to the wild. But when she approached this time, she barely believed her eyes at the sight of a vast expanse. Half the breadth was a tangle of thick plants slowly being driven back by the ranks of young saplings arranged in a disturbingly unnatural formation.

Selene turned to the King's Sword. "The King is letting them replant the whole forest?"

Jason grunted in a tone she had long since deciphered as affirmative.

"It's important the Silk City stands united with Toria," the King's Orator casually interjected. "Remember that you mustn't do anything to jeopardise that."

Strange. The King always spoke of the Silk Regent with vitriol. Selene considered Ophelia's vague command, thinking of too many possible interpretations.

"So must I bend to Regent Aristippus's every desire?" Selene asked.

The question had Ophelia scrunching her nose in disgust. "Certainly not. He's a lecherous weasel. But never speak in anger to him."

That order was far clearer for Selene to obey, and the dread in her gut at the thought of disobeying was enough to compel her to follow the instruction to the letter.

She took off her cloak as the midday sun beamed down on her with a heat that made her hair painful to touch. In her old life, she'd never fathomed why this area was rarely treated to a breeze.

"Aren't you hot?" she asked the King's Sword, desperate for conversation to distract from the imminent trial.

The King's Sword shrugged but, unusually for him, removed his cloak a few moments later. As he did, she spotted a faint glimpse of a mark on his arm that he quickly covered again with the sleeve of his tunic.

"How did you get that scar?" she asked. In all the times she'd seen him fight, no one had ever landed a blow.

The King's Sword frowned before placing his hand over where the mark lay under his sleeve. Then he shrugged in reply.

They continued along the road in silence until closing in on a large group of people at the edge of the new forest.

"Is that the Silk Regent?" Selene pointed to a man strutting in thin, golden robes while half-naked slaves hacked at wild undergrowth.

"Yes. It's Aristippus," the King's Orator replied. "And I see he has company."

Selene scanned those nearest the Silk Regent. Next to him stood another finely dressed man who, despite a beard inches longer than the last time she'd seen him, she recognised from one of Selene's old memories. He was an algus from a lesser house of Selene's former home, and his name currently escaped her.

The Silk Regent spotted the approaching party and moved to greet them while muttering something to his guest. Once closer, he fell silent and beamed at them with his gold teeth sparkling in the sun. According to Ophelia, while his dark, handsome gaze left many women weak at the knees, his reputation made most clamp both legs together, weak or not.

"I see you got my message," he said. "I wanted the King's Envoy to see for themselves the progress we've made."

The King's Sword grunted, apparently unimpressed, and Selene had to suppress a grin of amusement. But the disinterested reply did nothing to dampen the Silk Regent's smugness.

The King's Orator moved away from them to inspect the labouring slaves more closely, leaving Selene to her first test. It was time to act, and impressing these two men would get her one step closer to revenge. Judging by the Silk Regent's reputation, a little flirting was the best way to win him over.

"It's a pleasure to be back." Selene slowly walked towards him with a seductive swing in her hips that drew in Aristippus's dark eyes.

"I had no idea you missed me," the Silk Regent said. "I confess, I was a little surprised to hear you were alive and not with your sister in that rakkan city."

Selene huffed. "Don't mention her to me. She's a disgrace to our race."

"Quite." The other algus stepped from behind the Silk Regent. Lines ran through his sun-kissed skin and aged him by

211

more than however many years had passed since Selene had last seen him.

She paused and frowned slightly at the man's face. *Come on… What's his name?* She hesitated for what felt like minutes, but the drops of sweat had only made it halfway down her temple when the name suddenly surfaced.

"Clymenus!" She painted a grin on her face and stepped forward to kiss him on the cheek. "Glad to see you again."

"Yes, though in such unfortunate circumstances."

Selene morphed her expression into one more solemn, just as Nikolaos had taught her. "Yes. But don't fret. We'll rebuild our city one day."

Clymenus smiled wistfully while the King's Orator watched from the corner of her eye with a satisfied grin.

The Silk Regent's gaze, which had lingered on the lower half of Selene's body throughout the conversation thus far, finally rose. "Absolutely. Why, just look!" He whirled around with a grand sweep of his arm across the bands of slaves roaming with a sluggishness of people that didn't rest more than a few hours a day, including sleep. Some cut at the brambles twisting around the landscape while others dug deep holes, ready for the steady line carrying mulberry saplings.

"It's almost three decades since our forest was burned and poisoned," the Silk Regent said. "Not a single tree was allowed to survive. All that rose from the ashes were nettles, crawling vines and grass. Yet now, the trees will thrive again, thanks to the King."

It was the King who scorched it in the first place.

"We'll soon have wealth beyond all comparison." The Silk Regent's smile was visible even from the back of his smug head. After only a few minutes, Selene already wanted to strangle the man.

"I hope you'll help us rebuild our city with some of that wealth," Clymenus said.

But the Silk Regent carried on speaking as if the man hadn't spoken. "The rains have been kind to us this year. The trees will thrive, as will I."

Behind his back, Clymenus looked at Selene with a grimace to convey a feeling she probably should have shared. But she didn't, and would rather change the topic of conversation.

"How long have you been staying here?" Selene asked Clymenus quickly.

"A few months," he replied. "I left Laltos with the last wave of refugees but didn't travel with the main group. I evaded the Xavalan cavalry and came here later after showing my allegiance lay with the King."

"You're lucky," Selene said. "I was captured by the Viridians and would have died with them if not for the King's Sword."

Clymenus frowned. "That's what happened to you? You're not in as bad shape as their usual prisoners."

"You see only what I allow you to see." Wounds could be covered up and agony masked beneath a blank expression.

"Hurry up!" the Silk Regent yelled at his slaves. "I want to see twice as many trees here when I return." He turned while the slaves gaped as if they'd been sentenced to hang. Perhaps that would have been a more pleasant end for them. Oblivious, the Silk Regent now scanned Selene's whole body with a quizzical look, as if he could see beneath her clothes.

"So…" the Silk Regent said, "will you enlighten us as to why you requested this flying visit?"

Selene opened her mouth to lie, but the King's Sword silenced her with a hand to her chest.

Jason shook his head.

"But why ask for Clymenus specifically?" the Silk Regent asked. "And why the secrecy?"

The King's Sword answered the question with only a glare.

"Selene has been through a lot," the King's Orator replied, stepping back towards them and into the conversation. "As we were already passing through, we thought she'd feel more at ease seeing a familiar face for the first time in months."

The Silk Regent threw a nervous glance at the King's Sword. "Very well. I've arranged a secluded dwelling for you. Our feast tonight shall be sparsely attended. I do hope you'll join."

"We'd be delighted," the King's Orator said, although her tone showed little pleasure.

Selene couldn't wait. Whilst training in Toria, her drink rations hadn't been large. And with enough wine in these men, her test would be that much easier.

They left with one of the Silk Regent's personal slaves, who showed them back to the city and into a small inn near the town walls that had been emptied of its inhabitants. After a bath, nap and change of clothes, Selene rejoined Ophelia and Jason, then they made their way through the side entrance to the palace as the sun set above them.

They entered a dining room much smaller than a great hall but far larger than it needed to be, nonetheless. Exquisite artwork decorated the walls and ceilings but was spoiled by the vulgar, erotic scenes depicted, something all too common in this city. The three of them sat at one side of a long table, helped themselves to a few olives, and soon after, the Silk Regent and Clymenus joined them.

"Wine! Meat!" Aristippus barked, and collapsed onto his chair. Slaves scurried away while Clymenus sat next to Selene.

"The food here is good," he said in a hushed voice, "but it's not the same as we had at home. The bread leaves a lot to be desired."

"I've heard the olive oil isn't much better," Selene said.

Clymenus smiled wistfully. "You remember that? My grandmother?"

She suppressed the confusion and surprise wanting to show on her face while digging through old memories. "Ah…" She forced a smile. "Yes, she pressed her own olives. Wouldn't let a slave near them."

When the words brought a full smile to the man's face, Selene breathed again and poured herself a deep cup of wine.

"I think I get my perfectionism from her," Clymenus said. "Only the best, and thankfully the Silk City is likeminded, though I'd also advise you to avoid the bison. The Regent only allows it to be served bloody."

"Thanks for the warning."

"Has any of your family joined you?" Clymenus asked. "Or are they all in Margalvia?"

"Margalvia," she said. "They've all been tricked by Lex into thinking the rakkans will help them, but I know better than most what they're really like."

"So it's true? She betrayed us?"

"Yes." Selene let out an angry breath. "She's worked with them for years, and I suspect she's been working with the Viridians too."

"So, tell me what happened," Clymenus said in a low voice. "How did they capture you?"

Aristippus belched loudly. "Wine good enough for you, Selene?"

She'd almost forgotten the Silk Regent was there. "Splendid." She took another ladylike sip while eyeing the lewd man before turning back to Clymenus.

"I was taken in Laltos," she said. "They dragged me away when news of the Xavalan counterattack filtered through." She made her voice weaker. "Then they took me into the Uncharted Mountains, and they…" She quivered her lip and took a deep breath.

"Don't trouble yourself," Clymenus said with a wince, refilling her cup of wine. "I shouldn't have asked."

The King's Orator grinned slightly while chewing and looking at her plate as if unaware of the conversation. Selene had done well. Sometimes there were benefits to being a woman, and Nikolaos had taught her to use them to full advantage.

"It's fine," Selene said.

"What's fine?" The Silk Regent raised his voice while slowly chewing what looked to be roasted swan.

"We were just discussing my captivity," Selene said.

"Ah…" The Silk Regent pouted. "It must have been so hard for you, my dear. I know what they do to women, even those less fair, such as yourself. I trust you've clawed out any mongrels that might be growing inside you as a result."

Clymenus choked on a mouthful of food and coughed violently, and Selene almost dropped the cup of wine in her hand. A second later, when she'd digested the insolence of the words, she had to restrain herself from throwing the wine over the man. There were so many curt ripostes she could have made, but she recalled the words of the King's Orator: "Never speak in anger to him." What Selene felt wasn't anger but infernal rage. So she was forbidden from speaking.

"Really!" Clymenus said. "You shouldn't speak to a lady like that, especially an algus."

216

Selene slowly took a sip of wine while the rest of the table waited for her to say something, to rebuke the man's vulgarity as the dead Selene would have.

But she did nothing while anger lingered within her. To disobey Ophelia's command would lead to… The woman was already frozen mid-drink and eyeing her with the keenness of an arbiter.

The King's Sword shifted in his chair and went back to picking at olives as if bored by the conversation. But Selene knew it was an act.

"What?" The Silk Regent picked up another chunk of swan and peeled the skin from the juicy meat. "You can't be too careful." The man's lips curled into a grin.

By now, Selene had calmed herself the same way she did when getting one of her headaches; Nikolaos had trained her not to react to that sort of stress. Finally, she was allowed to speak in words the dead Selene would have used.

"There's only one half-breed you need to concern yourself with," Selene said. *You.* With what beast had this man's mother mated with to spawn such a foul specimen?

"Is that so?" he replied. "You mean your boyfriend?"

This time her face heated, and she couldn't prevent the flush.

"Ah, so the rumours are true," the Silk Regent said. "You did mate with the Slayer."

"That's quite enough." The King's Orator stood with a commanding panache that stole everyone's attention. "We did not come here for impolite conversation."

The King's Sword froze with an olive in hand, watching the only person he ever seemed to revere besides the King himself.

"My apologies." The Silk Regent chewed on some swan skin as if thoroughly pleased with himself. "I hadn't realised you'd become so protective of her; I thought you had sympathy for no one. Or is it the King that has grown protective of her? I had no idea he was into sloppy seconds."

This time Clymenus threw down the knife he'd been using to cut his meat, and the handle cracked his plate and sent vegetables all over the table. "Selene, I've suddenly lost my appetite and could use some fresh air. Would you care to join me for a stroll?"

She gently cleared her throat, thankful to have an excuse to leave. "Some air sounds good."

21

King's Orator – Xavala

Ophelia silently watched as Selene and Clymenus stood and prepared to leave. Without needing her instruction, the King's Sword grabbed a handful of olives and got to his feet too while Ophelia brought her attention back to the Silk Regent. Although usually brash, his words had been abnormally sardonic. His gaze soon wandered to the grotesque nude paintings on the wall, across the women's bodies that seemed to evoke no reaction from him. She should have known his mind was too lurid to focus on anything of importance for long.

After a few moments, the three others left via the door behind Ophelia. Being without the King's Sword never used to make her anxious, but Selene's task was of such gravity that a stone had permanently settled in her stomach.

"Let's speak frankly, Ophelia." The Silk Regent's dark gaze lost all the carefree, wine-induced joviality it had held. It was a look Ophelia knew all too well. She'd been right to suspect the man's comments weren't those of someone bored and entertaining himself with the discomfort of others. They were premeditated scrutiny.

Ophelia poured more wine into an already full cup while every slave left the room so quietly someone less canny than her wouldn't have noticed.

"What's wrong?" she asked in a calm yet authoritative voice.

"I was about to ask you that. Why are you here?"

Ophelia frowned. "The King made our purpose clear."

"The King makes nothing clear. Why Xavala? Why now? Why Clymenus?"

"You'll have to ask the King. I'm not privy to—"

"Don't lie to me." The Silk Regent shoved away the plate in front of him and leaned forward. "You're not as adept at deceit as you think."

"Deceit?" This miscreant wouldn't take a hint. If mentioning the King wouldn't deter his questions, an explicit threat would. Not even a regent would be foolish enough to defy the King or his orator.

But something gave her pause. Having been privy to the King's communications with Aristippus, she'd noted the forced politeness on Toria's part. Clearly, the King wished to avoid using the rod to beat this man and preferred to use bait and charm to control him. And when all else failed, flattering the man's excessive ego secured whatever the King desired.

Ophelia cleared her throat, trying to cough out the disgust that wanted to lace her words. "Regent, I would not lie to an esteemed man such as yourself, but there are things which the King would rather others didn't know. If a loyal servant such as I were to repeat them, I'd be better off dead, so I know that you understand my silence on certain matters."

The Silk Regent's mouth curled into a subtle grin, and it struck her far deeper than his threat had. This was the prideful smirk of a man who knew something, and she needed to discover what.

She continued, "But I'm sure someone with enough intelligence"—she leaned her head a fraction closer to him—"would be able to infer my reasons for being here, and I'd be unable to conceal all my reactions if they were put before me." She gave the Silk Regent a slight raise of her eyebrows, falsely conveying her willingness to cooperate with him.

His smile only widened as he likely dwelled on how intelligent he considered himself. "The King told me that Clymenus was a traitor and that you are here to deal with him."

Ophelia opened her eyes slightly, mimicking fear. "He's indeed a traitor."

"I know he won't return from his walk with the King's Sword." The Silk Regent leaned back in his chair with a shake of his head. "I don't believe such a simple man would side with rakkans. Which means the King wants him dead for another reason."

Perhaps Ophelia had misjudged this regent. He must have had some form of brain after all if he'd figured out that much.

"Why else would the King want Clymenus dead?" Ophelia asked, knitting her brow in false confusion.

The Silk Regent twirled a curl of his dark hair whilst staring at the ceiling. "A simple man isn't a threat to a king because he wouldn't know anything of importance… I confess I've puzzled over this ever since the King informed me of his intentions, but now that you're here, it's obvious."

Ophelia held back the urge to swallow. When had the King notified Aristippus of his intentions? Why hadn't *she* been involved in that?

221

"If you've figured it out, why ask me?" she said, eyeing Clymenus's carving knife still lying on the table. If only she were an algus and could use it.

"I'm not as ignorant as the King thinks." The smugness had returned to Aristippus's expression. "I know a goman lives."

Ophelia's body froze, rigid by force of will so it wouldn't betray her fear while she deepened the furrow in her brow. "Archimedes? I can assure you he's dead."

"Don't lie to me." The strain in the man's voice grew with every word, betraying the fact that he wasn't certain of what he said. "You know very well I don't speak of Archimedes."

"If a goman really lived, why wouldn't the war be over?"

The question weakened the man's conceited grin. "But Selene's so…different. She used to go to every effort to appear unattractive to me. Now she flirts, and I confirmed my suspicions." His own words reinvigorated his confident posture. "I knew she was a spirited woman, so it wasn't difficult to provoke her. Selene wouldn't let my invasive comments go unchallenged, even if they were the words of a regent. However, for the Numbered, hierarchy is everything."

Ophelia chuckled in a well-rehearsed fashion. "My apologies, Regent. I don't mean to laugh, but this is all so fantastical. Wouldn't you expect a woman who underwent months of torture to act differently? Of course she's more timid."

Aristippus scowled. "But—"

"And if the King had a goman, wouldn't he already know you'd discover the secret and have Jason run his sword through your shrewd mind?" That's the first thing she'd ask the King when she wrote, as soon as she was done here. She had no escorts of her own to use, but she'd brought her most trusted algus with her. His sparrow had carried news from her spies that must have led to the deaths of thousands of opponents by now, and hopefully Aristippus would be the next casualty.

But why hadn't this pompous regent been killed already? Did the King just want to avoid repeating the short but devastating War of the Two between the cities? It had been the *human* King Medus—before the goman's arrival—that had won that war, but not without cost.

The Silk Regent frowned as doubt overcame his expression. "But Selene's changes in behaviour…"

The latch on the door behind Ophelia clicked and almost stopped her heart. She turned to see Selene and the King's Sword stride through the doors and head back towards their seats. By the blank look on their faces, one would have been forgiven for thinking nothing of interest had happened outside, but there was no Clymenus, and the lightest of blood splatters spoiled the white tunic of the King's Sword.

Ophelia sighed and relaxed a little now that she was back in Jason's presence. Then she looked to Aristippus and did nothing to betray the fact that the Regent's next words could invite Jason's piercing blade. If he mentioned gomans one more time…

The Silk Regent's eyes narrowed as he watched the two new entrants. "Enjoy your walk?" he asked.

Neither of the pair answered him, and he again stared at Ophelia. His next words were uttered with assiduous precision. "I'm glad to be rid of a traitor. Now that your business here is done, when will you be leaving?"

Ophelia would have left that very minute if she could. "Tomorrow."

"A pity. I'd have liked to enjoy this last night with you, but I'm afraid I have important matters to attend to. I'll have swifts ready for you at sunrise. Forgive me if I don't see you off."

While the Silk Regent bade his farewells to the three in turn, as any formal host did, Ophelia suddenly realised how stifling the air had become, thick with the aroma of the sweaty man's perfume. She needed a stroll herself to clear her mind. As hard as it was to believe, this had been Selene's easiest challenge before the real trial to come.

22

Sulla – Margalvia

The drizzle soaked through Sulla's cloak as he watched Varro kneel and tear away the grass that had encroached over the granite tombstone. The Warlord ripped a few clumps until the word "Brutus" saw the starlight again. Despite trying to discuss Darius and Lex with Varro for a while, there never seemed an opportune moment, and this certainly wasn't it. For days, Varro had been complaining of not having found the time to finish building his brother's tomb out here on the hillside, in the lower lands north of Margalvia. Anyone foolish enough to offer help had met with a quick rebuke. Only family built tombs. Customs were there for a reason.

"The men are almost ready," Varro said to the cold, dead stone. "We march for battle tomorrow." Finally, the time had come. The Warlord would return to the only place he dominated, where his confidence would reign supreme and he'd unleash the vengeance he never admitted he craved—the battlefield. The towering walls of Denehill stood firm in the distance, in rakkan hands since Sulla's men had stormed the fortress. But that victory had only been half as impressive as Varro's at the Battle of Uxon almost two decades ago. To have seen the then commander in that battle…many had mistaken him for a god.

"Issue word to the Azure Legion," Varro said with a slight turn of his head to indicate he no longer spoke to the dead.

"I'll send a pigeon," Sulla said. "What should we say?"

"Warn them of our intention to retake the mine. I don't want them getting caught in the fight."

"And what of the Branzians?"

Varro's voice was as toneless as ever. "Tell them nothing."

"As you wish, Warlord." Sulla would again join Varro in their next battle, but he was a poor substitute for Brutus. How they needed Brutus's words of solace now, but instead of recalling the rakkan's many wise sayings before a bloody fight, all Sulla remembered was what he'd been told of Brutus's last words when bleeding into the mud: "Varro, it's cold." The Warlord really needed to finish this tomb to give the burial site shelter on the breezy hillside.

In the ancient tongue learnt in their youth, Varro began chanting a prayer to Brutus's grave in a tone so soft and gentle it blended into the wind. Apparently, the true beauty of the chant wasn't in the unknown words themselves but in the elegance of the sounds, the tones, the music. But Sulla was probably too feral to appreciate it.

As the pair silently watched the grass shake in the night, the air shifted behind Sulla in a manner that told him someone was approaching. *Why can't people ever give us a moment's peace?*

"Warlord," Sulla called, turning to see Regent Hera, wrapped in an exquisite cloak that clung to her figure in all the right places to make a man hot.

Varro slowly rose from his knees. "What is it? What couldn't wait until our meeting with the men?"

"It's best others don't hear this." Hera glared at the Warlord with a wave of rare anger. "I just heard the last of your kuraminium ore is gone."

"It's true," Varro said. "We'll manage until we've retaken the mine."

"Why wasn't I informed?" Hera stepped forward but gave the gravesite a respectfully wide berth.

"Your army doesn't use kuraminium," Varro said.

"It's still pertinent to the survival of this city."

Why did people have to use such big words Sulla couldn't grasp?

"He'll tell you next time," Sulla said before the Warlord could make the situation worse by being stubborn.

Hera swept her cloak to the side with a hiss. "We may be guests in your city, but I'm still Regent of the humans here. I should be informed of anything so vital to our defence as well as yours. Do not disrespect me again, Warlord."

Varro ran a hand through his hair, jaw visibly tense, but he gave no other clues as to his feelings on the scolding. "Your grievances have been noted. Was there anything else?"

After a pause, Hera said, "There's another reason I'm here. Someone wished to speak with you privately." Without elaborating, Hera spun with a flare of her dress and made her way back towards the city.

Sulla scanned the hills around for a sight of anyone while Varro turned his attention back to his brother's grave. Seeing nothing, Sulla eventually reverted to sparing Brutus a few moments' thought, his mind soon drifting to the one the rakkan had treated like a son—Darius.

Even though both he and Varro had pressing matters to deal with, they stayed a few more minutes in silence, listening to the breeze course between the thin vegetation around.

When Sulla was about to call it a night and go to prepare for battle, he felt another person approaching from behind.

As he turned, he barely believed his eyes and swore the stars played tricks on him. But slowly, the old man came closer and into focus.

"Eugenius?" Sulla said.

Varro virtually leapt up from his knees and peered at the man beneath the overgrown facial hair that was a few shades lighter than when they'd last seen him. If Sulla didn't know better, he'd have mistaken the old Warlord for a beggar. In those familiar eyes, he saw warmth and calmness.

"I thought it about time I paid you a visit," Eugenius said, "given everything happening within and without the Empire."

"Where have you…?" Varro began.

"I hear you're soon for battle," Eugenius said, seeming to ignore Varro's gaping.

The Warlord nodded.

"I didn't know whether you'd be pleased to see me, but I couldn't ignore something my grandson mentioned in passing."

Varro's jaw tensed again.

"What did he say?" Sulla asked.

"Something about Hadrian going after the Waif Magician. Is it true?" The calmness about the man suddenly gave way to a nervous twitch of his moustache.

"It's true," Varro said. "I've been trawling our archives for information about why, and I think he wants to use the Staff of Arria to find the Twin Blades."

Sulla had lost count of how many old fogeys he'd asked about the history of the Blades. Most knew of them only by thirdhand stories, or had lost their minds so completely they didn't remember you had to wait until you sat on a latrine to push. The few who had been youths at the time, and therefore were young enough to still have lucid thoughts, only recalled that the last overlord's rise to power was clouded in secrecy.

"Hadrian's building an algus army," Varro continued, "in order to take on the Magician. From what I've read, the Staff and the Blades are bonded in some way, antagonistic to each other yet attracted at the same time."

The revelation had the former warlord twitching even more. "I see…" He strode to Brutus's gravestone, deep in thought. "I heard about your brothers… I know the pain of loss and how it can cloud a man's judgement." Eugenius focused on Varro with a hint of the menace he'd borne as warlord. "Are you hindered?"

"I am not," Varro said.

Eugenius seemed to study the Warlord intently before saying, "You're wrong. Hadrian doesn't want the Staff to find the Blades."

"Then what does he want?"

"The Staff of Arria doesn't help you find the Blades; it allows a warlord to *take* them."

Sulla stiffened. As if they needed more urgency in defeating the fiend. "You mean it…"

"Quells the Blades' fire. A warlord must battle through the Staff's weakness and take hold of them. Once in his hands, they're subdued and bound to his will. It's how overlords in past centuries took them."

And once they were Hadrian's, the Law of the Blades said that every living rakkan had to bend the knee to him. Sulla cursed.

"Things are worse than you know," Eugenius said, ever more urgency in his voice. "Hadrian isn't searching for the Twin Blades."

229

"Of course he is," Varro said. "That's one thing we can be sure—"

"He doesn't need to search for them. He knows where they are."

The next curse to leave Sulla's lips was so foul that Eugenius grimaced.

"How can you be sure?" Sulla asked.

"He was there when they were lost."

"That was so long ago," Varro said. "He can't have been more than a teen at the time. Surely he wouldn't remember."

Were they willing to bet the fate of their city on that? Not by half.

"Do *you* know where the Blades are?" Sulla asked Eugenius.

"Only that they were seen with the last overlord at Mount Psilos. I was only a lowly legionnaire at the time, not the grandson of a warlord, like Hadrian, who was there when the humans attacked."

"You didn't fight in the Battle on the Mount?"

"No…"

This was the last thing they needed on the cusp of battle, when they had no warriors to spare.

"You can't let Hadrian get the Staff," Eugenius ordered.

"Easier said than done," Varro said.

"You know what you need to do."

"Do I?"

Eugenius strode up to him and grasped the Warlord's mantled shoulders tightly. Fire swelled in his eyes. "Hadrian cannot take the Blades if another takes them before him."

Varro shook off the man's hands. "Don't be absurd. I can't—"

"You must." Eugenius's voice rose to the harsh growl of the warlord Sulla had known in his younger days.

"I don't want them," Varro said. "The horns on my helmet are enough of a curse. What more weight will those etched blades bring?"

"Any who want them are not worthy of them. Our fate is what we make it and not always what we wish for. Did Trogus want his wife to be betrayed? Did he want her power leeched into a staff? Did he want to sacrifice himself to try to destroy it?"

"You speak as if that legend were true," Sulla said. Surely the ever-sceptical Eugenius knew the story was made up to entertain children by the fireside.

"It doesn't matter," Eugenius said. "The Staff exists. The Blades exist, and you *must* take them before Hadrian."

Usually, going up against the Magician would be a suicidal challenge only Sulla would be up for. But now, Varro had a large number of algus to draw upon. Perhaps he could be persuaded, and Sulla could finally rejoin Darius.

"I agree with the old man," Sulla said.

But Varro scoffed. "I can't thin our numbers for retaking the mine just to get closer to gaining a power I have no interest in. Whatever Hadrian's plans were, the Magician will evade capture, as she's done all her life."

"Bet our lives on that?" Sulla said. The Azurians may have only caught the briefest of glances of her over the years, despite actively hunting her, but Hadrian had algus.

"The mine is my first concern," Varro said. "After we have it back, I'll consider how we act."

Sulla huffed. "But there isn't time. If—"

"This isn't a discussion." Varro stepped up to Sulla with a deep breath that effused authority. He was warlord, and Sulla had no more appetite for disobedience. Not yet, at least.

Eugenius cleared his throat. "I've said my piece. I'll visit again when you've returned from battle to give you all I know on how to get to Mount Psilos and the Blades."

Varro gave the old man a nod. "Until we meet again."

23

Lex – Uncharted Mountains

Lex leaned forward to give her back a rest from the jagged bark of the tree behind and pressed her head against her knees, trying to ignore the thumping of Darius's boots as he paced up and down. She couldn't, and the tension in her head only tightened like an iron vice on her temples.

Drops of rain from a shower long since past fell from the needled canopy above onto her head, the only thing cooling her sweats and temper. When she looked up, the line of muddy boot prints and crushed plants under Darius had deepened further. She'd have yelled at the man, had a rakkan camp not been nearby, and had she the energy for a row. He'd never been so agitated before.

"Would you like another drop of tears?" Nasrin whispered beside her.

"No." Lex gave the carer as much of a smile as she could muster, though it must have looked as pathetic as it felt because Nasrin winced with more worry.

"It's been two days," she said.

As if Lex needed reminding. But her head had to remain clear. Pain focused her attention on avenging all those she'd lost and protecting all those she cared about. For weeks, she'd tried to think of a better way to disable the Magician's sight but always failed. The metal powder she'd found had been a good start, but only something brighter would do. There had to be something that burned faster.

Under the rotting remains of a nearby uprooted tree, Lyra lay beside Gorgias's escort—just in case the whiteback tried to burrow away—and the freed children lay close by, shrouded by fronds. If only she hadn't sent Tiro with an update for Sulla, she'd have a better view of their surroundings.

Darius ceased his pacing and prowled towards the children, kneeling beside the boy he'd dubbed "Lionheart" and whispering some words that brought a sigh of relief from the child. But the rest of the children shrank away from the Slayer next to them.

Lex stared at the pair, at the boy that could have easily been her son yet clearly wasn't an algus or Numbered. Having all these children around only made her dwell on the two she'd never give up fighting for, and the distraction weighed down her mind until it felt like iron in her skull.

But this time, her focus lingered on Darius and his almost fatherly treatment of them. Ever since she'd had to finish off Omid in Laltos, the man hadn't been able to see a suffering boy and not react. The old Darius had never shown such care; a harsh life had blunted his empathy. Now, with that washed away, had Archimedes revealed the person who had been beneath all along? Keeping her distance from the old Darius had been tough because he'd exuded power and might in a way that seduced many women, but his magnetism now wasn't through his strength—well, not entirely. Those shoulders… If only he'd shave that beard.

After speaking a little more to the children, Darius came back with fear etched into his face. "Gorgias should be back by now."

True. A few more hours and the sun would set, leaving them no choice but to move away and start a fire. But that wasn't what unnerved her most. After thinking Selene was dead for so long, what if Gorgias really did come back with her? How would Lex explain the fact she'd given up on her own sister?

The whirring of her mind brought a familiar exhaustion. Clearly, she'd get nowhere again today. She needed a distraction to clear her head.

"Darius?" Lex patted an empty patch of dry dirt beside her and waited.

The man took the hint, and so did Nasrin, as she stood and sheepishly wandered away towards the children. Only she seemed to be able to approach them without the poor things quaking.

"Something wrong?" Darius said, dropping with an inelegant thump onto his backside. He was such a gentle, graceful man.

"I need to pick your brains," she said.

He snorted a laugh. "Shouldn't take long."

"This is serious. I need something that burns very fast and very bright."

The man sighed and ran a hand through his beard. Usually, she hated facial hair on men, but he avoided looking feral somehow.

"Charcoal?" Darius said. "Ferven?"

She waited for a further response, but none came. He'd been right. It hadn't taken long.

As talkative as ever, he moved to stand again, but she grabbed his arm and held him in place.

"Sorry," he said, "but I don't have anything else to suggest. Nasrin already told me everything you tried burning, which covers a list far more extensive than my knowledge."

"I have something else to discuss." And the truth was, she'd wanted to broach the subject for a while. "I want to talk about you."

He coughed and lowered his head nervously. "What about me?"

"You're…different since your exile."

"Ah," he sat back down beside her and swallowed. "I hope that's a good thing."

"It is."

Her reply chased away the grin that had been forming at his lips. He frowned, almost as if he didn't believe she'd pay him a compliment. That was only true *most* of the time.

"How am I different?" he asked.

Even his letters over the last year had sounded different, more mature. "You make decisions, think for yourself rather than just listen to others. You're more like a…" *Commander.* "More like the old Darius."

He nodded, and a little warmth returned to his previously fretful stare. Building his confidence wouldn't come easy, and she'd hardly exuded poise herself after Laltos, but if she didn't do it, no one else would.

Despite the old Darius being gone, her hopes for him as a warrior hadn't changed. In a war, inspiring soldiers was half the victory, and who would be afraid when charging alongside the battle cry of the most fearsome slayer to walk the Empire? At the

Battle of Laltos, she'd seen a glimpse of the commander Darius could become. Impressing men with courage when certain death faced them was a skill she'd seldom seen in anyone, including veterans that had lived through more war than he had.

But the man before her now wasn't ready or willing for more. Yet.

While she tried to think of something to fill the tense silence that grew between them, he suddenly went for his sword.

"Someone's coming this way," he whispered. "And they're not alone."

Lex struggled to her feet and drew her sword. She gave Nasrin a signal to hide with the children while Darius planted his tense body in front of her.

Moments later, two men stepped out from between the firs, and one of their heads bore Gorgias's signature black hair. The other had a stocky build and a large head that was mostly a hairy chin. Although neither man had a weapon hanging from his belt, Lex never took any chances by making assumptions.

Darius pointed his sword at the pair, and they stopped a few yards away without the need for a threat.

He growled. "I didn't know being trapped in a Viridian camp made a woman grow stubble."

"I c-can explain." Gorgias held both his hands out, and his friend mimicked the gesture—though with a surly reluctance.

"This had better be good," Darius said.

Lex scanned the forest behind the pair for any trace of an ambush, but all that stirred were the forest sprigs, offshoots and raindrops falling from leaf to leaf.

"I made it into the camp," Gorgias said, "and I searched everywhere, but Hadrian has already left. So I instead began asking about Selene. I spoke with plenty of algus, more than a s-sensible man should have. I was lucky they didn't catch—"

"Get to the part about your burly friend," Darius said.

"R-right." Gorgias swallowed. "I'd searched the whole camp and didn't find her, but then asked Ninety-seven here about her on a whim, and he said he'd seen her."

Darius's sword almost slipped from his finger, but he caught himself just in time. The shock on his face reflected a hope that Lex didn't share. She couldn't bring herself to believe her sister lived until she saw it with her own eyes. A lifetime of disappointment left one cynical.

"Where is she?" Darius asked.

"Well." Ninety-seven cleared his throat. "I said I'd met someone of her description a couple of days ago."

Unable to put up with these fantasies much longer, Lex pushed past Darius and strode to Ninety-seven with a scowl. "Did you speak with this woman you claim to have seen?" With any luck, *he'd* crush Darius's hopes.

"A little," Ninety-seven said. "She was in a rather dire mood but said she was a survivor of Laltos."

"And where was she?" Lex asked.

"I…don't know the name of the place."

"Foltara," Gorgias said, his face damp with a sheen of sweat. "It isn't far. Only a few miles along the road to Dolthea. It's a poor village the Viridians haven't bothered to occupy and would be a good place to drop off the young ones, regardless. They could get passage to the east if we have the money."

"We?" Darius said. "I never said you could join us."

Gorgias's face fell, and he stared at the ground like a child that had suffered a rebuke and a rod to the backside. "And what else would I do? Surely you wouldn't leave me here alone…"

Suspicion emanated from Darius's face as he studied the broken man.

Gorgias was far from Lex's primary concern, but as she pondered their next move against the Magician, Darius turned to her.

"What do you think?" he asked.

Broken people weren't to be trusted, but another algus would make their search and eventual "discussions" with Shirin easier.

"I haven't the energy to keep an eye on him," she said. "If you do, he may come in useful."

"And is this village worth searching? If some of the Subdued are mixing with humans, perhaps Selene is there."

The last strand of Lex's patience snapped. "It's a fool's quest. There must be thousands of women who look like Selene in the Empire. And I hardly think former algus mixing with…" Her thoughts trailed off as something suddenly connected in her fatigued mind. *Mixing.* Why hadn't she thought of mixing *powders* before?

"Lex?" Darius raised an eyebrow.

She ignored him and reached to get her bag from beside the tree. She tore it open and rummaged through the contents desperately, knowing she had some supplies of the metal powder there but doubtful she had the one thing it made sense to mix first. Sure enough, her hands reached the bottom of her bag without finding anything.

She cursed and turned to Darius. "I need sulphur."

He stood silently with his head tilted back, staring into the canopy above them.

"Darius?" she snapped.

He flinched as if waking from a dream. "Sorry. I saw…nothing."

She sighed. "I need sulphur."

"All right. I don't have any on me."

"Of course not." But where could they get it? Perhaps some of the larger towns or villages.

Darius gave a frustrated grunt and again peered at the branches above for a brief moment. Before Lex could ask what was wrong, he looked at Gorgias and Ninety-seven, still brandishing his sword.

"Where did Hadrian go?" Darius asked.

"I'm not sure," Ninety-seven said. "Likely a camp in the north, not far from Foltara perhaps."

Darius narrowed his eyes at the man before raising his voice. "You'll lead us to this village, and you'd best not try anything. Do you know who I am?"

"Yes," the Numbered replied, his face stiff but his voice less so. "The Slayer."

"So you know what I'll do to you if you cross me."

Ninety-seven nodded.

"You'll stay away from everyone except me," Darius said. "You'll sleep apart from us, and you'll do exactly as I say. Both of you."

Gorgias bowed his head. "Yes, master."

Darius gritted his teeth but held his tongue.

Meanwhile, Lex plotted a new course in her mind. A village would hardly have stores of sulphur, but any one of the nearby towns might.

For the first time in weeks, her pain eased of its own accord.

24

Darius – Northwest of Dolthea

Darius watched the boughs and twigs high above him as he went over to Nasrin and told her and the young ones the plan. Half of them were too pale with dread at the prospect of seeing anyone new again, but the other half—Lionheart among them—had a hopeful brightness in their eyes he hadn't seen before.

But his attention didn't linger on the youths. Although not within sight, Lyra sensed the pteron had been lurking for hours, always staying among other birds to evade detection—until now. There it was, perched on the loftiest branches of a fir tree, barely possible to detect if he hadn't been searching for it. It had never lingered this long before, and ever since Gorgias had returned and mentioned Selene, the creature had flapped its scaled wings at every suggestion of travelling to Foltara. Whatever the signal meant, he suspected going to the village was the only way to reveal the truth.

While he pondered, a sudden pang of fear gripped him. Lyra sent warning of something else moving within the surrounding thicket.

He scanned around with an obvious concern that had some of the more alert young ones huddling together nervously. His focus flitted to every shake of a frond in the wind, and he even threw back his cloak to expose his sensitive arms. But whatever lurked was moving with a lifeless stealth that evaded him. It couldn't have been a Viridian, then; they were louder than a drunk man in a brothel.

"What's wrong?" Lex called. Her hand moved to the hilt of her sword.

"Get down," Darius whispered to Nasrin and the youths.

Was this an ambush? He waited for a few moments for arrows to begin flying, but again his rakkan skin felt nothing, and eventually, Lyra's heart calmed, although she glared at him as if urging him to do something. Maybe she'd been spooked by the wind.

"It's nothing," Darius said, although his words seemed to bring no consolation to the young ones.

Was it something connected with the pteron? Perhaps he should have asked Lex to send Tiro after the thing long ago, but he hadn't seen her escort for a while. And besides killing the pteron, what could the falcon do? If captured, it wasn't as if creatures talked, and scaring it away would only stop him from getting answers.

Every time he thought of killing the thing, Lyra growled at him with alarm. Whatever he did, she did *not* want the pteron dead.

It took a while for everyone to calm down, although Darius wouldn't allow himself to, but they set off as soon as possible. Gorgias and Ninety-seven led the way ahead of Darius and his permanently unsheathed gladius. They purposely cut a long path around the Viridian camp and through parts of the woodland so dense it often took them minutes to hack through a few yards, feet catching on brambles and creeping vines all the way. After a few hours, Darius was ready to torch the whole damn forest to get out, but he just about managed to keep his patience until they approached a glade. Lyra slipped through the undergrowth with irritating ease but still bore a knot in her stomach, ever aware of the spying escort tailing them.

After reaching the clearing, they set up camp for the night and rested until way past dawn the next day. The young ones took a while to rouse, and disturbing what appeared to be a deep sleep made him feel like a monster, but when they'd woken and foraged a light breakfast, they set off again for another day's hike.

Evening had fallen by the time the forest completely opened up with glades of flat grassland, dotted with streams, ponds and the odd heavy copse. Darius didn't see anything else moving, but Lyra caught the scent of prey in the area. Dark clouds above threatened yet more rain to wet his long hair, and the odd patches of visible sky now shone a deep shade of orange.

Many of the youngest wore grim faces and kicked the dirt as they grouped up behind Lionheart and his freckled girlfriend, probably bitter with the same ache that rumbled in Darius's stomach.

"They need a proper meal," Darius said to Lex. "Lyra senses prey close."

Lex nodded. "It's a good place for animals to graze and quench their thirst."

While the two conversed about their plans for both food and the next day's travel, a herd of ferrow deer emerged at the far side of the clearing. Standing at least the height of a man, the beasts numbered a dozen and ambled far enough away not to be perturbed by a group of humans. But they were close enough to make out the white stripes and spots that covered the tawny fur of their backs. Ferrows ran briskly and nimbly, a prey even Lyra hadn't often hunted with success unless she stalked them to within a few yards. Thankfully, Darius had a fine archer beside him.

"Lucky day." He spotted a large doe at the back of the herd. "Shoot the fat one."

While he watched, the creature twitched its head in an odd way that brought a shocked gasp from Lex.

"What is it?" he asked.

She studied the beast carefully for a while before answering. "A deer."

He snorted. "*Thank* you."

"I don't feel like hunting. Can you get it?" When she looked at him, it was with a curious mischief in her eyes that he had no idea of the reason for, but at least it made a difference from weariness and fatigue.

Lionheart's girl also gaped at the animals with a keen interest that she hadn't shown in anything other than her boyfriend up to now. Her frown deepened the more she watched, then she spoke for the first time in a voice as high and coarse as steel scratching steel.

"You won't get that one," she said. "That's a—"

"Darius is capable of hunting things far more fearsome than a deer," Lex interjected.

The girl drooped at the interruption and returned to the arms of her boyfriend with a flush to her mottled cheeks.

"Don't worry, Freckles," Darius said. "You'll sleep with a full belly tonight." But he swore Lex suppressed a smirk at the words.

244

"Lyra," he said. "Stay with Nasrin and the young ones." She'd do a much better job of protecting everyone than Gorgias and Ninety-seven.

"We'll find a spot to rest in the forest," Nasrin said, then she led all the young ones into a thick ring of trees that would cloak them from the wind as well as the sight of anyone passing by. Gorgias and Ninety-seven didn't follow but made their way to a nearby spot at a distance from the young ones they'd been permitted to sleep.

Meanwhile, Darius still eyed the doe, suspicious. What was Lex not telling him?

"Can I have your bow?" he asked her.

She raised an eyebrow. "Why? Can a deer outrun you now?"

Of course it couldn't, but something told him she'd enjoy watching whatever was about to happen. He held out a hand and sensed the wind rushing from the glade into the forest. Grazing upwind, the herd wouldn't have caught his scent.

He pulled his cloak as tight behind him as possible—making his body appear smaller—and pulled his hood low over his face, obscuring his predatory eyes. Then, with slow movements, he crept into the clearing as the evening's darkness deepened. Regardless of the favourable environment, the deer would see him coming well before he got near, but he didn't need to be close; he was just saving himself a long sprint.

He crept sideways with his body facing away from the herd, and when they finally pointed their eyes and ears towards him, he'd made it halfway into the clearing. His nonthreatening stance worked. A few went back to grazing after only a glimpse—the fat one among them—and he eased closer, sword ready for when they bolted.

Moments later, most of the deer skipped away, but the fat one still munched with its head down and ears back. It wasn't

245

until he was within a few yards, all the other ferrows having fled, that the fat one finally lifted its head and showed him its big, wide eyes as dark as a rakkan's. It was a pity to slay the innocent beast, but hungry youths needed nourishment.

He bent his knees and readied his sword, then with a swift lunge, he surged forward and aimed for the neck of the doe, the target his gladius would strike with a lethal blow. But as soon as he swung his sword, the doe sprang to the side with a flash of blue in its eyes.

Darius pivoted and tried to follow, but the beast tore into a sprint with a haste he'd only ever seen from one other creature—a swift. And in his haste, he lost his footing and skidded on the wet ground, almost toppling over.

Only a few seconds later and the doe was nothing but a springing blur as it whisked through the rest of the glade and disappeared into the woods.

Instead of pursuing the doe, Darius stopped and gaped at the deep hoof prints left in the mud. How had he never come across these magical creatures if there were more of them? Soon, a plethora of questions filled his head, and he trudged back to Lex.

How long would her mocking last? Would he be spared the brunt of it if he simply ignored her?

When he reached her, she was sitting against a tree with a more relaxed posture than usual, and he noted the spot gave her a perfect view of everything that had unfolded. And she wasn't clutching her hip or wincing for a change.

"Go on…say it," he said.

"Say what?" she said, casually picking at her nails.

"Whatever wisecrack you've prepared."

"I wouldn't dream of worsening your embarrassment." She cast her gaze down to his feet and raised an eyebrow. "Was treading in its dung some sort of animalistic show of dominance after it humbled you?"

When he looked down, he noted the mess squelched under his boot. *Oh, you little…* He should have charged after the thing. Once he'd scraped his feet clean across a thick tuft of grass, he sat down beside Lex with a sigh.

"Thanks for that," he said. "What was that thing?"

"A ferrow."

Although the remark was no doubt intended as a quip, he had to wonder whether the creature had been a deer after all. "How was it so fast?"

"It's like us, like swifts. Some are born with the gift, but it's exceedingly rare. People claim it originated in humans, and these creatures are a consequence of bestiality by people millennia ago."

That evoked mental images best forgotten. He'd always assumed swifts were a specific breed of horse. "What about rakkans? Can they be born with it?"

Lex shook her head and gave him a mirthless grin. "For whatever reason, you're unique. You have your human half to thank for your algor."

That meant thanking his mother, a prospect that made him turn up his nose. "If it's just animals, why don't people use more of them? Seems like they could be useful as escorts." Just imagining Lyra with his gifted agility gave him a rush of excitement.

"As you've seen, they're evasive, low-profile, and far rarer than human algus. You don't want to know how many horses they breed in the east to produce enough swifts for the Royal Roads and cavalry. As for escorts, the Chief Priest of the Order refuses to bond such animals."

"Why?"

She shrugged. "He's a…unique man. Perhaps he has a reason. Perhaps not." With a groan of effort, she struggled to her feet and took her bow. "I'll get supper."

"No." He leapt up and swiped the bow from her grasp before she could argue. "You rest. I'll find something else, something in my league this time."

A heaviness seemed to overcome her body again, and she slumped back down. "Fine."

As he went to collect the arrows, his bond with Lyra suddenly deepened. His stomach dropped. This time, it wasn't just pangs of fear she sent him but a rush of energy, a threat, a fight. She pounced at something—or rather, someone.

He whirled around to catch a glimpse of the others but couldn't see anyone through the greenery.

"Something's wrong." He tossed Lex her bow and opened his mouth to say more, but a clash of steel rang through the forest that had him rushing forward at once.

He bolted towards the others as more twangs reached his ears. Lyra's emotions surged through him too, angry and fearful and violent. A heartbeat later, algor flashed between the tree trunks and illuminated a pair of swords, lines of blue light among the dull gloaming. Had Ninety-seven turned on them? Had *Gorgias* turned on them?

But that didn't make sense. Surely they'd attempt to kill *him*, which was why he and Lyra never slept at the same time.

He sprinted past tree after tree, and the clashing figures between them quickly came into view. Half shielding himself behind a tree trunk, Ninety-seven parried a blow from an algus while another lay beheaded at his feet.

With each swing the enemy algus took, his long cloak flailed, a quivering sheet the colour of bark and leaves, and revealed a white-and-black tunic underneath. Hatred burned in both men's eyes, and although the foreigner's clothes moved too quickly for him to see clearly, Darius presumed the man wore the King's eagle on his front.

Meanwhile, Gorgias and Lyra fought with a male and female algus in similar colours. One enemy's sword arm was crushed and bloody inside Lyra's gnashing jaws while the woman swiped at Gorgias's head in a flurry that sliced through his hair and skin.

But Darius ignored them all and instead raced towards the ring of trees behind. When he neared the gap in the trunks, he spied Nasrin and the young ones pressing their bodies tightly together in the centre. The carer shielded as many as she could through a brave yet futile spread of her arms while Lionheart attempted to do the same with his scrawny figure.

Stalking towards them, a woman held out a dagger pulsing with algor and took aim. Darius sprinted but was too far to do anything other than watch.

The shield clutched in the algus's other arm gleamed as she tossed the dagger with a cry that told of the malice behind it. While the blade spun through the heavy air, Nasrin winced and shifted her arm into its path. But she hadn't enough skill. The dagger cut across her elbow, passed Lionheart's thin neck, and lodged into the collar of Freckles behind him.

The girl screamed and would have fallen backwards if not for the youths packed tightly at her back who steadied her.

Without time to reel, the enemy algus ripped her sword from its scabbard and rushed towards the helpless souls in front.

Darius was still too far to intervene, so he took a giant breath and spat a guttural roar that had the algus skidding to a halt and gaping back at him. Horror contorted her ugly, pockmarked face, and she reacted faster than most.

She bolted to her side, away from him and towards the edge of the thick ring of trees. She was caged, like a wounded animal in the sights of an apex predator. Within seconds, she hit the branches with a crunch that slowed her a fraction, and her flailing cloak came within Darius's reach.

He grabbed it with a strength that tore it from her body. The pull jerked her back, not to a halt, but enough for Darius to stab his gladius into the woman's shoulder. She yelled in pain but pressed on through the branches of the trees in front, sending them whipping back across his furious face.

Darius swung again and cut clean through the back of her thighs.

This time, her scream was shrill, and she tumbled to the ground, tossing leaves, branches and dirt into the air. Darius coughed and bore down on her, pressed his foot onto her belly and watched her try in vain to writhe free. With his off-hand, he seized her arm and pressed it to the dirt, then he stabbed his gladius through her bicep using such strength his sword sank into the ground until the hilt crushed her arm.

"I'm not finished with you," he growled before leaping off her and heading back to the others.

Screams pierced his ears from behind, but he trained his focus onto the two algus with Lyra and Gorgias. Grappling with his panther, the male enemy's sword arm was shredded to bone, and before Darius could help, an arrow tore through the man's head and ended his struggles for good. Although Darius couldn't see her, Lex must have been close.

It took only a glance at Ninety-seven to see he'd vanquished his opponent, which left only one of the King's algus. She loomed over Gorgias as the man weakly parried her strikes from the ground, and her cries thundered with such rage that she didn't react to Darius sprinting until he reached out and grabbed her sword arm mid-swing.

She gasped before he squeezed and crushed the bones in her wrist. A second later, Gorgias slashed her inner thigh from below, scoring a savage and mortal wound. Blood flowed heavy and red, disturbing Darius somewhat, but not as much as it would have done a year ago.

With a snort to rid his nose of the coppery stink, he turned and ran back to the now shivering and sobbing huddle of young ones. Nasrin had the freckled girl in her arms while Lionheart stroked her sweaty head, whispering "*Ssshhhh*" over and over with a numb stare at the disturbed ground in front.

Darius came to a halt just short of them and spied the bright scarlet gushing along the embedded knife. The smell of blood sat even heavier in the air here. "Is she…?" *Dying?*

Nasrin raised her teary gaze and nodded.

Why? Why would an algus go after a group so young, unarmed, unthreatening?

With fire now burning in his throat, he turned to the algus he'd pinned. He'd damn well ask her.

But as he stalked up to her, something was wrong. The only sobs and groans were those from the young ones behind. The woman lay unmoving, and when he reached her, the volume of blood squelching under his boots told him she was dead. A wide cut split her throat, with a knife and a limp hand resting just beneath.

He grunted, fire spitting from his nostrils. "You didn't deserve such an easy death."

Once again, he questioned who had been the target. He'd crossed paths with enough Torians in the last year to know they had no qualms about killing children and terrorising whatever humans struggled to eke a living in these war-torn lands. Had the woman just been a coward, too afraid to face Gorgias and Ninety-seven?

He watched the two Subdued as they joined the young ones and nursed their scrapes and wounds. If he hadn't seen the pair fight with such fervour and passion, he'd have suspected they'd planned this ambush. Were these algus from the King the same foes Lyra had sensed near the Viridian camp?

Bitterness tainted his thoughts as he rejoined the others. This time, he'd spare them the gruesome sight of him wetting his arms with blood. No one was fussing over the girl any longer, and the only mournful sobs were from the others. Lionheart's face was stony and dry as he clung to his girlfriend's body, but the quivering of his lip betrayed the anguish he was keeping caged.

Darius had freed these youths, and for what? Death? He'd failed to protect them. He'd failed to feed them well. He'd…failed.

"Torians," Ninety-seven muttered, not sensing that silence was needed to calm many frayed nerves. "The Viridians forever complained about them. The only purpose of these groups is to sow fear in workers and slaves. They even—"

"That's enough," Lex snapped.

Another hush fell over the group while Nasrin bandaged herself and all the other wounded. But eventually she struggled as the fading sun offered too little light to work. And Darius feared the night hadn't seen the last of violence.

"Let's move," he said. "We'll go to the other side of the clearing. From now on, these young ones don't venture far from me. And you." He turned to Ninety-seven.

"Yes?" the man said.

"Go catch us a meal. Everyone may have lost the will to eat, but we need our strength."

252

Ninety-seven nodded and wandered away with his bloody sword, and as he did, Darius spied the pteron watching from a high branch of a tree. *I see you.*

Lex stood opposite him, focused on the children with her bow in hand. It would be so easy to bring the winged creature down.

But as soon as he thought of it, his panther growled with an anger that set the young ones shuddering again.

Fine. I won't do anything. Perhaps he was being foolish, but Lyra had always been the smart one.

25

Rufus – Uncharted Mountains

"Out!" Hadrian bellowed at two centurions who had dared move too close to him.

Three Viridian Guardians rushed from the Warlord's side and dragged the centurions out of the tent, almost knocking over the bloody heart that rested on a plinth made of bones at the centre. At least the men knew better than to resist.

"I wasn't done questioning those men," Rufus muttered. There were only a few that had been scouring the Azurian Glacier, and he needed all the information he could get.

As the tent flap opened, a breeze swept inside and sent dust scattering both in the air and across the thick carpet that had been laid, forcing Rufus to conjure a little ferven in his eyes to shield them. The light helped him assess the maps on the table in front of him, although he was the only one there who seemed interested. His father was busy sitting on his stone throne, eyeing everyone that moved, and around the edges of the tent, thinly clothed women had prostrated themselves in quiet devotion, not moving a muscle and no doubt praying the Warlord would choose them next to prove their piety.

Meanwhile, Rufus's brothers laid back on reclined chairs, picking the dirt from under their nails, acting relaxed but pale with horror. Apart from them and the Viridian Guardians, few were allowed to sit in the Warlord's presence these days, and it had only worsened after the Dreaded One's attack on the camp.

None of the men rested without worry, their eyes often flitting to the fresh heart at the centre and the dripping bones that lifted it for all to see. An hour ago, the organ had beat in the chest of one of Rufus's older brothers, a rakkan who had dared to walk in here without taking off his dagger. *The clod always was forgetful.* At least his father seemed a little less paranoid since the sacrifice. Hopefully, that would make the Warlord more reasonable in their important investigations.

Rufus cleared his throat. "Can we at least invite in the legionnaire from Dolthea who claims he has urgent business?"

"No! They lie. They only mean me harm; I know it." Hadrian grabbed his injured arm and rubbed it. "They all sense my weakness."

The Warlord's constant touching probably only made the pain worse, but Rufus was damned if he'd say so. If anything, he wished the rakkan would retire to his bed, even though it was barely past midnight.

"Fine," Rufus said, going back to aimlessly scrutinising maps as if a blot of ink would suddenly materialise to pinpoint the location he sought. "Maybe we're searching too far south. The Magician has been sighted in the Uncharted Mountains more recently, or she could even be hiding north of Azuria in the Forest of Whispers."

None of his brothers answered him, but the Warlord finally took notice.

"You think she's that brave?" Hadrian mused.

"I think she's not one to believe in tales of spirits, whether the stories are true or not." After all, a foreboding forest was the perfect place to hide. No human or rakkan ever ventured there, and it would spare her the chills of the Glacier that only rakkans tolerated.

The Warlord mused no further and instead looked down at the lump missing from his left arm, flexing the muscles with a grimace when they didn't contract all the way without tremors.

With a sigh, Rufus collapsed onto a chair. "This would go a lot faster if we asked the Branzians to help in the search."

"Never," Hadrian growled. "They can't be trusted. I'm still reeling from you letting them take ore from our tunnels in the mine."

"It's to deter a Margalvian attack. We're not supposed to *like* it. But they haven't mined more than their fair share."

Hadrian waved a dismissive hand. "Regardless, only we will search for the Magician."

Sometimes Rufus doubted the Warlord had a cogent plan at all. "It would help if I knew where we were going after we've got the Staff. Is it far into human lands?"

Hadrian murmured to himself for a while before answering. "Yes."

"And you know the precise location of the Blades?"

"Why do you question me?" The Warlord's eyes narrowed with a disturbing fright.

Rufus sighed. "Come on, Father. Surely you don't think someone as scrawny as I intend to challenge you?" The same couldn't be said of his brothers, and many had now stopped fidgeting enough to let Rufus know they were listening even if they acted disinterested.

The Warlord seemed to notice too and growled. "All of you, get out!"

When Rufus stood to leave with a discreet roll of his eyes, the Warlord pointed to him. "Not you."

Did that mean Rufus was finally going to get some answers? It was a little late but better than nothing. As his brothers trudged out of the tent, huffing and groaning, the women filed out in silence with tiny steps. Meanwhile, Rufus sat quietly and shrank into his chair to appear as physically unthreatening as possible—not that he needed much help. The Warlord could outmatch him with only one arm.

Hadrian took a giant gulp of water before he spoke again. "The Blades shouldn't be an issue. They're far into hostile territory but in a barren area."

That matched the little Rufus knew of where the last overlord was seen with them before he'd fallen.

"You've never told me the story before," Rufus said. "All my brothers say you regaled them with the tale, yet never with me. Is it because my mother was one of your lowly worshippers?"

Hadrian scoffed. "I told them when they were children, told them of the glory I would one day have."

"Yet not me…"

The Warlord surveyed him with wary eyes, but thankfully, they weren't fearful. "I never told you because I knew you were different. That lot are fools who've forgotten the details I told them as boys. With you, I knew you wouldn't forget."

That could be the reason, or it could be the fact the Warlord had barely been around when Rufus was growing up—not that he was complaining. Now that he knew the man, he counted it a blessing not to have had to tolerate what Cordus, the late but treasured eldest son, had.

"It seems important that I know the story now." Rufus slid down in his chair another inch.

Hadrian sighed. "There isn't much to tell. The rakkan war had been long and costly, and your great-grandfather hadn't come out on top. It was a Margalvian who commanded the Blades when all was said and done, but I'll be damned if I can remember his name. Tensions had all come to a head at Mount Psilos of all places, disagreements about useless lumps of something religious… Can't remember that either now."

"Aeternus?"

Hadrian murmured. "Could be. In any case, the humans caught us unawares, and the Overlord retreated while the legions banded together and fought off the attackers."

"But if we won, how were the Blades lost?"

"Because he fled like a coward. Who knows whether the humans got him or whether the Blades sensed his weakness and consumed him. It doesn't matter. All I know is where he retreated to, and I kept the location to myself, knowing my day would come."

"You didn't even tell your grandfather?"

Hadrian chuckled. "I always knew that one day I'd be lauded more than Hadrianus the Great himself."

Ignoring the Warlord's amusement, Rufus gazed at the map again. This time he traced all the human settlements and lands they now controlled, but they didn't stretch east far enough to come close to Mount Psilos. The Silk City now commanded most of the territories that guarded the mountain.

"How do you plan on getting to Mount Psilos?" Rufus asked.

"Behind the shield wall of the Viridian Legion. How else?"

It was typical of a brute to think force was the answer to every problem. "I think we'd have more success being covert. After all, we don't expect to meet resistance there, do we?"

Hadrian growled. "I suppose not, but we have to be swift. I don't have enough decades left, you know."

I'd say you had too many. "We can decide closer to the time. We have matters that are more pressing at the moment. Can I invite the legionnaires in now to give us their information? I fear Dolthea is in trouble from what I've heard." But what else could be expected when the Viridian warriors had slaughtered most of the people living there instead of enslaving them? Who did they think was going to work the fields or herd cattle? As it turned out, their few slaves weren't enough. Cattle starved, fields dried and rotted without harvest, and the lazy warriors either complained at having to do labour or starved too.

Just recalling the blunders made a tense headache grow in Rufus's skull. It wasn't like he hadn't told them all before, including the Warlord—numerous times. Bloodlust was rarely a good long-term strategy.

"Invite them in one at a time," the Warlord said, straightening in his chair.

It took Rufus a second to recall what they'd been speaking about. "Very well. Bring in the first legionnaire!" he yelled to the guardians outside.

A few moments later, a rakkan walked in—a tall, burly legionnaire from Dolthea. Rufus led the conversation while the Warlord never took his eyes off the man.

"How many died?" Rufus asked.

"Around a third, Commander," the legionnaire muttered.

"A third…? What have you damned fools been *doing*?" Rufus tugged on his hair a little. "Who gave the order to work the slaves that hard?"

The legionnaire eyed both of them nervously before muttering, "Our centurion, Arius."

Rufus cursed. *Not that cretin again…* Not only had the rakkan been idiotic enough to work their labourers to death, but he'd sent a legionnaire clearly without enough loyalty to lie or feign ignorance of his incompetence.

"Take slaves from the nearby towns and villages." Rufus waved his hand, ending their talk.

"But what if—"

"Dolthea needs them more. We need the harvest from its farms, or we'll struggle this winter." Why was everyone a buffoon that needed the blatant pointed out?

Hadrian relaxed a little while the legionnaire left. "I want you to go and sort out that town personally."

The request didn't entirely surprise Rufus. *But why must I always be the one to clean up everyone's mess?* "If that's what you wish, Warlord. Does that mean you want me to cease helping with tracking down the Magician?"

"For now. Cut off this Arius's head while you're at it. Perhaps it'll make him smarter." Hadrian chuckled.

Rufus took no amusement from the remark, instead focusing on the aggravation and death this centurion's folly would cause. "I've got a better idea. I'll send him in chains to the mine."

Hadrian laughed again, only this time with a sinister delight. If given a choice, prisoners always chose the executioner's axe over the mine.

While the pair waited, another legionnaire was ushered into the tent. This one had dented armour that looked decades old, and judging by the smell wafting in, that was when he'd last bathed too.

"Who are you?" Rufus asked.

"Bellus, Commander. I was one of the salvagers sent to Laltos a few weeks ago."

Hadrian let out a resonant grunt. "I thought we'd finished salvaging months ago."

Bellus shrugged. "I went where I was told to, Warlord."

"Probably another centurion using his own initiative." Rufus sighed, already longing to lie in his bed for the rest of the night. "Why are you here?"

"I…err…" Bellus looked down at his sandals and folded his arms together.

"'Err' is not an answer," Rufus said.

"Apologies, Commander." Despite speaking, Bellus didn't make eye contact again. "A friend and I were in Laltos collecting armour and didn't have much luck. We thought we might find some buried in the collapsed tunnel, so we spent a few days finding a way through and searched around. After that, we passed all the way through to the Cliffs of Aphatos."

That explained the man's nervousness. If Rufus hadn't sensed there was something significant about to be said, he'd have had the rakkan flogged for not sticking to his task.

"Get to the point," Hadrian ordered.

"Point…yes, Warlord. We saw her. I raced here as fast as I could to inform you." Bellus finally looked up sheepishly.

Hadrian groaned. "Saw who? Your mother?"

"No, Warlord. The Magician."

Hadrian leaned forward so suddenly his throne creaked underneath him. "At the Cliffs?"

Rufus bolted up from his seat and scoured the map again. "Why would she be so far east, so close to Laltos and the Silk City?"

"I'm certain, Commander." Bellus took a step back. "She took my friend, and I only escaped because I…hid in some thick clumps of grass."

Hadrian grimaced. "Coward. Show us where on the map and be gone."

Bellus hurried forward, quickly pointed to a spot, then scurried away while Rufus placed a skull marker there.

"That explains why we haven't found her," Rufus muttered. Both the Azurian Glacier and the Forest of Whispers were hundreds of miles west of the Cliffs.

"Call all our hunters back at once," Hadrian said as if they could simply sound a horn and do it in an instant. It would take weeks.

"And do what? The Cliffs of Aphatos are far too deep in human territory for us to march there without an army. The Xavalan Cavalry patrol there and would cut us down."

"I'm not afraid of cavalry." But the way Hadrian gazed into space after saying the words made Rufus doubt their truth.

"Then let me lead the expedition," Rufus said. "I'll ensure our men and Subdued amass within the ruins of Laltos without the humans noticing. Then we'll—"

"No." Hadrian shook his head and scoffed. "You're an administrator, not a battlefield commander. Those who can fight will march to the Cliffs."

Not this argument again. "A commander doesn't need to fight. Strategy and tactics are more—"

"Guardians!" Ignoring the argument, Hadrian waited until the two guardians stationed outside entered. "Summon my sons. We have a new plan."

"Yes, Warlord," the guardians said before racing out of the tent.

Rufus collapsed back onto his chair and studied the map again, at all the places he could be of so much use other than Dolthea. At least securing the town would ensure the Viridians had a viable road to the Cliffs, so the task he'd been set wasn't entirely pointless. But why did no one see his worth—because he rarely picked up a sword?

"I'll leave tomorrow night," Rufus said through gritted teeth.

"No. You'll leave within the hour."

That left him little time to assemble the men he wished to take. He'd better get to it. Standing up with clenched fists, he muttered, "As you wish, Father."

26

Darius – Northwest of Dolthea

The night after the ambush, Darius rested beside Lionheart, but neither of them slept. Fears of Lex, Nasrin or the youths being attacked circled Darius's mind, and he had to keep opening his heavy eyes to calm himself. He lay staring at the odd star shining through the dark tangle of the forest canopy above him. Insects buzzed to join the quiet snores of the young ones and the others, and occasionally, the roar of a big cat somewhere in the hills disturbed the noise, but as full as his ears were with the wild, the darkness felt empty. The only thing that allayed his fear was the thought of the village, the thought of Selene.

Perhaps he was a fool for entertaining the idea Selene lived, yet he'd gone over and over the first thing he'd say to her. Enough time had passed for him to sort of forgive her for handing him over to be tortured, but still… He wouldn't be able to look at her the same way. When such love and resentment clashed inside him, any resolution seemed impossible.

After the squawking birds announced the rising sun, Darius hurried to wake the others and get them ready to travel. The shaken young ones picked at the last of the hog meat Ninety-seven had brought back the night before, then they set off again, staying within the thickest parts of the woods and away from the road.

Fir and pine trunks rose from the ground in columns dozens of feet tall before so much as a branch broke the smoothness, and each tree sprouted at such regular intervals on such flat soil that it was almost as if this place had been manufactured. Each turn of Darius's head brought into view a landscape indistinguishable from the opposite direction, so it was a good thing they had Gorgias and Ninety-seven to guide them.

He walked well behind the lead pair, alongside Lex and the others, always with one eye above, where Lyra knew the pteron followed even if neither of them could see it. Since Tiro was still nowhere to be found, the creature hadn't taken a break from its tracking.

Tired of his ruminating mind and the grating silence hanging over everyone, he asked Lex, "Where do you plan on getting sulphur?"

She shrugged. "I don't need much. One of the towns will have some. Then we'll find the Magician."

The mention of the name seemed to wake Nasrin from a walking sleep. "Then we should head back into the mountains. Shirin never cared for forests and always preferred to be close to rakkans for her…experiments." The carer lowered her head with a look of shame.

Darius grunted. "Don't be embarrassed. We can't choose our family. Sometimes they're just wretches that kidnap and torture people."

Lex shot him a glare, fierce and biting, like he'd impugned her honour. A few seconds later, he realised what he'd said could have applied to Selene arresting him.

Nasrin scoffed, a harsh sound she rarely made. "I hate what she's become, but you don't know her past."

That was true, but there were many with tortured pasts that didn't act as heinously as the Waif Magician. Perhaps he was biased because she'd tried to kill him.

"Enlighten me, then," Darius said.

Nasrin adjusted her bag as if the strap had dug into her neck. "*You* know what it's like to be hunted by algus for your whole life, just because you're a hybrid and because kings and regents fear you. And you're every bit as bitter and vengeful as her. But I don't judge you or her either. I saw a different side to her, as I do with you. I'm the only family she has left, and she was never anything but kind to me."

How could Nasrin compare him to that witch? He murmured and took a moment to rein in the derisive response that first came to his mind.

"Even the wicked treat their family well," Darius said. "But you have a point about bitterness." The same spite festered inside him, and he'd indeed killed many over the years.

"Staying in contact with me put her at considerable risk," Nasrin said.

"You must have been useful for something, then," Lex said flatly, staring at the brown needles under her treading feet.

For the first time since Darius had met Nasrin, her eyebrows forked in anger. She bit her bottom lip but said nothing.

"Whatever Shirin's reasons are," Darius said, eager to pass over the comment, "it's clear we know too little about her. What does she do with those she kidnaps?"

"I only know the same stories as you." Nasrin's voice grew tense. "I haven't seen her for a while."

According to the tales, the Magician was working on a weapon already dubbed the Staff of Shirin. Whether its existence would be a good or bad thing was hard to judge. Nasrin carried on regaling them with stories of when she'd met with the old woman, but no details seemed helpful to their hunt. Lex still mined the carer for information, right through the times they stopped to eat and even when the sun's rays weakened in the sky.

Just as Darius was about to suggest calling it a day, a muscle in his stomach twinged. He turned to Lyra, and a knot grew inside his belly in a fashion he sensed originated from her.

His panther shifted her eyes skyward towards what he knew meant the pteron, and when he peered up and spotted the silhouette against the orange sky, it wasn't trailing directly above him as the creature often did, but circling to the side, adjacent to where they trekked.

For the first time, something perceived by Lyra told him the creature wanted him to follow it. And that wasn't his only new sense. Once again, his insights into Lyra's mind deepened for a moment. She smelled something in the forest air—fire.

At first, Darius ignored the two beasts and carried on walking. The pteron might still be responsible for the ambush, and he'd head directly to the village on even a slim chance of finding Selene there. But eventually, the knot in his stomach wound so tight that his steps pained him, and Lyra gave his leg a swipe with her claws to remind him it ailed her too.

He stopped, pressed his fingers deep into his lower abdomen and massaged.

"Something wrong?" Lex halted.

Nasrin soon rummaged in her bag for no doubt some foul-smelling herb against stomach pain.

"I'm fine," he lied, "it's just…" He surveyed the area the pteron circled, then lowered his gaze to Lyra. *Do you really trust that thing?* Far more readily than usual, her eagerness to follow became transparent. Maybe if he'd listened to his cat's urging the last time, the ambush wouldn't have happened.

Then again, if he left the young ones now and history repeated itself…

"Just what?" Lex asked.

"I…" The more he pondered, the more he recalled that his panther rarely led him astray. "I think we're heading the wrong way. Lyra smells a fire coming from this direction. We should check it out."

"Fine." Lex whistled to Gorgias and Ninety-seven without any further need for argument.

While she waited for them to track back, Darius whispered to her, "Stay behind me with the young ones and Nasrin, but not too close. And make sure the other two do too. At any sign of trouble, call for me, all right?"

She nodded.

As tempted as he was to leave Lyra there too, he needed her stealthy skills. Beckoning her to head out in front, he began treading the path highlighted by his winged stalker—which had once again hidden itself.

As soon as he'd taken a step, the knot in his stomach unwound and was gone. But every other muscle in his body now tightened, ready for enemies to appear at any moment. After a few minutes' walk, the fog of silence that had fallen on the forest deepened further. Birds ceased chirping. No squirrels scurried through the undergrowth.

If this goes wrong, I'm blaming you, Lyra.

But his panther's feral alertness showed she had no time for humour. Her body dropped lower, each step becoming calculated and feline. She'd caught another scent.

He signalled for the others to hold back before following a few yards behind his escort. Stealth was hardly his strength. She'd tell him when she needed him.

A smoky aroma soon filled his nostrils, thin but unmistakable, and its source came slowly into view through the numerous columns of tree trunks. Ahead was a clearing in the forest marked by knee-high grass and young saplings sprouting. At the centre, a newborn fire sent orange flames whirling around a short white tree whose every branch had been shaved clean off. A few figures skulked around the trunk, wearing dark metal helmets and cuirasses, and the odd patches of skin they showed were pale white and highlighted by green bands on their biceps. *Why are Viridian Legionnaires in the middle of nowhere? And why would a pteron lead me here?* His mind wasn't designed for puzzles like this.

He crept behind the closest tree large enough to conceal his figure and studied the sight before him more closely. Including those without an obvious weapon, he counted at least a dozen rakkans and only one human, who received a couple of backhands from the legionnaires in quick succession. The person slumped while Darius continued surveying. There were no tents or obvious signs of shelter. The band must have roamed free and light.

Lyra, prowl to the other flank. See if there are any others hidden.

As she did, he dared to creep closer, one tree at a time, until he reached a trunk wrapped in strangling vines and so rotten that half the inside had been eaten away. Now able to see every facial expression of the rakkans, he found them as he'd come to expect—as twisted and ugly as warthogs drinking vinegar. Next to a heap of chains and restraints, piles of weapons lay stacked for sharpening by a rakkan without a rank, and thick, black sweat dripped from his chin while he ran a whetstone up and down each one. Whatever they were preparing for, it didn't take an oracle to foresee it had something to do with the nearby village. Even if it didn't, did he need a reason to slay Viridians? Especially with so many under his guardianship close by.

Judging by the comfortable way the rakkans moved in armour, the band was made up of veterans. Darius had slain enough rakkan raiders this far west to know the bloodlust in their hungry eyes, but the open fire was something new. Curiously, the dancing flames touched but didn't so much as singe the tree. He recalled something the boy Omid had said once, that some of the trees of these woodlands were immune to ferven. But surely that didn't extend to all fire.

A shout from one of the men reminded him of his enemies. By now, he'd noted which warriors moved with the most laboured gaits, which had bandages and injuries, and the thickest boned he'd need to slay first. When he attacked these bands, his challenge wasn't usually in staying alive; it was in slaying every last one before they escaped. Twelve rakkans running in twelve directions would be a stretch, and even one escaped enemy could slaughter a human village.

Lyra reached the other side of the band and confirmed there were no Viridians lurking out of his sight.

Stay hidden. Rakkans were still off-limits to her. One lucky strike and they'd flatten her skull.

Darius drew both his gladii and slipped the cloak from his back, uncovering the rakkan skin on his arms. Meanwhile, half a dozen of the warriors huddled into a group with grunts and jeers at one another, arguing over something that didn't interest

Darius. All that interested him was who were the strongest and fittest among those gathered.

He peered up at the pine tree in front of him. Despite its sickly base, the top reached the very heights of the forest and still bore enough weight to crush a man—or six, he estimated. Silently, he crouched and dug the points of his swords into the trunk, flat side up. He stabbed them in, and the bark and rotten remains of the centre yielded enough for him to wriggle until his hilts hit the trunk. Then he heaved, lifted up with all the rakkan strength in his legs and back. Groans emanated from the wood as the flats of the blades budged up a fraction. It was a good thing kuraminium was the strongest thing the world had ever produced.

The trunk tilted, threatening those below with its colossal mass. But Lyra saw the Viridians hadn't noticed anything amiss, so he kept pulling until his knees locked straight.

Branches above snapped. He ripped out his swords and now shoved the trunk, boots scraping across the ground until they finally found buried stones to brace against.

The groan became a low, thunderous howl, and finally, the rakkans gaped up to see tons of wood smashing through the surrounding canopy and hurtling down towards them. As soon as Darius felt gravity take over the force from his arms, he ceased pushing, then raced around and towards his foes with fury coursing within him.

The six that had grouped dove to the sides with a haste that blinded them to his approach. Three rolled onto the ground and into his fatal path. They hadn't even caught sight of him before he swung his swords and cleaved their necks in a flurry of bane and surgical accuracy.

A shudder passed through the earth as the tree collided, sending shattered splinters that he conjured ferven to incinerate as they struck his face. With a leap over the trunk, he found two more marks with their legs trapped. They gaped at his flashing kuraminium before they became nothing but blood splatters on the ground, splatters that once would have sickened him but now only fuelled his fervour.

Three of the rakkans were already fleeing without having bothered to arm themselves. The rest grouped together out of fear rather than forming any strategic defensive formation. Their swords shook so violently they almost fell from their grasp, and Darius rushed towards them undeterred. One broke away into a run, but the others screamed as Darius's swords danced and cut thighs, arms, shins without so much as a successful parry. After ending them all, he raced after those retreating and caught them as easily as Lyra caught rats.

A slash to the back of the legs was all it took to bring each down, and a stab through the neck finished them. When it was over, he paused, wary of silence whenever it fell. Neither his eyes nor rakkan skin sensed any further movement. His deep breaths in and out gradually eased, and only then did he search for the human that had been with the band.

While Lyra went back to check on the others, he strode towards where he'd last seen the person, towards the flames now weakening near the still unblemished tree. It wasn't long before a face-down man became visible through the long grass, blood staining both the back of his shaggy head and the soil underneath. A nudge was all Darius needed to know the man was dead, when the fractured skull wobbled.

Lex hobbled up to him, assessing the carnage. "Are you going to tell me how you knew they were here?"

"I told you," he replied, "Lyra caught the smell of the fire. Why isn't it harming that tree?" As far as he could see, there was nothing unique about the young, hacked birch.

Lex didn't even glance at it before she answered. "It was started with rakkan fire. These trees are immune, and this isn't the first time I've seen Viridians attempt some sort of blood sacrifice to end whatever magic protects the forest."

This was Darius's first time, but then, he rarely paid attention to Viridian rituals because he hadn't the patience to wait before slaughtering them.

Gorgias, his friend, Nasrin and the children soon joined them and didn't seem fazed at the further blood and death.

"Are you satisfied, Darius?" Lex asked. "Can we head back and make our way to this village now?"

This time, Darius used his connection with Lyra to sense whether the pteron still lingered above him. A second later, she confirmed it.

"No," he said. "Let's carry on this way and make our way around. Can we do that, Gorgias?"

The algus scanned their surroundings for a moment, looking for who knew what because every direction was identical, but eventually, he nodded his head. "It's not much farther. We'll be there by tomorrow."

A nervous twitch returned to Darius's stomach when he realised what that could mean. Tomorrow, he might confirm whether Selene was alive or not.

27

Darius – Foltara

After another day and night of trekking, Darius and the group came within a few hundred yards of the entrance to Foltara. The clay huts that made up the settlement only numbered a few dozen, and none had the scars of war that other human villages this far west seemed to bear. Most were only a single storey, with white walls and thick thatch roofs, but one bell tower stood largest in the centre, like a village hall or the house of a wealthy local. At least it wouldn't take them long to search the tiny place.

As Darius studied the area further before entering, something moved atop the tower. Although too small to make out the shape, Lyra knew what it was at once—the pteron.

Gorgias and Ninety-seven waited beside him with far more relaxed postures than at the Viridian camp.

"You're sure there are no rakkans here?" Darius asked, keeping the flying creature's presence to himself for now.

"I'm sure," Gorgias said.

"How about hostile algus?"

"We can't be sure." Lex strode forward with a hand close to her sword. "The King's colours still fly."

Darius spotted the eagle emblem on a flag hanging limply in the weak breeze from one of the huts. Of the few people Darius could see in the streets, most wore the rags of slaves and the sunken cheeks of those underfed. But none bore wounds or signs of Viridian oppression.

Gorgias moved to follow Lex, but Darius caught his shoulder. "Wait. Why would Selene be here if there's no Viridian presence?"

Gorgias frowned as if the thought had never occurred to him, then turned to Ninety-seven expectantly.

"We often stopped by places like these," Ninety-seven said. "Sometimes for respite, sometimes to speak with Xavalan or Torian algus from whom we could glean information. Even so, they're more hospitable places than the Viridian settlements for an algus, even for the Subdued."

A hand touched Darius's arm, and he turned to see Nasrin with the young ones and a dispirited-looking Lionheart behind.

"Are you ready?" Nasrin asked with an apprehension that seemed to mirror his own.

"Don't know," he said, "but I can't let Selene wait any longer."

They set off together with the young ones close by. Lyra followed a few yards behind the group with her ever-alert eyes and ears tracking everything that moved. Lex led them on a winding route through the streets at first, which only seemed to draw the attention of the poor people around. Although they'd disguised themselves as rugged travellers, Lyra gave at least one of them away as an algus. But Darius was damned if he'd leave her apart from him. Besides, most of the civilians seemed to cower away from them once they'd seen the hulking panther. They probably assumed he was the King's algus. Whatever Toria or the Silk City were doing here, he wasn't sure he had the mental energy to learn of new horrors. Hopefully, it would be safe enough to let the young ones finally go free.

Even Gorgias scanned every street and corner, and they'd almost canvased the whole place within half an hour. Lex looked ready to give in, but Darius knew the pteron still watched from atop the bell tower. Did it want him to enter that building?

Lex came up to him and rested a hand on his shoulder. "You shouldn't have got your hopes up."

Perhaps, but they still hadn't checked inside every building yet.

"I'm not ready to give up," he said.

"Then let me know when you are." Lex retracted her hand. "I'm going to buy the children safe passage east."

Safe? Nowhere in this wretched empire was safe for those who hadn't the strength to fight. Darius walked towards the pitiful young ones, watching the tops of their small, bowed heads and the thin hair on top. Only one had died, but he'd rather that were zero, and if he was to part with them now, he could only pray their future was brighter than the last few days had been.

"You all stay out of trouble," he said, patting Lionheart lightly on the back. Why could he never think of something good to say at important times? "People say 'farewell' in moments like these, but knowing what awaits you out there… I'll just say 'fare better.'"

"Does it get easier?" Lionheart asked weakly.

The poor boy didn't know what hell life dealt to most. "Time heals," Darius said, "or at least helps you forget."

Nasrin pulled Lionheart into a hug that brought out tears that the boy had suppressed for so long. Just the sight reminded

Darius of all the times he'd broken down, when he'd been unable to take any more.

Gazing at Lyra, it took him a moment to refocus on the few good things in his life that made the fight and pain worth it.

Leaving his panther to guard the others, he began walking towards the bell tower, keeping his head low and obscuring most of his face with his shaggy hair. The featherless pteron spied from above as he reached the door and pushed it open with more force than he'd intended. The handle clattered into a wall and sent a bang echoing through the large open hall immediately before him. Inside, around two dozen heads all swivelled to scowl at him. Rows of wooden stools were laid out facing the front, where a priest in grey robes stood before an altar bearing a figurine of a winged woman alongside an icon that matched the one hanging from Darius's neck.

A service. Just my luck. The Diagathic Order often met in ad hoc places like this, though he'd never sat in on their rites. He scanned everyone's heads but found no auburn-haired women, and he could see only one other room at the back of the place, probably where the priest made his preparations.

Why had the pteron led him here? Perhaps to pray for Selene. Perhaps to accept she was dead.

"Either come in or don't, my friend," the priest said, "but in either case, please close the door." The smile on the man's face looked genuine, as if the interruption didn't faze him and had been expected. His long, grey hair didn't seem to have been cut a day in his life, and as Darius took in his tanned, unblemished face, he could have sworn he'd met the man before. But where?

Without the time to ponder, Darius eased the door closed and took a seat at the back next to a beggar. Although Lex and the others were busy outside and might need him, there was an odd serenity about the room that made him want to linger for a while, either because of the gently hummed tunes from a couple of choristers at the side or the floral scent of incense smoking on the altar to create a heavenly mist.

"Welcome," the priest said, "to faces both familiar and new." He grinned at Darius, who had to prevent himself from responding with a roll of his eyes. In his experience, those who acted friendly had to be treated with more suspicion than enemies.

The priest continued with some incantations, or prayers, or…something Darius wasn't sure about, and the minutes passed by with him getting ever more uncomfortable on his seat. But the longer he sat, the more he…sensed something. It was almost imperceptible at first, but when the songs began and the chanting filled his ears, he noticed. Music was so foreign, so alluring; it roused feelings that only confused him. Whatever these emotions were, they made his sensitive arms feel the air all the more. Could it be a draught? Or perhaps anxiety over admitting the woman he'd loved was dead? *Damned if I know.*

After what seemed an eternity, everyone in the hall stood, were blessed by the priest, then began to file out of the place.

Shaking off his earlier fascination with the rites, Darius inspected those leaving just to be sure, but Selene wasn't among them, and soon he was the only one left in there, alone with only a strange emptiness that filled the space instead of songs.

He'd preferred the smell of the poor men and women to incense. He was a little surprised how downtrodden the people here were because he'd always assumed the Diagathic Order was a religion of the affluent.

A quick circuit of the place confirmed a lack of anything interesting there, which left only the small room at the front, into which the priest had retired.

Despite being sure he'd find nothing, he strode up to the door. But as he lifted his hand to knock, it opened to reveal the expectant priest.

"Ah, there you are," the man said. "It's such a pleasure to see someone new, especially an algus that isn't here to steal our food or to take our young men to war. Forgive me if I don't kneel, but I do not treat mortals as gods like others do."

Darius paused after the man spoke. Should he ask how the priest knew he had the powers of an algus? *Better not.*

"I'm searching for someone," Darius said.

"Oh, aren't we all. Tell me her name."

"… How do you know it's a woman?" While gazing into the man's grey eyes, into the wisdom and youth they held, Darius suddenly recognised him. Over a year ago, he'd brought Lyra bleeding in his arms to Dolthea, and this man had saved her life.

The priest grinned. "I'm a prophet and know many things. But the one you seek clearly isn't here."

Darius peered past the silver-haired man yet saw nothing but a small, bare room behind him with no place for a full-grown woman to hide. It seemed the pteron was only causing mischief.

"Sorry to have interrupted you," Darius said. He could afford to waste time no longer.

"Don't you want to know where she is?"

Darius raised an eyebrow. "Don't even think of pretending you know. I didn't even give you her name or description."

"I had a feeling a man would come. You're fortunate I know someone who can help you."

Although he had little patience, Darius gave himself half a minute to humour the priest. "Keep talking."

Instead of answering, the man walked past him and planted his backside on one of the stools. He tapped the seat next to him.

"I'm fine standing," Darius said. "Just get on with it."

"Charming. I go by many names, but you may call me Aran, of the Diagathic Order. And you are…?"

Darius glared at the man. "Someone it's dangerous to lie to."

If Aran was moved by the threat, he kept it well hidden behind his pleasant smile. "Well, you seem to be in a hurry, so let's not waste time. During my daily prayers with the Goddess, she informed me of someone important who would cross my path."

This time Darius clenched his fist before holding himself back from thumping the man. "Goddess…? That's who you're speaking of?"

"Of course. Dianoia knows all because she is the mind behind everything."

"I see. And she just so happens to want to help me?"

"Of course she does." Aran gaped. "She loves you."

Darius snorted. "She has a funny way of showing it. Did she care while letting men torture me?"

"But surely you must believe, or else why wear her husband's figurine around your neck?"

Darius looked down at his chest, at the necklace and pendants that had come loose over this tunic. Usually, he would have ignored the priest's ravings as those of a madman, but something gave him pause. This mad priest had saved Lyra's life when she'd have died in the hands of most others.

"And how does the Goddess want you to help me?" Darius asked.

"A couple of weeks ago," Aran said, "a woman came here in ghastly shape. I was moved to assist her. I had an inkling someone would soon come looking and that it was important I help them."

Darius wasn't sure whether to hope that was Selene or not. "Where is she?"

"A local family took her in on the east side. She won't be hard to find."

"Thanks." Darius took a silver crest from his pocket and flicked it to the man. "I'll come back for that if you've lied to me."

"My, my." Aran's expression morphed into one of pity, like the way one looked at a starving dog. "You're so cynical and full of rage and anger."

"Well, you got that right." At times, those emotions were all that gave him the energy to carry on, to the point he'd been insufferable even to Lyra.

"Sorry for being a grumpy arse," he said to the priest.

The man chuckled. "It happens to the best of us, especially when we're in a hurry. So… I won't keep you. Goodbye, for now."

Darius gave the priest a final "thank you" and left, using the sun above to tell which side of the town was east. This time when he trudged, there was no pteron watching, and Aran's words replayed in his mind and only confused him. Why would the Goddess want to help a rogue like him? Or was it Selene who deserved help?

Was he being foolish? Perhaps he'd have spared himself pain if he'd given up all hope of Selene long ago.

After whirling around a corner, he bumped into Gorgias, who had an exasperated flush to his cheeks.

"There you are," Gorgias said. "Where have you been?"

"Don't ask," Darius grunted. "But I have a lead. I saw someone—"

"I've been looking for you." Gorgias gasped a little, as if the next words wouldn't come from his mouth.

Don't tell me something happened to the young ones. "What is it?"

Gorgias paused nervously. "We found her."

281

"You…" *Found her?* The last two words he only mouthed, as if he dared not utter them lest it make them false. Gorgias had to be joking…but he wasn't that cruel or foolish.

Darius tried to speak again, but his voice was gone. He had no words to say, no coherent thoughts or emotions as his mind spun.

"You're sure?" he finally rasped.

Gorgias grimaced. "Yes. Come with me."

Darius should have been elated, but the Subdued's troubled expression made him dread what he was about to see.

28

Lex – Foltara

Lex gaped at her sister for so long she must have appeared rude. But despite her best efforts to summon the words and express the emotions tearing at her insides, nothing came to her lips. Selene's once auburn hair hung tired and dull, not even shining with vibrancy in the candlelight. Her withered body poked angular and bony from her baggy tunic, and worst of all, the hazel eyes that had once beamed with an enthusiasm that could cheer even an icy soul such as Lex's were now hollow and vacant. It was the same haunted aura that had plagued Darius after his capture in Laltos, and it only brought Lex more grief, more guilt. She should have been joyful to find her sister alive again, but all the reunion did was add another failing to her long list.

Selene sat hunched in a small bedroom belonging to the villager who had kindly taken her in. The place hadn't even floorboards to keep the chill of the ground at bay, and the cold was only worsened by a line of dripping clothes hung right across the room, leaving a trail of puddles at the foot of the mattress.

"Lex?" Selene whispered, with a timid shame that only Lex deserved to bear.

How could she have given up on her sister? If only she'd searched, perhaps Selene wouldn't be so harrowed now. The guilt reminded her of her son, the one she'd lost all hope of finding. Except he was likely still alive, walking around as a man she wouldn't know or recognise. After many years of praying he should be dead, she regretted every word she'd uttered to the Goddess now that Archimedes was gone.

With a deep breath that did nothing to calm the trembling in her hands, Lex finally spoke, "Selene… I'm sorry."

Tears already began wetting Selene's eyes. She'd never been much of a weeper, but who could blame her now?

"I should have searched for you," Lex continued, awkwardly keeping her distance to give her sister space. "But I thought you were…"

"So did I." Selene's head drooped. A tear fell and splashed into one of the puddles at her feet. "Many times, I prayed I soon would be."

Unable to bear separation any longer, Lex stepped forward and took her sister's hands, crouched until her knees were soaked, and met Selene's teary gaze.

"How did you survive Laltos?" Lex asked. "Where have you been?"

"The Viridians. They captured me and other algus, then took us with them in the sortie back to Viridia. I've been all over, through the camps, the trials, the…" A shudder passed through her.

"It's fine," Lex said. "Don't speak if it's too upsetting. I'm just glad you escaped." It took all her restraint not to ask Selene how she'd managed it. Perhaps the broken woman had traded Viridians her body for freedom. The thought brought up acid to burn Lex's throat.

Another long, drawn-out silence followed, where all Lex heard were the drips of water and Selene's heavy breaths. Her sister's hand squeezed hers hard, probably thankful for the newfound safety now so foreign to her.

The stink of vinegar from whatever primitive methods the villagers had used to treat Selene's wounds stung Lex's nose. For the first time in months, Lex closed her eyes and said a prayer to Agathos, the God of Justice, thanking him for sparing Selene and calling for his might to pass into her and Darius to avenge this and all the other heinous crimes in the Empire. *Why keep me hindered by pain? Unleash me. I'll enforce your justice.*

But like all the times before, the pain in her hip continued stabbing, her plea ignored by the God.

Turning her attention back to Selene, a curiosity struck her. Despite Selene virtually sacrificing her life for Darius the last time she'd seen him, she hadn't asked about him. Or anyone else.

"Do you know what happened at Laltos after we left you?" Lex asked softly.

Selene nodded. "Father's dead."

Lex waited for more, waited for Selene to ask about her *daughter*. Granted, the now broken woman had only met Cynthia mere hours before her capture, but Lex would never forget such a thing had their situations been reversed. Still, Selene just stared at the puddles soaking into the ground, blinking with every drip splashing.

Had she told any of her torturers about Cynthia? A chill of terror ran down Lex's spine. Pain seized her hip and forced her to stand with a gasp. No one was supposed to know. After seeing and hearing of the hell Darius and the Magician had lived through, there was no way she'd risk exposing her daughter, even if the girl had no algor to make her as lethal as the other infamous hybrids.

As inappropriate as it was to interrogate Selene right now, Lex couldn't wait. "What did you tell the Viridians?" she asked.

Selene frowned with a bite of her lip. "Nothing important. They didn't want much. Laltos was already in ruins." The nervous shift of her eyes said otherwise, though.

"I don't care if you gave them military secrets," Lex said. "I need to know whether you told anyone about Cynthia."

Selene froze, displaying not a trace of the emotion she usually would have when thinking of family. "Of course I didn't." Her face contorted into a scowl. "Who do you think I am, to betray my own niece?"

The anger in her voice gave Lex a little peace of mind. "I'm sorry. I had to ask." Awkward silence once again stretched out, which still wasn't filled by her sister asking about Darius. Something was amiss. Surely she couldn't have been…Subdued?

Before a further question formed in her mind, a knock at the bedroom door disturbed them.

"It's us," Gorgias called.

Selene didn't react to the voice.

"Darius will be with him," Lex said.

A spark of fear lit Selene's eyes for the briefest moment before a mirthless smile spread across her mouth.

"Don't fret." Lex leaned down and squeezed her sister's hand a final time. "He's forgiven you." And the way he'd been preoccupied with Selene over the past year told Lex that his feelings were deeper still, even if he didn't admit it.

29

Darius – Foltara

Darius stared at the door for so long he counted every knot in the wood. Still, he didn't open it and wouldn't until he was ready. Would he ever be?

"She's in there," Gorgias said again.

"I heard," Darius muttered. He glanced around the kitchen as if it would help him summon some courage. The tiny home they stood in had been tidied in a hurry, with piles of dirty plates and pots stacked in the corner. The owners had been kind to invite Selene and them in and now fussed over a steaming pot in the clay oven while Lyra watched. Although the spicy aroma usually made him salivate, now he only felt like throwing up. What was it he feared he'd find in the bedroom? How she'd react to seeing him? Or was it how he'd react to seeing her?

"All right," he said.

"I'll let you know when the food is ready," Gorgias said.

"Lyra, come." His escort padded to his side as he took the handle and eased the door open. The room beyond was indeed a bed chamber, but the first person he spotted was Lex pacing towards the door without acknowledging him.

His first instinct was to stop her and ask her what was wrong, but then he spotted the woman lying on the mattress at the far side of the room—or rather, the back of her head, because she lay on her front facing away. But he'd never mistake that hair.

Lex slipped past him without a word as his panther stayed tight to his heel. After they'd both stepped gingerly inside, he eased the door closed again, thankful for the separation of the two sisters who played on his mind. As the latch snapped shut, the woman on the bed shifted her head around and faced him, removing any doubt he'd had.

He opened his mouth to say something, but all that came out was a gasp soon lost in the *drip*, *drip*, *drip* from the clothes hanging across the room. The intense look she gave him radiated pain, even though it was one of surprise. But deep down, her traces of fear were unmistakable, the same fear he'd shown when he'd studied his reflection after Laltos.

Yet, even afraid and weary, she was every bit as beautiful as he remembered her, and old feelings he thought were dead now roused.

"Darius?" she asked.

By the Creator. If she had to ask who he was, what hell had she been through? Or perhaps his beggar disguise was that good. He quickly checked the room, noting she had no weapons to hand—most unlike her old self—and there being no other windows or doors besides the one he'd used to enter.

"It's me," he said, though the words only came out as a whisper. Finally summoning some courage, he paced over to her,

288

batting aside a pair of wet breeches, and touched her hand, verifying she was real and not a spirit.

"I never thought I'd see you again." Her eyes welled up.

"I feared so too." Despite asking about her, he clearly hadn't sought hard enough to find her.

She sprang up from the bed and dove into his arms before he could untangle his emotions. Her hair brushed his cheek, flat and greasy, and nothing like the soft and fragrant curls he remembered.

He wrapped his arms around her and squeezed, just like he'd dreamt of doing for so long, but she gasped, stifled a scream, and tried to pull away suddenly.

Damn him. Only two seconds in, and he'd already hurt her. "I'm sorry… I forget my strength."

A knock sounded on the door, followed by Lex's voice. "Is everything all right in there?"

"I'm fine." Selene shook her head with a grimace, then lowered her voice. "It's not your fault."

"Then why…?" Darius asked.

She wrapped an arm around herself and rubbed her back, wincing at even her own light touch.

Now he realised why she'd unnaturally lain on her front like he'd had to do after torture in Laltos. The fact she had put him in that cell was a grudge he'd never shaken, and one day he might have the fortitude to take it up with her, to unleash the darkest gripes that made his anger linger. But that day wasn't today, not after what she'd been through.

A growl resonated in his throat while his forehead burned. "Who did that to your back? The Viridians? Hadrian?"

Selene sighed and staggered back down onto the mattress. "His warriors. But it takes more than beating to break me."

Although she was one of the most headstrong women he'd ever met, she'd been a captive for over a year; Darius had considered himself broken in a far shorter time. But perhaps she was more stubborn than he. Her sister sure was.

At the thought of Lex, Darius's anger quickly died, replaced by dread and guilt. Over the last few weeks, he'd realised where his true feelings lay. Lex had never deserted him, had saved his life when it had endangered hers and even her daughter's. Such devotion was unmerited and underserved, but he'd do his damnedest to be worthy of it. He couldn't allow anything he'd once felt for Selene to jeopardise that.

With a shake of his head, he sat next to Selene and tried to ignore the old lustful feelings that being next to her stirred, beckoning Lyra over for some added resolve.

"How are you?" he asked as Lyra nuzzled her head into his hands.

"Better, now I've seen you."

He was shocked to see a slight smile on her face.

"How long has it been since you escaped the Viridians?" he asked.

"A few weeks. I've mostly been regaining my strength to travel east. The Order have been kind enough to arrange care for me."

Darius murmured to himself. If only he hadn't gone after Hadrian, perhaps he'd have found her sooner. Once again, the *drip*, *drip*, *drip* filled his ears and almost had him tearing the wet clothes down.

"Is something wrong?" Selene shifted her body closer to him.

"A lot of things. Where did they take you? What did they do to you?"

Her expression filled with anguish. "I…please, don't make me talk of it. It's too…too—"

"Stop. You don't have to. I shouldn't have asked." He wrapped an arm gently around her shoulders, not knowing what else to say, so he remained quiet and tried to enjoy being close with her again, tried to focus on her being free rather than the anger rising within, focus on the warmth of her thigh sliding against him.

He stroked her shoulder while Lyra sat and looked at Selene without blinking. The panther had a strange air about her, a reserved posture she only usually had with someone she didn't trust.

Something wrong with you?

Lyra didn't break her stare. If anything, her golden eyes narrowed slightly.

"What have you been doing?" Selene asked. "Since Laltos?"

"Searching. Killing." *Despairing.* "I've been like that for what feels like a lifetime. I almost don't know how to feel now. It's like I…forgot how to be relieved, happy."

She reached out and took his hand. Only then did he catch sight of the scars on her wrists, pink and fresh. Somehow, things had been a little easier before he'd found her, when he could at least hope that she hadn't been through a worse, more prolonged torment than what he'd suffered.

"How did you stay sane?" he asked. "What did they…?" He ended the question when he recalled she'd already refused to answer.

She withdrew her hand and began shakily unfastening the lacing on her tunic. "I can't speak of it, but I can show you."

"No, I don't want to—" Before he could plead not to see it, she was slipping her tunic over her head.

As soon as she began, he worried that seeing her exposed flesh would provoke a craving too great for him to resist, but those fears dissolved as her first wounds became visible.

Darius winced at every inch of revealed skin until he was gaping at her whole back, still purple, red and raw, with splits straining to open against stitches. That delightful spine down which he'd once ran his tongue would never be the same again.

He turned away, feeling his fists tremble and tighten so much he'd have crushed iron. *Drip*, *drip*, *drip* sounded again, and he'd had enough. He reached out, grabbed a fistful of a cloak and squeezed it so hard his thumb almost tore through the fur as water splattered down onto his boots. Lyra growled and bared her teeth as he desperately tried to harness his rage, dampen it enough that it didn't spill over into his escort's emotions any further.

"Darius?" Selene whispered.

Finally, her soft voice was enough to make him fight back and control himself.

"Yes?" he asked. When he turned, she was facing him again. Perhaps her bare chest being less mutilated than her back should have relieved him, but it didn't.

"Do I disgust you?" she whispered.

"No! No, no, it's just…no." He closed his eyes. "It's just painful to see you so hurt."

She stroked the back of his hand, the touch of her gentle fingers taking him back to all those times he'd lain in bed with her.

"You must need a lot of the weeping plant's tears to cope with that," he said. "Be careful. I've seen some people overdo—"

"I'm not taking anything. I was forbidden to."

"You…" Darius opened his eyes and gaped at her. "Nothing?"

"Just vinegar on the wounds for infection, but I'm letting them breathe and dry at the moment."

Darius knew the sting of vinegar too well. "You know, you can take tears. You don't have to follow the Viridians' orders anymore."

"Oh…yes… Sorry." She flinched away as if ashamed.

"Here." Darius took a vial from his pocket and handed it to her. "A drop will be enough for now."

Selene looked a little hesitant to take it from him, as if she were still afraid her torturers would burst in at any moment and whip her for disobedience.

"Take some. You're safe." Darius placed the vial gently in her palm. "The Viridians won't hurt you while you've got the Dreaded One as your protector."

She opened the vial gingerly. "You'll…protect me?"

Again, if she had to ask, he questioned whether they had broken her in part or completely.

"Until I die," he said.

Her lips curled a little into a grin before she swallowed a drop of the tears. All the while, she eyed him, almost as if suspicious, but then she slowly slid closer again.

"Thank you," she whispered in his ear, and let her warm lips touch him, sending gooseflesh down his neck.

"It's nothing."

"Not to me… Can I ask something of you?"

"Of course. Anything."

She leaned in and dropped her voice. "Can you hold me? I just want to feel safe."

Although hesitant, he had just said "anything."

"All right," he said.

Before he moved, she'd swung a leg over him, straddled his lap, and pulled him head-first into a hot embrace. He didn't dare touch her again in case he opened more of her wounds, so he kept his hands awkwardly at his sides while she squashed her bare chest into him.

"You're safe," he whispered.

"Do you know how much I've missed you? I knew you wouldn't give up on me."

He didn't have the heart to tell her he pretty much had.

Without warning, she kissed his forehead and let out a heated breath that swept down his neck and chest, triggering carnal thoughts he didn't want to have again. But this embrace was different from the ones they'd shared in Dolthea. Back then, her body had been loose and relaxed, so much so that he'd always held the back of her head whenever he picked her up from the clinch and brought her on the bed for more. But now, a tension throughout her core left her rigid and firm. Was he more off-putting these days? He supposed that with the beard, he did look like a yak's rear end—and probably smelled like one too.

Carefully, he grabbed Selene's hips and tried to lift her off him, but she clamped her thighs.

"Selene," he said with a sigh, "we can't—"

"I just want to feel safe. Please, I don't even remember what it's like for a man to hold me gently." Tears were now spilling down her cheeks and into his beard, yet he couldn't look away this time.

Whatever the stories behind this trauma, he didn't want to hear them lest they enraged him beyond control. Yet he waited and would willingly take the brunt of anything she needed to unburden herself of.

"You're safe." He squeezed her hips with his strong hands. "No one will do this to you ever again."

"You can't promise that. No one can."

"I…" Darius trailed off. She was right.

"Will you stay with me? Sleep with me?"

He took it she meant that literally. "I'll sleep at the foot of your bed, if that's what you want."

"You don't mind?" Her tears had finally stopped falling, but her wet eyes pleaded with him.

"Anything you wish," he said.

"… Anything?"

That hadn't been the best choice of words considering she was half-naked, straddling him.

"Anything to protect you," he clarified.

She ran her thumb down his cheek, just like he used to do with her, right over her light freckles.

As the heat of her thighs burned his lap, she leaned in and kissed his forehead again. "Thank you."

The tingling in his skin was unfamiliar but welcome as he savoured the embrace.

Then the latch on the door clicked, and Darius turned his head to see Lex stride into the room with a bowl of steaming broth in her hands.

"Selene, I brought some—" Lex froze as the three locked eyes.

Nasrin and Gorgias came up behind Lex but stopped dead.

"You don't waste time…" Gorgias snorted.

Darius suddenly felt Selene's weight on him all the more while Lex's shocked expression twisted into a vicious glower aimed solely at him.

Lyra, don't let her kill me. Lex wouldn't believe they hadn't been doing anything even if he tried to tell her.

30

Paulus – Cliffs of Aphatos

"Empty yourself!" The Magician's wicked cackle raged along with the inferno in Paulus's palm.

He clutched the metal staff in his hand more tightly and flared ferven all the harder, trying to expel every ounce of magic in his muscles and bones into the thing as it glowed white beneath the fires.

At the other side of the cavern, the Waif Magician eyed him greedily, without the Staff of Arria for the first time in two days. Had he possessed enough strength, he'd have rushed over and crushed her skull. But she'd cut off his left hand after he tried the first time. Even without the Staff, a single ageing rakkan was no match for an algus, never mind a half-goman.

"Do as I instructed!" the Magician shrieked. "Imagine this staff will save your sister, will save the son stolen from you, if only you imbue it with your power!"

But with a wail of exhaustion, Paulus's energy ran dry, and he collapsed to the ground, plunging the once blindingly bright crevice into the darkness of night.

A few seconds later, a blue glow seeped into the place as the Magician flared algor. "You've failed me for the last time, you pathetic man."

What else did she expect? Now even without the Staff stealing his strength, he hadn't the energy to push his chest from the rough ground, never mind make the new staff she'd imagined.

"That was all I had." Paulus's weak rasp echoed loud in the quiet place. All he wanted was to rest and never wake to this witch's face again. As he closed his eyes, the darkness pulled him instantly, but before he fell under, a cold blade stung his throat.

"You don't deserve a peaceful death," the Magician said. "You're as great a failure as all the other rakkans, and now my patience has run out. If only you knew what you've done, Azurian, what I now must do. If you did, you'd have made greater efforts to help me."

But he'd tried everything to prevent the torture. He'd longed to expel his ferven and life force into the new staff, to feel the sweet release of death. And now that the moment had arrived, he was calmer and more at peace with his fate than he'd thought possible. He'd done what he'd set out to do—save his sister. This old hag clearly had no one who cared for her like that, and the only one to blame was herself, despite her lamentations to the contrary.

"You must be…" Paulus began, "a lonely, pathetic woman…to converse with a prisoner so—"

The sword cut his neck with a sudden, painful slice. Warmth flowed under his body as a new darkness began to fall, one that would be eternal. Finally, he was free.

31

Lex – Foltara

The pot of vegetable stew burned Lex's hands more and more by the second. But all she could do was behold the pair of them locked in each other's arms and fight back the urge to hurl the steaming broth into Darius's flushed face. Lucky for him, she wouldn't risk her half-naked sister getting scalded or risk Nasrin seeing her outburst.

"I'm sorry," Nasrin said. "We should have knocked, but we heard voices and…"

Darius lifted Selene off his lap with his rakkan strength and lightly placed her back on the mattress. Meanwhile, Lex shook her head as if it would rid her mind of the scene she'd just witnessed. Her sister was alive and in need of care. That's all that mattered.

"Perhaps I should leave you all to it," Darius said.

"No," Lex said flatly. "Stay. Make yourself comfortable."

As if sensing her sarcasm, Darius lowered his head and quietly slipped past her with Lyra at his heel.

"Don't go far," Selene called after the man as he left. Then she thankfully grabbed her tunic and covered herself again.

Lex should have given Darius a slap to the back of the head on the way out. Of course, she'd wondered whether the pair would get together again as soon as she'd found her sister, but she hadn't reckoned on it taking less than half an hour.

Men... They were only interested in one thing—well, two, if you counted sleep. Nothing good ever came of romance.

Lex turned to Gorgias. "Keep an eye on him. Make sure he doesn't go around unclothing more women."

Gorgias grinned. "What if they unclothe themselv—"

"Just go." Lex shoved the smarmy man outside with her elbow and kicked the door shut. Then she turned to her sister. "Are you hungry?" She tried to make her voice far calmer than her riled insides.

"Yes, thank you." Selene eyed the meagre, soggy food with more eagerness than an algus ordinarily would. The poor woman must have been starved for a long time.

Lex handed her the bowl and spoon, then sat down next to her while Nasrin floated between the wet clothes hanging in the room.

"How are your wounds?" the carer asked.

"A little better," Selene said. "Darius gave me something."

I'll bet he did. Lex swallowed. "Are you fit to travel?"

"I've done so with worse injuries," Selene mumbled through a mouthful of food.

The unladylike conduct took Lex aback. Even when her father had adopted Selene as a slave, the girl had observed good manners.

But months with the Viridians changed people. The tortured face of Lex's late husband came to mind, the burns that had brutalised not only his eyes and mouth but his soul, and as if on cue, her hip sent a jolt of pain through her bone. She gasped.

Nasrin frowned at her. "Mistress, are you—"

"I'm fine," Lex lied, flattening her grimace. "Selene, we'll get you somewhere safe, but we can't linger here. We have something important to do."

Selene froze. "But…you can't leave me. I want to go with you and Darius."

"You're in no fit state, and it'll be dangero—"

"No!" Anger flashed across Selene's face. "I'll travel with you."

Lex slid back an inch, having expected her sister to resist them leaving but not to insist on coming with them. Yet, as much as she hated herself for it, Lex had no urge to argue against Selene joining them. If her sister came, she wouldn't have to convince Darius to hunt Hadrian and the Magician with her rather than escort Selene.

"As you wish," Lex said. "But you can turn back at any time. Are you sure you can travel soon? We can give you a few days."

"It won't be easy," Selene replied, "but I can."

Good. Unfortunately for them both, they had neither the luxury nor the time to deal with pain. "Then we'll leave soon and search for the Waif Magician."

Selene smiled.

But Nasrin shook her head. "I think you both need—"

"We're fine," Selene snapped.

Daughters of Theodoros weren't easily cowed, though Lex bet Selene was putting on a braver face than she was.

"Fine," Nasrin said. "We should start our search in Dolthea. Shirin often bought supplies from there when desperate."

300

"Dolthea is under Viridian control," Lex said through gritted teeth, recalling the stories of its fall shortly after Laltos's destruction.

"Yes…" Nasrin scrunched her nose for a moment before she shrugged. "But I don't think that would deter her. We can let Darius search there. He can act as a slave, and he can handle himself should his cover fail."

Usually, Lex would rather have slid down a hill of broken glass than send Darius undercover after the last time, but this hunt was too important.

"I'll go with him," Lex said. Dolthea was the best place to buy sulphur as well.

Selene opened her mouth to speak.

"Alone," Lex added. "You can wait outside the town. I think you've been around rakkans enough, don't you?"

Selene nodded but had a sullen expression that told Lex she was thinking far more than she was saying.

"Would you give us a minute?" Lex asked Nasrin.

The carer nodded and left the room while Selene looked sheepishly at her sister as if bracing for the strike of a rod. It was a look common to ones held captive for so long, but it held a familiarity that Lex couldn't quite put her finger on.

"How are you, really?" Lex asked.

After a few moments, Selene closed her eyes and whispered, "Hurting."

Who knew such a simple word could make someone feel so helpless.

Lex took her sister's hand firmly. "You aren't alone. It'll take time, but things will get better for you." She had to believe that for herself too; otherwise, why suffer through life?

"I hope so, but not before I see justice done." Selene's voice became hard, bitter. It was a foreign tone from her mouth, but not unexpected.

"And what of Darius?" Lex asked. "Are you comfortable around him?"

Selene's expression didn't change. "Yes. All I've thought about for a year is seeing him again."

Whatever that meant for the pair, Lex wasn't sure—but she'd been the one who pushed Darius away in the first place, to spare herself pain. She shouldn't come between them.

The sisters carried on catching up until they were interrupted by a light knock at the door.

"That's probably the priest." Selene sighed. "He checks on me from time to time."

"I'll get rid of him." Lex stood and opened the door.

But the face that greeted her on the other side left her momentarily lost for words. It wasn't just any priest but the Chief Priest himself. "… Aran?"

The Chief Priest's flowing silver hair shone beautifully and blended with the colour of the inexpensive but neat tunic he wore. As always, he donned a pair of gloves that seemed sewn to the fabric of his sleeves to protect that unique pair of hands with a power no others shared. His grey eyes sparkled with their usual hopeful delight, and his unblemished skin glowed as youthfully as ever. No one knew how the old man cheated the signs of ageing, but that was hardly his most impressive gift.

It had been a long time since she'd seen Aran without a disguise—if in fact this was his real appearance—and she suddenly wished she still wore her Agathos pendant around her neck. But what was the leader of the Diagathic Order doing in a tiny village? Hiding again?

302

"Alexandra." Aran gave her a broad, genuine smile. "What brings you here?"

"Nothing pleasant, unfortunately."

"My, my. I'm rarely surprised, but I never thought I'd see you in these lands again. And they call me a prophet…" He chuckled.

That was hard to believe. Every time they'd met in the past, it had been far from a coincidence.

"It's good to see you," she lied. The truth was she'd given the Order far too little of her time recently to feel anything other than guilt at the sight of the holy man.

"What brings you here?" Aran asked again, with a glance over to Selene.

"My sister, of course."

"Your…" Aran frowned. "Forgive me. I never realised. Had I known, I'd have tried to inform you at once."

Lex turned to her sister. "You didn't tell him?"

Selene blushed and shrank away. "I didn't want the Viridians to find me."

"Oh, it doesn't matter. We're all here now, and it seems your sister is being well looked after." Aran's gaze swept across the hanging clothes, then over the women as if searching or studying. "If only…I… Oh, dear." He grimaced as if he'd suddenly been stricken with pain, eyes now focused on Lex's neck. "You look as tense as a Dolthean farmer. Don't tell me the pain has returned."

If only it had ever left. But it was definitely worse. "I'm fine," Lex said. "Just had a long journey."

The Chief Priest raised an eyebrow in a way she knew meant he saw through her lies.

"Very well," Aran said. "In that case, could I be rude and ask you to do me a favour"

"What? Now?"

"Yes. It's most urgent."

Whatever. After all, she had promised Selene she'd get rid of the man. "Fine," Lex said. "But let's talk outside. My sister needs rest."

The Chief Priest only spoke again once they'd left and the bedroom door was closed, leaving them alone in the small kitchen. This time when he spoke, his tone became as solemn as when he said prayers. "Are you sure you're well? I'm worried about you."

"Why? Do I look like I need worrying over?"

"Yes."

Lex scoffed. "I'm insulted that you don't think I can care for myself. Now, what's this favour?"

"I'll come to that. But first, the Goddess wishes me to help you as well as insult you."

Usually, when he said such things, Lex assumed he wasn't being serious, but his voice had no trace of joviality.

Unsure how to respond, she simply said, "Really?" Would the Goddess care about her after she'd lapsed for so long?

"I don't need to be a prophet to know your pain." Aran held out his hands. "Would you like me to help you?"

At this point, she'd exhausted her patience in seeking healing, even resorting to superstitious rituals—predictably unsuccessfully. "I'm fine."

"Doesn't it tire you to put on such a tough façade?"

"I…" The words resonated, and the exhaustion that was always a minute's rest from catching up to her crept in again. "I…" Perhaps it was time to be honest with someone. "It does."

The Chief Priest's expression softened as if he knew her pain and worse. "What ails you?"

"My hip. It won't give me a moment's respite, and I can't fight with such a hindrance."

"Ah. Is it the same as before?"

If only. "Worse."

Under Aran's sympathetic but silent gaze, a calmness began to come over her, so subtle she could have been forgiven for not noticing it. The feeling took her back to the first time she'd experienced it in a service of the Order, where she'd gone in her last search for hope. On that day, she'd found it in the axe of the God of Justice, a realisation that had passed her by despite years of attending prayers prior to that.

"Is it really your hip that's the issue?" Aran asked.

"Yes. It stops me fighting to avenge my fallen city." She couldn't even bring herself to say the name after her failures.

"It also stops you thinking, stops you feeling the true weight of the loss."

"And so would soaking myself in Viridian blood."

Aran winced. "You forget who you're talking to. I don't approve of such bloodthirsty ambitions."

Lex stepped back from the man, clenching her jaw. "Tell me, does Agathos brandish an axe or a flag of surrender?"

"*You* are not the arbiter of justice." Aran's demeanour lost its softness, but the shake of his head was one of pity and disappointment. "I pray you realise that before…" His voice trailed off while he regarded her as someone would a dying woman.

Whatever went through the minds of devout men was a mystery to her. With regular men it was easy; they undressed her and imagined themselves indulging their carnal desires. But she highly doubted those thoughts ran through Aran's mind.

"I thought you said you could help me," Lex said.

"I just did. But I take it you're referring to your pain. For that, I know a remedy, but I shall need the wilds to provide the plants. Pray that the Goddess may decide to make you well by helping me find what I need."

"I have prayed," Lex said, although Aran's warning of a greater pain lurking beneath the distraction bore a ring of truth. But she'd battle through hurt. Anything that made her fit to fight. Of course, that was if the man spoke the truth. She was still sceptical after having tried begging the Goddess to spare her the burden countless times.

"May Dianoia's will be done," Aran said confidently, pushing together his gloved hands in a sign of prayer. "And now I must request my favour because I don't believe it's by chance I've happened across you today."

Why not ask the Goddess your favour? She didn't dare voice the mocking question to a man who had always treated her fairly. "Ask it."

"I am needed in Dolthea. The people there have suffered greatly, and a new commander has arrived who has loosened control enough for me to conduct services in secret. The people need hope."

"Then I don't see how I can help."

"I merely need an escort."

Lex raised an eyebrow. "Is that a deliberate pun?" Aran was the only man in the Empire capable of bonding people to animals.

The Chief Priest grinned. "It was. Tell me, how is Tiro?"

Lex started. "You remember his name?"

"Of course. It's hard to forget someone as angry as you were."

Did that mean Aran would recognise Lyra and realise that the scruffy-looking man with them was Darius, the Slayer of

Gods? But she doubted it; their bonding had taken place well over a decade ago.

Then again, did that matter? Darius thought himself disguised, but when a man went around slaying groups of algus or cavalry, it didn't take a genius to put a name to him.

"I'm not sure," Lex said. "We aren't…" The lie she'd been about to tell disappeared from her lips under the man's once again sympathetic eyes. But there was another reason she considered letting him travel with them. Aran was a man who rarely did anything without a motive. The question was, what were his motives now?

She'd rather have the Chief Priest close by while she discerned whether the suspicion in her gut was unfounded or not. It wasn't as if they had to fear him. He was no algus and didn't even know how to handle a sword.

Plus, they were heading to Dolthea anyway, and how would she feel if she later discovered the Chief Priest was murdered or kidnapped on the road? The Viridians would love that, which was reason enough for her to prevent it.

Lex gave Aran a nod. "We'd be happy to escort you."

32

Sulla – Ruins of Gerunda

Sulla and Warlord Varro waited patiently as algus and commanders filed into a crumbling room that had once been the heart of the rakkan city of Gerunda. Razed by Archimedes a decade ago, it had holes dotting its walls, the scars of ballistae bolts, hammers and more. And the roof had fared no better. Dust leaked from cracks, threatening a collapse at any moment, as if the building savoured the agitation it caused in the algus inside it.

Sulla enjoyed their nervous peering up. Rakkans didn't fear such puny stone, mainly because they had the strength of bulls in the mating season, but also because the Margalvian architects had checked out the room beforehand and deemed it safe. Sulla had "forgotten" to mention that to all the humans, though. After decades of them fighting and killing his kind, they were due a little unease.

But the roof wasn't the reason Varro was wearing his bull-horned helmet, a sight that struck terror both on and off the battlefield.

"Shall we begin?" Commander Julius slurred his words through his swollen jaw.

Sulla wasn't sure whether to be happy or disappointed the commander had survived the battle waged to secure these ruins. But the most important battle was to come, and Julius had a good head—not that Sulla would ever admit that to his face.

"We'll wait longer," Varro said.

Without asking, Sulla knew what the Warlord waited for—an answer to one question: Had their army's movement been seen? There was only one woman who knew for sure, and her absence struck Sulla as troublesome.

At least Lex and Darius were making some progress if her last message was anything to go by, but Hadrian still wasn't dead yet, and the Magician evaded them. If only Sulla had gone with them, the world would probably be saved by now. Probably. After the upcoming battle, he'd finally tell the Warlord his plans.

Interrupting his ponderings, Regent Hera entered the room with a confident walk that drew most eyes to her. "Sorry I'm late."

"What news do you bring?" Varro asked before she'd even reached the rest of the encircling warriors.

"Good and bad. The movements of your small companies through the mountains seem to have gone unnoticed by the Viridians. Our escorts see no reactionary mustering of warriors."

It had taken them much longer than a simple march, but the element of surprise was their goal.

"Good." Varro turned to Julius and the other commanders. "Are we at full strength?"

Julius grinned. "Almost. We're awaiting the last few centuries."

"The Militia's swords are accounted for and whetted," Sulla added.

Varro turned back to Hera. "And are the algus ready?"

"We are," she replied. "But there's still the bad news."

Sulla could only hope it didn't interfere with Varro's carefully laid-out battle plan, one so meticulous it was guaranteed to go wrong. But that was when battles were the most fun.

"Go on," the Warlord said.

"Our escorts haven't been able to get into the tunnels or the mine."

Varro cursed and spun to face away from all those present.

"So we betrayed the location to you humans for nothing?" Sulla said with a sarcastic scoff.

Hera's regent posture slackened, and something like offence filled her expression. The weeks of arguing between the commanders came back to mind over whether they could retake the mine without algus. Thankfully, Varro had decided: "Why not include them?" It wasn't like Margalvia had the Treaty to obey any longer.

"It's not good enough." Varro's voice echoed from the wall in front of him, shaking more dust from the roof. Then he spun to face them. "Sulla, your men will break a way into the tunnels for the escorts. We need to scout."

"Aye, Warlord," Sulla said. "But as soon as the rest of the Legion is here, we should attack regardless."

Varro's helmet swung for him to survey all the commanders there, and all but one nodded in agreement.

"Very well," the Warlord growled. "When the last of my men arrive and are fed, we strike."

Battle couldn't come soon enough.

33

Darius – Northwest of Dolthea

Despite Darius's pleas to both Lex and Selene that they rest longer, they only spent a day in the village before setting off again. The morning air was crisp but clear, rays of sunshine breaking through the forest canopy to warm his head and shoulders as they trekked. Even their new priestly companion couldn't disturb the peace that had finally calmed Darius's heart.

Now that they'd said their farewells to Ninety-seven, Lionheart and the rest of the surviving young ones, Darius breathed easily once again with only the five of them and Lyra to protect. The stress that had come from worrying over a large group was something he'd never miss. Even the pteron had left him alone again as if it understood his beleaguered mind needed a break. Or was it because he'd found Selene?

Yet what brightened his day the most was that Selene was alive and finally safe, and as they chatted amongst the trees, he saw glimpses of the woman he'd loved coming through the layers of torture. Sunlight glistened from her hair, giving the curls a fire they hadn't had before. She even hiked with a less encumbered gait than Lex, although it was plain that her worst injuries were in her mind.

But he soon realised her hazel eyes had lost the allure they'd once held, even if they'd lost none of their beauty. Now they only reminded him of how hateful they'd been when she'd chained him like an animal. The many months of fearing her dead hadn't revived his lost affection. Granted, he still loved her more than most people he'd ever met—although that wasn't saying much, considering most made him want to ram his fingers in his ears—and the way her hips moved as she walked roused subconscious urges he hadn't satisfied in too long. But that was just because he was a man.

Gorgias led from the front again, and Darius watched the algus as he chatted more with Selene, trekking ahead of Lex, Nasrin and the Chief Priest. They soon reached a stream and quenched their thirst, then made their way along the bank towards the water's source. The edges burst with thick plants and flowers that threw out a fresh scent that almost masked his sweaty odour. But most of all, he enjoyed the quiet trickle of the stream.

He could have walked in silence along there with Lyra at his heel all day, but he had too many questions for Selene to hold his tongue.

"How's your back?" he asked. Just the memory of the chafing during his trek after the Battle of Laltos made him wince on her behalf.

"The bandages are helping, thanks," she said, "as are the herbs the carer gave me."

Does she not know Nasrin's name? "I'm surprised you can stomach them. She made me some kind of mulched herbs the

312

other day…" He shuddered. "I'd rather have spooned the contents of a latrine into my mouth, vomited it up, then eaten it again."

Selene chuckled, a sound that usually would have come as natural as breathing but right now baffled him. Darius considered Gorgias again; the man had barely broken a smile since they'd been reunited, and she'd been captured far longer. Was she that much mentally stronger?

"Can I ask you about the Viridians?" he asked in as gentle a tone as he could.

She swallowed but nodded.

"Did they ever make you…do anything?" he asked. "I mean…hurt someone else." Gorgias's sobs replayed in his mind.

Her skin paled. "They did. I'd rather not speak of it."

"Fair enough. I don't mean to pry." He needed to veer to another subject. "How are you sleeping?"

She shrugged. "My back makes it difficult to lie down, and I have other pains not so obvious, but I've been so tired lately that I doze off eventually."

No nightmares? No waking drenched in sweat having relived her torture? "Glad to hear it," he muttered. He should have been relieved she hadn't suffered as he had at first, but it struck him as rather odd.

Lyra prowled beside him and must have sensed his musings because she eyed the woman suspiciously as well.

"We'll be in Dolthea in a few days," she said. "Do you remember the first time we stayed there?" A wistful smile lit up her face like the morning sky.

He'd overlook the locking-him-in-chains memory. "How could I forget? I worked my charms on you."

"I think you'll find *I* was the charmer. Honestly, you couldn't take a hint. It was like being a teen again. I had to give signals

313

more obvious than a Torian fisherman." She gave him a playful shove, but her analogy puzzled him.

"Do they give obvious signals?" he asked.

"Of course. The delta is too rough to shout or use anything but wild gestures to communicate on the boats."

"If you say so. Then I hope I was worth all the effort it took to seduce me."

"Oh…" She bit her lip. "You were."

A prideful grin curled his mouth. At least he'd done something right in those days, although he supposed repelling the Viridians from Dolthea had been pretty good too, despite the freedom he'd won not lasting.

Selene brushed her hand against his as they walked, the touch as gentle as the trickle of the stream beside him, so gentle he didn't know whether it had been deliberate.

"I hope you aren't planning on visiting any brothels this time," she said.

"Brothel? When did I…?" He stopped walking, the warmth of the sun suddenly leaving him with a shiver. *Bita.* How had he never given a passing thought to Omid's mother since then? "Was Bita in Laltos when…?"

Selene took his hand and shook her head. "No. Don't worry. I sent her to help my birth family on the northern coast. The Viridians haven't bothered that region. There's little of value."

"Oh. I'm glad." The air warmed a little again, but with it, he caught the smell of something rotten. "Is that—?"

"Dead horse ahead," Lex said behind him, so close he flinched away and pulled his hand from Selene's grasp. "I can see the flies buzzing from here."

He should have known wearing such a thick cloak and blocking his senses was unwise—anyone could sneak up on him. But without it, his rakkan armour was too obvious.

314

"I'm glad I haven't drunk from that stream recently," the Chief Priest said, stopping beside Lex with a frown.

They carried on and, sure enough, a decaying horse lay in the middle of the water with a dense cloud of flies buzzing above. They walked around and carried on upstream for a few minutes until they reached a large pool churning at one side under the point of a tall, thin waterfall. A rainbow hung across the mist from the riling water, a spread of colours that blended into a plethora of flowers flirting with the pool's edge.

"I hope we don't need to climb up there," Darius said, casting his eyes to the top of the rock from which the water cascaded.

"No," the Chief Priest said. "We can head west, away from the stream."

That would probably give Darius no chance to bathe over the next few days. He opened his cloak a fraction, and a slight sniff was all it took to confirm he needed a wash.

"I'm going to bathe," he said, imagining the crystal-blue, inviting water on his skin.

"There are places to bathe in Dolthea," the Chief Priest said.

But Darius would rather not spend another few days stinking around Lex and Selene. He began slipping off his boots while the others discussed what they'd like to do.

Gorgias showed no interest, never willing to bathe with anyone, and Darius doubted the Chief Priest wanted to strip off—the man hadn't so much as removed a glove so far.

Nasrin walked up to the water and dipped in her hand but ripped it out with a yelp quickly after. "It's like ice. It must be straight from the top of the mountain."

Darius shrugged. "Doesn't bother me. If you're not interested, wait close by. You're not moving on without me."

Lex raised an eyebrow at his demand, which usually meant some insults were running through her head, but this time she almost looked…pleased with him.

After waiting for the others to move away to the other side of some thick bushes, Darius pulled off his cloak, armour and tunic.

Lyra, stay with them. Don't let them wander. She was the last one to go, leaving just him, the crisp air and the calming fizz of the waterfall. He shook off his trousers until he wore only his necklace and pendants, then stepped up to the water. Fancying a little fun, he conjured algor on the soles of his feet then touched the top of the pool with them. Veins of ice shot from his toes, and after a few seconds, he put his weight on the frozen water and felt it hold. He carried on stepping slowly, shakily keeping his balance, until standing in the middle of the pool with a circle of ice stretching a few yards around him. The cold mass rocked back and forth, not deep enough to find support at the bottom of the pool.

"Having fun?" a voice called from behind.

He turned and almost slipped onto his backside. Standing by the bank, Lex stood stripping off her gear.

In an instant, he flared ferven across his legs and dropped as the ice beneath him disintegrated and steamed away, plunging him into a soon roiling, bubbling bath. He extinguished his ferven and tread water, glancing back at Lex, who was now in only her underwear. Although the odd scar marred her otherwise smooth olive skin, they stole nothing from her elegance. If anything, they made the woman even more breathtaking—the marks proved her tenacity, her love of the ones she fought for and the pain she was willing to bear.

He'd never seen her so bare and open before; she'd never been shy, but even so, she didn't usually undress in front of him.

Quickly averting his gaze, he called out, "I thought I'd be alone."

She didn't respond, and he dared not look when splashes of water sounded. Even without ferven, the water still steamed around him.

"Would you like me to head downstream?" he asked, risking a look at her from his peripheral vision.

She stood half-submerged, slender and bare. "Do you want to smell of dead horse?"

"That would still be an improvement." He weakened his kicks until the water reached his nose, then scratched under his arms to wash. Without intending to, his body twisted to face her, and his eyes latched on to her body, unable to resist the temptation. He breathed a sigh of relief when he saw her facing away.

As she splashed water to wet her skin, the muscles of her back flexed, strong from years of archery, and left a groove down her spine where water trickled from her wet hair all the way down to her backside, the skin there lighter than her sun-kissed face.

"Don't you know it's rude to stare?" she said, still facing away.

Darius blinked. Could she see behind herself now? The water suddenly became chilly, and he scanned the air and trees around, not taking long to see her falcon perched close by.

You little... When had he returned?

Breathing out, Darius sank and submerged his head, taking as long as his remaining breath held in the hope the embarrassing moment would be forgotten. But when he came up, she was neck-deep and swimming straight towards him.

At least now that her captivating body was underwater, he needn't avert his eyes.

"Sorry," he muttered.

Rubbing his body clean again, he expected her to stop and wash at a distance, but she carried on until she was only a couple of feet from him, where the crystal water no longer hid her body.

"I need to ask you something," she said.

It took him more effort to keep his gaze up than it did to slay a hundred men. "Go ahead."

"But I need you to do me a favour first."

"What?"

As if a mask fell from her face, her expression dropped and seemed to age her a decade. "The Chief Priest couldn't help with the pain, and I've taken as much medicine as I dare. It's almost unbearable."

He grimaced and instinctively looked at her hip but snapped his gaze back up when he realised the nude area he was staring at. Thankfully, she didn't react.

"What can I do?" he asked.

"When it's like this, a hot bath usually helps. Can you warm me up?"

His first thoughts on how to get her hot would earn him a slap if she knew them. And the imaginings stirred something below the water that he prayed she didn't see.

"I'll go slowly," he said. "Tell me if it gets too hot."

She smiled painfully and nodded.

As carefully as he could, he conjured ferven on his toes. The water fizzed and bubbled, and Lex drifted until she was right above the heat, so close he saw everything, even in peripheral vision.

She closed her eyes and sighed. "More."

He obliged, gradually conjuring more on his feet, then calves. When her shoulders relaxed, and she showed no signs of discomfort, he flared even more. Soon the bubbles churned with such strength he began rising from the water, drifting apart from her, so he reached out and grabbed her hand to keep her near.

She gasped but soon let out a long, satisfied breath that was almost a moan. After a while, the hot current began whirling them, but Darius kept his energy flowing, feeling even the muscles in her hand relax. Enough time passed for his escort to begin relaying her restlessness to him, but he'd give Lex as long as she needed.

Eventually, she opened eyes that were relaxed, sky blue, stunning. "So…we need to discuss Selene."

The name put a sudden barrier between them, and Lex waited as if measuring his every reaction to her words.

"Go on." He eased the ferven on his legs.

But she frowned. "Don't stop."

"Sorry. So, what about Selene?"

When the bubbles returned, her expression melted again and lost the edge it had held. "There's something off about her, but I can't quite think what. Have you noticed anything?"

"I guess. But compared to Gorgias, she's far more like her old self. It's almost like he's a different person, whereas Selene has lost far fewer quirks."

"Don't you think that's suspicious?"

"Not really." Was she trying to wedge some distance between him and Selene with the questions and her body?

"But…" Lex said, "she didn't even ask me about you when I first spoke with her."

"… She didn't?" The revelation struck a blow deeper than any he'd taken in his fighting life. Even if Selene had known he was alive, how could she not ask how he fared?

"I guess…" he continued, "she has been acting a little *too* normal at times."

"That's what I mean. She's clearly broken, but there's something different about her compared to Gorgias."

Whilst he agreed with Lex, where was she going with this?

"No two people are the same," he said, "but perhaps we should watch her carefully."

Lex opened her eyes and immediately stared at his chest muscles. At least, he hoped she was looking at his chest.

"I have an idea," she said.

"Uh…I don't think this is the time or place."

She rolled her eyes. "That bear claw. Perhaps we can test her with it."

My necklace… A new heat rose in his face, a flush he hoped his beard covered. Being naked and so close to Lex while wearing a treasure her sister had given him in love was *not* something he'd have planned.

"Test her for what?" Darius asked. "What do you think's wrong with her?"

Lex opened her mouth a fraction to speak but paused for a few seconds before saying, "I know a lot about that claw. I could use it."

"Use it how? What could have happened to her?"

"Just… Do you trust me?"

He murmured under his breath, "Of course I do. Do you not trust me enough to tell me what you're getting at?"

"I do. But I'd rather not put worries into your head that may be unfounded. Maybe I'm being paranoid."

Putting worries in my head? The talk triggered a thought—goman magic. He banished the ferven from his body and let the water around them still once more. If Lex was thinking of cogi, he was no longer in any mood for warmth.

"As long as this test won't hurt her," Darius muttered.

"Of course not." Although her words were reassuring, something lingered behind her gaze that he couldn't decipher.

As much as he trusted her and her instincts, Selene being compromised was too foul a thought to seriously contemplate.

"Is your hip better?" he asked.

"Yes. Thank you." She gave his hand a light squeeze as if she were going to leave, but she kept holding him, never breaking eye contact in a way he wished could last a lot longer than it likely would. Something about the feel of her skin, even in water, made him wish he'd spent much more time with her in the last year. If only Varro hadn't been so damn spiteful, Darius could have been beside her throughout the pain.

Eventually, she loosened her hold with a smile, then began swimming away. "We should get to it. Do you mind not looking at me this time?"

"I didn't mean…" He turned away and considered conjuring algor to encase himself in ice, a fitting frigid end to what had been up to this moment his first pleasant day in a long time.

But maybe Lex was worried about something different with Selene than him. The only goman in the Empire was dead.

So why did the thought set his heart racing?

34

Lex – Northwest of Dolthea

After Lex and Darius had dressed, he handed her the bear claw with a grim look she took to mean he had the same suspicions about Selene as she did. He went to rejoin the others, but she lingered by the water for a moment, running her thumb across the claw and recalling the moment she and Selene had retrieved it, the moment of anguish they'd shared. If a goman had tampered with her mind, they'd have to alter that memory because she'd never shown Selene a greater act of love. Choosing to save Selene's life over her own escort's had inspired a loyalty that nothing could overcome. A goman would have to erase any emotional connection to that event.

She prayed her fears weren't true, and that she wouldn't have to spill her sister's blood. Sadly, it wasn't a fate unknown to her. Omid had been the last but not the first person she cared about to have their mind erased by a goman. At the memory, she rubbed her hip, out of habit more than pain. The hot water had worked, but the relief wouldn't last long, judging by past experience.

After gathering the rest of her weapons and items, she made her way towards the others. As she passed around a bush, the Chief Priest stood waiting with a smile and a mix of thin, serrated leaves in his hand.

While they'd been apart, he'd changed his appearance in subtle but effective ways: used berry paste to add colour to his hair, smudged a little dirt on his face to catch the wrinkles and make them more pronounced, and even turned his cloak inside out to get a new shade and a rougher material. Although the disguise was thin, she barely recognised the man. The only things unchanged were his gloves, now mostly covered by his long sleeves.

"Feeling refreshed?" Aran asked.

Refreshed wasn't the word after such a steamy dip, but she definitely felt something, something strong.

"Yes, thank you." She moved to step around him, but he shifted himself into her path.

"I have something for you," he said.

"I'm a little preoccupied with—" She stopped speaking when he held out the leaves and waved them under her nose.

"I just found them," he said. "My prayer was finally answered, so I can make a tea that should help you."

She peered at the leaves and recognised a few different plants. The only one that might help the pain was the yellow-stemmed holthorn, but even that was only used by herbalists for a mild headache.

"They won't work," she said flatly.

"Not on their own." Something twinkled in his grey eyes as his smile widened. "But I've been mixing these things for a long time, and they're quite potent. For instance, this shillbane"—he picked the longest straight leaf from the bunch—"calms the mind, and that will help you more than anything prescribed for pain from an injury. And this—"

"All right." She moved to shove his hand and the plants aside, but the man flinched away with nerves suddenly turning his face pale.

"I'll drink your tea," she added. There was nothing poisonous there, at least. What harm could it do?

"Excellent." The man turned on his heel and scurried off.

Strange man. When she rejoined the others, the Chief Priest was speaking with Darius and handing him a cup while the rest sat taking the chance to eat some of the various berries and fungi they'd foraged along their travels. Selene sat quietly, nibbling on mushrooms while listening to the others muttering.

The sight only deepened Lex's suspicion. Although they could hardly be fussy over food, Selene would never eat something she disliked unless it provided heavy nutrition. And mushrooms did not. How would a wise woman approach this conversation? Lex didn't want anyone else around, should things turn ugly.

"Selene," she said. "Can you help me with something back at the water?"

Her sister's reaction was one of curiosity, but Selene eventually nodded and stood. She picked up her sword belt, almost as if arming herself for a fight, though it could have been from habit.

As she followed Lex back down to the waterfall, Darius caught wind of them leaving. After saying a word to the Chief Priest, he hurriedly caught up with them and handed Lex the cup with a noticeable tremor in his hand. He obviously worried more about her sister than he let on. *Sensitive soul.*

With a gentle grasp, she closed her hand briefly around his and took the cup, a sudden heat in her hands. Her touch calmed his trepidation as she'd intended. If only she could calm her own.

Steam rose from the cup, and its aniseed aroma turned her stomach. But she took a sip anyway and almost retched when it tasted worse than it smelt. Or was the sickness due to what she had to now do?

Selene wandered up to the water and dipped the tip of her boot in, sending ripples out to join those spreading from the base of the waterfall. Sometimes her behaviour was so like before, such as now. Lex cursed under her breath. *Am I being paranoid?*

"What do you need help with?" Selene asked, tossing her hair back and running a wet hand through it.

Lex said nothing. A little paranoia couldn't hurt. She walked towards the bank and sat down with her tea and the bear claw clasped tightly in her hand. Selene followed her lead and sat cross-legged across from her sister after laying down the sword to her right.

But Darius remained standing, looming over them like a dark, lethal cloud.

After taking another sip of her tea, Lex said, "I told Darius something that happened with us, and he doesn't believe me." She scowled at the man to sell the ruse.

He scoffed and played along. "The details don't make sense to me. I think you're hiding something."

Lex looked back to her sister, whose frown bore not only confusion but also anger for some reason.

"Can you tell him the truth?" Lex asked.

"About what?" Selene asked.

"This." Lex placed her tea down and held out her palm, the bear claw in the centre like a giant black thorn.

Selene's mouth fell ajar. "Is that…"

"Your escort's."

Selene took the claw and peered at it up close, a smile coming to her face. "Philippos. But I gave this to Darius…"

Darius shot Lex a quick glance with as stoic an expression as she'd ever seen from him. Unfortunately, the white knuckles on his clenched fists betrayed his tension. Selene had remembered one inconsequential thing, but it didn't mean she was whole.

"I just took it from him," Lex said, "and regaled him with how we collected it. Would you like to confirm to him what happened? He doesn't believe I'd ever be so selfless."

It took Selene a few seconds to respond, the claw stealing most of her focus. "What did you tell him?"

"No," Darius said quickly. "Tell me your version, and I'll see if she embellished any of the details. Wouldn't be the first time."

Lex groaned. "Will you stop! Why would I lie?"

"I don't know. To impress me?"

Lex's ears burned in genuine anger. "You're becoming as arrogant as the old Darius every day, and that isn't a good thing." She supped a long gulp of tea, getting the ghastly fluid down as quickly as she could, but the aniseed nettling her throat almost made her throw it back up again.

Selene lifted her head but wasn't focusing on either of them. "Very well. I've already told Darius how my first escort died—about the murderous rakkan I showed mercy to—but I'll start from the beginning. Lex and I were tracking a band of Viridians deep in the Uncharted Mountains. Food was running out, so we'd split up to forage."

"Just the two of you?" Darius asked.

Selene nodded. So far, the memory was whole. "My escort was digging for roots in a patch of shrubs we'd found on the otherwise barren slopes, so deep his head must have been underground. I was distracted, focused on a mountain goat I was stalking with my bow. The next thing I heard was…" Her voice trailed off, and her head fell, sending her curls across her face.

With a piteous sigh, Darius sat down beside her and wrapped an arm across her shoulders. Perhaps he was just being sympathetic, or perhaps he still had feelings for her, but Lex noted he'd sat down on top of Selene's sword, preventing her from using it.

For a while, a heavy silence hung, and Lex finished the last of her tea if only to keep her hands busy. The taste didn't grow on her.

"So…" Darius cleared his throat, and his next words were as soft as a father's to his newborn child. "You heard your escort?"

Selene nodded, her sagging hair quivering. "He was dead before I found him, and a bony rakkan had already seared and bit his flesh." She went on to describe the scene, fight and ultimate conversation she'd had with the rakkan, all with the same small details Lex could recall from that time. It was all a little *too* accurate.

When Selene had finished, Darius winced. "I don't know how you found the heart not to slay the fiend."

"You didn't see him as I towered over his defeated, shuddering body," Selene said. "Rakkan eyes are usually vicious and cruel, but this one's had…a brightness in them. Perhaps it was the algor of my sword. But for whatever reason, I pitied the starving man, believed him when he said he'd thought my bear was a wild animal. So I let him go."

Lex hadn't understood it at the time and still didn't. The rakkan wouldn't have had time to arouse pity if *she* had been there first.

"When I found Lex," Selene continued softly, "it all caught up with me. The rush of battle left me, left me in a state. I could barely walk, barely hold my sword. I just felt so…empty."

Lex focused on the rushing water nearby, unable to watch her sister's grief-stricken tears when they looked so like they had before. And she'd shared that grief later, shared the void an escort left when the bond was shattered. If her daughter hadn't been born the year before, that might have been the final wound to destroy Lex's will. But she'd had to keep going for Cynthia.

"But Lex wouldn't let things lie," Selene said, a new edge to her tone. "She pulled me up, and we returned to my escort's body. And he wasn't alone."

Darius frowned. "You told me the rakkan got away and killed some algus a few days later."

"It wasn't him, but others must have sensed the kill. Dozens were there, biting and gnawing at his corpse. The smell of roasted meat carried on the wind, as foul as anything I've ever smelt." Her face twisted into an ugly grimace. "So we attacked."

While Selene took a moment, Darius gave Lex a subtle glance of regret, as if guilty they were subjecting the girl to something torturous and unnecessary. But just because this conversation was painful for her didn't mean it was avoidable. The details were correct so far, but they hadn't arrived at the crucial one.

The silence continued far longer than Lex would have liked, but she wouldn't interject, so she sat still, shifting occasionally to clear the leaves from her empty cup, waiting for Darius to nudge Selene into speaking again.

It took him a while, but he finally cleared his throat and said, "Did you kill them all?"

Selene nodded with a grim scowl. "But not without cost. More came soon after. I can't even remember exactly what happened. It was a blur."

Excuses. Lex leaned forward, inched a hand closer to the hilt of her dagger.

"But they overpowered me," Selene said. "Next thing I knew, I had an arm around my neck, and a squeeze would have ended me. That's when Lex saved me." Selene looked at her with a sisterly warmth so flawless it stole Lex's nerve. But it couldn't be genuine. She'd missed the most important detail.

"How did Lex save you?" Darius asked.

"She was fighting nearby and heard my shriek. Her sword was as swift as I've ever seen and stabbed the rakkan through the eye."

"I told Darius about my escort," Lex said. It was time they got to the point.

"Ah…yes. Well, Lex's brantari fought alongside us and…" Selene swallowed.

"Brantari?" Darius said. "As in, the tiger?"

Selene nodded.

But "tiger" was an insult to the size and strength of the fabled brantari. Standing at twice the weight of a large cat, it was one of the few animals with the mass and power to take on a rakkan one on one, and thanks to its elongated, razor-sharp canines, one bite was all it needed to end a foe. It was as if the God and Goddess had created the monsters for the sole purpose of fighting alongside the humans.

"I thought there were none left," Darius muttered.

"There are a few," Lex said. "And they cost a fortune." Not to mention the tons of meat they chomped through.

"So what happened to it?" Darius asked.

"*Him.*"

329

Darius gave Lex a look of apology, but she knew he hadn't meant anything by the remark.

"It's hard to recall," Selene said, with a dismissive shake of her head.

"Try." Darius's voice had nothing of the sharpness in his stare.

Something changed in Selene's posture, subtly but not invisibly. Her back straightened, eyes widened, and she was still, deathly still, like a cat about to pounce.

"That's the part I don't believe," Darius said, his arm still around her shoulder but his fingers now tense and ready to latch on to her.

"I remember him crushing the head of one rakkan in his jaws," Selene said, "then another rakkan took hold of him from behind."

So far, that was true. She was almost there.

"But then the rakkan had me," Selene continued, "and all I heard was a piercing screech from the cat, and when I looked, a rakkan had it in its grasp. Lex didn't have time after saving me to prevent the rakkan from… We were both devastated by the losses."

Lex's forehead burned. Didn't have *time*? She said it so matter-of-fact, so callously. The Numbered could feign emotion, go through the facial motions and shed a tear or two, but they had no understanding of the internal.

The truth was not what her sister described. When the rakkans had taken hold of her escort and Selene, the pair were seconds from death, and even an algus hadn't the gifts to save them both. Those seconds had passed like hours frozen in a time when Lex had been forced to choose between saving her sister and her escort. And, of course, she'd chosen Selene. Any sister would. The choice was obvious, and the Numbered knew it.

But they thought that made the choice *easy*, not even worth relaying, passing over it like it wasn't even a choice at all. They didn't know the pain, the guilt, the months of wondering why it couldn't be *you* who died instead of your escort. She and Selene had even travelled together to get new escorts shortly after, praying new bondings would relieve the holes inside them and becoming devastated when they didn't. Those moments on that mountainside had bound the two sisters with a fire that the two decades before hadn't, and they'd both taken a claw of their fallen escorts to remember that day.

As thoughts ran through Lex's mind, she kept her expression stony and unreadable. If Selene had been manipulated by a goman, their situation was far more dire than Lex had feared. But how could there be a goman in the Empire with no one knowing? It beggared belief. Why not use such a formidable force? And even if a goman did exist, why tamper with Selene?

Selene almost certainly wouldn't know if it was true. If Lex asked, the mind blocks would set in, and even torture wouldn't break them.

Whatever the truth, they had to assume the worst. Too often in her life, Lex had taken the chance with a Numbered and seen the bloodshed that caused. Not this time. They had to deal with Selene, and Lex saw no other option. She'd seen too many Numbered over the years to hold out any hope. She'd confirm her suspicions beyond doubt, then do what had to be done.

But a doubt gnawed her stomach as she watched Darius, the long-haired man who wasn't the same as before falling to a goman, yet who wasn't too dissimilar. Was there something she was missing? He'd been a special case, touched by Archimedes for only a few moments and with rakkan blood in his veins to frustrate the goman's cogi.

331

No. She couldn't afford to be weak. Selene had to be neutralised at once. Since they'd all stopped speaking, the woman's hand had inched closer to her sword.

Darius caught Lex's stares, and a wave of dark anger washed over his eyes. He'd seen her intent. And he wouldn't let her do what she needed to. She had to be fast.

35

Darius – Northwest of Dolthea

A tough gust sent ripples across the water and tossed Selene's soft hair onto Darius's hand, a gentle touch that barely registered as his whole body froze in a numb, painless sensation of sinking into the ground. A murderous fire sparked in Lex's eyes, rendering it unnecessary for him to ask whether Selene had passed whatever trap her sister had set. But how could Lex be sure?

"So…" Selene gave him a smile that, for a moment, almost filled the hollow feeling within. But then it only reminded him of the woman he'd known. Surely, regardless of what had happened to her, that woman was still inside.

"Did Lex tell you the truth?" Selene asked in her sweet, playful voice.

"Not the whole truth," he muttered through gritted teeth. Under the hand still resting on her shoulder, he felt her muscles tense as she shifted her weight away from her sword arm. He spied the flats of her feet firmly planted on the soil and the coiled energy within her legs. It couldn't be true… But it was.

He forced as genuine a laugh as he could and moved his weight discreetly on top of her sword. "I think Lex should stop speaking so rashly and think more about things before she reacts."

Lex tensed. "Sometimes fate doesn't give us the time to stop and deliberate."

"But sometimes it does. You take pause *sometimes*. I'm living proof."

The pair glared at each other for so long that Selene fidgeted and seemed to sense something was amiss.

"Shouldn't we head off again?" Selene grabbed the hilt of her sword, but Darius didn't move from atop the blade. "Darius?" she whispered. "Are you going to tell me what this was really about?"

Darius closed his hand around Selene's shoulder, and it took only a little of his strength until she flinched and gasped.

"What are you doing?" she asked.

"I'm tired of lying," he muttered. "Come out with it, Lex."

Lex ripped her dagger from its sheath, a sudden move that made Darius twitch. But rather than use her weapon, Lex placed it carefully on her lap.

"You aren't the Selene we knew." Lex's tone and phrasing brought a familiar acidity to Darius's mood. She'd spoken to him with the same disdain after Archimedes had tampered with his mind.

"What do you mean?" Selene asked, her voice flustered. "Let go of me!"

"Tell us the truth, Selene," Darius said.

She suddenly twisted and tried to rip herself free of his grip, but it was futile. No matter how hard she struggled and writhed, he only needed a single hand to lock her. Her flailing arms struck him over and over and tried to push him away. The strikes barely registered, but they wounded another part of him; he'd rather have bathed in a sea of blood than feel her struggle against him.

When her writhing didn't cease, he pushed her back to the ground and swung his body to mount her. A second later, he pressed his weight onto her hips and clasped her arms to calm her struggles, a dominant grappling position even if he hadn't had rakkan strength.

"Get off me!" Selene screamed, a sound so shrill and grating he had to face away and pretend it wasn't her he was manhandling.

"Just tell us everything, Selene," Darius shouted above her cries.

"She won't tell you," Lex said, storming over and towering above the pair. "She probably doesn't even know herself. That's not the Selene you knew."

Tears stung his eyes as he gazed into Selene's, watching the hazel beauty now fearful and angry.

"So what do we do?" he asked.

Then he felt the air shift as Lex's sword arm moved, so he released one hand and caught her swing before it landed.

"Don't," he said. "If you harm her, I swear by your gods, I'll—"

"You can't be serious!" Lex grimaced. "She's *not* our Selene."

Selene used her free arm to prise away the fingers that held her in a death grip, and her grunts of frustration when she couldn't budge him only further darkened his mood.

Darius and Lex froze in a stalemate he had no idea how to resolve. Soon after, the Chief Priest and the others rushed through the thicket and gasped in horror when they saw the scene before them.

"What's happened?" Nasrin asked.

"Selene's been wiped out by a goman!" Lex spat.

Selene kicked to try to twist free, but Darius was far too heavy a mass. He grabbed her other arm again, then fell forward and pressed her wrists to the ground above her head.

"Get off!" she shrieked. "My back! My back!"

As if being whipped himself, Darius felt the pain of lashes with every one of her screams. He was a monster for even doing this.

"Have you been warped by a goman?" he asked.

Selene did nothing but writhe further.

"Come now," the Chief Priest said with a troubled look at the woman. "Is this necessary? There hasn't been a whisper of a goman being in the Empire—other than Archimedes—and I would know. Even if she'd been manipulated by a goman, she'd have mind blocks to prevent you from getting any information from her."

The reminder of the blocks sparked something in Darius's memory. Lex had said the same of him, and that he'd forgotten things and grasped his head when it had happened. But Selene had never done that, not even with all the accusations of gomans being thrown at her.

He sat back up and released her arms, still straddling her waist to control her but allowing her to push her wounded back free from the ground. She winced, tears now wetting her cheeks and stealing his resolve.

"Maybe you're wrong…" He turned to Lex with a new terror gripping him. Was he torturing the woman he'd once been in love with?

But none of the fire had left Lex's expression. She crouched to Selene's level and spoke in sharp, harsh words. "Tell us where you've been for the last year."

Selene gasped. "I have. I told you, I was with the Viridians, then I escaped. Then I…I rested with a woman in the mountains for a few days before finding the priest in that village."

"What woman?" Darius and Lex said together.

"I don't know…old, short, sort of crippled. She had dyed red hair and a nasty temper. I didn't like her, so after I'd eaten and regained enough strength, I snuck away in the night while she slept."

Darius's skin chilled to ice, sending shivers through his very bones, and Lex's face contorted with the same horror.

"Why would the Waif Magician tamper with her mind?" he asked.

The Chief Priest stepped forward, nervous hands fidgeting like he wanted to help the poor woman under Darius's weight but didn't know how.

"If I may," Aran began, "the Waif Magician could not change someone as radically as you're suggesting. Shirin *can* tamper with the mind, possibly even pervert a simple beast's mind to control it, but a woman like Selene—there's no way Shirin can replace decades of memories and warp her like a Numbered."

Darius frowned, eager to believe the man but conscious of his own bias in wanting it to be true. It would explain why Selene still recalled seeing the woman, though.

"What makes you so sure?" Darius asked.

"Because the Magician would have done it already. She'd have an army of algus, just as Archimedes had." The Chief Priest's kind eyes widened apologetically, pleading.

And Darius believed him, unable to argue with the logic. But that left the question of what exactly the Magician *had* done to Selene. Because something had clearly changed.

Darius looked at the woman beneath him. "If I let you up, do you promise not to try anything?"

Selene nodded, so he carefully lifted himself off her while keeping one hand firmly clasped around her wrist, then they both stood. He studied every movement she made, every fearful glance she shot him. Her terror was real, and he hated himself for having evoked it.

"We can't trust her," Lex said, her tone barbed with frustration. "We need to take her somewhere to lock her up."

"Imprison her?" Darius said. "She needs the people she knew and loved. She needs to remember the real us, not rot in a cell where her bitterness will fester." Unfortunately, that was something he'd learned through experience. "And she'd only be safe in Margalvia. That's weeks away."

Nasrin came forward with a silent frown and went to Selene's back. She pulled at the collar of the algus's tunic and glanced down her neck, rousing even more guilt in Darius. How much additional pain had he caused Selene?

"Whatever the Magician did," Darius growled, "she can undo it."

Nasrin eyed him with suspicion. "I can't say I understand why Shirin would do this, but if I speak with her, I'm confident I can have her reverse it."

But Darius wasn't sure he'd even let the carer try. First, the Magician had tried to kill him, and now this? That witch didn't deserve to breathe, and any discussion would take place with her on the sharp end of his gladius.

Lex stalked beside him and put her mouth to his ear. "Optimism is dangerous. We should assume the worst."

"Like you did with me?" he spat. The harshness with which she'd treated him when his memories were first erased was hard to forget, an experience he'd prevent Selene from sharing.

He caught Gorgias's eye and recalled the man's wife, Fourteen.

"You've more intimate experience with the Numbered than most," Darius said.

The algus gulped. "I guess."

"Do you think she is one?"

"I haven't seen enough to make me think that, but I can ch-check." Gorgias came forward and studied Selene's face with such focus, it was as if the algus had found his calling in life. "A goman altered your memories," he said while he scrutinised her reaction.

Selene retracted her head a fraction, but that could have been due to the algus's juvenile face being an inch from hers.

"You really are Selene," he said. "Lex is your real sister, and Darius really did love you."

Again, the words barely evoked a response.

Gorgias turned his head towards Darius while his gaze remained on Selene. "I don't see any signs of a mind block," Gorgias said. "And all the Numbered had them. None were able to learn that their minds had been warped by a goman. They were all lost forever, believing themselves to merely have the appearance of someone that others would recognise."

"It's not enough to be sure," Lex said.

But it was enough for Darius. "The matter's settled. Selene isn't going to a prison. She's coming with us, and when we find the Magician, we'll make the witch undo whatever she did."

Lex snarled in anger but walked away towards her bag while Darius turned Selene to face him reluctantly.

"I'm sorry for being rough," he said. "But you need help, and I'm going to get it to you. But we'll need your help too. You must tell me where you stayed with the old woman."

Selene nodded, but her jaw was tense. And who could blame her for being angry after what he'd just done?

"It…" she began. "It's hard to say. I'd never been there before, and I'd lost a lot of blood, so my memory is rather hazy. It wasn't far off the road to Dolthea. If I saw the place again, I'd know it."

It would be unusual for the Magician to hide so close to a settlement, but with her cogi foresight, Darius supposed she'd be relatively safe regardless.

Lex stormed back up to them and thrust a set of shackles and chains into Darius's chest with a force that would have bruised a human.

"*You* can stay chained to her," Lex said. "Only carry a kuraminium weapon, and either you or I must be awake at all times. No one else is to go near her."

He took the shackles and inspected the steel clasps and few feet of chain connecting them.

"Why does she need to be restrained?" Darius asked. "You didn't chain me after Archimedes had tampered with me."

Lex's glare darkened. "I would have if I could. But I was alone with you, and I didn't have the strength to contain you like you have over Selene."

From the few years he recalled knowing Lex, he knew her bared teeth meant she'd never back down on this point, a stubbornness born of fear rather than malice.

"Fine." Darius began fastening the shackles to his and Selene's wrists. "Why do you have chains anyway?"

Lex raised a thin eyebrow, and he suddenly regretted asking. They'd been for the Magician, for the scenario he wasn't supposed to remind Nasrin of.

"Are we still heading to Dolthea?" Darius asked.

"Yes." Lex focused all her attention on Selene as she spoke. "We'll find out the truth."

36

King's Orator – Toria

Ophelia brushed the flakes of skin from the himation draped over her left shoulder. She usually enjoyed such formal attire because the large sheet wrapped ceremonially around her body was warm and flattered her otherwise straight figure. Plus, the cream silk was the most comfortable in the Empire. But today, she'd rather have been dressed in sackcloth if it meant she could speak with the King. She awaited the King's invitation to join him and receive her next task, but the ruler had been unusually isolated of late.

As it was, she had to make do with the two in her present company, only one of which she adored—the King's Sword. Then there was the *other* King. The human Medus II. The puppet. The forty-year-old adopted namesake of the late King Medus I. *The spoilt brat.*

Trying to forget her frustrations, she surveyed the pair and the rest of the hall around her. Hundreds of guests, both honourable and dishonourable, mingled and danced with stuffed bellies stretching the wrap of their colourful himations. The sea of bodies was a melting pot of reds, blues, oranges—every ghastly colour of nature, and it seemed only the Torians in attendance had the class to wear light shades, led by their king—at least, the Puppet King—who donned a brilliant silver himation wrapped across his muscular torso.

Dozens of musicians stood tapping their feet and strumming their lyres and kithara to send an angelic chorus to bless everyone's ears. Overhead, hanging below the tall and vast ceiling, were a thousand candles, bathing the symposium below in a tangerine light that almost rivalled the sun. Slaves weaved through the guests in the hall with trays of both salted and honeyed snacks, and they ensured the numerous spillages of wine on the waxed marble floor were mopped up in an instant.

"Ask them to change the song," the Puppet King said with a yawn so wide that the jewel-encrusted crown on his head slipped back.

"Of course, my king," Ophelia said with a slight bow. His terrible taste in music hadn't changed since before the arrival of the goman, since the ascension of the one who in Ophelia's eyes was the real King, someone worthy of her servitude and adulation.

Ophelia raised her hand lazily, and a slave boy scurried to her side. "Tell them to play 'The Stampede of Alogos.'" It was one of the Puppet King's favourites and the least offensive to Ophelia's ears. The real King's summons couldn't come soon enough. *Why does he make me wait?*

The King's Sword turned his head to her, a look she knew all too well. The man hated the Puppet King's taste in music too. She allowed the side of her mouth to curl into a grin, one that he returned.

As the only citizen at the symposium to wear his slate-grey algus tunic rather than a himation, the King's Sword stood out like a blood-soaked warrior in a temple and had created an empty circle around the three of them that no one dared enter for fear of the old, dangerous eyes underneath his hood. *And aren't we better off for it.*

Ophelia stepped closer to the algus and whispered, "I wish you'd dressed in what I suggested. You could have worn the garment over your arm to hide the scar."

Jason merely grunted in reply, but the subtle inflexion of his tone meant he'd scoffed. He didn't deserve to stand out—almost like a slave—but she enjoyed the fact he scared away the supposedly most influential people in the Empire and delayed the monotonous pleasantries she'd soon have to make. It also spared her having to pay attention to the Puppet King's conversations. The fool believed himself king, and the real King's influence was far more subtle than relying on mind blocks or other obvious signs of interference. But Ophelia still had to be vigilant because the Puppet had a habit of making promises *she* then had to keep.

A few moments later, the musicians' drums began pounding, and rhythmic thunder announced the impending belting of the choristers. The crowd cheered and stamped their feet, provoking a familiar headache that Ophelia masked with a smile.

She whispered again to the King's Sword. "Has the King told you when we're to meet him later?"

Jason grunted again, a deep sound that meant "no."

Within the dancing crowd nearby, one of the nobles set her sights on the Puppet King and swaggered towards them. The delicate, shadowed colour around her eyes made her ooze the confidence of a siren and was matched in allure by her brazen red himation. As if that were not enough to assault one's eyes, a weighty diamond hung from her neck, a treasure passed down in her family for three generations. The woman clearly wanted to display her trust in the King and his invitations by wearing treasures that might be easily stolen, but Ophelia knew her too well to be fooled. The display was as shallow as a summer puddle.

Ophelia stepped in front of the Puppet King and intercepted the new arrival with a wide smile and a bow. "Regent Berenice, how lovely to see you. And might I say, you're looking radiant."

Berenice smiled, though the pleasure didn't extend to her eyes, which still focused on the Puppet King she'd had an affair with a decade ago.

"Ah, Berenice." The Puppet King nudged Ophelia aside and went to kiss the Regent on each cheek, a touch that made Berenice blush.

"So nice to see you again," she said. "It has been too long since you hosted a banquet or accepted my invitations to visit Alogos! My people and my swifts miss you."

"Alas," the Puppet King said, "the troubles in the west demand all my attention."

Ophelia suppressed a roll of her eyes. The only attention the man gave was to whores and the false reports she fed him.

"You work too hard, Medus." Berenice ran a hand across the Puppet King's chin, and Ophelia had to quickly grasp the sleeve of Jason's tunic as he reached for his sword.

"Now, now, Regent." The Puppet King took a step back. "This is a formal occasion. You cannot address me so familiarly."

"Oh. I'm sorry, my king." But her seductive tone showed the apology to be a lie.

"If you're feeling some particular…urges, Regent," Ophelia said, "then we do have men and facilities for that."

Berenice scowled at her and opened her mouth to no doubt issue a sharp reply when the King's Sword cleared his throat. The sound scared the Regent's voice away, and she turned her attention back to the Puppet King.

"I hope the foals I brought have been to your liking, my king," she said.

"Indeed." He slapped his full belly. "Very tender and fattened this year. Have you been rearing them differently?"

"How astute of you to notice. We've been hard at work breeding more swifts for your army, which has left far more useless foals that have nowhere to graze. Without anywhere to move or exercise, their meat becomes particularly tender."

"You'll have to send them more often."

Ophelia checked the entrance to the banquet hall to see whether anyone arrived to summon her to the real King. But it was empty, except for slaves.

"King Medus! There you are." The familiar voice behind them sent a shudder of revulsion through Ophelia's spine. Without turning, she sniffed the pungent aroma of the Silk Regent's musk, and even Berenice grimaced in disgust and walked away at once.

The Puppet King spun on his heel with a disgruntled growl. "It's rude to interrupt me, Aristippus."

"Apologies, my king." The Silk Regent bowed with a smug grin, and his golden chains dangled with such a weight he might not stand again. "I didn't see the esteemed Regent of Alogos."

Ophelia didn't need to read any cues to know the man lied like a rakkan. If only the King had heeded her warning and ended the reprobate…

She put her mouth to the ear of the King's Sword and whispered, "He bothers me."

Jason gave her a glance before turning to face the Silk Regent square on, pulling his shoulders back and drawing in a long, deep breath that took more than a few thunders of the drums to finish. The lyres hit a high, fevered pitch.

The Silk Regent paused, still bowing but with his gaze now firmly on the most feared algus in the Empire. Such disquiet was a pleasant sight that almost alleviated Ophelia's restlessness. After a few moments of hesitation and silence from both him and the Puppet King, the Silk Regent took the hint. He quickly rose and turned to scurry away, only to hit a slave girl carrying a tray full of cups of wine behind.

The girl shrieked, and the cups tumbled in all directions, splashing red wine over her, the Silk Regent, the King's Sword, and almost over the Puppet King himself.

Aristippus yelled a curse. Slaves rushed over with towels and began dabbing the men dry. One boy took hold of Jason's left sleeve and dried the wine dripping from it, but the slave pulled it too harshly, and the fabric tore a fraction.

Ophelia's heart almost stopped, and Jason jerked his arm away, shielding the scar on it at once. Thankfully, the sleeve still covered the mark and nobody saw.

Lost in his own madness, the Silk Regent gaped down at his once fine ivory silk himation now splashed with ugly red, then at the slave he'd barged into. "You stupid girl!" A murderous scowl overcame his face, and he backhanded her across the cheek, sending her crashing down to the marble.

Ophelia needed no further excuse, and hopefully, this would be the pretence she needed to end the reprobate. She nudged Jason in the back.

The algus's sword sprang from its sheath before she saw Jason move and flashed in the candlelight before halting when pressed to the Silk Regent's treasured groin. The man panted, sweat beading his brow as the polished steel threatened his manhood. At least perspiration masked his perfume.

Ophelia longed for the slimy man to make a move, to give her friend an excuse.

"That's enough, Jason," the Puppet King said. "It was only a slave."

The King's Sword didn't even move to breathe until Ophelia gently cleared her throat. Then the algus loyally retracted his weapon.

It was only then she realised the music had stopped, and the chatter of the hall had died away, bringing unwanted attention.

She turned her furious gaze to the musicians. "Play!"

Shocked back into action, the choristers sang once more, and the drums boomed.

"My apologies, Aristippus." The Puppet King cast a scowl at his bodyguard. "I don't know what comes over the man sometimes."

"Is he an imbecile?" the Silk Regent asked, a flush to his cheeks that matched his stained clothes. "Or just a fool?"

"Definitely simple-minded."

Ophelia clenched her teeth. If she had possessed claws, she'd have ripped out the gullets of both spoilt men long ago. Jason was twice the man they were combined, before and after the real King had changed his mind so drastically.

"Did you know I found him in the dungeons after my father died?" the Puppet King said. "He'd lived there since he was nine."

The Silk Regent snorted. "Perhaps he belongs there."

"He's a most useful asset to the King," Ophelia said, unwilling to dull the sharpness of her tone. But the truth was, Jason was far more than an asset.

As she seethed, the music and pounding of dancers' heels continued harassing her ears.

"I read more in my father's diaries," the Puppet King said lazily as if the algus's life was only of fleeting interest. "He captured Jason in the early years of his reign, during the troubling threat of Hadrianus the Great's last push east. My father made Jason fight for sport in the dungeons. From twelve years old, even the most seasoned algus couldn't best him. But it's only in the last decade Jason's been willing to follow orders. Before that, he was feral."

With a smile more forced than any that day, Ophelia turned away to check the entrance again. It was still empty, which meant she had to continue listening while the two men talked about Jason. She'd visited the man in the dungeons soon after becoming one of King Medus I's most trusted advisors. At roughly the same age, she'd bonded to the reserved fighter like no other before or since. He hadn't looked at her ugly skin with disgust. She hadn't needed his fear for him to treat her with respect and not ridicule her. For that, she vowed to give her friend her undying loyalty and hated that—despite her best efforts—she'd never managed to convince the late King to release him from the prisons.

Thankfully, the real King had arrived and allowed it to happen.

The Silk Regent eyed the King's Sword with newfound courage. "I'll bet you Torians wished you'd trained your dog before the War of the Four. You'd have gained your empire far more easily."

Ophelia snapped. "Toria needed no additional help in that war."

The Silk Regent grinned without sensing the venom behind her comment. "You can never have too much help in a war."

"You speak to her as if you've been in one," the Puppet King said, casting his gaze across the crowds as if bored. "And without her, my father never would have won that war."

The Silk Regent lost his sneer while Ophelia's mouth widened with a newfound glee. It was time to have a little fun with the smarmy visitor.

"You're too kind, my king," she said. "It was a difficult war, and the sacking of Laltos brought significant challenges but great rewards."

The Puppet King shook his head, still facing away. "You must be mistaken. Laltos and Alogos surrendered under siege. Xavala was the city that was sacked."

The comment brought the murderous glare back to the Silk Regent's face, aimed directly at the side of the disinterested Puppet King's head.

Of course Ophelia remembered it had been the Silk City sacked, before the time Aristippus was handed the regency. But her comment would have been far too obvious a jibe for her to say it outright.

"Ah yes," Ophelia said as if speaking purely out of interest rather than riling up the weasel before her. "I was getting confused with the War of the Two. Xavala was left fairly intact after they surrendered to you in *that* war."

"If you don't include the forest we burned," the Puppet King muttered.

As if his head were about to spark ablaze, the Silk Regent gritted his teeth, then spun around and stormed away before saying something that would cost him his life.

Ophelia grinned at the preened back of his head as the song ringing in the hall reached its best part—the end. *Such a pity I never got to reveal it was my idea to scorch the mulberry forest.*

Now granted some respite again, Ophelia checked that Jason's sleeve still covered his scar and readjusted it herself while he murmured at her. But no one could be allowed to know the truth. No one could see the half-skull on his arm, a brand only three siblings in the Empire had ever borne. No one could know who his hermit of a sister was.

If only Jason had the same powers to manipulate the mind as the Magician, Ophelia would send him after the Silk Regent. But despite years of trying, the only cogi the King's Sword had shown was twofold: a lethal foresight spanning less than a minute ahead, and the ability to delve into people's minds—to perceive, not alter. It was far short of the power the King displayed, and Ophelia wouldn't even describe it as reading minds. But with a touch, Jason could sense some of a person's darkest secrets.

While the three silently watched the crowds again, someone approached behind her. "Excuse me, Orator."

Ophelia turned to see a messenger holding out a slip of parchment. She snatched it at once and dismissed the boy. After ripping it open, she breathed a sigh of relief to see the real King's handwriting.

You must leave at once to bring her an important message. Come with Jason to collect it in person.

At last, she could call this symposium to a close and have the Puppet King retire for the evening. If she and the King's Sword were to deliver a message to Selene personally, that could only mean the King's plan was about to bear fruit.

37

Selene – Northwest of Dolthea

For the rest of the journey that afternoon and evening, Selene followed Darius like a dog on a chain. The early night was warm, and as the forest cleared a little, stars filled the sky above in a show of brilliance. As dull as the woodlands had become to her, at least she wasn't still in Toria. She'd take slipping in mud and dung over Toria any day. If only she could be without Darius's persistent questions.

"Do you remember anything changing after you'd stayed with the old woman?" he asked for a desperate second time. *This is what the Slayer of Gods was like when he was with friends?*

"I told you. No!" She was glad to have a reason to vent her genuine disgust at the man. Hiding it was difficult. Just the touch of his hands made her skin crawl, and her mind replayed the memories of him beating her and flaying her back with his whip.

But she sealed that pain and hurt deep in the recesses of her mind. Her new body protected her from that side of him, and she still had a task to concentrate on. How could she have suffered such a setback so soon? It had only taken them days to undo months of intense work with Nikolaos. Clearly, the man hadn't known the dead Selene well enough. If it hadn't been for his line about the old woman, she'd probably be dead.

"Don't worry," Darius said for the thousandth time. "You're not alone. I had to go through the same after Archimedes got to me. He'd…" The man's mouth continued to move, but the words no longer registered. A familiar tension seized her head, but her training overtook any impulse to grasp it, and she merely forked her eyebrows in annoyance while all sound ceased.

After a few moments, as if waking from sleep, they'd skipped forward several hundred paces, and she couldn't even remember what the man had been talking about.

"Do you understand now?" Darius asked.

"I'm not a fool," Selene snapped. "And I wish you didn't have to drag me chained." Although the King had ordered her to get close to Darius, that definitely didn't involve being restrained. The last time Darius had chained her, it hadn't taken long for his true cruel nature to surface, like a lurking monster beneath a shallow but opaque sea.

So what were her options now that she'd failed? Should she remain or return to the King for further orders?

She quickly studied the dagger at Darius's waist out of the corner of her eye. It was only the length of her forearm. Would she be able to lift the kuraminium weight while he slept, if need be? As soon as she thought it, Lex caught her stare, eyes narrowed like a predator's. Nikolaos had warned that her sister would be the hardest to fool. At least he'd been right about something.

If she was going to get out of these restraints, her best choice was to convince Darius or Lex to release her, and to do that, she'd appeal to the emotional attachments that made them weak. Escape and return to the King could only be her fallback option.

"I suppose this is poetic justice," Selene muttered, letting her face droop to feign sadness. "Perhaps I deserve this after what I did to you."

"No." Darius moved closer to her, and his voice became quiet but so tense it rasped. "Look, I don't want to talk of torture, and I'm sure you don't either, which is why I don't mention it. So I'll only say this: What you did has scarred me forever and killed a part of me that treasured you more than anything or anyone. I can never forget. Maybe I can never forgive. But still… I'd rather have died than let you suffer as I suffered. The Viridians won't know the meaning of *wrath* until I make them pay for what they did to you." His words sent a wash of fiery breath across her face, a mere taste of the rage of that violent sea monster.

Selene forced a mirthless smile. A weaker woman would have fallen for his lies, but she was not weak. "If I swear not to escape, will you stop tugging the shackles so roughly?"

He became sheepish. "Sorry. Sometimes I forget my strength. But if you want to swear it, I'd rest a lot easier."

Selene scoured the memories in her head, trying to find the perfect one to help repair the man's confidence in her. And she found it, a confession he'd made at his most vulnerable.

"I do swear I won't try to escape," she lied. "And I hope you'll realise that I'm still me. While I'm still the woman who betrayed you and deserves your hate, I'm also still the woman who invited you into her bed; I'm still the first woman who ever saw you for what you really are."

His puzzled frown came as he asked, "What am I, really?"

She walked closer to him and took his hand gently, recalling the exact words he'd once said to her, the reason he'd loved her.

"I see the *man* beneath the warrior. I don't just see the Slayer everyone else sees," she whispered.

The words seemed to steal his voice and thoughts, but the warmth in his eyes told her she'd spoken wisely. It was a start, but winning him over wouldn't be easy. A dark anger still burned inside him. If she saw a chance to escape, perhaps she'd best take it.

38

Lex – Northwest of Dolthea

After a few days of trekking through the hilly forests and drinking plenty of disgusting tea, Lex awoke one day feeling a foreign numbness. It took her a few moments to realise what was different. She grasped her hip, pressing her fingers deep to the bone just to check she wasn't still dreaming. But she wasn't. The pain had reduced to nothing but a dull ache. She should have been elated, finally unencumbered enough to protect and avenge, but how could she be, when her sister lay in chains and was possibly lost forever? Fate was cruel to gift her the joy of reunion only to doom her to suffer loss a second time.

Lex cursed. Without pain, her mind was too free, bringing an endless stream of worries and guilt to the forefront. *Focus on Cynthia. Focus on something good for a change.*

But unable to do so for long, she quickly roused the others, ate, and got them moving again towards Dolthea. Now less than a couple of days away, they joined the road, a welcome respite for her feet after the uneven terrain where every root had seemed determined to snare her ankle.

But her relief was short-lived. Without the shelter and cloak of the trees, Lex constantly scanned her surroundings, watching and listening for sounds of horses or hunters or rakkans or…magicians.

Something about what Selene had said didn't make sense. Would the Magician stay so close to rakkan-dominated territory? Her audacity was famous, as was her liking of rakkan prisoners, but still…

The rain from the previous day left a familiar smell of wet lavender that lined the road in these less dense areas. Women usually loved the floral scent, and Lex had once, but now it only roused uncomfortable memories of searching for her husband's killers in these parts.

Every snap of a branch in the wind drew her gaze, and it wasn't just unseen forces that unnerved her. Why couldn't Darius see the danger he'd put them in by insisting her sister stay with them? Perhaps she'd taught him to listen to his heart over his head *too* much. At any moment, Selene could turn on them.

While keeping her keen eyes on her sister, Lex slowed her pace a fraction to join the Chief Priest as he walked at the back of their group. He'd fashioned a new disguise for himself that morning and now had a fresh blackness to his hair that knocked a few decades from his apparent age.

"How are you finding the tea?" Aran asked.

"I can't say I like it," Lex replied, "but my pain is much better today. Thank you."

"Don't thank me. Thank the Goddess for providing me with the ingredients."

Perhaps she should have, but Lex still couldn't bring herself to thank the overseer of this world just yet.

The pair continued while Lex mentally reached out to her peregrine circling above them, confirming he hadn't spotted anything ahead on the road.

Lex made polite conversation for most of the day, breaking only to eat and occasionally check in with the others. After the evening meal, she placed herself at the group's rear with the Chief Priest again.

"I appreciate you travelling with me," Aran said. "To have one algus is a blessing, but three… I feel like a regent, particularly with your larger friend. I daresay his scowl would be able to scare the fiends out of hell."

Well, he can't be speaking of Gorgias. "Don't let him hear you say that," Lex said. "I've just about convinced him he's not a god, but if you carry on, he'll have people bowing down to him like the Viridian Warlord." He'd be almost as insufferable as he'd been at times in the past.

"I'll keep my lips sealed." Aran chuckled. "By the Goddess, we can't have more mortals thinking of themselves as gods in this world… So, will you all stay long in Dolthea?"

It wasn't the first or even the second time the man had asked of their plans: what they were doing or where they were going afterwards. The questions were growing too inquisitive for her liking.

"I don't know," she replied, now watching Selene and Darius deep in conversation again. The man's concern had been apparent for most of the day, and gave away the conflict within him, but at least he was suspicious and constantly questioning the woman. Would he be able to confirm whether a remnant of the real Selene was still present?

"Are you all right?" The Chief Priest raised a now dark eyebrow.

"Sorry," Lex said. "My mind is wandering." At least that was true. She was still reluctant to lie to a holy man, even if she suspected he wasn't always truthful himself. "Did you say something?" she asked.

"Nothing after asking how long you will stay in Dolthea. I take it you're going there to bring hope to the people, and it sounds like it's very much needed."

"I'm not sure," Lex said. "Depends if we're exposed as algus or not."

"I sincerely hope you aren't discovered." The Chief Priest glanced ahead at the others, although Lex noticed his attention lingered on Darius in particular, the algus he'd so far not mentioned much. If Aran had recognised Lyra, he was keeping it to himself.

"Something wrong?" Lex asked.

"Huh? Oh, no." Aran quickly turned to her with a little flush on his cheeks. "I'm just tired. It's almost dark. Will we stop for the night soon?"

Usually, Lex would be reluctant to camp so close to a road after dark, but she'd rather arrive in Dolthea under the blazing sun that thinned the Viridians' numbers.

"We could go for another hour," Lex said, "then we—"

"No, please. I've got awful blisters on my heels. A humble priest such as I cannot afford the same level of comfortable footwear as you."

When Lex looked down at his feet, she couldn't see any changes to his gait, only that his boots were indeed old and worn, not to mention looking a little ridiculous together with his robes. At least they were more practical than the sandals priests usually donned.

"Fine." Lex hurried and caught up with the others. Once sure the Chief Priest couldn't overhear, she told them to head back into the forest for the night.

Meanwhile, she kept Aran in her peripheral vision and couldn't help but notice him scanning the shrubs and trees around them.

"I'll have Lyra prowl and find us a spot," Darius said when Lex had finished speaking. "I'll stay up overnight. You get some rest."

"No," Lex said. Her gut told her she needed to be awake tonight. "My pain will keep me up anyway, and I have Tiro. You should ensure you're at your strongest for Dolthea."

"Oh." Darius glanced down at her hip with a sympathetic wince. "Is the tea not helping? Why are you still drinking it, then?"

He was always perceptive at the most inconvenient moments.

"The Chief Priest says it takes time," she said, "and you can't argue with a holy man."

Darius scoffed. "Of course you can argue. I'll go over there and argue with that *holy* man right now."

"Just forget it. Get some rest."

"All right," he mumbled. "I can stay up with you if you'd like, and take your mind—"

"We can't afford to both be tired." But his concern warmed her even more than the bubbles in the pool had.

"My escort and I can stay up with you," Gorgias said. "I don't sleep well anymore either."

"No, I can," Nasrin interjected. "She's my—"

"Enough!" Lex snorted through her flared nostrils. "I'm neither a child nor a decrepit old woman. I can bear a night up alone."

They all threw her a sheepish look before skulking after Lyra to find a dry and sheltered spot to sleep.

Meanwhile, Lex waited for Selene to catch her eye before asking, "How are you doing?"

"*Great.*" Selene gave a wide, sarcastic grin and strode after the others, tugging at Darius and the chain.

Such a response was certainly consistent with the old Selene.

Darius followed without argument, as did Lex soon after, and the panther didn't take long to find them a quiet place. Wasting no time, Lex found the best vantage point to begin stowing her belongings, and after a few minutes, the Chief Priest came up to her, yawning.

"I'm ready to retire for the night," he said.

"Don't go too far." She hadn't even seen where he'd prepared his sleeping spot, only that he'd emerged from behind a bushy pine tree close by, a convenient area blind to her.

"I'll be close," he said. "Will you be keeping watch?"

Something told Lex he wasn't just asking out of fear they'd be ambushed. "No." She had to force out the lie, and she hoped it wasn't transparent. "My escort and Gorgias's will alert us of any danger."

"If you're happy we're safe, then I'm happy." He left and walked past the others with similar biddings of sweet dreams.

She leaned back against the tree and positioned a branch to dig into her spine. There was no way she'd risk slumbering tonight. As she watched the Chief Priest disappear again behind the thick foliage, she reached out to Tiro, who was scouting ahead in Dolthea. *Return. I have a job for you.*

***

The gentle patter of rain joined the buzzing insects to fill the night air. Despite the long journey on foot, Lex hadn't had to worry about drifting off. Her head hadn't lolled once, perhaps because she no longer took the weeping plant's tears.

Every time the leaves and branches around rustled, Lex scanned while keeping her head motionless, and usually the disturbances were nothing more than the wind. But finally, in the dead of night, she saw what she'd feared. Only the faintest of lights glowed in the forest, but enough to make out the source—the Chief Priest clutched a tiny candle and crept out from behind the tree to which he'd retired. First, he glanced at the others slumbering, then at Lex.

She kept her eyes half-closed but fixed on the man as he stalked a few yards through the undergrowth and disappeared from her sight.

Tiro. Track him. The bird obeyed and set off from his perch. Although not as silent in flight as an owl, he was sufficiently quiet to evade a human. Meanwhile, Lex slowly rose to her feet, sword in hand, and proceeded the way the Chief Priest had crept.

She moved silently, sacrificing speed for stealth, but let her escort guide her. Soon enough, she spotted Aran again. While venturing for a few minutes, he kept scanning the surroundings, looking in Lex's direction a few times with a pause, but she made sure to always remain out of sight. After trekking away from the camp, he finally disappeared into a thick bush.

Lex paused and didn't break cover. Whatever the Chief Priest did in the bush, he emerged a few moments later with something clasped in his hands. She crept to a closer tree and carefully leaned around the trunk until she spied the man kneeling while handling a bird on the ground. It certainly wasn't Tiro, and at this distance, all she could make out was that it wasn't large enough to be a bird of prey.

But as soon as her falcon soared to a new vantage point and got a proper look, he knew. Pigeons were his prey, and the longer

Lex stared, the better she saw the Chief Priest grasping at the bird's legs. It must have been wild because there was no chance Aran could have planned to be here. And he was meant to be uniquely gifted in taming and bonding animals. The question was, why tame this pigeon?

Lex dared to move closer, now with her whole body away from the tree that had just hidden her. The patter of rain concealed the sound of her movements.

Suddenly, Aran looked up in her direction.

She froze, like a wild animal spotted by a human, while the Chief Priest continued staring. But he wouldn't be able to see in this darkness. It wasn't as if she'd been foolish enough to conjure algor.

The man's stare continued for what felt like minutes, but eventually, he focused his attention back on the pigeon's legs. He was sending a message.

It could have been innocent. But there was no way Lex would take that chance. *Tiro. Climb. Be ready.* The falcon obeyed and took off to join the grey clouds eddying up high.

Meanwhile, Lex took a few steps to the side until once again concealed by the trees, except for her watching eyes. She waited. Usually, her attention focused only on her pain, and even now that pain was reduced, her mind still dwelled on the area, as if by reflex, and the attention only amplified her discomfort.

But finally, the Chief Priest finished and released the bird into the night sky.

Lex focused so hard it hurt her eyes.

Above, Tiro wheeled and had the pigeon in his sights.

As soon as Aran's focus had shifted back to the ground, she sent the command. *Get it!*

Tiro dove, and she could almost sense the air and rain pelting his feathers as he gained more pace than any predator that lived, a speed no pigeon could match. But catching prey was easy. Tiro's task was far more difficult. She didn't need to give the order not to kill because the falcon was well-rehearsed at intercepting. But even he wasn't infallible.

She closed her eyes as the falcon's claws reached and caught hold of the flapping prey. The pigeon struggled and writhed so much Tiro had to sink his talons deeper and still almost lost his grip. But he didn't, and while the Chief Priest made his way back to the others with the only light for miles in his hand, Lex waited.

A minute later, Tiro landed close by with the dazed pigeon underneath him. Lex rushed forward and covered the bird's head with part of her cloak while taking it in her hands, and when Tiro let go, the wet feathers smeared blood across Lex's hands. Daring to risk conjuring some algor, she took a closer look and cursed when she saw the left wing bent out of shape. Although she was no expert fancier, a child could have spotted it wouldn't fly again.

You failed. She pulled the note from the poor bird's leg, then placed it gently on the ground, still blinding it with her cloak. *Finish your supper.*

Tiro darted across and, this time, sank his claws and beak into the prey's neck, ending its struggles quickly. Meanwhile, Lex unravelled the note. It wasn't addressed to anyone and wasn't signed.

> *I trust this message finds you well, and I hope the war is treating you more kindly. If not, then take heart in this. I am where I set out to be, with the ones I sought, and I now see reason to believe my prophecy may become more than a desperate hope. These people I now enjoy the company of are weary but steadfast. I see their hunger, their pain. Liberation has been won with less, and I will do what I swore I would do.*

But do not forget my warnings. Do what I suggested at once,
or what will transpire will be worse than the alternative. Darius
is more bitter than I'd anticipated, and has worsened since one of
his companions has apparently been compromised. If he's to
prevail, it must happen at the Mount.

Lex read Darius's name thrice, each time with more algor to shed light, just to check she'd read correctly. *If Aran knows who Darius is, why not say anything?* It didn't sound like the Chief Priest opposed them, but he'd sought them out. What game was he playing? She was of two minds whether to tell Darius about this message or not. He might kill the man. And if not, he was hardly the best at keeping secrets. If Lex was to ever discover the Chief Priest's intentions, they ought to play ignorant for now. Plus, perhaps she owed the priest the benefit of the doubt after he'd healed her pain. After all, he was hardly friendly with the King and had no love of rakkans either.

With the pigeon dead and Aran's message never to find its home, the Chief Priest's warning would go unheeded. She'd have to confront him soon, but she'd give it a few days.

To ensure this wasn't lost should something happen to her, she needed to let someone know. But who? She preferred conversing with Brutus or Sulla, but one was dead, and the other was too rash to trust with something like this that required a considered approach. The last thing they needed was to upset the Chief Priest and the Diagathic Order. While the loosely organised group was without political power, many of the common folk—the life and blood of the Empire—followed its wise teachings.

That left only Hera and Varro as people she trusted to act wisely, and at the thought of the Black Warlord, old and bitter memories turned her stomach. It had taken so long for her romantic feelings for him to die, but they had.

Tiro hopped forward and gave her a violent nip on the thigh.

"Ouch," she whispered. "What was that for?"

The bird cocked his head at her, and she knew the answer immediately. She had far more important things to do than wallow in misery. Her pain had been a useful distraction from such things.

I'll send a message to Hera. Although Varro would probably still read it. *Tiro, I hope you had your fill. You've a long way to travel.*

39

Darius – Northwest of Dolthea

Darius awoke to the dawn sun blinding him through the trees, a thankful end to a night of disturbing dreams. He shifted his head into the shadows with a silent curse and looked over at Selene, who was still dozing. Was it fate's sense of irony that left her chained this time rather than him?

Lyra and the others rested close by as well, although he couldn't see them all. His relief at not having young ones to protect had been short-lived, and now he spent every waking moment grilling Selene in as gentle a way as possible. Days of talks had only convinced him further that she was still in there. Some signs of tampering were apparent, but they were more likely forgotten memories or the usual fogginess after living for so long under torture. Whatever the Magician had done, it was subtle and certainly not enough to let Lex take Selene to a prison without a fight.

If he could pinpoint exactly which memories seemed off, then he might get more of a clue as to what the Magician did and why. So far, her most suspect recollections were the ones where they'd been closest, those passionate nights, the times he'd saved her from death, when he'd first pronounced his love for her. Whenever she recalled them, there was no fondness or wistfulness in her expression like there had been before.

After mulling things inconclusively, he roused fully and woke the others to ensure they got a full day in Dolthea. Lex was already awake and didn't appear to have slept if the dark circles under her eyes were anything to go by. Nasrin, Gorgias and the Chief Priest fared better, and even Gorgias's whiteback badger came to join them in eating some nutritious roots for breakfast. At least the animal seemed to enjoy the food far more than Darius did. Perhaps he was fussy, but was it too much to ask to eat something that didn't taste of soil?

"W-we'll be in Dolthea in a few hours," Gorgias said, nervously stroking his escort.

It still puzzled Darius why Gorgias hadn't left with his friend and the youths, but he'd given up on asking the man. They needed the extra help, especially considering how dangerous Dolthea might be.

His thoughts reminded him of another fear. Walking into the town chained to Selene would only attract unwanted attention, and it might be best to stay outside the walls with her. Yet he couldn't stomach the thought of sending Lex in there alone. All he imagined was Viridian Legionnaires charging at her in too great a number for her to handle. Or worse, Lex suffering the same torture as Selene without him to fight for her. If anything happened, he'd never forgive himself.

"What will we do with Selene?" Darius asked. "I doubt she wants to go into a place teeming with rakkans."

Selene opened her mouth to argue, but Lex cut in. "You two are staying out here together. Nasrin and I will go in and ask if anyone has seen the Magician."

"Really?" The Chief Priest's face fell. "You two will split up? Surely it would be safest for both of you to come to Dolthea."

Lex narrowed her eyes at the strange man but said nothing.

"Are you that afraid of the Viridians?" Darius asked. "You're hardly a threat, and they'll never recognise you."

"They don't need many reasons to mistreat someone," Gorgias muttered. The welts and bruises on his face might have healed, but the fear clearly hadn't.

"Quite," the Chief Priest added. "Please come with me."

Darius would have thought his presence was more a risk than a benefit, but protecting Lex was the most important thing. Whenever he'd crossed paths with Viridians recently, they never recognised him anyway unless he revealed his unique blend of powers. He rarely left Viridians alive to describe him to others.

"I'm coming with you, Lex," he said. "You can't argue with a holy man."

Lex folded her arms. "I thought you said you could."

He smirked. "I've had a change of heart."

"Convenient… And what about Selene?"

From what he'd seen, her mind hadn't been altered enough to make her a flight risk, and he trusted her vow—although he'd never admit that to Lex.

"I'm not arguing." Darius stood and began fastening his sword belt. "I'm not letting you go alone. Gorgias and Lyra can look after Selene."

"M-me?" The Subdued paled. "What if she tries to escape?"

Darius eyed Selene's bow, which the algus had been carrying for the last few days. "Use it," he muttered. "In the *leg*, if you must. Then Lyra will make sure she doesn't evade us."

Selene shot him an ugly scowl, and he realised he should have made that remark in private.

Lex tightened the band holding her hair and took a few deep breaths as if ready to argue.

But before she could, Darius held out his hand. "The key…"

With a resigned sigh, she tossed him the key to the shackles, and he began searching for the most strongly rooted tree he could find. He spotted one with a thick trunk that would still allow Selene room to move, then stooped down to whisper in her angry, red ear.

"I'm sorry," he said. "I hope you understand why we had to do this once we've fixed you."

She huffed, making the same high-pitched noise she always had. But before, it had been playful rather than acidic.

"Do you want me to take you somewhere to relieve yourself before we go?" he asked.

The daggers shooting from her eyes gave her answer.

"Sorry," he repeated, and led her to the tree to secure her there.

While the others collected their belongings, he pulled Gorgias far aside and whispered forcefully to the man, "Protect her with your life and from herself if you must. The bow is a last resort, and if you need me, talk to Lyra."

Gorgias nodded in a weak fashion that gave Darius little confidence.

So he grabbed the man by the shoulders and shook him. "I'm trusting in you. Are you up to this?"

Gorgias's face brightened as if he'd been given a glowing compliment. "Yes, master."

"Hey. What did I—?"

"My apologies. Force of habit. With all the torture I went through, it's hard to—"

Darius lightly shoved him away. "Really? You already used your sob story this morning to get the last of my water. At least only use it once a day."

Gorgias grinned while Darius crouched and gave Lyra a rough scratch behind the ears. *Keep an eye on them both.* He sensed some nerves in her belly that his strokes to her neck eased a little, but then he realised it wasn't just fear for Selene and Gorgias. Their little flying friend had returned—the pteron.

"Darius? Are you ready?" Lex called.

"I…" He glanced up but couldn't spot the creature above. Perhaps he was taking too large a gamble, but if the pteron stayed near Lyra and Selene rather than follow him, his escort would know, and it might give him a clue as to what the reptile's purpose was.

"I'm ready," he called to Lex and made his way over.

The Chief Priest finished packing away his things, then he, Lex, Nasrin and Darius got underway and rejoined the road. After a few minutes, Lyra stopped sensing the pteron, and it wasn't long until Dolthea's wooden walls became visible at the end of the road.

The stained brown wood hung cracked and loose in places, as flimsy as Darius remembered and about as protective against rakkans as a wall of grass would have been. But it did ironically give the *Viridians* a helpful defence against algus and cavalry, and judging by the fresh scars on the wood, the rakkans had already put it to good use.

Now closer to the town, there were a few other people on the road for them to lose themselves amongst, and although Darius was dressed like a beggar, he looked like royalty compared to some people in their drab rags.

Dark figures patrolled the top of the gate, which now had a large sheet suspended overhead. Below, many rakkans leaned in the lines of shade and watched the people coming and going into the town.

"Stay close to me," Darius said, leading the way and pulling his thick cloak further around him to cover his weapons.

Lex hurried her pace to stride alongside him and said, "What have you been speaking with Selene about?"

"Just this and that, all our secret plans, Margalvia's weaknesses, the location of the mine… The usual things."

Lex's silence conveyed her displeasure at his sarcasm more than words ever could.

"She's been asking me things too," Darius said.

"About what we're up to?" Lex asked.

"Not so much. More about where I've been, from the human cities I visited to all the rakkan lands I stalked. I guess she wants to know how I was, questions I'd have expected Selene to ask."

Lex murmured to herself. Was there nothing that would give her peace of mind?

As they approached the town's gates, they joined another couple of travellers at the rear of the group and tried to mimic their laboured shuffling.

"Are you ready?" the Chief Priest asked, his usually cheery tone now drab.

Darius checked his sword was within easy reach under his cloak. "I am."

"Be careful of your supplies," Aran said. "Don't show the people you have food, or you'll attract thieves. My friends say the Viridians have taken a lot of the harvest back to Viridia."

At least it would make the townsfolk easier to bribe for information. This was the first time Darius had considered what he was about to see, a realisation that made him curse his self-absorption. Witnessing the scenes of Viridian savagery hadn't ended peacefully in the past, and that was before he'd seen the wounds on Selene's back. His infamous temper simmered under the surface.

"I thought you said the new rakkan in charge here was more lenient," Darius said.

"He is," the Chief Priest replied. "But a lenient oppressor is still an oppressor."

Darius would have to see for himself and decide whether it was best for the rakkan to continue breathing or not.

"Thank you for accompanying me here." The Chief Priest forced a smile. "You're welcome to join me for my first service this afternoon. I'll be…" Aran huddled close to everyone, whispering, "I'll be performing a bonding between a young algus and the animal she's chosen for her escort."

"We haven't the time," Lex said.

But Darius wasn't so quick to decline. He'd only heard of such bondings in stories and was curious to see one. Surely it couldn't take too long. Plus, it only just struck him that the Chief Priest might be the one person who could tell him why his connection to Lyra had been occasionally deeper lately.

Aran seemed to notice his interest, as the man's grey eyes bored into his.

"Where?" Darius asked.

"Under the surgeon's abode. Midday."

"I'll be there," Darius said, and immediately hushed as they approached the gate. The forest had been hacked to stumps around the walls, and hundreds of hoof- and footprints had long ago been baked into the soil. This wasn't the first time Darius had entered a town undercover, and nowadays, the prospect didn't faze him. But with Lex and Nasrin here for him to guard, he found his body grew sweatier by the second.

When they walked past the Viridian Legionnaires, the rakkans barely paid them attention and seemed more preoccupied with sheltering their bodies from the rising sun. Entering the town soon deepened the pit in Darius's stomach. Although under Viridian control, most of those wandering around were human. People hobbled or sat in the streets, baggy-eyed and skinny. Plenty of gore, both fresh and old, stained the road, and Darius couldn't help but hope he found an excuse to add rakkan blood to the blots during his visit.

The buildings themselves were mostly intact, having suffered from neither Viridia's eventual victory nor the counterattacks by the Torians and Xavalans. Once deeper into the town and away from most Viridian guards, the Chief Priest bade them farewell, then the others discussed where was best to begin asking around.

"I know the places Shirin would most likely come undercover," Nasrin said.

"I'd like to find out what the Viridians know too," Lex said. "If she's nearby, they'll know."

Darius grunted his approval. Interrogating rakkans sounded more like a job that suited him.

When the street they were in had quietened, Lex waved to a woman begging nearby. "You there. Want to earn a crest?"

Her two thin children nudged her forward as she shuffled closer, one hand shaking on her crooked walking stick.

"What can I do for you, travellers?" the woman asked with a hoarse voice that sounded riddled with sickness.

But regardless, Lex walked forwards and lowered her voice. "Who's the Viridian Commander here now?"

"His name's Rufus. He stays in the old town hall."

Did it really matter? Whatever the rakkan's name, it would be no tragedy if his neck happened to meet Darius's sword.

"Do many guards patrol these streets during the day?" Darius asked with a glance over his shoulder at a passing Viridian Legionnaire. Thankfully, the rakkan's eyes were half-shut.

"They come in groups," the woman croaked. "Seems to be at random times."

That was annoyingly unpredictable. "How many warriors are garrisoned here?"

"We're not here to fight," Lex hissed.

The woman frowned at the pair of them. "Are you here to liberate us?" Despite the hope the thought should have instilled, a horror came over her sagging face. "Please, not again." She grabbed his sleeve. "The Viridians leave us no choice but to work the fields. We don't want to give them our harvest, honestly."

"Relax." Darius took her hand and shifted his body so that it blocked her panicked face from the nearest rakkan's view. "We're not here to do anything. We're just looking for someone."

"You fear liberation?" Lex asked.

By now, a couple of other people had stopped to investigate them. Thankfully, Nasrin had enough wits to wander away and make their group less noticeable.

"How can we not fear?" the woman whispered. "The Xavalans… The Torians… They slaughter us in the fields to deprive the Viridians of slaves and have the gall to call it our liberation."

Darius grunted. "Yet they don't meet the rakkans in battle. Cowards."

Lex gave him a look of warning that he knew too well meant for him to seal his mouth. Lucky for her, he wasn't in one of his stubborn moods and would oblige.

"There's no one to save us." The woman's tone became more like a wail with every word. "No one has helped us since…" She pressed her lips shut and timidly looked down.

"Since what?" Lex asked.

The woman's voice dropped to a whisper. "Since…*he* saved us."

"Who?"

She leaned in closer to the pair of them. "Darius."

He had to suppress a nervous laugh.

"We never thought we'd pray for *his* return," she said. "That's how bad things have got."

Darius obeyed Lex's earlier hint and kept his mouth shut. Lex whispered some comforting words to the woman while handing her two crests and sending her on her way.

Only when they'd rejoined Nasrin and were walking deeper into the town did Lex speak quietly again. "Don't get big-headed."

Darius baulked. "I'm not. To be honest, I'd forgotten. I save so many towns these days, it's hard to remember—"

Lex batted his arm with a roll of her eyes, to which he snorted a laugh.

"You really think I'm that arrogant, don't you," he said. "You know I'm not being serious."

"It's hard to tell. And don't mistake Toria's ruthless tactics for cowardice. The King is no caitiff, and what he's doing makes sense while he's without the Staff of Arria. The Viridians haven't farmed for so long that they rely on the skills of these humans."

But that made the slaughter no less dishonourable and cowardly. Darius reached to his neck and touched his keepsakes there. The smooth stone of aeternus met his fingers first and reminded him that Brutus would have never resorted to such tactics.

"Sorry," Darius said. "Didn't realise you had such admiration for the King."

"Must you always be a sarcastic arse?" Lex snapped. "Just remember, we're here for information on the Waif Magician, or Hadrian, not to make our allegiances obvious to everyone, or to display more *heroics*."

He hated it when they had a disagreement and she ended it with a salient point. "That beggar seemed harmless enough."

"A mother is never harmless. She'd sell us out for a single meal for her children."

That was too true. Trusting in strangers, or in their good nature, was a sure road to catastrophe, especially when people found out he was far from a hero. He'd learnt that in this very town.

"Let's help Nasrin ask around," Lex said.

"Must I?" He'd discovered long ago that, when it came to speaking with people, he had about as much charisma as a rectal worm.

"Yes." Her tone meant she'd tired of him. "Don't be too obvious, and don't use your real name, even if you think they'll help you."

Darius cocked an eyebrow. "Do you really think I'm that brainless?"

Lex opened her mouth to reply, but he cut her off.

"That was a rhetorical question."

A trace of amusement flashed across her face before she walked away. It had been so long since he'd seen her with a pleasant expression that it stopped him in the middle of the street while she approached a vegetable seller who had set up a shabby stall at the side of the road. At least he could still brighten her mood as well as darken it. What he wouldn't give to see her smile again, even if it was to seduce some snot-nosed algus to get something she wanted. But these days, she didn't even grin for that.

As he moved towards another group to begin asking questions, a Viridian Legionnaire barged into his shoulder from behind and almost knocked him forward.

Damned cloak. It stopped him feeling others approach.

The legionnaire's head turned, and he glared through his visor's narrow slit.

Darius's heart picked up. A human would have fallen to that blow. He dropped his hand near his sword's cloaked hilt.

40

Darius – Dolthea

Darius tried to appear as fearful as he could while the Viridian Legionnaire fixated on him. Thankfully, the rakkan kept walking, without the brains to be suspicious.

Skulking around a nearby corner as quickly as he could, Darius checked for any other rakkans and breathed deeply. That had been too close.

For the rest of the morning, he set about wandering and talking to the odd person while ensuring he never ventured too far from Lex and Nasrin. They all made it into a large road with market sellers and their carts in a haphazard spread that seemed designed as a challenge to navigate. Barterers shouted out deals and made hand signals to one another while hagglers argued angrily over carrots and other vegetables. Meanwhile, a few Viridian Legionnaires, stalking around and surveying their subjects through dark helmets, reminded everyone who had authority here.

Darius made what hopefully seemed like idle chitchat with people to get titbits of information about the Viridian Warlord and any old red-haired women who might have visited the town, but he had little luck. The hours passed, and his head soon hurt from the noise and exertion. After another failed attempt with a young boy, he happened across a storefront displaying a surgical sign outside that had almost become lost within the carts.

He recalled the Chief Priest's invitation and concluded it would be a waste not to experience a bonding, given how rare they were. After all, when only one man in the Empire could bond a human to an animal, who *wouldn't* be interested? What was so special about Aran?

He spotted Lex's raven hair in the crowd and made his way back to her, just as she turned away from a red-faced seller with a scowl.

When she saw him, he murmured with frustration, "Any luck?"

"Nasrin hasn't gleaned anything, but I might have. Someone mentioned the Viridians moving large numbers of troops through here not long ago."

He cursed. "Why do I always arrive late?"

"Bad luck, *Saviour*."

He gave her a sarcastic smile. "Moving troops might not have anything to do with *her*, but perhaps we missed the 'Fire God' again. Let's get the sulphur and try searching outside the town."

"Not yet. We'll try to find the Viridian Commander here once Nasrin's finished."

It was no trouble for him to make a few rakkans talk, but first, it would be a wasted opportunity to not take the mysterious Chief Priest up on his invitation.

"Do you want to go to this bonding first?" Darius asked.

"No. We don't have time," she said, predictably.

"Why? How long does it take?" he asked.

"Usually half an hour or so."

Darius scoffed. "Is that so bad? Can't you just do this for me?"

"Why? Aren't you brave enough to go alone?"

"But… Not if it means leaving you."

A foreign look of bewilderment and nervousness came over the tough woman.

Darius continued, "And something about our new *friend* coming here with us felt a little convenient for him. Don't you want to check out what he's up to here?"

It took her a few seconds to respond. When she did, her voice was almost gentle. "Fine. But then we're heading straight to find the Viridian Commander."

"Since when do I need convincing to take on Viridians?"

She responded with a slight curl of her mouth, and they went to get Nasrin and headed towards the surgeon's abode. Despite the bustling street outside, the building was dead inside except for a gruff man at a desk, cleaning congealed gore from some saws and knives. The man didn't look up when Darius bashed the door shut behind them. The room was windowless and gloomy, with only a single clay lamp casting a yellow glow across the walls.

Darius cleared his throat, and when the man still didn't lift his head, he said, "We're here for it."

"What's 'it'?" The man breathed on the steel blade in his hand and polished it some more.

Darius wouldn't say anything explicitly, in case this wasn't the right place or there were Viridians and the Subdued eavesdropping. It wasn't a stretch to think the rakkan occupiers of the town wouldn't approve of algus gaining tamed beasts here.

"Aran said it was here," Darius said.

That name brought the man's rugged glare up. "Did he now…?" the man said.

Darius bashed his heel a couple of times on the wooden floor and heard the echo of a space below. This had to be the right place. "Yes."

The man grunted and put down his cloth but kept the dagger in his hand. "Password."

Why hadn't the Chief Priest warned them of such security? Or given them the password? Darius looked at Lex and Nasrin, but both shrugged and offered no further help. How could he prove they were invited? Showing the man he was an algus wouldn't help given how many Subdued the Viridians had, and fighting his way through would only draw unwanted attention to the building.

"We don't have a password," Darius said.

The man stood up from his chair and leaned forward, both fists pressed into the table. "Then push off."

Perhaps Lex had been right, and this was a waste of time. It certainly wasn't worth causing a fuss over. He cursed and turned to leave, but as he did, a door at the back creaked open, and a familiar voice said, "I knew you'd come."

Darius looked back to see Aran's head poking around the corner.

"Come in." The Chief Priest pulled the door open wider.

Obliging, Darius made sure to scowl at the man who had blocked his way. "You missed a spot on that knife."

He kept Lex and Nasrin close by and followed the Chief Priest into the room at the back, then to a trap door hidden underneath old crates.

"You'll need to be quiet down here," the Chief Priest said.

Like I needed telling… "Why does everyone think I'm a fool?"

"I guess you just have that look about you," Lex said as she disappeared into the basement.

Darius followed while murmuring curses to himself. Once below, there was little lighting again, but his rakkan eyesight gave him a view of the two haggard people watching, both wearing unblemished, white robes as pure as Aran's.

The Chief Priest's secrecy made sense of why so few had been invited, but why then were the three of *them* welcome?

"You didn't say there was a dress code," Darius whispered to the Chief Priest.

Aran smiled. "White is only for the pure. But you could have tidied yourself first…"

Lex and Nasrin kept close and led him to a vacant bench near the front. Ahead of them was an altar made of what seemed to be an ordinary stone dug up when excavating for the basement, but the otherwise grey surface was mottled with odd shades of purple and green. In front of the stone, a young woman sat with an adolescent tiger chained at her feet. As she moved, her braided hair rattled with decorative beads of gold and white, and the beast's fluffy striped fur showed the male hadn't reached maturity, like her. The chain around his neck was short and kept his fearsome jaws close to the ground. And with good reason, because every time the girl's hand went close, the beast bit at the air. *Cats…* It was a good thing she was an algus and could move with enough swiftness to evade it. For some reason, though, the beast was completely silent, not even emitting a soft growl.

After a few moments, the Chief Priest swept to the front, and everyone stood. In the silence that followed, Darius could feel the tiger's deep breaths, and it reminded him of when Lyra rested beside him. He reached out to her in his mind and was relieved to know Gorgias and Selene were both safe and discussing something.

When Darius's attention came back to the room, everyone was stood listening to the Chief Priest's whispers. Darius joined them and copied the ceremonial gestures and mutterings of those around him as best he could.

The service was too quiet for him to follow much, and most of the chants the man whispered were of poetic prose whose meaning eluded Darius. Despite being quiet, the tune was pleasant yet had a haunting harmony that unsettled him.

The chants seemed to go on and on, stealing not only time but also some of the heat from the room. But eventually, the Chief Priest motioned for the young woman to kneel beside the tiger.

As she did, Aran bent down and hovered his gloved hands above the pair's heads. "Do I have your permission to lay my hands on you?"

The girl nodded, and the Chief Priest slowly slipped off his gloves, then lowered his hands. At his first touch, Darius swore the soil beneath him inhaled while Lex and Nasrin froze in awe.

When the Chief Priest next spoke, his tone had become deep and authoritative, like the voice of law itself. "Do you reject the false gods of this world—the algus and all others who elevate themselves?"

"I do," the girl whispered.

"Do you swear to fight for the cause of Agathos, God of Justice, and recognise him as the only *true* king in this world?"

"I do," the girl whispered.

With tenets like that, it was no wonder the priest needed to travel in disguise. Darius guessed the tiger didn't get much say in these vows, but the cat was oddly at ease with Aran's touch, as if looking up to its master.

The Chief Priest continued. "And do you swear to be guided by Dianoia, Goddess of the Mind that binds you, to let her guide you in determining what is fair, right and just?"

"I do," the girl whispered.

The Chief Priest closed his eyes. "Then, by the gifts the Goddess has given me, I bind you." The last words bellied a quiet force that commanded the very air.

The girl gasped. Her spine went rigid. The tiger twitched as well and turned to her with wide eyes. At first, the girl's panting seemed to be caused by pain, but she smiled and closed her eyes as if savouring a feeling so joyful it lit the room around her. Soon, Darius couldn't tell what was real and what was in his imagination. One moment he saw a mist rise from the pair's bodies, but as soon as he blinked, the light cloud had vanished. The Chief Priest's eyes had paled to a shade of grey so light it was almost as if they'd rolled back in his head.

Was this how it had been for Darius and Lyra? Lex's look of wonder only deepened as if this was the most marvellous thing she'd ever seen.

"I thought you'd seen this before," Darius whispered in her ear.

"I have, but it's so…" Her voice trailed off as more breaths and gasps filled the room with the force and hush of the wind. And on it went, as he watched something he neither understood nor believed at times. Then, after what somehow seemed like both an age and a fleeting moment, the girl panted one last time, and the Chief Priest ripped his hands away.

Darius could have sworn a curtain of darkness fell over the basement. The tiger was now wide-eyed and alert, yet calm—tame, even. The girl ran her hand through his stripes, and this time, rather than try to bite off her fingers, he leaned his head towards her. While the two enjoyed their first moments connected, the Chief Priest slipped his gloves back on and released the chains holding down the tiger.

After a few chants of praise and blessings for the pair, Aran gave some lengthy final words of wisdom before the other two guests bowed and quietly filed out of the basement.

But Darius couldn't pull his gaze away from the girl and her once wild beast. The Chief Priest's gift was definitely real, and he claimed the Goddess had given it to him. Did that mean she existed and that her husband, the God, did as well? That unnerved him more than the thought of facing a legion of gomans.

Soon, the Chief Priest came over. "Are you all right?"

"How did you do that?" Darius whispered. He'd seen much he couldn't explain in the world, but this really puzzled him. "Did you make that tiger tame, or did the Goddess?"

"I didn't do anything to the tiger." The Chief Priest admired his work with a sigh of pride. "Their minds are linked, and now he no longer fears the girl or sees her as prey."

Maybe Lyra had once tried to sink her teeth into him. "I have a question for you," Darius said.

"I'm sure you do, but I'm afraid I must be rude and rush to another appointment. Perhaps we can meet up again later today?"

Darius wasn't sure whether he'd still be in this town, but this was a conversation he was loath to miss. "Very well. I'll find you."

"It would be best if *I* found *you*. Until then, I wish you luck on your search." The Chief Priest left the room, and soon after, so did Darius, Lex and Nasrin to rejoin the market street.

"What did it feel like for you," Darius asked Lex, "when you were bonded to Tiro?"

"I don't remember much about it. It's almost like being in a trance, a beautiful, wonderful dream."

It was a shame he had no memory of his bonding, and the longer he dwelled on the loss of that moment, the lower his mood sank.

Turning his mind back to the task at hand, he asked, "Shall I go to find this commander, then?"

"*We* shall," Lex said.

That was what he was afraid she'd say. But this wasn't a job for more than one person. "You need to get Nasrin somewhere safe. We can't bring her along, and we can't leave her roaming this town alone."

As much as Lex looked like she wanted to argue, it only took one glance at the sweet carer for her to nod. "You're right. But as soon as I get her to Gorgias, I'm coming back."

"I'd rather you left this to me."

"I'd rather you stopped treating me as a child. Just because Selene got captured doesn't mean I will."

The words stung him. Did Lex blame him for Selene's abduction?

Nasrin rolled her eyes. "It's a wonder you two get anything achieved at all. I don't know which of you is most stubborn."

"I'm not stubborn," Lex said without a hint of sarcasm. "I'm just decisive."

She was both. And it was one of the things he admired most about her, even though they were often butting heads. If anything, his own stubbornness had increased by having spent so much time with her.

"If I can't change your mind," he muttered, "just be careful."

Lex snorted with a shake of her head. "You don't need to keep worrying over me."

"Maybe not." *But I always do.*

He walked with them towards the exit to the town, past many Viridian Legionnaires that thankfully didn't see through his

387

disguise, and only once he'd seen the women walk through the gates did he turn and begin striding to the town hall, to the commander they'd called Rufus.

41

Sulla – Urukan Mine

The flaming pickaxe heads of the miners rose and fell on the rocks that had closed the mine's entrance years ago, pounding like blazing drums of war in the night. Sulla gripped the hilt of his sheathed sword to relieve some of the energy coursing through him while every algus and commander around joined him in watching. Finally, the time for battle had come. The Red Militia would avenge their defeat at Laltos, bolstering the unstoppable might of the Black Legion. And they'd avenge the Viridians' betrayal in the mine over a year ago, when Sulla's former Militia Chief had taken a mortal wound.

The old Gerundan entrance to the Urukan Mine had once been the largest way in—as tall as an ancient tree and as wide as dozens of Margalvian roads—although, without standing directly before the opening, it was hard to see amongst the loose boulders and overhanging rocks in this part of the brittle mountains. But now, the entrance was a pile of rubble, as if someone had crushed the peak above it, leaving only a black-faced crag and giant shards beneath.

Sulla remembered the day when all the rakkan legions had banded together to cave it in, the roar of thunder that had shaken the mountains and sent dust clouds to choke all those involved. With Gerunda in ruins, they hadn't risked leaving it for the humans to discover the way into their most valuable resource.

The miners had made it some yards in, but a few had already been crushed by collapsing boulders even a rakkan couldn't withstand.

Picks pounded continuously while rakkans at the front fired the rocks with ferven until they were glowing and weak. Stones fell and were quickly shovelled and hauled away. And awaiting a few yards back, rows upon rows of Black Legionnaires fed on the last of their rations, now only hungry for Viridian blood.

"Any word from the rearguard?" Warlord Varro asked Regent Hera.

"They see nothing unusual," she replied. "We only need to worry about what's ahead of us."

"Revenge," Sulla growled. Out of the many escort spies who had eventually gained access to the mines, only a few had returned. The escorts now with the algus near him had been the most successful, but the details they'd provided weren't close to what was required.

Not that it fazed Sulla. He'd have charged in blind.

The Warlord had prepared the men for any eventuality, as had Sulla. Relaying messages to the commanders throughout the maze of narrow tunnels would be impossible. Each centurion was responsible for his own century's actions once the battle was raging.

And that moment couldn't come soon enough.

"We're through!" one of the miners called from inside the new tunnel.

Sulla's muscles twitched, ready to charge. Not long after the first rakkan had shouted, what started as a small gap became a wide entry, short but large enough for ten legionnaires to march abreast, better than Sulla had hoped for.

"We're ready, Warlord," Commander Julius said.

Varro held out a hand and took his shield from his servant. "Give the order," he muttered.

Julius and Sulla ripped their swords from their scabbards and held them straight up, flaring ferven like beacons. The men knew what it meant—advance with haste.

The front line was already moving forward before Sulla dropped his arm. There were no roars as they set off, no yells to dampen the fear in their fellow men. The attack would be sudden and swift, and the Black Legion needed no aids to rouse the urge to fight. This brawl was long overdue.

Each unit set off with their centurion at the front. Commanders and algus mixed in with the most elite warriors that would head straight for the central veins of the mine, where they'd meet the fiercest resistance. As for Sulla and the Warlord, their group was the most battle-hardened and savage of the lot. They'd push straight towards the Viridian entrance to the mine. They'd cut off the retreat before most within the mine knew of the attack, and routed Viridians would find sharp kuraminium guarding their path home.

The line in front of them set off, and Sulla began pacing forward. Every thud of his boots brought more and more of the rush of battle to his limbs. It was almost serene. When survival was a man's only instinct, he never felt more alive.

They soon scratched their heads across the stones as they passed through the gap the miners had made. It went on for more yards than Sulla thought it would, but they finally emerged into the grand tunnel. Most of the rock inside glowed a dark blue from the low shimmers of algor that the algus used to find their way.

Enclosed on all sides and above, the walls made the *boom* of the march echo. They moved with haste, deeper into the mountain where the air tasted stale and thick, but eventually, the march slowed. The tunnels had begun to fork and narrow.

Varro watched with a grit and steel in his strides that gave Sulla chills. It had been too long since he'd seen the Warlord do what he did best—fight.

"The centuries are parting," Hera said. The woman was too short to see ahead of the mass of black helmets, but her escort hovered above.

Sulla's century veered down a tunnel to their right that led straight to the Viridian entrance, followed closely by Hera, the Warlord and his elites. This passage was narrower, forcing them to squeeze and rush with only three side by side. The algor from the algus chilled the tunnel and misted the wet air, and it took them almost an hour before Sulla heard the noise he'd longed for—the ring of steel and kuraminium. Not long after, the roars began. Red flames burst in front of them and sent a wave of heat that wafted Hera's hair beside him.

"No mercy!" Varro roared as he veered to an offshoot tunnel on his right. Sulla followed, the two heading the century behind, and soon the tunnel widened enough for them to swing a sword. And just in time, because their first victims came into view, a group of miners with a single Viridian Legionnaire to protect them.

The yells and screams of his men chanting "No mercy!" echoed all around them. With a roar, the Warlord flared ferven across his shield and gladius and crashed into the Viridian Legionnaire with a force that knocked the rakkan from his feet.

As he fell, Varro's gladius skewered his throat with a stab that retreated as swiftly as it had mortally wounded.

Sulla leapt over the fallen legionnaire and barged aside the miners into the black wall of the tunnel as he raced onwards. It wasn't long until the air shifted in the passage before him, rushing into his face and heralding the arrival of the enemy.

All he saw was a blind corner, but he carried on regardless while those around him slowed and raised their shields.

By the time Sulla reached the bend, a Viridian Legionnaire stood waiting and swung at his head. The gladius bounced off the visor of Sulla's helmet and knocked him with a force that brought bright spots to his vision. He dropped lower and to his side, partly from the blow, partly to angle his sword under the enemy's shield before stabbing the man's ankle right below the greave.

The legionnaire roared and thrust his shield into Sulla's head again, knocking the metal against his forehead and grazing it across the skin.

As Sulla reeled, a burst of cobalt-blue light flared and flashed before his vision with such speed he barely saw it. Blood suddenly gushed from the Viridian Legionnaire's neck while Hera bolted past him and stabbed a dagger into the back of the rakkan's spine for good measure. The icy fury in her grimace bore a pain Sulla understood all too well—vengeance.

As Sulla got back to his feet and rushed ahead with the century once more, a warm trickle came down his forehead and into his right eye, blinding it. *Damn it.* It never took much to open the weak scar tissue on his face.

A stink of sweat and burning blood now filled the narrow tunnel, and he almost choked as he coughed. Mines were hell enough without battling in them. But this was what his old Militia

Chief had gone through before the end. Sulla would finish what Claudius began.

Sparks suddenly sprayed in front of him as a wall of Viridian Legionnaires met Hera's furious blade. She stabbed one through the eye but hadn't the room to manoeuvre. Another scored a cut across her chest before Varro and Sulla arrived and charged shields-first at either side of her and knocked the rakkan away. Once she'd passed between them, Sulla and Varro came together and braced for the testudo ahead of them. The Black Legionnaires followed close behind and shoved them in the back as they'd been trained for thousands of hours to do.

The two shield walls collided, and suddenly Sulla's own strength wasn't enough to avoid the crush between the shields in front and behind. The blow would have forced the air from Sulla's chest had he not been wearing a cuirass, but he left the metal to do its work while slashing his gladius low at the boots of the Viridians. Every movement was like trying to swim in a sea of metal shards intent on crushing him, but he swung wherever his arm had room to move.

One Viridian in front faltered as Sulla's sword sliced off his toes, then Varro's gladius beside him found a narrow gap between the shields and struck the rakkan's throat.

More blood spilled and fizzed as it hit the scorching ferven on the shields, sending a sickening black steam that made Sulla retch.

He dug in his heels and shoved, feeling the Viridian line move back a fraction while spears glanced off his helmet. Then he heard the pounding.

Daring to raise his head above his shield, he looked beyond them in the tunnel and saw flaming pickaxes striking upwards into the roof.

"They're caving in the passage!" Sulla yelled at Varro.

But the Warlord didn't respond amidst the deafening roars and rings of hacking metal.

It was up to Sulla. They had to get through these men. With a curse, he began a flurry of strikes at the Viridians' legs again, mostly hitting their greaves or the bodies of his own men with his elbow as he tried. But he scored a few cuts, and suddenly the Viridian shield wall lurched backwards.

If it hadn't been for the men behind him, Sulla would have toppled over, but they shoved him forward with such momentum that his legs barely needed to take his weight.

The Viridians turned and fled as the Margalvian century roared "No mercy!" again and slashed at their backs.

The miners who had been trying to destroy the roof dropped their tools and retreated before the charging warriors. But as they did, another mass of metal and flame appeared in front of them.

A Black Centurion howled a war cry and charged head-on at the routed Viridians while Sulla and the Black Warlord charged from the opposite side. The Viridians stopped and braced, and a second later, a violent clap of thunder rang down the passages as both sides hammered their enemies, shoved with shields, stabbed their spears and gladii in a sea of sparks and flames and blood. When the last of the mauled Viridian resistance fell to the ground, Sulla stepped over the dead and patted the centurion on the back.

"Good timing," he said. "Now let's get to the Viridian entrance."

The band of warriors pressed onwards. Blades of gleaming algor soon flashed at the front as the algus rushed ahead and displayed their swiftness.

More Viridians came, and some tunnels had caved in entirely, but Varro had taken all the maps of the tunnels to memory. He ducked through offshoots, pointed at walls that they smashed through with ease into adjacent tunnels, and finally, they made it to a wider passage with a hint of daylight seeping through the thick air. And from the other side of the curtain of mist, more Viridian Legionnaires charged.

Varro and the rakkans raced forwards as the algus cut through their enemies, now with room to dance and strike with the ease of men training swordplay with novices.

The closer they got towards the Viridian entrance, the wider the tunnel became. When Sulla sensed they neared, he called out to the algus, and they dropped behind. The strongest and most ferocious of the Black Legionnaires formed their shield wall facing the road to Viridia with the Warlord not far behind. Then they spied the Viridian testudo outside, a wall of metal spiked with spears three ranks deep.

Sulla dropped to the back of the century, where all the Margalvian miners followed, then glanced up. This tunnel hadn't the height of the Gerundan passage, but its curved ceiling gave it a strength that would take them hours to weaken safely. But they faced greater casualties if they didn't block reinforcements.

"Ready your picks," Sulla called. "Militia, form a rearguard!"

The warriors nearby barged aside any Viridian miners trying to flee and formed a rear testudo facing back into the tunnels.

"Javelins!" the Warlord yelled at the front.

Those behind the front shield wall drew back their weapons and launched them into the Viridians outside. Most only crashed into their enemies' scuta, but a few found the gaps and speared the shoulders and necks of Viridians. The injured and dead fell away, leaving ever larger holes in the defence, but the Viridians broke into a charge.

"Swords!" the Warlord yelled when the impact was imminent.

Most of the men needed no instruction, gladii already unsheathed.

Sulla turned back to the miners. "Climb! Melt the rock as quickly as you can!"

The miners sprinted to the sides of the tunnel, flaring ferven across their hands and feet, and began clawing their way up the curved passage walls.

Despite being at the rear, the clash of shields at the front set Sulla's ears ringing again and was followed by yells and grunts. Sulla watched as yard after yard the Margalvians dug in their heels and pushed, with only dead and dying Viridians slowing them.

Brave miners now hung from the ceiling and used their ferven to drill their arms deep into the rock above. Lava dripped below them as a dark, blazing red spread from the miners like vines of fire creeping out across the top of the tunnel, just a hint of the heat and depth to which the ferven was penetrating. Sulla watched so intently he didn't blink. At the first sign the roof was coming down, he needed to give the order to retreat. Miners weren't unskilled, and the fewer that died, the better.

After a prolonged fight with each side slowly whittling away at the other, the Viridians at the front lost their nerve first and turned to flee. Varro's algus chased and cut some down easily but eventually fell back into a quieter tunnel. The panting and gasps of the tired and injured Margalvians filled the silence along with the odd grunt from the miners above, and finally, some fresh air wafted into the space from outside.

The Warlord strode back from the front line, the metal of his helmet, cuirass and sword dripping dirty blood that wasn't his own.

"How long?" Varro asked.

The rock above let out a deep-bellied moan.

"There's your answer," Sulla said. "Pull the century back inside."

"To the rearguard!" Varro ordered.

Those algus and centurions still fit enough fell back and organised their men to strengthen the shield wall facing into the mine. The line of defence stretched for the entire width and drove their shields deep into the rock.

Meanwhile, the injured Margalvians hobbled to a safe spot behind while others scrambled to stem ruptured legs, severed and broken limbs. Sulla did a quick count, and fewer than a quarter were either dead or injured—fewer than he'd expected.

A miner above yelled and dropped from the ceiling as a shard of rock gave way and speared down into the floor, the tip shattering on impact. The other miners hollered and let go at once while molten lava spilled from cracks and new fissures began opening.

"Come on!" Sulla yelled, waving for the miners to join him. But less than half fled in time.

42

Darius – Dolthea

It wasn't until twilight that Darius got his first glimpse of the commander, and the hours of waiting outside the old town hall had stiffened his back something fierce. *When did I start becoming an old man?*

He'd almost missed the rakkan walking in the street, given Rufus's lack of stature. The slender man's flat arms didn't look used to wielding a stick, let alone a sword—which was probably why he carried none—and only the bands of rank on his bicep convinced Darius that he was indeed the one in charge here.

But the two guards that walked with him were a different matter, two giant rakkans with shoulders so large they swallowed their necks.

Lex had met Lyra and Gorgias a while ago, so she must have been back in Dolthea by now. But he hadn't seen her, despite being vigilant. While watching, he'd spotted a crawlspace in a less busy side street that would allow him to sneak into the town hall.

His plan was to get in and make the commander talk by force—a simple task given the rakkan's size. What unnerved him, though, was the pteron; it had reappeared and now perched on a nearby rooftop with a placid indifference to the fact that Darius saw it.

He couldn't wait to get inside, alone with the commander, but it seemed fate had decided to vex him today—probably with a grin, considering how most people, including gods, hated him—because Rufus didn't enter the hall and instead walked down the road towards the northern gate of the town.

Darius followed the man and his guards at a safe distance, and thankfully there were enough vagabonds in the street for him to get close enough to eavesdrop without looking out of place. Given the evening was still young, there weren't enough legionnaires around to stop him should he have rushed in with a plan of force. There was definitely enough space in the wide road for the humans to flee and leave him room to use his sword. But who knew what repercussions that would have for the town.

"How many did the message request?" Rufus snapped in a harsh tone.

"Two centuries," a guard replied nervously.

"That's ridiculous. They're needed here."

"I don't think it was a request, Commander. The Warlord demands more men."

Was Hadrian planning another offensive? That would be most unlike him. All he seemed to care about recently was the Waif Magician.

"The Warlord doesn't know the full picture," Rufus said. "We lost almost an entire century in the last Torian raid."

"If you don't mind me saying, Commander, you didn't *have* to defend the slaves."

Rufus stopped walking and gaped at the man as if he'd been foolish enough to declare the sea was violet. As he did, his gaze met Darius's for the briefest of moments.

Darius quickly looked down, as any regular human would when faced with a hostile ruler.

When he lifted his head again, Rufus had turned without another word and continued marching towards the northern gate. The commander only stopped once the street had opened into a large square just before the north exit, a place where wagons and carts normally offloaded their products to the surrounding warehouses, but currently, there was barely a hoofprint in the dirt.

Rufus met with two centurions, and they grouped together at the centre, discussing something. There were fewer humans on this side of the town, and Darius was forced to divert his path to the edge of the square, behind some stacked crates outside a boarded-up building. He joined some other rough sleepers who were fashioning themselves a place for the night out of old sacks and planks, where the wind wouldn't chill them. None noticed him—or if they did, they didn't care. Judging by the stench of unwashed bodies and urine, Darius probably fit right in.

His position wasn't ideal—Rufus's stare as he conversed with his guards and centurions was levelled almost directly towards Darius—but he was hidden by the crates. The distance made it difficult to hear, but still, he only missed the odd sentence, given the quiet the commander seemed to have unwittingly imposed on every human nearby. The Viridians' conversation began with mundane matters, rotas and defences, but finally the topic turned back towards Hadrian.

"The Warlord probably doesn't realise," a centurion growled. "Food stocks are lower than he'd hoped. We need to save all rations for ourselves."

"And who will work the fields when the slaves starve?" Rufus asked.

Even Darius knew that was a rhetorical question best not answered, but the centurion did so anyway. "Slaves are expendable. I'll take my men and get some more, raid farther east."

Darius dared a glance around the side of the crate and took in the full sight of the brawny centurion bearing down on the slight commander, almost with a look of derision.

If Rufus was fazed by the rakkan's sneer, his calm expression did nothing to show it. He turned to one of the guards he'd been walking with before. "I think I've found a centurion I can spare to send on the Warlord's suicidal mission."

The brawny centurion scowled for a moment before his strained face became composed. "I would be honoured to serve my warlord. The Twelfth Century fear nothing."

Rufus narrowed his eyes. "Good. Give the Waif Magician my regards."

Darius almost gasped and lost his composure. What had that meant? Was Hadrian close to her? Did it mean the Viridian Warlord was close to Dolthea? Darius prayed so.

Given the brawny centurion's prior lack of composure, it was no surprise that fear quickly filled his expression. And the other Viridians noticed, chuckling to themselves while looking at their commander. Yet Rufus showed no trace of amusement. His scowl was tough and cruel, making it clear the edict was not a display of authority but of pure malice.

Although Darius hadn't thought much of the man before, he was now a little more hesitant. But he leaned forwards, eager not to miss whatever was said next. *Just mention the location.*

"I'll give you your orders before dawn," Rufus said. "Report to me then."

"Yes, Commander," the brawny centurion muttered before skulking away.

Darius shifted his body back behind the crates and out of sight. It wasn't what he'd hoped for, but it was better than nothing. All he had to do was grab this centurion after the meeting with Rufus and he'd have the time and place to find Hadrian and hopefully the Magician. Finally, fortune had favoured him.

After waiting a few moments for the centurion to build up some distance, Darius stood and moved to follow the rakkan.

But as he went around the crates, he was startled by Rufus, who didn't look in the least bit surprised when they almost bumped heads.

Darius staggered away until he was in the square, ensuring that his sword wasn't making a bulge under his cloak. "My apologies, Commander."

"Where are you from?" Rufus asked in a tone as sharp as his keen eyes.

"Sorry, I don't understand," Darius said. "Do you mean where was I born?"

The rakkan's eyes narrowed further. "I mean, where have you come from? You're too well fed to have been living here for long."

Darius wasn't exactly the largest man, but now that he recalled how feeble most of the humans appeared, he wished he'd realised how out of place he looked. "After the invasions, I fled to the forests and foraged there for a while."

"And why did you come here?"

In addition to the commander, his two giant guards, centurions, and at least a dozen legionnaires in the surrounding square were close enough to hear cries of pain should Darius use his sword. A few of them were even watching him with suspicion.

"I didn't come voluntarily," Darius said. "Some of your men found me, Commander."

"Interesting…" Rufus turned and made a gesture to a centurion.

Darius had no idea what it meant, but the centurion wasted no time hurrying away.

"You know, I never forget a face." Rufus turned back to Darius and began pacing like a cat around its prey. "I've never seen you here before."

Darius tried to turn his head to keep the rakkan in his vision at all times, and when he noticed Rufus paced in ever wider circles, he moved his hand closer to the hidden hilt of his sword. The commander had no weapon, either concealed or otherwise, as far as Darius could see. He didn't want a scene, or he risked losing what could be a lead on the Magician.

"I stay out of sight," Darius said. "If you'd like me to move somewhere else, I will."

"I do. We need strong men like you."

"For what?"

"To guard the fields during the day, when my legionnaires prefer to be out of the sun."

Would that involve whipping the humans that were slacking too? *Probably.* Was it best to feign an interest, as any starving vagabond would?

"We pay the most effective defenders well," Rufus added.

Darius raised an eyebrow. "You pay slaves?"

Throughout the conversation, Rufus's intense stare had focused on him like an archer's lining up a shot. Yet the rakkan's voice was still unthreatening and seemingly genuine when he said, "Yes, we pay. You'll eat and have lodgings."

It annoyed Darius that he couldn't find more things to hate in this rakkan. It would have made it that much easier when the time came to slay him.

"I'm sorry," Darius said, "but I wouldn't know how to fight. I'm a labourer." He bowed and turned to leave.

But Rufus called out behind him. "I'll pay you upfront."

Darius tried to make it look like he'd stopped, but every shuffle of his feet took him farther away from Rufus. With each passing moment, this conversation struck him as more bizarre and suspicious. "I'm sorry, Commander."

Rufus's eyes narrowed again, and it was only then that Darius realised the centurion behind the rakkan had returned, along with dozens of other legionnaires. They lined up, shields and spears ready.

"What is this?" Darius asked. It was a strange reaction to a suspicious beggar. Even if they suspected him of spying, they had no reason to fear a human. Unless they thought he was an algus.

"Here. Take your pay and go to work." Rufus fished a pouch of coins from his pocket and tossed it towards Darius.

It soared straight for his nose, and he had no option but to catch it to avoid a bash to his face. But as soon as he closed his fist, he felt the deception, the heaviness of the kuraminium coins inside. Gasping with the best false pain he could, he dropped the pouch. But it was too late. He'd betrayed his strength by halting it for just a heartbeat.

Rufus grimaced. "I knew I recognised your face. And only a rakkan would call me 'Commander,' Dreaded One."

Knowing the ruse was over, Darius released the cloak from his back and ripped his sword from its scabbard in one fluid movement. As he did, horns blared from multiple directions, as if they'd all been ready, waiting. The sounds were soon followed by the pounding of boots as legionnaires scrambled in the streets.

Keeping well clear of him, they flooded into the square and fanned out in a large semicircle.

"We're under attack!" a rakkan shouted before another blare of his horn.

Humans began charging out of buildings at the noise. Women grabbed teary-eyed children and ran towards the legionnaires while the men followed. They didn't dare go close enough to be within striking distance of the rakkans, but rather than flee, they huddled close by their occupiers, using whatever walls they could for added protection to their backs.

The behaviour shocked Darius more than the fact he'd been found out. He'd known they feared liberators, but to seek the protection of the Viridians…?

Around Darius, everyone left a wide, dirty space, and he now slowly spun and waited for any to make a move. The civilians close by the Viridians would make it that much harder to slaughter so many legionnaires, and his sword was only a short gladius. A longer spatha would have been more useful. But it wouldn't take him long to get one from a defeated enemy.

"What do you want?" Rufus strode out in front of his men.

Darius's first impressions of the man really had been wrong. He'd have bet anything that the rakkan would hide behind the shields of his warriors at the first hint of trouble, yet any man that met him face to face while knowing who he was earned his respect.

"I'm not here on behalf of Xavala or the King." Darius bellowed every word to reassure the humans.

Looking around, he searched for a suitable escape. A few of the roofs nearby would be easy enough to jump up to.

Many of the townsfolk began whispering to one another, and some spoke loudly enough for him to catch the gist of what they were saying.

"It's *him*."

"He's come to save us again."

Suddenly, the humans began edging away from the Viridians they'd once sought as protectors and instead huddled closer to Darius, although keeping at a small distance.

If only he *had* come to save them. But by the sound of it, they were all better off if he left these rakkans alive. This situation wasn't too dissimilar to when he'd slain Archimedes, which had left the west in the mess they now suffered.

Whatever the right thing to do was, Darius didn't know. He turned to face Rufus. "I want one thing. Give it to me, and I won't slaughter your men."

"Slaughter?" Rufus said. "You think you can kill so many?"

Darius shrugged. "I've overcome greater numbers."

The commander murmured to himself for a moment. "I think not. Testudo!"

Every rakkan around him lifted their scutum and pressed sideways into one another, forming long, tight shield walls with spears jutting in between. Behind the front ranks, rakkans lifted their shields to complete the defensive shell. It took the men only a few seconds to arrange themselves into uniform and strict regiments, and the front line stamped their tall shields into the ground, creating a shrill clap that made all the humans flinch.

"My men are well trained." Rufus still stood in front of his army's formidable wall of kuraminium. "They will not rush in to let you cut them down. They fight as one. Your speed will not be enough to overcome them. You've bitten off more than you can chew."

Darius shrugged. "I'm not worried. I'll spit you out after."

He was tempted to try just to prove the rakkan wrong. But this commander was far more cunning than most of the leaders Darius had happened across, and he'd only ever seen such discipline at the Battle of Laltos. Had Viridia's successful tactics been down to this man rather than Hadrian?

Rufus raised his hands. "I suggest you surrender or flee. You're alone against many."

"He is *not* alone!" a woman cried behind him.

Darius turned, expecting to see Lex, but instead, it was the girl and her young tiger escort from the ceremony, beads still swaying in her hair. She had a steel sword in her hand and a face as ferocious as her tiger's, but she had no armour, and judging by the way she gripped her sword, she was a stranger to it.

"Don't get involved," Darius barked.

But the girl ignored him. "I stand with the Saviour of Dolthea."

More nicknames? He was losing count of them now. And this one didn't even make any sense. If he'd saved Dolthea, the town wouldn't be occupied by rakkans.

"As do I!" This shout was an unmistakable, commanding blare. From within the crowd, Lex emerged, armoured with scaled sleeves and ready for a battle.

"You're still outmatched," Rufus said. This time, he backed up to the shield wall of his men.

Darius's safest option was to flee, and it wouldn't be difficult. But he had an idea. He waited for Lex to join him while studying the testudo in front of him. One of the legionnaires on the right flank held his scutum too high and left his leg exposed, and the rakkan next to him had his spear extended further than the others. It was the weakest point of the line, ripe for attack.

Lex walked up behind him with fury in her breaths. "If it's come to this, we should slaughter them all."

"This isn't what we're here to do. *You* said that, remember?"

"I've had a change of heart."

He leaned closer to her and dropped his voice. "I have an idea. The commander mentioned a message they've had from Hadrian. I can keep them busy here while you look for it in the town hall."

She scowled. "I can't—"

"They mentioned the Magician."

Her scowl faltered. "You're sure?"

"Yes."

"All right." It took a few seconds for her to turn her lethal glower away from the rakkans and disappear through the cowering humans.

Once she was gone, Darius called over to the girl with the new escort. "Hey, Tigress."

She turned with a steely determination in her stance that was brave but amateur.

"Don't follow me," he warned before taking a deep breath and turning to face the shield wall head-on.

43

Darius – Dolthea

When Darius stepped towards his enemies, a few flinched despite being at a safe distance. Each stride he took was careful, finely balanced so that he was ready to dodge should the Viridians begin launching javelins at him. But most of the warriors behind the shield wall stood like grunting statues. Only a couple moved, turning to gaze at their commander. *Must be fresh recruits.* Veterans didn't need to look.

The air in the town hardly stirred, and every nervous twitch from the surrounding people sent waves to the skin on Darius's bare arms. He was ready for whatever came.

Rufus did nothing but watch each step Darius took closer, with an intense and unnervingly wise stare. Only when Darius was within a few yards did Rufus speak. "Ready!"

A row of legionnaires behind the front line lowered their shields and hoisted their javelins over their shoulders. As they did, Darius felt the shifting air as the humans there finally realised they weren't safe. They instead shuffled into the street to his left, gaping like spectators at the gladiators' arena. Now all that stood behind him in the square was the wooden wall of a single-storey warehouse. With his rakkan jumping ability, it wouldn't be hard to climb.

Scanning the tight formation of his enemies, Darius saw a few options for engaging them, but it would be a lot easier if he had some projectiles of his own. So he opened his arms wide, inviting the Viridians. "What are you waiting for? I'm right here."

Most of the warriors looked at their leader, who merely stood in a measured and piercing silence.

Darius would have to force some action. He bent his knees and prepared to sprint, bouncing up and down lightly, tightening his grip on his sword, using his keen rakkan sight to study the eyes of each Viridian on the front line, searching for the rakkan with the most fear in his gaze. And he found a man looking twice at his commander within only a few seconds, about a third of the way to the left, at an angle sharp enough that he could evade the thrusting spears more easily.

He paused a few more moments, letting the dread and anticipation cloud his enemies' minds, tighten their muscles. One man couldn't defeat such a close formation with skill alone. But fear? That could defeat an entire legion. And at the right moment, he pounced.

With a sudden burst of speed, he surged towards the shield wall. The fearful rakkan he targeted flinched as he neared but held his nerve. All the defensive spearmen moved and tried to angle their weapons towards him and score flesh, but they hadn't the time or space behind their shields to turn far enough. He batted three spears away with his sword as soon as in range, let another two spearheads glance from his cuirass, then kicked at the shield of the rakkan he'd set his sights on.

His blow landed like a charging bull crashing into a metal fence, sending a ripple out and behind the rakkan that only shook his enemies. Sensing the solid defence as his kick landed, he pushed off and leapt back to a distance safe from their spears less than a heartbeat later, eyes already scanning the testudo for his next target.

A few of the Viridians shuddered like bells after a hammer strike, but he hadn't weakened the kuraminium façade one bit. These men were far better trained than most Darius had faced. Maybe they'd even force him to break a sweat.

He rushed in again with another angular attack that had spears bouncing off his armour before his boot collided with the shield of another rakkan. The legionnaire's knees buckled as Darius thrust himself away again with a fiery snarl that none dared return. Even Rufus stood watching, unmoved, as if studying for an opportunity to counterattack, waiting for the moment of Darius's weakness or mistake. Men always thought you had to rush to win a fight, but this commander obviously knew better. Unfortunately for him, Darius wasn't foolish enough to tire himself out.

The last of the day's light faded and cast a deep shadow across the square, broken only by the odd lamp the humans lit on Darius's flank. It was enough to see the sweat dripping from the arms of those rakkans ready to toss their weapons.

Without giving his enemies time to steel their nerves, he darted in again, this time at the opposite side of the shield wall, to the one spear he'd spotted protruding too far. He raced across the front rank, dodging as the spears thrust out but too slowly to take him by surprise. When he reached his target, he dropped and skidded along the road, under spears as they flew down at him without the strength to do more than glance off his shoulders. He reached and grabbed the farthest-reaching spear, dug in with his heels and surged back away from the shield wall, bringing the weapon and the rakkan behind it flying forward. The legionnaire tumbled and yielded the spear as Darius once again got to a safe distance, this time with a weapon long enough to threaten the lives of the men.

"Now!" Rufus yelled.

Before Darius saw anything, his skin sensed dozens of javelins launching towards him. He dropped his spear and dove to the side head-first, leaping out of the path of the incoming wave before they crashed into the road with a loud clang of metal and speared dirt.

He landed on his stomach, skidding along the street before rolling and getting back to his feet. His trousers had torn and left a scratch on his right knee. In the square, dozens of javelins either lay or stood skewered in the road, clustered together so closely they could only have come from warriors with formidable accuracy. He had to be swift.

With a rush of speed, he darted towards the javelins. Rufus barked more orders too late, and Darius already had two projectiles in hand when the shield wall lurched forward and began to charge.

Darius tossed a javelin at the commander, but the rakkan merely dodged to the side. Darius's next throw was aimed at the legionnaire straight in front of him, too covered by armour and shields to sense the air, and he scored a blow straight through the eye-socket of the rakkan's helmet.

Now only a few yards from the tide, Darius turned and bolted towards the building behind him. The humans screamed. More javelins came at him and forced him to dodge to his side but hadn't the accuracy of the well-measured earlier throws.

A few speared deep into the wooden wall, and when he reached them, he leapt and bounced from them, as agile as a squirrel, and was up on the roof within moments. The shield wall of the charging legionnaires crashed into the building while those behind raised their spears and glared at him above. They were at least five ranks deep, and those at the rear lacked shields, ripe for an attack.

But Darius saw the obvious trap. Another two lines of warriors had stayed with Rufus and made a second shield wall. If he leapt to the area behind the advanced group, he'd be sandwiched and crushed.

"Bring the building down!" Rufus yelled.

Darius's heart pounded, impressed and fearful for the first time. Lex had better hurry.

A crash boomed from below, and the whole warehouse lurched, almost knocking Darius off-balance. After regaining his footing, he sprinted to his right, readied his gladius and leapt from the side of the building, at the flank of the attackers.

By the time the Viridians turned to face him, he'd already landed and sunk his gladius into the thigh of one, soaking himself in enough blood to know he'd hit a major vein. With his other hand, he grabbed the roaring legionnaire's shield and ripped it away. Gore continued splattering over him, and he blocked two spears with the scutum a second later.

Swinging his gladius low, he scored the legs of two more and stabbed into the groin of another who rushed in. Sword and arm now red and hot, he pulled back and readied for the next attackers.

But instead of rushing forward in a battle rage, the Viridians fell back and formed a shield wall again, spears ready. They panted and wheezed with fiery breaths under their heavy armour, and Darius saw he could keep this up for far longer than they could.

"Must we do this?" Rufus yelled.

Darius glanced at the rakkan as he stepped forward, albeit still at a distance where Darius couldn't threaten him.

"Are you ready to surrender?" Darius called mockingly.

To his surprise, the remark stirred no anger or change in the commander's demeanour. He merely paused before shouting, "How about we parley? It would be a shame for all these poor men, women and children to suffer for your foolhardiness." He waved his hand at the humans still watching in the dim light. The Tigress stood tall and defiant at the head of the group but wouldn't be able to protect the people.

Perhaps Darius should have fled when he'd had the chance, when the commander hadn't used the blood of bystanders to threaten him. Now his options seemed limited. But at worst, a parley would buy Lex more time.

"Very well," Darius called out to Rufus. "But you must meet me alone."

The legionnaires closest to Darius backed up slowly to rejoin the others while the commander had a discussion with his centurions. After a few heated moments, Rufus began walking forward alone.

As feeble as the rakkan looked, he was braver than most Darius had happened across. Darius followed the commander's lead, and every Viridian Legionnaire behind the front line of the shield wall readied their javelin and prepared to skewer him. He prayed Rufus was more honourable than his warlord.

The pair met in the middle of the bloody square, a couple of yards from each other, close enough for Darius to suppose they wouldn't risk tossing a weapon into their own man. While he pondered, Darius surveyed the red at his feet. Compared to what he'd spilt in the past, it was but a drop.

"Why are you here?" the commander asked.

It was hard for Darius to think of an answer other than the truth. The only other reason to be here would be to drive the Viridians out, but then it made no sense for him to come alone. This commander was far too sharp to believe such a lie, and the longer he dwelled on the rakkan's question, the less reason he saw to hide his real motives. The Viridians were already searching for the same woman, so they'd hardly alter their plans upon the revelation of his quest.

When Darius answered, he kept his voice low enough that none would overhear. "I want the location of the Waif Magician."

Rufus's eyebrows lifted, the first sign of surprise the commander had shown all evening. "Ah. And here I thought you were going to demand I leave this town."

"Well, maybe we'll get on to that."

"And why do you want to know about the Magician?"

"Don't pretend like you don't know. Will you tell me willingly or not?"

"What makes you think I know where she is?"

Darius growled under his breath. "Spare me the lies."

"Even *if* I knew, you realise that telling you that would be my own death sentence?"

Darius shrugged and kept his voice low. "Who will know it was you? Tell me, we'll fight a bit more for appearances, then I'll flee the town, and you can claim a victory over the Dreaded One."

Rufus paused and stared into his eyes for a few moments. When smart men did that to Darius, he was always unnerved, as though they saw things about him that even he hadn't realised.

"You're nothing like I imagined you'd be," Rufus said. "I've only ever seen you in battle before."

"Yes; I'm a unique guy, charming and cuddly when you get to know me. Now, will you tell me freely, or do I need to make you bleed first?"

As Darius had now come to expect, Rufus was unmoved by the threat, or else masked any nerves well. "If I bleed, so will all these humans. The choice is yours."

Darius thrust out his blade with a burst of speed and stopped it only when the point pricked the rakkan's neck. All the legionnaires drew back their spears with curses.

"You'd be the first to die," Darius said. "What's your life worth to you?"

Rufus glanced down at the blade without a trace of nervousness. It was enough to make Darius's stomach drop.

"You'd violate a parley?" Rufus asked.

As much as Darius wished running the man through would prevent a slaughter, it wouldn't. He lowered his blade with a grunt of frustration and threw a quick glance back to see if Lex had reappeared. But she hadn't.

"It seems we're at an impasse," Rufus said. "If you will not surrender, then we have no option but to fight."

The last thing Darius wanted was the blood of all these humans on his hands. The longer he looked at the disciplined legionnaires, the more he knew he wouldn't be able to stop them all. But there was one detail he couldn't yet fathom; the commander hadn't taken a sword or shield, even when the fight had broken out. Even if the man wasn't used to weapons or preferred not to use them, he'd still hold *something* if he were seriously contemplating a battle. Rufus had been the one to call a parley, and he was smart enough to know that if he ordered a bloody slaughter of this town, Darius's fury would be directed squarely at *him*. Either Rufus was willing to simply roll over and die, or he was bluffing.

417

Well… Two can bluff. Darius glared at Rufus and let the ferven rage in his eyes. "A fight it is, then."

The commander's only reaction to the words was a bulge in the veins in his neck.

That was all Darius needed to up the stakes. "I've changed my mind. I'll be sure to take you alive. Can't have my lead on the Magician dying on me too quickly."

Rufus studied him for a few more moments before he grimaced with a curse that revealed his real mood for the first time. "I hate it here, and I resent ever being sent. I could fight you, and perhaps I would triumph. But what do I gain from it? A dying town that kills more of my men than it feeds. But maybe I could do it purely for the glory..."

"You don't strike me as a man who craves reputation."

"Reputation, perhaps not. But do not think me unambitious or benign, Dreaded One. The most dangerous people in this world never wield a sword."

That was true of many, and Darius thought them all the more cowardly for it. Yet he'd never say that of this rakkan.

"They may not wield a sword," Darius said, "but when I'm finished, they'll die by one."

"And for those enemies we have in common, I wish you every success."

"Well, first on the list is your warlord. Do I still have your best wishes?"

As unexpected as the evening had been so far, nothing surprised Darius as much as the slight grin his sarcastic words brought to the rakkan's face.

"I have a proposal," Rufus said. "I have no wish to lose more of my men in this town—they'll be needed for much greater battles when the time comes. And I doubt you'd like to see the slaughter of these women and children. So I propose a mutually beneficial arrangement whereby we can part ways, both saving face from any reputational damage and minimising our losses."

Darius frowned at the man for a few moments. "Those are a lot of fancy words to say 'I surrender.'"

Rufus shook his head. "This is no surrender. I'll leave this town peacefully."

That wasn't a lead on the Magician, but Darius doubted he'd get a better offer. "What's the catch?"

"We'll obviously need to take the food with us, but the people will still have the fields."

"And you won't return?"

"No. This town is only a weight around my neck."

At least the people would have their homes back, and Darius could track this commander and his men to get information from them at a later date. Or perhaps Lex had already found the message the Viridians had mentioned.

"You can take half the food and not a grain more," Darius said. "You have an hour to leave before my sword gets bloodier."

The veins in Rufus's neck bulged all the more as he glared, but finally, he sighed and said, "I'll have my men collect the grain, and we'll take our possessions from our—"

"No." Darius flared algor in his cold eyes. "Take the grain from the granary. Everywhere else in this town is no longer your jurisdiction." That would buy Lex more time if she needed it.

Rufus's eyes narrowed, but after a long pause, he nodded with a slight grimace. "Very well."

The commander had agreed to that too quickly. *I've blundered somehow.* If only Darius knew what the commander was really gaining from this.

After those words, the two parted, and Darius was relieved to see Lex emerge from the crowd when he rejoined the humans.

A few of the other townsfolk came and huddled around him, but none he recognised besides the Tigress.

"They don't want a fight," Darius said, loud enough for everyone to hear. "I agreed to let them take half the food stores if they go peacefully."

"But the harvest is almost over!" someone shouted behind them. A gaunt man stepped forward from what seemed to be his family and brought all the townsfolk into the conversation with him. "We won't have enough this winter. Why can't you just slay them all?"

It took Darius a few moments to take in what the ungrateful man had said, but when he did, algor flared from him once more. "I'm one man. Not a god."

"Just a man who slays gods…"

Darius opened his mouth to give the gaunt man an earful, but Lex grabbed his arm and pulled him down to whisper in his ear, "I found the message. The Viridians are sending men to the Cliffs. She's there."

All his irritation fled in an instant, and he turned to her to see the same fierce satisfaction that rose inside him. "You're sure?"

Lex nodded, but with a firm determination on her face.

The Magician must have moved on after tampering with Selene. As he was about to reply, someone grabbed his other arm and tugged, saying, "Hey, Saviour?"

He swung around, ready to bark a reprimand at them, but saw it was the Tigress looking up at him timidly.

"What?" he asked.

"The people are worried." She turned her attention to the shivering humans around, all too thin to survive a stiff breeze, never mind a cold winter. "We won't have enough food if the Viridians take half."

Darius murmured, "What can I do? You heard them threaten all your lives. Do you want to fight? Because it won't be my blood that waters the weeds on Dolthea's roads if we do."

"I…" The Tigress's voice faltered as if her age and wisdom still had a way to go to catch up to her bravery.

Thankfully, Lex stepped forward and raised her voice to the crowd. "Those who are strong enough will have to leave. There are villages to the north that the rakkans haven't claimed."

"But the Xavalans still raid there!" a man shouted from the back.

Even Lex lost the words she'd been about to say.

"You could go to Margalvia," Darius muttered.

The mere utterance of the city's name brought a horror to the people's faces that the Viridians hadn't evoked.

"Or not," Darius said.

"What if we come with you?" the Tigress said. "We can march with you to somewhere safe."

Darius exchanged a glance with Lex and knew from her expression that they weren't heading anywhere "safe."

"I'm afraid I can't," Darius said.

"But…" the Tigress said. "Then we'll follow you anyway. We'll assist the Saviour of Dolthea wherever he goes."

And what? Have hundreds of hungry people to look after and die, just like those children? There's no way he could focus on what needed to be done with that kind of responsibility.

Lex cleared her throat. "We could travel—"

"No," Darius said, surveying every person so they'd know he spoke to all of them. "You will not be safe. You will not be comfortable. You will not survive. Where I must go now is no place for civilians."

The Tigress's face twisted as if he'd stabbed her in the gut. "But you're the Saviour—"

421

"I'm the saviour of no one!" Now, ferven blazed from his eyes and cast hot rays over the people that had them squinting and backing away. "I'm one man, a warrior with no home and fewer allies than I can count on one hand. I couldn't save the woman I loved. I couldn't save my adopted father. I couldn't save all the children that I've had in my ward. I cannot be what you hold me to be!" His hand shook, and he squeezed his sword more tightly to abate the tremors.

The people's expressions became ugly, loathsome, disappointed. Even Lex frowned at him with her nose turned up. Should he have fought Rufus to keep more of the food stores? Perhaps Lex would have negotiated better. She was more suited to being a leader than him, and a smarter man would have waited for her to discuss the terms of the Viridian withdrawal.

But he'd done his best and would have battled if it might have helped these people. It wouldn't have, though. And they were wrong to praise *his* name when it hadn't been him who saved this town last year. Many algus had fought, led by Selene. All he'd done was reveal he'd been lying to them for weeks. Selene had been the real saviour, yet to see her now…

"Do not harass this man," someone called from the back of the crowd, a voice Darius only recognised when the man spoke again. "You do not know how close you just came to a massacre. This half-rakkan saved you."

The crowd parted, and the Chief Priest strode through its midst, now dressed in clean pearl robes that set his skin aglow in the evening. He stood beside Darius's bloody figure without an ounce of hesitation.

"He is no god," the Chief Priest continued, "not even a slayer of gods. He cannot protect so many of you, yet he has delivered you from your occupation in a way your wicked Torian overseers haven't."

As soon as the man began speaking, the crowd's anger dampened.

"How many stories of Viridian surrender have you heard told?" the Chief Priest continued. "Any? None? It shouldn't come as a surprise because it seldom happens, let alone without bloodshed. Accept your deliverance. Violence is not the answer."

The people looked from the Chief Priest to Darius, only this time, the anger and dissatisfaction on their faces had been replaced with shame.

Darius marvelled at how a man had changed their attitudes so swiftly with only words. But that wasn't the only thing that dwelled on Darius's mind. Aran was acting as if the revelation of Darius's true identity came as no more of a shock than finding a twig in the woods.

The Chief Priest smiled at him. "I told you I'd find you."

A shift in the air above caught Darius's attention, and he looked up as a pteron dove towards them without showing a hint of slowing down. But as Darius held his sword ready to defend against whatever it was attempting, the pteron veered away from him and instead landed on the Chief Priest's shoulder.

Aran gave it a quick stroke.

"That's yours?" Darius asked.

"Indeed." The Chief Priest smiled as if he didn't see the ferven escalating in Darius's glower.

44

Darius – Dolthea

Of course Aran had an escort. Darius was a fool for not realising it sooner. Why wouldn't the only man who could bond animals do it for himself? But still…why have the pteron follow him?

"Don't you dare move." Darius had many questions of this man, but first, he turned to the Tigress. "Keep an eye on the Viridians for me and let me know if they try anything."

The girl hurried away without hesitation while Darius and Lex squared up to Aran from opposite sides.

"Look who's popular." The Chief Priest grinned. "I have to say I'm pleasantly surprised at what you've achieved here without innocent bloodshed."

But the man's amusement vanished when Darius grabbed his arm, smearing his pristine robes with gore, and began tugging him away from the townsfolk.

"You mustn't touch me!" the Chief Priest said with an uncharacteristic fear in his pitch. Darius ignored the man and led him into one of the buildings that had been abandoned earlier. As the Chief Priest's pteron flapped away from his shoulder and returned to the sky, Darius pushed the man inside a small kitchen with Lex following.

He closed the door carefully while Lex strode closer to the Chief Priest and forced him to back up into a table to evade the point of her blade.

"You've not been truthful with us," she said.

"I resent your accusation." The flustered look of annoyance on the Chief Priest's face seemed genuine as he readjusted his gloves. "I've answered every question you asked truthfully."

"And what about those we didn't ask?"

"What? You expect me to guess?"

"Don't play the fool because you're anything but. You've known who Darius was all along."

"But of course," the Chief Priest said. "My memory may not be what it once was, but it's hard to forget such a bonding. Darius and Lyra were a well-matched pair, and it caused me considerable distress to see her so injured last year."

Darius growled under his breath. "And you neglected to mention then that you knew who I was or that your pteron has been following me for months."

Lex blinked in surprise. "It has?"

"Was it important?" Aran's face flushed.

"When I'm the most hunted man in the Empire?" Darius said. "I'd say so."

"*I* do not hunt you."

Darius baulked. "So why was your pteron following me? And how the *hell* did you know to use a pteron?"

The Chief Priest winced and looked down, shamefully. "Hell… You shouldn't speak of such a ghastly place without fear, and if you aren't careful, you'll learn that only after the God of

Justice's axe has fallen. And I fear the place as well because I have done a heinous thing to you that I swore I never would do to anyone. I saw no other way, but that doesn't mean there was none, or that my actions are forgivable."

A sinking dread and anger churned in Darius's stomach. "What did you do to me?" Was this something to do with Lyra sensing the escort?

"I spied on you," the Chief Priest said with almost a howl of shame. "I used my powers to bond an escort and intrude on you in a way that no one should. You're an important man, and I used my pteron to guide you where I wanted you to go, to rejoin Selene, to attack the party intent on raiding Foltara, and so that you could bring me here. What you did here today is only the beginning of what you're capable of, but many paths lie before you. As long as I care about any of the people in this world, I must do all I can to help you. You're unique."

The man was too flattering to be truthful, although his pteron had never done anything other than observe.

"I don't buy it." Lex angled her dagger upwards into the man's chin. "What are you really after?"

The Chief Priest swallowed. "There's no need for that."

"Easy, Lex." Darius came forward and gently pulled her arm away from the leader of her religion. There would be time for punishment once they knew the truth.

"Why didn't you just say you knew who he was?" Lex asked in a tense voice.

"You wouldn't have accompanied me, and I knew it was vital to get Darius here. The people needed a savio—"

"Don't say it," Darius growled.

"Why? Why do you hate praise or reverence so much?"

It was a question he'd rarely considered, but the inflexion in the man's voice made Darius suspect the Chief Priest thought *he* already knew the answer.

"You tell me," Darius said.

"You don't think you're worthy."

That was definitely part of it, but it was also the unwanted attention such accolades drew to him and how others relied on him in a way that only ever led to their suffering.

"But do you know what?" The Chief Priest came forward, his eyes serious and unblinking.

"What?" Darius said. "I'm wrong? That by thinking I'm unworthy it shows how worthy I am?"

"No. You're right. You're not worthy."

Darius snorted a laugh. "At least you're being honest now."

"*None* of us are worthy. Only the God and Goddess are worthy of such praise."

"Are they?" Lex's face twitched nervously. "Those that leave so many people to face slaughter and injustice deserve applause?"

She had a point, and judging by the Chief Priest's lowered head, even he knew it.

"Your charge is a fair one," Aran said. "They could intervene, and they do not. But do you know why?"

Lex scoffed. "They don't care?"

"No. They most certainly do, or they would not have created us to care also. No, they do not intervene because they will not take away our freedom to choose. They do not want a world of Numbered that obey their commands. They want a world of free people."

"Why?" Darius asked, a genuine question whose answer he couldn't fathom.

"Because without freedom, there can be no love. And what greater good is there?"

The words made Darius consider things he never had before, and the longer he did, the more he sensed a ring of truth. He'd give up anything—his powers, his strength or even his life—for the sake of Lyra, or Lex, or Selene.

The Chief Priest spoke again with a new firmness directed at Darius. "And some are called to use their freedom to lead, to end tyranny. I may have defended you out there, but those people are right in one thing—they need you."

Lex's expression had softened at the Chief Priest's words, but soon her scowl returned. "Stop distracting us from your conniving. Who were you informing of Darius's situation?"

Darius started. "What are you talking about?"

However, the Chief Priest showed no surprise. "Ah. So it's *your* fault my message never made it. I was conversing with a friend in Menara. I'd told him that he should expect Darius to return to the town soon."

"He should?" Lex asked.

"Return?" Darius added. He didn't even know where the place was, let alone when he'd last been there.

"It doesn't matter whether you believe me or not," the Chief Priest said. "Your path will take you there before your search is complete; mark my words."

"What makes you so sure?" Darius asked.

"I can't be certain," the Chief Priest admitted. "I have few talents. You have seen my greatest gift, to connect people with the animal world. But I also hear things others do not, a chatter within the birds' songs, a muttering in the reptiles' croaks."

This conversation was getting more bizarre by the minute. Lex rolled her eyes, and Darius considered asking the man what language lizards spoke to check his sanity.

"What did this message say?" Darius asked Lex.

She took a parchment from her pocket and read it aloud to him, ending, "'Do what I suggested at once, or what will transpire will be worse than the alternative… If he's to prevail, it must happen at the Mount.'"

At least it seemed the Chief Priest wasn't against him. But perhaps there was some hidden message in the text that he was blind to.

"So?" Darius turned to the man. "Explain."

"I…" The Chief Priest's gaze flitted between the two of them. "I mean you no harm, or I would have called your enemies upon you long ago, and I would not have helped to end Lex's pain. I only withheld what I knew because you wouldn't have come to Dolthea otherwise, and I was…afraid of you. I have many enemies, including a king unhappy with some of my thoughts on his rule, and I put myself at considerable risk by revealing myself. But I know what you seek and believe it's my duty to assist you however I can."

The man made a decent point. Darius didn't trust him, but he'd done enough to save his life for now. "And what do we seek?" Darius asked.

"You think you're after Hadrian and the Waif Magician, but that is not your end. You may not know it yet, but many do, both friends and enemies. Hadrian is seeking to take the Twin Blades of Trogus." The Chief Priest paused, and Darius recalled when Selene had told him about these fabled weapons a year ago. He was about to ask what that meant when Aran continued. "Find them, and you will find your quarries. And find them you must. If the Viridian Warlord is successful, it isn't just your old city that will fall. Every settlement in the Empire will suffer the same fate as Laltos, and the King will be powerless to prevent it. Humanity will be enslaved. Every rakkan will bend the knee to Overlord Hadrian, and the 'Dreaded One' will be executed. You may have given Dolthea hope for now, but there will be none for this land until the end of time and the final damnation."

"You really know how to sour a small victory." Darius glanced at Lex, who again showed little surprise at the revelation. "Did you know about this?"

Lex nodded. "Sulla said they suspected, but it doesn't change our plans."

"Right. Only changes the fate of humanity as we know it."

The Chief Priest said nothing for a few moments as if giving his pronouncement of doom more time to sink in. But all it did was waste their time.

"So, where are these blades?" Darius asked.

"At Mount Psilos," the Chief Priest replied. "It sits near the south coast, a couple of hundred miles east of Margalvia. You need to head there at once."

"And you know this how? Divine inspiration?"

The Chief Priest stared for so long that Darius suspected he was preparing a lie.

"I have many ears," Aran finally said. "If you take me with you, I can help."

"Well, I'm convinced," Darius muttered sarcastically.

"We aren't going to Mount Psilos," Lex said. "We're heading to the Cliffs of Aphatos."

"Is that the place behind Laltos we tunnelled to last year?"

Lex nodded, and Darius saw no need to waste more time. He retreated into his mind for a moment to check Lyra and the others were safe, and once he'd confirmed it, he came forward and grabbed Aran's arm again.

The Chief Priest winced. "Please, do not—"

"Touch me, yes, yes," Darius muttered. "I got it the first time."

"I have more questions," Lex said.

"Then we'll interrogate him on the road," Darius said. Thrusting Aran forward with a strength that almost lifted the man from his feet, he made to rejoin the others.

45

Sulla – Urukan Mine

Sulla tossed the dead Viridian Legionnaire in his arms onto the pile, adding to the barricade of limbs, armour and entrails now standing waist-high a few yards in front of the Margalvian defensive line. It wasn't like they needed help defending the tunnel since they'd only lost a dozen more men over the last few hours, but Warlord Varro was never one to take a risk.

Sulla picked up one of the fallen shields and tossed it to a Black Legionnaire, who swapped his own for the scutum marked with Viridian colours. Now the whole testudo sported their enemies' shields. When the Viridians retreated here from the interior of the mine, already battered and bleeding, they'd think themselves safe before suffering a death swifter than they deserved.

But no attacks came for almost an hour. The passing time let the rush of battle fade all too quickly for Sulla's liking, and as it did, his stomach turned at the stench of sweat and blood and disembowelled men growing by the minute. Even the most battle-hardened of his soldiers coughed and spat. Now that the outside of the tunnel was blocked by fallen debris, the fresh air wafting through was too thin and feeble to wash away the foulness.

Their only clue as to what was happening deeper in the tunnels became the odd cry carrying from the depths. The wait passed like an age. But eventually, another band of warriors rounded a bend and started coming.

Sulla leapt back behind the shield wall as they moved their spears aside for him, then every warrior braced with their weapons again. They all stood still, waiting, hiding like predators.

The approaching group leapt over the heap of bodies and hadn't landed before the testudo lurched forward in a silent and well-rehearsed push. Shields parted and out thrust spears, skewering the Viridians before they'd even seen the Margalvians behind. The points pierced necks, thighs and arms, and those that didn't die by the spear soon felt the bash of a shield followed by the sharp stab of too many gladii to parry.

After that group, they came in sporadic clusters. Some were miners who had only their picks to use when they realised they had rushed towards enemies, but most were legionnaires, who in the dim light had a look about them that seemed to set Varro pacing nervously behind his men.

"Something wrong?" Sulla asked, dropping back.

"Yes." When the tunnel had quieted again, the Warlord pushed through the ranks of his men until in front of the shield wall and inspected the recently slain. Sulla followed and gaped when he saw the armbands. He cursed. They weren't all green.

"Branzians?" Sulla asked.

"Yes," Varro muttered.

But how? Their warriors had been given strict instructions, and the centurions had memorised maps of the tunnels. They shouldn't have ended up anywhere near Branzian areas. Yet almost half the corpses bore their bronze colours. Thankfully there were no Azurian warriors, or they would have turned every legion of rakkankind against them.

"We need to go in there," Sulla said, "to see what's happening."

"Indeed." The Warlord turned to one of the centurions. "Stay with your century here. Sulla, bring your men with me. We'll push deeper."

Sulla gave a nod to his own centurion, and the two set about barking orders to their men. They arranged them into separate groups while Varro turned to Hera and her algus.

"Stay here and defend," the Warlord said. "Slay anyone that comes, regardless of their colours."

Sulla guessed that made sense. It wasn't like they could do more harm than had already likely been inflicted on Margalvia's relations. Giving his men a wave, he led them across the heap of bodies besides the already amassing century with Varro. A quick count confirmed they had enough warriors, then Sulla set off at the front, the pounding boots of his century behind.

At first, they met only weak resistance that Varro alone cut down, but soon they were deep in Viridian tunnels and faced a tightly packed group of both Branzians and Viridians.

Without a care of what colour they bore, Sulla rushed towards them, raising his shield and gladius. Varro did the same, and his blade scored first blood on a Branz Legionnaire that charged forward. Sulla knocked a Viridian back with his shield, then stabbed his gladius through the rakkan's flailing leg. The man yelled, but Sulla's bloody sword slashed his neck a heartbeat later.

Meanwhile, Varro cut down three Viridians with a flurry of strikes that even a seasoned algus would be proud of. When all their enemies lay bleeding at their feet, over half wore bronze bands around their arms.

This couldn't be right. Even if the Margalvians had somehow wandered into the Branzian areas, they wouldn't have flushed warriors so far into Viridian territory.

"I don't like this," the Warlord muttered.

"Really?" Sulla shrugged. "I've never felt better. Do you smell that Viridian blood?" He took a long drag in through his nostrils, having waited too long for this moment.

They set off into the tunnels again, hacking and slashing a path through whatever bodies stood in their way and trampling over the weaker shield walls. After another hour, every man in the century was coated in blood that wasn't their own. But Sulla wasn't tired, and neither was the Warlord. Finally, Varro was in his element. Countless more fell, eviscerated by his blade, each strike like revenge for Brutus that he'd never vented until now, releasing a violent and hardened demon.

But Sulla knew nothing would ever dampen his rage until he'd slain the one responsible.

After slaughtering another group of Viridian warriors, they rounded a bend in the tunnel and met a blood-soaked Julius leading his men. The commander almost slashed the Warlord's thigh by mistake, but Varro blocked the strike by raising his greave.

"Apologies, Warlord," Julius huffed. "Wasn't expecting to see—"

"What resistance have you met?" Varro interjected.

"Fierce." Julius grimaced. "I've lost a third of the men with me, but few have escaped us. But there's something you should know. We've come across Branzians. They've been too intermingled to avoid clashing with them. We did our best to avoid causing casualties, but…you know."

"This can't be a coincidence," Sulla said. It was a deliberate ploy, one that the Warlord shouldn't take as anything other than alliance against Margalvia in the war.

"Do we pull back and avoid them?" Julius asked.

Varro let heat rage in his eyes. "No. Slay every Branzian you see."

Julius gave a grim nod and left with his men while the Warlord pulled Sulla aside.

"You need to get back to Gerunda," Varro said. "Get a message back to Margalvia and tell them to prepare. I don't want them to be caught unawares should the Branzians try anything."

Sulla hadn't slain enough for one day, but thinking of Gerunda gave him an idea.

"Varro, this war is getting out of hand," Sulla muttered in a low voice. "We can't take on Viridia *and* Branz."

The Warlord's horned helmet dipped. "I know."

"But I see a way out."

Varro looked up. "How?"

"A way to bring both these legions to heel without a long, painful war. You must do what Eugenius suggested and take the Blades."

The Warlord's growl resonated in his helmet, giving it a steely ring. "We'd need the—"

"Staff of Arria, yes. That's why I think I should go to help Darius and Lex. They're searching for the Magician, but on their own, what hope do they have?"

"And what can you do? Rakkans cannot stand in the Staff's presence."

"No, but we can help if they run into Hadrian's men. Who knows? We might even cross paths with the bastard himself."

Varro's gaze dropped to the dead Viridians and Branzians again for a long while; the only sound from him were his deep breaths spitting mist from his visor. But finally, he turned to Sulla and said, "Very well. Go to Gerunda and send word to Margalvia first. Then find them. But you'll take only your century."

"And I'll need algus with flying escorts to find Lex," Sulla said.

Varro nodded and waved over a few young men from his century. "Take them all."

Sulla gave his warlord a slap on the back and muttered, "Give them hell. I'll get word to you when I know more, but be ready to head to Mount Psilos. If Eugenius was right, that's where we'll see you."

The two parted, and Sulla was soon racing back through the tunnels to Gerunda. He hoped Lex had sent Tiro with a recent update, otherwise, he had an entire Empire to scour in order to find her.

46

Lex – East of Dolthea

When Lex and Darius left the building and reached the gates of Dolthea with the Chief Priest in tow, night had blanketed the town in darkness, and even the moon didn't grace them with light. For now, Lex just wanted to get back to their camp, but at the earliest opportunity, she'd get Aran away from Darius and begin a real interrogation, one where her dagger would be unchallenged.

The three were met by what appeared to be a mob at the gates, again requesting to travel north with them to some of the smaller towns.

"We can't," Darius said for the umpteenth time. Each time his voice became more of a bark in the night. "We're heading east, into a far more dangerous place than here."

"Then we'll come with you!" The girl with the new tiger escort came forward, no longer in disguise as a ruffian but wearing chain mail and a scabbard at her waist.

Darius grimaced so hard his head shook, and Lex shared his frustration.

"No." Darius's glare darkened, as close as ever to the murderous look he'd had when Lex first met him—or rather, fought him. With a shake of his head, he pulled the Chief Priest's arm and began striding out of the town and onto the dark road.

The crowd deflated with one long, heavy breath that seemed to shake their raised torches. But while Lex shared in their pain, a new hope arose in her as she watched the surly man stomp away. He was finally making decisions, and the way the people looked at him stunned her into silence. A couple of years ago, the mere utterance of the name "Slayer of Gods" would have had every man, woman and child here quivering. Yet now, they called him their saviour and begged to join his cause. It was a reverence won with the blood and tears of many, and she'd often doubted it possible at all. But here it was, proof that her dream of united humans and rakkans could become a reality. Now they needed to extend it to the far reaches of the Empire.

Before leaving the town, Lex strode up to the young algus and whispered, "You need to stay with these people. If the Xavalans or Viridians come back, I suggest you surrender to them. If we achieve our aims, it won't be long until we can return and liberate you for good."

The girl nodded grimly while Lex made her way after Darius. Before catching up to him, she took a slip of parchment and a reed pen from her pocket, then crouched. *Tiro, come to me.*

While her peregrine descended from the sky, she wrote Sulla an update on where they were heading and that they were close to finding the Waif Magician. Then she strapped the message to Tiro and sent him soaring back to Gerunda. She hated being without him, especially in the night, and had been separated for many days throughout their hunt. But she had to keep Sulla updated. Three algus could hardly take on the Viridian Legion if it came to it.

She rushed and caught up with Darius once they arrived back in the forest where they'd chained Selene.

Lex's sister sat quietly, leaning against the tree, with the only light around coming from a faint glow of algor from her. It was enough for Lex to see there was no redness around her wrists near the restraints, which suggested she hadn't tried to escape. Her expression seemed almost bored rather than furious, as her real sister would have been.

Lex walked over to Gorgias and pulled him discreetly aside. "How was she?" Lex asked.

The algus lowered his voice. "She was fine. We just sat and reminisced. She has most of her memories intact, but something has definitely been done to her."

"Any signs of mind blocks?" Lex asked while inspecting her sister's demeanour further.

"Nothing like I've seen before. This bears no resemblance to what I've seen gomans do."

But that didn't make it impossible. Years of experience had taught Lex to assume the worst. The Numbered were cunning, and if she ever encountered her son again, she'd be forced to treat him with the same callous indifference she now showed her sister, however painful that might be.

Darius shackled himself to Selene again while Lyra rubbed her head against his legs. Meanwhile, the Chief Priest stood fidgeting, now freed of Darius's grasp but hardly difficult to catch should he attempt to run.

"We'll camp here for the night," Lex said. "Do me a favour and secure the Chief Priest." She reached inside her bag and withdrew a new set of shackles she'd bought in Dolthea in case

Selene tried anything, but now she'd use them on their second suspicious companion.

Gorgias took them and raised an eyebrow. "Why?"

"It turns out he's been spying on Darius for months, and I don't trust him. Be wary of anything he says, and if he tries to flee, stop him however you must."

The surprise in Gorgias's expression lasted a few seconds before he nodded and scurried away to do as instructed. Meanwhile, Lex went over to Nasrin and pulled her away from the salted meat she'd been preparing for them all to eat.

"What is it, mistress?" the carer asked.

"I found sulphur, but I need to test it," Lex said.

"Very well. I'll get Darius to light us a fire." Nasrin walked back over to Darius while Lex found a flat stretch of earth over a dozen yards to the nearest tree. She began scraping away all the leaves and branches with her boot, cursing more than once when the wind swept the potential kindling back into the area. But eventually, she cleared a spot. Now with a few yards square of nothing but damp soil, she went into the centre, dug a shallow pit and placed a dry, circular leaf down.

By now, the others were watching her in silent puzzlement, but she ignored them and measured some of the metal powder onto the leaf, a pile no larger than her small fingernail. Then she added the same amount of sulphur as Nasrin returned with a burning twig.

Using her finger, Lex mixed the yellow and grey powders together until they became a singular mustard pile.

Nasrin handed her the stick. "I think I'll get back."

"Tell the others not to look directly at it." Lex took the twig and, although it was almost a yard long, would have preferred to be farther away. As much as she hoped not to get injured, part of her wanted to. That would mean she'd found the right substance to blind the Magician.

She conjured algor across her body until the chilly film coated every inch, then stretched the small flame towards the powder.

When the fire first touched and buried into the pile, it did nothing but give a little fizzle, but as Lex drew a breath to sigh in frustration, the powder suddenly ignited into a brilliant white flash that consumed her entire vision. The blast ripped the stick from her hand and almost rocked her backwards, but her algor protected her from any heat. Most importantly, the whiteness that had overtaken her vision lingered, even when she banished her algor and expected to discern some vague shapes in the night.

Curses rang out from the others, and even Lyra growled with frustration. But after a few minutes, the white spots in Lex's sight faded enough for her to make it back to the others, whose irritation was plain in their frowns.

"I did tell them all not to look," Nasrin said, still blinking harshly herself.

"When someone tells you not to look," Darius said, "without explanation, how can you *not* look? It's human nature. We're curious fools like that. It's like if I said don't imagine Gorgias stripped naked and dancing like a drunk on hot coals. Can you imagine anything else now?"

"Algor didn't protect my sight," Lex said, ignoring the disturbing mental images Darius provoked.

"I had my eyes tightly shut," the carer said, "and I could just about see the shape of you afterwards."

Lex considered her next words carefully, given that Nasrin was here. "Then it should be enough to allow us to escape the Magician should things go awry. I have enough powder for a few of these, but only Darius will be able to light them with ease."

Darius nodded. "Let's hope the Magician doesn't have the Staff too close to prevent me conjuring ferven."

That was an issue of which Lex was well aware, but she had no solution to it at the moment. "Rest for the night. I'll take first watch." She'd rather make sure both Selene and the Chief Priest went to sleep. Already, every flutter of a bird in the trees around them made her flinch, knowing Aran's pteron was out there watching but not knowing what his real intentions were. Yet. Tomorrow, her grilling would begin, away from Darius and the others.

The rest settled down for the night while Lex fashioned some closed pouches of mixed powder ready for them to use. After a few hours, Darius awoke and took over the watch, but her sleep was rough and disturbed by every snap of a branch or rustle of leaves.

As soon as dawn broke, she rushed to her feet and roused the others.

"We should get moving," Lex said before most had two eyes open. "We'll eat and forage as we go." She didn't wait for a response before she strode over to the Chief Priest and began unlocking the shackles that fastened him to a tree, careful not to touch him as he always insisted.

The man frowned but offered no argument until he hobbled to his feet and she shoved him towards the east.

"Please, don't… You can just tell me where to go rather than manhandling me." Aran pulled apart the silver hair that had fallen across his face.

"Maybe I'll stop when you've answered my questions," Lex said. She quickly glanced over her shoulder to check the others were far enough away they couldn't hear. They were still collecting their things but wouldn't be long before following, so she carried on.

"What questions?" the Chief Priest asked. "You want to know why I'm helping you?"

"You call spying '*helping*'?" She'd only met the man a few times before but never would have thought him capable of doing something so underhand. Clearly, she didn't know the man as well as she'd thought, and it was time to make a decision about him. She slowly pulled her dagger from its sheath when Aran wasn't looking and clutched it by her leg where he couldn't see.

"I know I used the wrong methods," the Chief Priest said, gazing regretfully up at the dew-coated firs around, "but doesn't the outcome speak for itself? I could have had Darius killed or captured more times than you know."

Lex's hand twitched. Maybe it would have been wise to end this threat for good, but the man before her was the leader of the Diagathic Order, of which she still counted herself a member—even if she'd cast away her religious pendant in a moment of angry madness.

"Don't you preach about the God of Justice?" she asked. "About the importance of the good? Does deception fall under that?"

The Chief Priest blew out a hefty sigh. "I know I've failed by my own measure. But when we're faced with doing the wrong thing for the right reasons, it's hard to turn the other way. You know that all too well."

This time her hand squeezed the hilt of her dagger hard. "I told you those things in confidence." All the people she'd killed, all the secrets she'd kept. One day she'd pay for those misdeeds, but they'd saved those she cared for, so it had been worth it.

"No one can hear us," the Chief Priest said with his usual reassuringly pleasant tone. "I'm merely admitting my guilt, not voicing yours."

"To whom? Agathos?"

"Him and you."

"Why? You saw how he forsook Laltos." They'd be able to see the ruins on their way to the Cliffs, a sight which just imagining brought back the pain in her hip. What kind of God of Justice watched over that slaughter and did nothing?

"I know of the powers I possess," the Chief Priest continued. "I know the powers you algus possess, which allow you to seek justice and to protect the innocent—even to falsely elevate yourselves as gods. Do not forget why I do what I do. Sometimes we are to help ourselves. Yes, not every algus is perfect, and not every escort I bond will be used to serve Agathos and Dianoia. But on the whole, despite the Order being unwelcome in most parts of the Empire, we make a positive difference. I would not do as I do and paint a target on my back if I did not believe that with every fibre of my being."

Lex recalled the long years she'd pondered these issues before she'd devoted herself to the Diagathic Order. Long debates and discussions with her father replayed in her mind, conversations she'd never have with the man again. The reminder brought a gnawing sadness that hadn't faded in a year. Every instinct for justice inside her told her the Order's teachings were true, yet at times, the uncertainty overwhelmed her. And if she allowed it to now, it would again.

"I wish to discuss something else," she said. "Tell me how you're allegedly going to help us and how you know so much about the Magician, the Blades…everything."

The Chief Priest regarded her curiously, his lips opening and closing repeatedly as if unsure whether to say whatever dwelled in his mind. When he did speak, he uttered each word with care and delicacy. "I can be of great help. I bond algus to a single escort to aid in the defence of the Empire, but I am only limited to that by my own volition. Personally, I have many escorts that are my eyes and ears, with a connection far deeper than I grant to most algus. It is how I know so much and how I have evaded those who hunt me for so many decades."

Lex's steps faltered, and she gaped at the man, with too many questions to know where to begin. She always did her best to stay abreast of every rumour and whisper in the Empire, yet she'd never heard a word of people having more than one escort.

Only once he was a few yards ahead did the Chief Priest seem to realise he was walking alone and turned to her.

"How can no one know that?" Lex asked.

Aran smiled wistfully. "Because I've never told anyone before."

Lex's jaw fell open, and she checked again that the others were too far behind to overhear.

"Please don't tell them." The Chief Priest's stare was suddenly overcome with a deathly seriousness that stole the colour from his face. "No one else can know. If others found out…"

"Then why tell *me*?" A woman he barely knew.

"Because I need you to trust me, and I know the only way to do that is to put myself at your mercy. My talents make me of interest to the King enough as it is. My gifts are valuable, and as much as I've tried to teach others to replicate them, only one other person ever managed it. My mother and father couldn't, and they tried profusely after I happened upon the talent."

"Who was the one?" Lex had never heard of another.

"… My sister. We practised together until she…" Aran closed his eyes with an anguished grimace.

Lex shook her head and began walking again before the others caught up. Her dagger hung loose in her hand as she struggled to piece together the implications of the revelation.

They trudged quietly for a while, disturbed only when a flock of pigeons raced overhead and gave her a start.

Their fluttering unsettled the windless forest, and amongst them could have been an escort, or numerous ones either from Hadrian's Subdued or the King's algus. *If only Tiro were here.* She watched the birds intently as they disappeared into the distance. Then she focused her attention back on the Chief Priest.

"Would you like me to bring a falcon to us?" he asked.

"Actually, I would." No pigeon would approach at the mere sight of something like that hovering above, and she needed to see he wasn't lying. "What else do you have close by?"

The Chief Priest muttered to himself for a while, before concluding, "A pteron, a falcon, a spider, a swift and a kynigi owl."

The last two creatures made her heart skip a beat. "How? A kynigi owl?" Most of the Empire thought them extinct, but it wasn't hard to imagine that being false given they could easily evade people for decades. Their legendary sense of sight and smell made them unrivalled at both avoiding danger and hunting prey from miles away.

And a swift? She'd never heard of anyone being bonded to a creature that displayed some of the same powers as algus.

"I cannot trust any human enough to wield too much power," the Chief Priest said, "so I limit my bondings to one per algus and never to magical beasts. To be honest, I was reluctant to give humans anything at first. But I grew up during the height of Hadrianus the Great's power. I saw how fearsome the rakkans were when led by a true conqueror. So I had to assist humanity in some way, even if the warlord himself was killed in my youth. If I'd known Archimedes would come to turn the tide in the war, perhaps I wouldn't have devoted my life to preaching, wandering from town to town, setting up small local communities that soon became the Diagathic Order."

This was all too much for Lex to take in or believe. Just how old was Aran? And why would the man be so open with her with such dangerous secrets? Usually, she would have observed him and figured out his motives, but Aran was far more dangerous than he led people to believe. If they couldn't trust him, they had to find out now.

Lex wheeled in front of the Chief Priest and raised her dagger to threaten his neck.

The man halted with a gulp.

"Why would you tell me all this if it was true?" Lex asked.

"Understand what I'm doing here," the Chief Priest said nervously. "I have a religion to lead, finally making traction in some of the cities, yet I've chosen to come with you, to stop spreading my teachings, to stop bonding more escorts to algus, to help the *Slayer of Gods* of all people. I do this because I see no other way. I see destruction in our future. I stood by and did nothing while Archimedes sought to exterminate a people. I stood by while the Viridian Legion razed Laltos. I thought the life of a pacifist would suffice. I thought the truth of my religion would be enough to bring harmony. But the vast majority of algus reject me and my insistence that they are not gods. And of those that don't, lots try to fool me and just go through the motions to get an escort. I've lost hope in peaceful preaching. This war needs to end, and there's only one man I've seen with the power and will to do that, no matter his flaws. I know you've seen his potential too."

Try as she might, Lex could see no hint of deception in Aran's eyes. As her next question formed on her lips, a noise came from behind her, very faint but distinct—a rapid thunder of hooves.

She whirled around, expecting to see a band of cavalry charging through the trees, but instead saw the blurred shape of a pale-brown swift race within the forest around a hundred yards away, tossing dirt and leaves in the air. As quickly as the beast had appeared, it vanished into the undergrowth.

Just as she was about to question Aran further, another shape caught her eye, this time silent and floating in the sky. Its wings rose, flapping above the nearest tree, not making so much as a whisper as the owl's pale blue and grey feathers melded it into the sky. The bird's body was no larger or smaller than a snowy owl, but its wingspan spread vaster and thinner, making it all the harder to pick out against the backdrop of clouds.

After a few silent moments, the owl too veered away and vanished once again.

The Chief Priest hadn't been lying, and Lex slowly withdrew her dagger with shame heating her cheeks. There was no reason for a kynigi owl to fly other than it was Aran's escort. And Lex could only think of the many options such a creature now gave them.

Perhaps she believed the man because she wanted to, because that owl could help them find Hadrian faster than a dozen packs of bloodhounds. But she'd take the risk and remain vigilant.

The Chief Priest gazed down at her lowered knife. "Am I to take it you believe me now?"

"Does your owl know the scent of the Magician?"

"I'm afraid not."

"How about Viridians?"

Aran paused before nodding in understanding. "I know what you're getting at. You want to know if she can find Hadrian."

Lex sheathed her dagger and nodded strongly. "Can she?"

The Chief Priest smiled. "I chose wisely in revealing my secret to you, Lex. If I had told it to any other algus, their first act would be to demand that I bond them to more escorts in exchange for silence, not to ask that I help them."

Lex couldn't say such a demand hadn't fleetingly crossed her mind, but she doubted the man would have obliged if she'd voiced it.

"I taught the owl Hadrian's scent months ago," Aran said, "though she hasn't picked up a trace around here. But if he's gone to the Cliffs, she can find the trail soon enough."

47

Rufus – South of Dolthea

Rufus awoke to the low churring of a nightjar in the trees overhead. It flapped its wings excitedly as another call rang out in reply, then it took off and left Rufus to hear only a hiss as wind and rain tossed the branches and needles. A thin spray fell across his body, but nothing would ruin the peace he enjoyed in his half-roused state. The sun had finally withdrawn its angry blaze and left a black sea above, lit up with a million specks of light. A few clanks of armour and mutters came from the centuries of men close by, but Rufus simply rested with his head on a tree root and gazed upwards through the forest canopy for a few moments.

One of his only memories of spending time with his father as a boy was looking at the stars and asking for their blessings. The older he'd grown, the more ridiculous the notion of praying to dead rakkans struck him, but the sight of those sparkles on the dark sheet above filled him with as much awe as he'd had as a child. However sceptical of the gods he was, he knew there was *something* up there, something greater than him or any rakkan, something that wouldn't bend to the will of the tiny creatures below.

"Commander?" a deep voice spat.

Rufus gave a great sigh and rose from his resting spot. "What is it?"

"Get up." Balbus, their most experienced centurion, stared down his scrunched nose as he grimaced in disgust. The black hair on his chin was wet, clumped and dirtied with old animal fat, and the hair on his head was no tidier. Still, his appearance was neater than his battle tactics.

"*I* give the orders around here." Rufus stood, still shorter than his centurion and with half the bulk, but that was the story of Rufus's life.

"We'll see," the centurion muttered with a snort of derision. "We're setting up an altar to make our sacrifices."

Rufus pulled his damp red mane back behind his ears and regarded the two centuries surrounding him as they roused. Many picked up the bowls of raw grain they'd left to soak in rainwater during the day and began gobbling down their slop. But some took wide plates in their arms and stalked around, taking significant portions from each man.

These damned sacrifices. It was always Balbus who initiated them. They needed to save every ounce of grain they'd taken from Dolthea if they were to get to where they were heading—the Cliffs of Aphatos and then Mount Psilos. Usually, Rufus allowed the men to indulge in their superstitions, but this time a sacrifice would see some starve in a few weeks. Foraging in the Cliffs would yield little substantial food, and the only animals to hunt weren't large enough to satiate a man for more than half a day.

"How many sacrifices to our warlord are you planning?" Rufus asked with false interest.

"Many," the centurion grunted. "We need to atone for your humiliating retreat. May Hadrianus the Great pardon us."

Rufus rolled his eyes when the rakkan wasn't looking. Leaving Dolthea had been a relief, with little left there of value. The truth was, Dolthea had been a lost cause months ago from the unrelenting raids. If the Warlord had focused on an assault on the Silk City instead of pursuing the Blades, they wouldn't be in this mess.

Rufus scanned around for any signs of his more trusted centurions and caught sight of two that he'd been with ever since his first trials. He quickly waved them over and was thankful when he spotted that they were both wearing their sword belts.

"We'll need to get the men moving quickly," Rufus said to the new arrivals. "We'll never make it to the Cliffs in time at this rate."

"The sacrifices will take at least another hour," one of the centurions said.

Rufus gritted his teeth and braced himself. "Call off the sacrifices."

Balbus scowled at him and squared up with murderous intent. "You can't be serious."

"I am," Rufus said with a calmness he most certainly didn't feel inside. "We don't have the time or the food to waste. We shall make our sacrifices later."

Balbus stepped forward until he was taking heavy, stinking breaths that stung Rufus's eyes.

"First, you're a coward," the centurion said, "now you're spitting in the face of our warlord. I should challenge you and rid these centuries of your cursed leadership."

The threat from the meat-headed brute hardly came as a surprise, and Rufus had enough honour to meet any challenge fairly, despite knowing he'd lose. But he hadn't gained his position via a challenge and wouldn't lose it in such a manner either.

He stepped back calmly, a smile playing on his lips as he unfastened the straps on his right armguard and let the kuraminium fall into the dirt. Then he brandished the skin that had been hidden underneath: a green tattoo of a bull-horned warrior god whose swords dripped green blood.

The grimace on Balbus's face faltered, and a trace of fear crossed his eyes—all Rufus needed to take advantage of this fool's beliefs.

"By all means, challenge me." Rufus took a step forward and was relieved when the centurion backed up to keep him at a distance. "Did you forget I bore this mark?" Rufus continued. "You know what was done to make it. But perhaps you don't know that it wasn't gained through just a rakkan sacrifice, but a child sacrifice to the Warlord. I earned this divine symbol through innocent blood, and that blood now lingers under my skin, giving me a power that mortals cannot challenge." Such superstitious nonsense made Rufus want to retch now just as much as it had when he'd been forced to partake in the child sacrifice at the time. But the terror the tattoo struck into Balbus now made such divine blessings more real than they had ever been.

"You're weak," Balbus muttered, although the inflexion of his voice almost made it a question.

"Find out," Rufus dared. "Challenge me. Feel the fury of the warlords of old imbued within me by my father."

The other two centurions exchanged nervous glances, but Balbus continued glaring, the implications of what was being said trying to coalesce into something sensible in his tiny mind. Eventually, Rufus tired of waiting for the dim rakkan.

Rufus's next words were deliberately slow, soft and menacing. "Call off the sacrifices."

Balbus snorted and grunted, glancing down once more at the tattoo Rufus's father had forced him to bear. Then, thankfully, he turned and began barking at the legionnaires carrying the sacrificial plates to stop.

The two other centurions came closer with a lift of their eyebrows and a hint of amusement.

"I don't know why you put up with him," one whispered.

"He comes in useful," Rufus said. "Who else of you would be foolish and proud enough to charge into a battle against insurmountable odds?"

The centurions chuckled.

"Get your men ready," Rufus said. "We'll go around the Cliffs and approach from the south. It'll take longer, but we'll be able to stick to the forests."

The centurions nodded and left to give their men the orders, leaving Rufus to his own bowl of slop for breakfast. His father was far ahead of them, but finally he had an excuse to join what would be Viridia's finest triumph.

48

Darius – West of Laltos

After leaving Dolthea, Darius did his best to try to forget all those people he'd left behind. For the next few days, he spoke to the others as much as possible, particularly Selene, who'd occasionally dropped her permanent scowl to laugh with him.

Tiro brought a message one day, bearing the best news he'd heard in a long while—Sulla was heading to meet them with a century of men. If even Warlord Varro saw the urgency in finding the Waif Magician, their task was more pressing than Darius had reckoned.

It only intensified the tension that had been gripping his head of late and made him wonder why his body always had to act up when stressed. Wouldn't it make more sense for his head to become clear and refreshed when trying to figure a way to solve his problems? It was almost as if a man's body worked purposely against him.

As they travelled, Lex and the Chief Priest led from the front, deep in conversation, while Nasrin and Lyra prowled just behind. At the rear, Selene and Darius made sure nothing snuck up on them. The forest was fairly sparse, with every other tree reduced to a stump by fiery rakkan axes. But among the ashes and dirt, new sprouts had emerged.

One day, the pair trod past a young fir sapling in the forest. The tree's needles shone a vibrant, lush green, and by the height, it looked less than a year old. It reminded Darius of something odd Selene had said a few days before that he'd tried to pry further into but hadn't got anywhere. It was time for another attempt.

He cleared his throat and made his tone casual. "You said the Viridians had kept you near the Uncharted Mountains for the last year."

"Yes," she said, kicking through a weed growing from the forest floor.

"I was around there several times, searching the Viridian camps to see if I could find Hadrian."

"Oh. It's unfortunate our paths never crossed," she said dryly, almost as if she was bitter he hadn't found her.

"It's just that yesterday you said something that sounded like you'd seen me at some point. I didn't know whether I'd been close and missed you." If only he'd been looking for her as intently as he should have been.

"No. I didn't see you," Selene said.

He was about to press further but spotted the forest opening up ahead. On a hill, the main road connecting Dolthea and Laltos cut through the tightly packed trees, a path that Darius knew the Silk City's cavalry utilised heavily.

They continued towards it while Darius kept his hand near his sword, and when they reached the stonework, Lex knelt and inspected some markings.

"What is it?" Darius asked. But as soon as he got close enough himself, he saw the fresh scratches of horseshoes, as well as indents in the mud to the side of the road that would have been soaked with the previous day's rain if they'd been stomped before today.

"Viridians," Lex said.

Darius frowned and looked again. "But the tracks are leading towards Dolthea." Did that mean the people weren't even going to get a whole week to enjoy freedom? He'd clearly made many mistakes in his handling of things there.

"Not the hoofprints. Rakkans." Lex traced her hand across a set of marks so faint they could have been made by anything from boots to deer.

"Why would Viridians use the road?" Darius asked.

"Speed," Selene said. "The Legion marches almost twice as fast on the roads, and Hadrian's Subdued have escorts that give him early warning to hide in the forests when necessary."

"They must have gone to Laltos," Lex said with a forceful certainty.

"Why do you say that?" Darius asked.

Lex shared a glance with the Chief Priest, but he quickly looked away.

"They must be reopening the tunnel we dug last year," Lex said. "And if they're heading to the Cliffs with such haste, Hadrian must be with them."

"That's a leap," Darius said. "Hadrian could have taken a different path to whoever marched here."

"No. We're on Hadrian's trail," Lex said, still no hint of uncertainty in her tone.

458

It was hardly uncommon for Lex's mind to defy Darius's understanding, and he guessed this was one of those situations because her conclusions weren't obvious to him.

"We'd be better off heading straight for Mount Psilos," the Chief Priest said quietly, almost as if testing whether anyone paid attention.

But Lex shook her head. "We won't need to go there at all if we can get to Hadrian before he finds the Magician."

Couldn't have said it better myself. These Blades, although intriguing, were a far lower priority. But maybe the religious man was aware of something they'd overlooked.

"What do you think?" Darius asked Selene.

Before Selene could speak, Lex rose and strode up to him. "Until the Magician fixes her, you don't ask her for advice, are we clear?"

"Not really," he muttered, partly to test how strongly Lex suspected her sister, but also partly because so much of Selene had remained that he had no reason to doubt *every* word from her mouth. In fact, he had to resist the urge to snap Selene's chains there and then to prove his growing faith in her to Lex.

A blue light sparked in Lex's eyes, but rather than display her usual annoyance at his questioning, she seemed almost pleased that he was resisting.

She broke off her stare and spoke to the others. "Gorgias, you walk with the Chief Priest and follow his directions to Laltos. If we hurry, we might be able to catch up to Hadrian. I'll stay with these two for now."

"Since when does Gorgias need directions to Laltos?" Darius asked.

But Lex ignored the question. Although he knew she was only walking with him to listen in on his conversations with Selene, he had to admit he'd be glad to spend time with her again, even if it was while chained to her sister. He had questions about the Blades and Dolthea but was a little afraid of the answers.

Darius watched Gorgias and his badger stride alongside the Chief Priest, still aware—thanks to Lyra—that Aran's pteron was always close by. Nasrin and Lyra followed, and when the group was far enough along the road to be out of earshot, Darius turned to Lex.

"How can you trust Aran?" he asked.

She shrugged. "How can you trust Selene?"

Selene let out a sigh that had lost all the anger it had borne when she'd first been shackled. Now it was despairing, resigned.

"You've known Selene for years," Darius said. "We've known the Chief Priest for days. And *you* never trust people easily."

Lex seemed to ponder his words for a moment before saying, "I've known him longer, and I trust him. Do you not have faith in my judgement?"

"You always have to make it about you." Darius grumbled under his breath for a moment. "Of course I trust you." Sometimes he suspected she baited him into saying those words because he noted her lips curling into a delicate smile at his admission.

"Your walk looks a lot more fluid," he said. "Is your hip doing better?"

"Yes, thank you." Lex's grin widened. "I picked up more tea leaves in Dolthea, so I have enough for a while. How are you two faring? What have you been discussing so intently for the last few days?"

Darius saw no reason to hide anything, so he went over some of the topics, from their time battling Viridians over a year ago to older memories Selene had been sharing from far before Darius's known time. He'd noticed specific points in Selene's recollection that had been manipulated and didn't share them with Lex, but he might later.

The discussion sparked more conversing between the women that lasted until they rested for the night, then began again when they set off the next day.

At times, it was almost as if the two women were sisters again, and Lex's obvious determination to regard Selene as a fraud faltered many times.

While they were still near the forests, Darius sent Lyra to hunt for dinner and had hoped to entice everyone back into the seclusion of the trees, but they still stuck to the perilous road instead. After Lyra came back with a deer in her jaws and they stopped to eat their fill, Darius and the two sisters trudged together again at the back, and he finally plucked up the nerve to raise a topic he'd put off until now.

"I have a couple of questions for you both."

They waited while he chose which one to ask first. He munched on some biscuits to give himself a reason to delay continuing. Finally, he decided the detail of the Blades was the least pressing issue and could wait until last.

"Lex, do you know what will happen to those people back in Dolthea?" he asked. Already, a tension gripped his head before the answer came.

The stiffness of Lex's walk told him she knew something but would probably conceal it from him.

"It's hard to know what the Xavalans will do," Selene said, "after seeing what they did to Laltos…" Her voice trailed off with a pain that Darius doubted could be false.

"It doesn't matter what they do," Lex said without a shred of the hurt Selene had shown. At times like these, it was easy to see they weren't blood relatives.

"What does that mean?" Darius asked.

"It means we had little choice, whatever the consequences for the Doltheans. A delay of even a few days could mean the difference between loss and victory, and they will all be far worse off should we fail."

"Those that survive, you mean." Darius turned to Selene. "How did you make decisions like this when we were there last year?" As he recalled, Selene had almost emptied their granaries to feed the starving in Laltos. But she'd also allowed anyone who wanted to accompany them back to Laltos to do so.

"With a heavy heart," Selene said. "Being a leader is seldom easy."

Darius grunted. "Maybe I shouldn't have let the Viridians take half the grain."

"Probably not," Lex said.

The quick remark struck him like a rakkan punch to the temple. If he'd failed at such a simple negotiation, perhaps he was best suited to being a mere warrior after all.

"Do you think we should have let some of them come with us too?" he asked.

"Depends on whether the Xavalans slaughter them all," Lex said flatly.

This time, Darius couldn't let the cold comment go. He took her arm and stopped her in the middle of the road.

"How can you…?" As soon as he clasped her arm, he felt her veins pulsing rapidly, saw the slight shine in her eyes of the tears she was forcing herself not to shed. She wasn't uncaring. That was only the act she presented to him and everyone else.

"Let go of me," she said softly.

He did, staring down at his worn boots, still stained with old blood. "I'm sorry."

"We all make mistakes," Lex said in a gentle voice she rarely used with anyone except her daughter. "I've killed far more through my failures than you, even if everyone in Dolthea is slain."

"And the girl with Lionheart," he muttered. "It's not only Doltheans I've failed to protect."

"That was no mistake. We were attacked. And it's not even clear you could have achieved anything better from Dolthea."

"Well, I'm done trying." He set off again and tugged Selene along with him before they lost sight of the others.

"You can't give up," Lex said.

"I'm not giving up. I'll just let one of you handle those things from now on. I'm the muscle, not the brains. I'll stick to being responsible for the deaths of soldiers and warriors, those who oppose us and deserve it."

"We should all strive to be both strong *and* intelligent."

"I'm not sure wit is something you can gain through effort."

"Oh, will you stop!" Selene's yell brought them both to a halt, and even Nasrin and the others ahead glanced back.

"You *might* have made a bad judgement call," Selene said through her clenched jaw. "Get over it. You've made plenty over the last year alone and hurt a lot of people. Do you feel as bad for those you harmed with your own hands? Clearly not! Leaders do terrible things all the time, sometimes intentionally, sometimes unintentionally. So don't pretend this is something new to you." She stormed away until the chain connecting them snapped tight, then tugged against it angrily with her back still to him.

Darius gaped at her. Although he'd spoken with her a little about what he'd done over the last year, he hadn't told her much. It was true; he'd committed a lot of gruesome acts, but to people who had it coming. Whatever Selene was speaking of, something told him the memory might not be real.

"What did I do in the last year?" He held the chain taut to prevent her from walking away.

Her shoulders rose and fell with her heavy breaths. "How do I know? I wasn't with you."

"You seem to think you know *something*."

Suddenly, her breathing seemed to calm, and when she turned, her annoyance had unnaturally gone, as blunted as a bronze sword after a battle.

"I heard stories from the Viridians," she said. "Maybe they aren't true."

She really had changed if she believed rakkans over him. What had happened to her saying "Gomans never lie, rakkans never tell the truth"? Her change of heart could have been a result of the torture, but this wasn't the first sudden shift in her emotions.

Dropping it for now so as not to get her defences up even further, he began walking and let her go ahead, feeling Lex's stare behind him as well. Perhaps he shouldn't have voiced his fears over Dolthea. And he didn't for the rest of the day. That night was the last they'd spend in the forest. All that awaited now were the dead and barren farmlands outside Laltos that fed nothing but insects and vermin these days.

The night was another wet and sleepless one for him, but at least it allowed Lex to get some much-needed rest. He didn't wake her to change watch, and instead stared at the black, spitting clouds above, longing for the day they'd meet with Sulla. At least then he'd have what had once been a commanding officer to him, and that might save him from his self-inflicted confusion.

The next morning, they ate and set off along the desolate road again, and this time, Lyra walked next to him rather than with Nasrin or scouting ahead, sensing his sour mood. It wasn't until the afternoon that the fractured ruins of Laltos rose over the horizon, and at first sight, Lex developed a limp that hadn't been there in recent weeks.

Darius knew the ugliness they were walking into better than them all. The only thing he could do to help at the moment was to distract her.

"Tell me more about these Twin Blades," he asked her.

"You know what wielding them means," she replied.

His real concern was what would happen if they prevented Hadrian getting them. The Viridian Warlord was last on his list of preferred candidates, but neither did he want Varro going after them.

For now, he instead asked, "Where did the swords come from?"

"What am I, your tutor on history?" Lex said.

If only Darius had read the scrolls Brutus had once given him, then he'd already know the story. But, like many attempts Brutus had made to impart wisdom unto Darius, they'd been wasted by his own foolishness. If only Brutus were here now.

"Tutor…?" Darius ran a hand through his beard pensively. "The title fits. Most of what I know is because you taught me. I'd be lost without you."

The compliment seemed to stun her into silence for a few moments before thankfully making her more cooperative. "Very well, though a rakkan could describe the story better, given it began as their myth of origins. The songs tell of the beginning of our world and the two tribes the Creator made—human and rakkan. The humans were led by the matriarch Arria and the rakkans by the patriarch Trogus. As leaders, the Creator gave them each a gift: Arria was given algor and speed, and Trogus was given ferven and strength.

"At first, the two wed, and the tribes lived in peace. They even had a son and named him Hakor. As a celebration of the

465

unification of the peoples, the Creator gave them a final gift. Hakor would also receive powers, anything of the couple's choosing, and their choice determined the fate of us all."

"Is this real?" Darius asked. "Or just a story?"

Lex shrugged and carried on. "Trogus and Arria asked for Hakor to share in the knowledge of the Creator: sight of the future and knowledge of what dwelled in the minds of others. So in their son's thirteenth year, the Creator spoke, and Hakor received his gift. The only condition was that Trogus would remain immune to his son's powers."

"At least the Creator had some sense." Darius sensed where this story was leading and didn't trust the "Hakor" character at all.

Lex continued. "Trogus later made Hakor a judge to settle any disputes in the land. Hakor's position soon rose to that of the 'Governing Man' when he foresaw a drought that allowed them to save food and water and survive it. But after a while, he was not content.

"Hakor came to resent that he alone was not the focus of the people's adoration. After all, as Governing Man—or go-man as they had begun to call him—it was he and not his parents who worked hardest in the tribe. The envy poisoned him like a fruit left to rot, and he devised a plot to usurp his parents.

"To do so, he needed the only one immune to his powers dead, and deemed his mother's gifts would kill Trogus and destroy the partnership that had ruled over him for too long in his eyes."

"I've heard of only children being spoilt," Darius said, "but this one is something else."

"After luring his mother to a secluded place," Lex said, "Hakor persuaded her that her powers would best serve the people if relocated into a staff. No one knows how long the conversation lasted or what Hakor promised her, but she eventually agreed. She took hold of the staff and willingly drained all her power, her algor, into it until empty. It was then that Hakor took hold of her and drained her very soul into the weapon, magnifying its power many times over.

"With her last words, Arria damned her son for his lies and cursed him to never speak another word. Then his mouth sealed shut as the go-man sapped the last of her essence."

Lex took a pause in the story as they ventured close enough to Laltos to see the old earthwork ramparts outside, the trenches, and the breached wall that had sealed the city's fate. Her steps became more laboured and would only get worse. Meanwhile, Selene's gaze seemed to point anywhere but to her old city.

"I'm guessing that's the Staff of Arria," Darius said, eager to focus the two women on something else. "So what did the goman do with it?"

Lex didn't respond and instead took a small waterskin Darius knew was filled with cold tea and began drinking it.

Selene's voice then broke the silence, the first time he'd heard it since she snapped at him. "Trogus learned of his son's betrayal, and Hakor was now ready for the fight he'd long craved. The two met, and Trogus discovered all too late the effect of the concentrated power in the Staff. He fought valiantly to avenge his wife but was ultimately overpowered. With the last of his strength, he thrust his twin blades into the Staff and willed all his power and might to flee from his body and into the weapons. The ferven obliged, and once all his rage resided in the blades, they ignited in an inferno, burning the Staff almost to ash until Hakor pulled it away just in time."

Suddenly those swords sounded more appealing to Darius. If they could damage the Staff of Arria, it was hard to imagine how much power resided in them. And if Hadrian got hold of them…

"So did Trogus kill Hakor?" Darius asked.

Selene shook her head. "Hakor recoiled, took his dagger, and thrust it into his father's heart."

Darius cursed. "And then what? How did the people escape Hakor's rule to get to where we are now?"

Selene shrugged. "The songs end."

"We only know one thing," Lex said, finally having found her voice again, "every rakkan that has wielded the Twin Blades of Trogus has bound every legion to obey them. No rakkan can resist—" Her stare suddenly shifted south.

The Chief Priest and Gorgias had stopped ahead and looked back fretfully.

"Xavalans?" Darius asked.

Lex nodded, and they rushed towards the others. Nasrin hurried too, with Lyra soon beside her and hysteria in her panicked dash.

"They have at least five hundred horses," the Chief Priest said, so quickly the words almost became garbled.

"How far?" Darius asked.

"A few miles. If we hurry, we might make it into the city without them seeing."

But Darius could imagine the pain being there would bring to Lex and Selene.

"Why go into Laltos?" he asked. "We can hide in the old farms as we pass the city and loop around to the Cliffs."

"But Hadrian's trail leads through Laltos," Aran said.

"The tunnel…" Lex muttered.

Darius studied the road in front of them, searching for Hadrian's so-called trail that had so far remained invisible to both him and Lyra.

"How can you know where Hadrian went?" Darius asked.

"My escort," Aran said, but there was a nervous flicker in his features.

"To the gate. Quickly!" Lex shoved Nasrin and the Chief Priest into a run, and everyone else soon followed.

49

Darius – Ruins of Laltos

The battered, mangled gates of Laltos soon came into sight as they sprinted up another old earthwork rampart. The road had ended a few hundred yards back as the former defences began. Although the winds and time had flattened many of the trenches and ramps, it wasn't enough to help the Chief Priest's wheezing as he lumbered up and down.

"How far away are the cavalry now?" Darius asked as Lyra bounded ahead of him. He'd known travelling on the roads was a risk.

"A mile at most." Lex gazed back at the road while she ran as if she expected the Silk City's army to appear at any moment.

Darius murmured to himself.

"Don't say 'I told you so,'" Lex said.

"Wouldn't dream of it." If only they'd listened to him…

He was barely at a jog, keeping behind Nasrin and the slower priest, who—with all his wisdom—had decided to wear a long robe for the journey that made it difficult for him to run.

Gorgias sprinted ahead with his escort clutched tightly in his arms and was the first to disappear into the city ruins while Darius searched the sky for Xavalan escorts. There was Tiro and some other birds, but who knew whether they were wild or not.

Were the Xavalans heading for the ruins or farther north, or perhaps Dolthea? Darius wasn't sure which to hope for.

The group finally made it through the old gates into Laltos without any sight of the Xavalans and headed straight towards the palace. Once deep inside the eerily quiet streets, they slowed their pace and allowed the Chief Priest to catch his breath.

The charred, beaten buildings around them were reflected in Lex's and Selene's wide eyes as they walked. Many buildings bore so many holes and scars that the stones looked ready to crumble at the first hard gust of wind.

The two women peered around and slowed to a creep as if the cavalry outside the city were of less concern than the horror now surrounding them. After a few ruined streets, Lex's gaze dropped firmly to the dust and scrap on the ground and remained fixed there while she tightened her hairband every minute. Selene, on the other hand, continued peering, touching the cuts in the stonework where a fired kuraminium sword had landed a savage slash. At some spots, her attention lingered longer, although her silent demeanour didn't give Darius a hint of the thoughts disturbing her.

After reaching a bridge over the main river through the city, Aran bent over and stopped, his pale grey hair dropping over his once youthful skin to conceal the old man he apparently was.

"Just a few moments," he said, "if you please."

Lex turned with a huff.

"Carry on and find somewhere safe," Darius said. "I'll stay with him. We'll catch up to you when he's ready."

The others agreed and left Darius and Selene to look out over the water. Only then did he notice the submerged bodies: humans, rakkans and horses looking eerily pale. The rains over the last few months had given the river a heavy flow and now fell from the sky again, sending thousands of ripples across the water to thankfully mask the death within. The sound erased the horror around and almost made up for the head of rain-soaked hair he'd have to put up with later. As he watched and tried to recall the calming waves of the southern sea he'd enjoyed weeks ago, Selene took his hand and squeezed it lightly.

When he looked her in the eye, at the raindrops dripping down her cheek almost like tears, he saw a kindness that meant the gesture had been for *his* comfort, not her own. She'd clearly lost none of her former selflessness, and he couldn't wait until they found the Magician and undid whatever had been done. Then this kind woman would be whole once again.

After a long wait idly watching the water, the Chief Priest finally summoned the energy to stand up straight again.

"Ready?" Darius asked. Even Lyra seemed frustrated at the man's poor form.

"Can we walk?" the Chief Priest asked.

"If it's quickly."

"Very well." The Chief Priest looked around at the wet ruins and dead remains with a grimace. "This place…"

Darius wished the man wouldn't draw more of Selene's attention to the painful memories in the surrounding city. The sooner they were holed up somewhere, the better.

"Sorry for making you linger outside more than you must," Aran said. "Being here must be difficult for you."

"It is," Darius said, looking around at the dead, wet city. "I bloody hate rain."

Aran gave a tired shake of his head, and they set off again in the same direction as the others, soon cloaked by a silence as unnerving as the last time he'd come here, as if the dead were listening. And flutters in his stomach came from Lyra too. He made sure to walk with Selene on his left and the Chief Priest on his right, with enough distance between the two.

"I wish you'd heed my advice," the Chief Priest said. "We should head to Mount Psilos. That is where your quest must end."

Darius grunted but would still defer to Lex for such decisions, as he had for days.

"May I ask you a question?" the Chief Priest asked.

"Sure. I've still got a few myself."

"Is it true you fear blood?"

Darius turned his face away from the man. "Why would I?"

"You tell me."

Just the reminder of the warm liquid made the rain chill him even more. He considered his reply to the man and tried to decide which of his own questions needed asking. So far, he'd extracted few answers.

"It wasn't your fault, you know?" the Chief Priest said.

"What wasn't?"

"You know."

Darius turned back to glare at the man. "If you don't stop speaking cryptically, I'll show you how tolerant of blood I've become."

The Chief Priest raised an eyebrow. "Charming."

"Well, it isn't like they call me 'Darius the Charming.'"

"No, just the Saviour of—"

Darius's scoff cut the man off. "Don't. I'm no saviour."

"Why do you say that? Because you didn't save *him*?"

Amid? This time Darius's glare bore more than frustration but a rising anger. "Because I don't save *anyone*."

The Chief Priest let a wider gap grow between them as they walked.

"Look, I'm sorry for being moody," Darius said. "The rain makes me irritable."

"It's fine," Aran said. "Tell me, do you believe in good and evil?"

"What?" The shift in topic took Darius off-guard, but at least it was better than the last. "Of course. I've had enough wicked things done to me to know."

"But do you believe they are objectively real? Was it evil to mutilate a child, regardless of your opinions on the matter? Would it still be evil if you, or everyone else, didn't care?"

"You should talk to Lex. She's interested in such high-brow questions."

"It's not her answer that I'm interested in."

Whatever the man's point, Darius couldn't see what the opinion of a lowly warrior was worth. But he didn't need more than a moment to ponder the question of whether Amid being stabbed in the gut was wicked, or whether the horrors that had taken place in the haunted city they walked through were wrong. He knew it in his core.

"I've seen evil," Darius muttered. "It's not an opinion."

At that moment, he sensed Lyra's anxiety to move faster, so he upped his speed and gave her a scratch behind the ear. "Easy, girl," Darius said. "We'll be out of this place soon."

When he looked back at the Chief Priest, the man was grinning with a new relief.

"How can you smile?" Darius asked. "*Here?*"

"Your bond. It pleases me."

"Admiring your handiwork?"

"My work? No. I bond the minds of people and beasts. It is they that choose whether to use that bond to build a fruitful relationship or an exploitative one."

Unfortunately, Darius had seen algus do the latter over the years. "While we're on the topic of escorts, I have a question for you. Every time your pteron is close by, Lyra can sense it."

Darius's words seemed to strike a horror that stole the man's former amusement and gave way to shame again.

"Yes…" Aran said. "I'm afraid that I broke my most important tenet: a priest only uses his powers on the willing. It was my most grievous transgression against you, and I've regretted it every day since. But I did what I did, and I've tried to at least make good come of it since."

Darius's voice dropped low. "And what did you do?"

"Our…escorts are linked—not bonded fully but in a much milder way. I have to confess that I did it to keep track of you."

Was it evil to give a holy man a backhand? Darius wouldn't test it. Yet. "You did something to her when I met you the first time?"

"I know…" Aran's words became rushed. "I never usually lay hands on people without their permission, even escorts, but I couldn't resist. I hadn't intended to, but there was something different about your connection, almost like you'd forgotten a part of yourself when you brought her to me a year ago. I take it the rumours about you and Archimedes are true?"

As unsettling as it was to learn someone had such powers over him when he was blissfully unaware, if Lex trusted this man, he should give him the benefit of the doubt. Darius doubted this revelation would change Lex's opinion, but it would be nice if she shared her reasoning with him for once.

Darius grunted. "The goman got to me, but I had the last laugh. I sleep better after slaying men that meddle with me like that."

The Chief Priest's face reddened. "Forgive me. It was just a rash, impulsive act. I'd been in the west for months. I'd seen what the Viridian Legion was doing, and I thought you were the only one that could end this devastating war—and I still do. But I didn't just link my pteron to Lyra. I had you and your escort close for the briefest moment, and I said a little prayer to repair what I could of your bond."

Darius frowned. Was that why his shared experiences with Lyra were occasionally deeper of late? "But I never felt any different then. It's only been since the Battle of Laltos that I…" Then it hit him. Up until that point, Lyra had either been unconscious or they'd been apart. He'd sensed some deeper connection to her while away, but he'd assumed that was some facet of their existing link.

"Would you like me to repair the bond in full?" the Chief Priest asked with a desperate lift of his eyebrows.

Lyra stopped suddenly and gazed at the man. A surge of excitement rushed through Darius that was both his own and hers.

"You can do that?" Darius asked.

"Of course. But maybe we should find shelter first, out of this 'bloody rain.'"

Perhaps Darius should have refused to let this man touch him ever again, but the offer seduced him and Lyra with too great a force to resist.

"Fine," Darius said. "But I'm not dressing up in white."

"Very well. White is only for the pure, anyway." Aran gave a weak grin that strengthened with relief when Darius snorted a laugh in reply.

They hurried along and followed Lyra's lead. Darius knew his panther had tracked Lex's scent and felt how strong and cherished it was by his escort. Eventually, she led them to the old Laltos Bank, and they found the others waiting inside.

Fragments of pillars still hung from the high ceiling like stained, grey stalactites. The stone archways that had once connected them formed wavy lines, and many bore cracks as if the mass of the building above strained and willed to collapse.

Gorgias and Nasrin stowed their things between some of the pillars that remained standing. Meanwhile, Lex sat cloaked in a shadowed alcove near the entrance, which gave her a good view of anyone approaching in the street or the lower city. Without rakkan eyesight, Darius wouldn't have seen her harrowed expression. He considered going to sit with her for a while but would have to bring Selene with him, and Lex usually preferred sitting alone with her thoughts in times like these.

Conversely, Darius wanted his mind occupied with other things, so he turned to the Chief Priest and said, "Are we doing this or not?"

Aran placed down his small bag next to Nasrin and sighed. "Yes. I'll need a few moments."

"Very well," Darius said.

"We'll rest here for the night," Lex said in a monotone that was almost like a Numbered's. "Tiro has found Sulla. He'll join us in the morning once the cavalry have passed. Then we'll go to the Cliffs, find Hadrian, and Nasrin can help us find the Magician."

At the words, Nasrin dropped the biscuit she'd been nibbling and shakily picked it back up. And she wasn't the only one hesitant to meet the Magician.

Darius walked over to her and asked, "Is that all right with you, Nasrin?"

She smiled, though her eyes betrayed her fear. "Of course. I'm sorry, I was just thinking about the Xavalans."

Darius sat next to her, with Selene following his lead, and rested a hand on the carer's shoulder, a touch that seemed to take her by surprise—a welcome one.

"Don't worry," he said. "They won't find us here."

"And if they d-do"—Gorgias smacked his fist into his palm—"we have the Slayer of Gods to smite them."

Darius rolled his eyes and murmured, "I'm not invincible. Five hundred horsemen would be a stretch." The sooner Sulla came with his men, the better. Not only did Darius need his friend, but they also needed warriors.

"No. But Gorgias is right." Nasrin's smile warmed. "It's the others who depend on our task that I fear for, those who will suffer if I fail to reason with Shirin. But I'm not afraid for myself. When we're with you, I feel safe and brave, even in this cursed city."

Had she forgotten he'd been there at the Battle of Laltos and made little difference? "I don't know why."

"You inspire us." Gorgias finished stowing his bag and weapons, then came over to them. "I saw you on the battlefield after we escaped Laltos. Men were ready to follow you to d-death, even ones as noble as me."

"Nobody had much choice about it," Darius said.

"They had a choice whether to face death with valour or terror," Nasrin added.

Lex and the Chief Priest showed little interest in the conversation, but Selene was watching him with curiosity. She hadn't been with him after they'd escaped Laltos because he'd failed to protect her.

"You should hear what the slaves in Dolthea said about you," Nasrin said.

"I'd rather not." Darius unfastened the ties on his armour and began stripping it to get comfortable.

"Do you know what it's like," Nasrin continued, "to have the man you fear most in the Empire suddenly fight for you?"

"I did that once."

"Twice now," Gorgias said.

"They've seen you for what you really are," Nasrin said.

"And what's that?" Darius asked, though he still wasn't sure he wanted to hear the answer.

"A defender. The only algus in the Empire to bear a slave's name."

It wasn't the first time he'd heard that said of him. All algus rid themselves of their old tribe names to adopt one originating from the ruling class. This was about as much undeserved reverence as he could take without retching.

"I'm not an algus." He stood, helping Selene to her feet too, and made his way over to the Chief Priest, who had since moved into a separate hallway and was busy scrolling through some short texts he'd brought. The hall must have been a corridor for slaves to navigate the building while remaining unseen because it was bare and so narrow that the light from outside hardly found a way in—much like the basement where he'd watched the bonding. Perhaps Dianoia preferred the dark.

The others now sat out of sight, and the breeze from outdoors whistled through the hall and brought a wet chill.

"You ready?" Darius asked.

"What? Oh, yes," the Chief Priest said.

Darius sensed Lyra leap up and bound over to them. It was only then that he thought Selene might not want to witness this.

"Are you happy to watch?" he asked her. "I forgot, Laltos is where you lost him."

She frowned. "Who?"

"… Paris." Darius still recalled the splatter of black blood as the King's Sword had sliced through her pteron.

Selene shuddered but smiled bravely. "I'll be fine."

The Chief Priest slowly slipped off his gloves and positioned himself directly in front of them with his clean palms raised and waiting. "Are you ready? Do you give me permission to perform this ritual?"

Darius nodded, and Lyra came forward, eagerly craning her neck.

The Chief Priest placed one hand on the panther's head and the other on Darius's, the touch as light and warm as a summer breeze. Aran then began chanting words that were either too fast to understand or in a forgotten language, and they ran on for so long Darius feared something was wrong. The room hadn't brightened. There was no mist clouding the Chief Priest's eyes. Nothing.

Darius looked to Lyra and could tell she felt nothing either.

Then he gazed at the priest. "Am I supposed to—?"

Something hit him like a wave of darkness that stole the room from around him and left him falling through the world into pitch black at a blistering pace. The Chief Priest's words still echoed around, but there was no source, no one else to hear. Until she came.

He sensed Lyra's presence at once like she'd tumbled from above and he'd caught her instantly in a warm embrace. He was lost in her dark fur as they plummeted together. Mist rose around them. Chants rang out like a deep chorus of a dark yet benevolent ensemble.

Time passed slowly, but he didn't care. Every moment brought him closer to Lyra until it was if his spirit had been thrust inside her body, merging them into one. He opened his eyes—only they weren't his own. He saw himself standing there with his shaggy dark beard and a thick cloak hugging a muscular, armoured frame. Did he always look so scruffy?

He hadn't the time to contemplate because he was suddenly ripped away and back into his own body. Gasping, he fell backwards, only avoiding crashing onto the ground when Selene reached out and caught his back mid-fall. But shock still gripped him. Suddenly, he was aware of everything his eyes and ears and skin sensed and more. Smells that he'd never noticed before registered, only he couldn't actually smell them. He knew the strained look on Selene's face behind him, shaking under his weight, but he couldn't see her. Whatever had happened, it wasn't anything like he'd imagined.

"Feel better?" the Chief Priest asked with a smile.

Finally able to collect his wits again, Darius staggered back to his feet and blinked a few times as if it would ease the overwhelming mixture of senses assaulting him.

"I feel…different," he said.

Lyra came and snuggled her head under his neck, and the sensation brought a warmth and unity he'd never experienced before, even when his body had been interlaced with Selene's in bed a year ago. Was this how all algus felt with their escorts? If so, how could some be so cruel to the creatures?

"You'll adjust," the Chief Priest said, answering Darius's unasked question. "But for now, it's best to keep your mind focused on something else and not get lost in each other's thoughts and senses."

Despite wanting to test out his new connection to its fullest, he could hardly argue with the advice of a man who had proven so adept up to now. Perhaps he should even reconsider the priest's advice to head to Mount Psilos rather than the Cliffs.

The Chief Priest left and nudged Lyra away with him while Darius stood shakily and tried to grow accustomed to discerning between his own sensations and those of Lyra.

"How do you feel?" Selene asked.

"Strange. Thanks for catching me. Maybe I should have left our bond as it was. I don't want to be distracted when the time comes to fight."

Selene came closer and fiddled with his cloak, which had become loose and skewed. "Don't fret. You're still the best fighter in the Empire. None can slay you."

If only that were true. "I'm not afraid for myself."

She gazed into his eyes with her breath held for a few moments. "Then who are you afraid for?"

Why did she even need to ask? "Lyra, Lex and you." Every day he spent chained to Selene brought a greater fear that the subtle manipulation of her mind wouldn't be undone. But he had to ignore those fears; he had to believe she'd be made whole once again.

She frowned and studied him nervously for so long that he worried about what was going on behind her eyes. Was being in this city too much for her to take? Darius hadn't focused on what lay ahead before, but every day they came closer to facing Hadrian was a day closer to Selene facing her torturers. Perhaps she wasn't ready and was pushing herself into something painful. Maybe the Chief Priest's plan would be better for her.

But there was also the possibility that the Magician's magic was working before his eyes.

"Are you all right?" Darius dared to touch her shoulder.

"Fine." But her lie was transparent.

"Come here." Darius took her hand and pulled her farther down the bare corridor and away from those in the next room. Once shrouded, he took both her hands and bent until their noses almost touched. "You can talk to me, be honest with me. You don't have to hide your scars from me because I've been there. Is it this place? Is it that you're not ready to face Hadrian? Because if you say so, we'll find another way to the Magician."

"No." Selene brushed her fingers against his cheek. "It's not that. I'm just…tired of being in these chains. I wish I could prove to you that I'm still me, and my feelings are still real, but I haven't dared because I see you're angry with me."

"I'm not angry," he said. The memory of her betrayal was the cruellest one he had, one never able to be purged from his mind, and one that came to the forefront whenever he gazed into her hazel eyes and recalled all the love the sight had once borne. But he was past being angry with her, especially after seeing her so plagued.

She placed another soft hand on his face, which sent flutters through his stomach as well as causing other areas to stir. Old feelings that had long lay dormant returned as if they'd never left. She was no less beautiful now than she had been a year ago. His desires were tainted by what she'd done but were suddenly animal-like and overcame rational thought. It took all his restraint to control himself, but he did. In the other room was a woman who had never betrayed him like that.

As he opened his mouth to explain himself, Selene suddenly pressed forward and kissed him. Despite his earlier resoluteness, a fierce rush of heat gripped him, a carnal desire to grab her hips, lift her from the ground, throw her against a wall and—

A deep growl from the corridor brought his wits back to him. He ripped his lips away and turned to see Lyra glaring at him from the entrance to the other room, thankfully alone.

Selene gasped and panted, back pressed against the wall. Her kiss was the same it had been in the past: a raw, intense craving that he'd shared at the time. It only proved to him again that her true nature was deep in there, battling to come out against whatever perversions were laid inside. How could he harbour bitterness for a woman going through such internal struggles?

Lust fired up Selene's eyes for a moment before her expression morphed into one of sorrow. "I can't believe you still don't trust me."

Lyra prowled forwards; her amber eyes narrowed on Selene. Darius's own gaze was drawn to the scars still visible on Selene's neck, the same brutal ones he had because of her.

"Just take me somewhere," Selene said, voice breaking. "Chain me to a pillar. I don't want to be near you anymore."

The guilt made Darius want to snap the chains with his hands there and then, but the logical part of his mind knew that would be foolish. So why was it so tempting? Why did he already have the chain in his hand, ready to flare ferven and melt it in an instant?

He nodded slowly, then silently took her back into the main room. He retrieved the key to the shackles from Lex and guided a sullen-looking Selene to a more secluded corner of the room, still within sight, but where the chatter of the others wouldn't bother her so much.

"Call me if you need me," Darius said.

She didn't respond and instead brought her knees up and huddled herself tightly, tears threatening to fall from her eyes. Darius couldn't bear to look, so he went over to Lex, who'd been watching her sister curiously throughout.

"What's wrong with Selene?" Lex asked.

"She's chained up," Darius said. "I don't think anyone would be happy about that. Or maybe it's this place and the prospect of facing the Viridians again. How are *you* feeling being here?"

Lex tried to give a nonchalant shrug, but her pain was evident in the crow's feet on her face.

"You're not as good a liar as you think," he said.

"Oh, really?"

"It's your eyes. They betray you."

They narrowed at him. "Then I must demand you stop looking into them."

"It's not so easy when they're so…" *Alluring*. He couldn't say the last word aloud and regretted even beginning the sentence. "So…are you going to collect any of your gold while we're here?"

Lex took a deep breath and broke her stare at the change of subject. "Not now, but I have my plans for it."

"I thought you might." Although she'd never tell him what they were. "So, now that I've spoken with Selene more, I…"

"Don't tell me you want to release her." Lex's tone made plain her objection to the idea, but despite partly agreeing with her, Darius's resolve was beginning to falter. They couldn't keep Selene chained somewhere if they found the Viridians. It would be too dangerous. Yet the other option bore not only a risk to him but Lex and the others.

"I'll leave her restrained for now," he muttered. "But we need a better solution for keeping her safe until we can heal her mind."

50

Darius – Cliffs of Aphatos

The next day, they ate and set off towards the tunnel carved into the mountain behind the palace in Laltos. Despite both Lex and the Chief Priest being sure they'd found Hadrian's trail, Darius spent most of his time ruminating on the Magician. Although he didn't like to admit it, he didn't care what bonds Nasrin held with that woman. Anyone that harmed Selene would feel the sharp end of his sword.

But if they had a lead on the Viridian Warlord, he supposed they'd be foolish not to focus on him first instead of the Waif.

As they passed through the gates into the palace grounds and made their way up the hill, Darius finally spotted tracks on the overgrown lawn that once ran pristinely alongside the street.

"Hadrian can't be far ahead," Darius said to Lex. "These boot prints are fresh."

"He isn't far," Lex said, all the while peering up at the shattered former home of her father. "But those aren't Viridian tracks."

Before Darius could ask anything else, he spotted figures standing in the deep shadow of the cliff behind the palace. The others wouldn't be able to see through the darkness, but he recognised Margalvian armour even in dim light.

For the first time in a long while, a smile spread across his face. He lowered his head and tried to hide it. After all, the withered corpses and city around him shouldn't have brought even the thought of a grin. But how could he not smile when all he now imagined was Sulla's wolfish greeting?

Darius upped his pace until ahead of Gorgias and the Chief Priest. Selene didn't thank him for the rush, but at least it distracted her from the surrounding dire memories.

As they approached, the rakkans noted their arrival and barked to the others. They came forward, readying their shields and spears, but stopped when Darius held up a hand with ferven and algor glowing from different fingers.

One rakkan pushed his way to the front of the other men, stepping out of the shadows to let the noon sun shine on the horns of his helmet.

"Look who finally turned up," Sulla drawled. He slipped off his headpiece, and his wide grin set dimples to join the folds and scars on his cheeks. A fresh cut to his forehead had been stitched up through the eyebrow but was far from the most brutal wound Darius had seen on the man.

Selene's steps slowed, and eventually, she hung back so far the chain attaching her to Darius became as tense as her shoulders looked.

"It's all right," he said to her as they approached. "These are the good rakkans." Slowing his pace to one Selene was

487

comfortable with, Darius made a rough count of the men Sulla had brought. They numbered a century of rakkans, and all wore the red bands of the Militia rather than black, but he wouldn't complain. Even the warriors of the Red Militia could rival Viridian Legionnaires any day, and these men bore many of the same fresh scars of battle as their Militia Chief. Along with the rakkans were half a dozen algus Darius didn't recognise, half with bows and quivers, the other half with only swords.

When he reached Sulla, the rakkan grabbed him in a strong hug that threatened to bend his cuirass.

"Easy, Chief," Darius wheezed.

"Too strong for you?" Sulla said, ruffling his hair. "You're too young to be growing weak, Dar. And what's with this fluff all over your chin? Someone get this man a razor!"

One of the warriors ran off, seemingly to do just that while Darius shook his head and pushed his friend away. "Whatever helps me go unnoticed."

Sulla scoffed. "Unnoticed? You should *want* people to recognise you. They've been telling stories of you, Dar. They say you slew a thousand cavalry a few months ago and an entire century of algus the week before. The Viridians are quaking."

Darius snorted. "Lies. Don't believe every rumour you hear."

"Oh, I don't. I was the one who started them!" Sulla gave Darius a stiff pat on the back and made his way over to Lex and the Chief Priest, bowing as he met them. "Greetings, blue-eyes. Who's the guy in the dress?"

"This is a ceremonial robe." Aran lifted his chin. "My name's Aran, and I'm a humble priest trying to help these good people how I can. Whilst my position is a lowly one, I have some—"

"Forget I asked." Sulla rolled his eyes.

Lex looked at the rakkan with a slight shake of her head. "Are you finished? Have you been in the tunnel yet?"

Sulla opened his mouth to reply, but one of his men stepped forward and spoke first. "It's been cleared recently. We found some food they must have dropped that wasn't too mouldy or rotten."

Lex nodded sternly. "That confirms what we thought."

"Then what are we wasting time for?" Sulla gave a hand signal to his men, and they immediately began moving, ready to march without having to pack up belongings or supplies. The little they had already hung from their backs but wouldn't last them more than a few days, so the algus must have been hunting for them as they went.

One rakkan returned while Darius mused and handed him a razor.

"You were serious?" Darius muttered.

"You *should* shave," Selene said when he hesitated in taking it. "Sulla's right."

Darius looked to Nasrin and asked her, "Will it help with the Magician if I'm still disguised?"

The carer shook her head so quickly it was almost a nervous shiver.

As they all made their way through the entrance to the tunnel, Darius began hacking away at his beard, tossing some water from his waterskin over it when trying to get the last half an inch. The task wasn't easy on the move, and soon he and Selene had dropped to the back of their new enlarged group while he made a mess of his hair.

"Oh, give it here." Selene snatched the razor from him. "You're botching it so much you'll look like a three-fingered drunk cut it. Let me; then we'll run and catch the rest up."

The pair stopped, and before Darius could decide whether it was wise of them to fall behind, Selene took hold of his head, twisted it to the side, and slowly ran the blade down his cheek with a delicateness that made his mind again return to their entwined bodies. He was so distracted by the thoughts that Selene had already knelt him down and moved to his head, cutting the hair to his usual length, when he realised she had a sharp weapon that could have slashed his neck in a heartbeat.

His reaction should have been that of any warrior: to shove her away and ready his weapon. But for some reason, her touch was warm and welcome and safe. If Lex had seen them, she'd have been livid, but thankfully she was deeper in the tunnel, where the only light was from the ferven of the rakkans lighting the way for the rest.

"There," Selene said finally. "Much more handsome."

Darius stood gingerly, wiping the loose hair from his head and shoulders, ready for anything, but Selene handed him back the razor without hesitation. He tossed it to the side of the tunnel quickly and gaped at her.

"You could have killed me," he said.

"I know." She turned to leave and pulled him along with the chain as if he were a fool for even dwelling on the realisation for more than a second. Perhaps she was right to be annoyed. So far, she'd never done anything to suggest she intended him harm.

They ran and soon caught up with the others, and as they emerged from the tunnel on the side of a hill, a sprawling landscape met them, dirty green hills rolling up and down like a stormy ocean. There weren't many cliffs within view now that they were at the top, but the occasional dark fragment of rock jutted out in places, giving a taste of the hardness beneath the greenery. And through the damp earth, the only hint in the terrain that people had visited here was a trail of heavy boot prints left by the Viridians.

"Darius. Sulla." Lex waved them both into a huddle and dropped her voice. "Given we have Hadrian's trail, we'll focus on him first and forget the Magician for now."

"And what about Selene?" Darius asked. As much as he relished the prospect of performing his new ritual with Hadrian's blood, he didn't want Selene chained for any longer than necessary.

Sulla glanced at him, then at the chain attaching him to her.

"About that," Sulla said, "do you want to secure her to one of my men? Doesn't make sense to have our best warrior out of the fight."

"That's smart," Lex said. "I'm surprised you came up with it."

Sulla grinned. "A good idea had to come sooner or later."

Darius watched Selene's reaction, knowing she'd heard, and her deepening frown indicated her disapproval. If he'd been in her place, he wouldn't have wanted to be handed off to a strange rakkan, especially after being tortured by them for a year. Unlike Lex, Selene had little positive experience of rakkans in her life.

"Only if Selene agrees to it." Darius tugged her chain and brought her into the conversation.

She didn't feign ignorance of what they'd said but gave a shrug of her shoulders. "Chained is chained. What difference is it to me?"

Although her reaction surprised Darius, he wouldn't raise any objection and risk changing her mind. Sulla was right. He needed to be free to fight.

"I'll put my most trusted man on it. Atticus!" Sulla waved over his commander.

491

"Yes, Chief?" the commander answered after marching over, his voice as calm and neat as his clothes and armour. Although not the tallest rakkan, Atticus carried himself with pulled-back shoulders and a self-confident swagger that made him seem twice his size amongst the other surly warriors, yet the scratches on his cuirass and armguards and lack of wounds proved his self-assurance wasn't just all show.

Darius only vaguely knew the rakkan from drinking with Sulla before he'd been exiled from Margalvia and trusted the commander enough from what he'd seen.

After they explained the situation to Atticus and shackled Selene to him instead, they set off and followed the footprints while Lyra—and now Darius through their bond—finally caught a trace of a scent. A deep-seated anger rose to the surface when Lyra recognised Hadrian's musk.

Now that the sun was rising in the sky, the rakkans sheltered themselves beneath long, billowing cloaks dyed with a dirty grey tone that melded them into the surroundings. The white tarnflowers that had once peppered the top of the Cliffs were long dead and didn't look to have bloomed in the spring just passed. Only thin grass remained, but not enough to cheer the dreary landscape. It evoked mixed feelings. As they roamed ever deeper, the hills became broken and scarred, split with scattered cliff faces and fractures in the ground that gave a sense of a giant staircase of gods, collapsed centuries ago. Yet that only made it feel that much more isolated, barren and dead.

The Chief Priest continued his advice for them to alter course towards Mount Psilos, but Darius's attention was now too focused on his target to even respond. Lex and Lyra walked beside him in silence, comforting presences that let him forget the people and drama of the last few weeks and instead focus on the merciless killer he needed to become again.

After a mile of trekking, the tracks led down a steep slope into a thick, deep crevice that cut through the landscape. It stretched as far as Darius could see and branched off several times, like a sketch of a colossal tree scratched into dry ground. At some points, it was no wider than a man, but at others, he couldn't have leapt across it.

"That's not good," Nasrin whispered.

"What?" Darius asked.

"This fissure was one of the places I was going to check for Shirin. It's where she met me once."

If the Magician had already killed the warlord for him, so be it. He turned to Lex. "Does Tiro see anything?"

"Vaguely," she replied. "There's someone down there, but the crevice is too deep to see much."

With the sun still rising in the sky, they could either wait until noon for the light to shine to the bottom, or Darius could go in. And he wasn't a patient man.

"We'll make too much racket if we all go down there," Darius said. "I'll scout first and see what I find." He took a step towards the gorge, but Lex seized his arm.

"Wait," she said. "Gorgias should cover from above, just in case."

If there was one person Darius wanted covering him from above in a narrow crevice, it certainly wasn't Gorgias. The last time Darius had seen him shoot a bow, he'd have been lucky to hit the ground if he was aiming for it.

"How about Selene?" Darius said.

Lex shook her head. "No. And I'm going with you into the fissure."

"I don't think that's the best—"

"If the Magician is there, you'll need me."

As much as he feared for her safety, she had a point he couldn't refute, and it wasn't like he was intending to get into a fight right now. Sulla and the rakkans wouldn't be able to help against the Magician, and he trusted no other algus there to have his back more than Lex.

"Make sure you have the powder ready." Lex slipped a hand into her pocket while Darius verified the pouch she'd given him previously was still stashed in his tunic. Once sure, he walked over to Sulla with Lyra following at his heel.

"Keep Selene safe," Darius said. "I want Lyra to go with her."

His panther growled with annoyance at the prospect of leaving him, but she'd obey his wishes. The last time she'd faced Hadrian, things hadn't gone well.

"Will do," Sulla said. "I'll send her with the carer, the holy man, and a dozen of my men to hide in those rocks over there. My algus with bows will stay by Gorgias while the rest of us will wait for you at the top of this ramp. Give us a signal if you want us to charge in."

Darius gave his friend a pat. "Will do." Next, he walked towards Gorgias, who stood by the fissure while Lex filled him in on the plan. Unfortunately, the nervous quiver in the man's lip hardly filled Darius with confidence. Despite that, Darius would rather have a man he trusted—at least, trusted as much as possible—watching over him than just the other algus, many of whom had probably enjoyed his torture in their city. And the irony of him trusting the man who had actually overseen the whippings and beatings wasn't lost on him. But that was then; this was now.

"Is that clear?" Lex asked Gorgias.

"Yes. I'll do what I can," Gorgias replied, doubt filling his voice.

"Don't mess this up," Darius said. "I don't want either me or Lex to die down there." But the words only seemed to paralyse the juvenile man with more fear.

Perhaps I need to instil confidence for once. Darius relaxed his posture and softened his expression to hide the tension gripping his innards, then placed a hand around Gorgias's shoulders.

The man flinched at the touch, but after a second, seemed to relax under it.

"We wouldn't ask you if we didn't trust you," Darius said. "But you've got to trust in yourself. You're the man who went into a Viridian camp on your own and got information on Selene. Compared to that, this can't be so scary."

"The *man*…?" After a few deep breaths, Gorgias's eyes fired with a newfound courage. "Yes, I did do that. Don't worry, I'll protect you both, mast—" His voice trailed away from the word as Darius shook a finger at him.

"That's right," Darius said. "I'm your ally, not your master."

Gorgias scoffed, but at the same time his lips curled slightly into a confident smile.

When Darius turned to head down the ramp and into the fissure, Lex followed, gaping.

"What?" he said, pulling out his gladius and checking the blade was still sharp enough to cleave Viridian bones. A nick to his finger confirmed it was.

"It's been a long time since I saw you inspire someone like that," Lex said.

"Well, don't get used to it," he said with a laugh. "Being nice makes me feel so dirty I want to shudder."

"I hope you're jesting."

He was, but couldn't fathom why she seemed to want him to be nice all of a sudden. *She* wasn't nice and was fine with that. And so was he, strangely.

He looked back to catch a last glimpse of Lyra prowling away with the others. The panther turned. *Keep them safe.* Without hearing any words in reply, he knew Lyra wished him and Lex the same.

Then he carried on down the dirt ramp into the rocky scar in the landscape, stepping in a pair of large footprints made however many hours earlier. He closed his eyes and emptied his mind, gripped his gladius to remember the stiffness of the challenge that might soon await him. He could afford no distractions if they came across the Magician.

The darkness of the crevice soon blanketed both him and Lex, with tall, flat faces of rock towering over them at either side, as if they were ants in a dry crack. His rakkan eyes saw as far ahead as the rocky corners in the path, and once in the narrow gap, the movements of the air ceased entirely, as stark a shock as the sudden silence that fell.

They stalked single file, Darius at the front, and reached a few forks along the way. But he followed the turns that led deeper into the ground, and eventually, he heard dull echoes that came from within, so faint and raspy he wasn't sure whether it was from people or monsters lurking in the depths. He allowed the briefest of moments to concentrate on Lyra and her new hiding spot above, checking the others were safely out of harm's way.

Turning his attention back to the crevice, he climbed onto a nearby ledge and shimmied through a narrower crack in the rock, now with only a slither of daylight far above his head. It was clear no one had taken this route, but soon voices became unmistakable, and he wanted a safe place to hide and listen, to wait for a time to kill should one present itself.

Lex followed behind him as silently as his shadow.

"Where is she?" someone called.

"Cease complaining," came a gravelly reply.

That voice… Darius had last heard it a year ago on the battlefield when facing down the Viridian Warlord. Although a distant memory, Darius would never forget the voice's malice and the jibes it had slung at the defeated humans. His face burned. He gripped his sword tightly, feeling the hilt slippery with sweat already.

After a pause to regain some composure, he eased forward again, wincing and halting every time loose stones crumbled under his boots and sent echoes that felt as loud as thunder. But eventually, he rounded a corner in the rock that gave him a view of a small opening below.

The ledge he stood on continued out to overlook a dark widening in the crevice many feet below. He froze, counting at least a dozen tattooed Viridian Guardians and Subdued crammed into the opening. They all stood to attention, surrounding a boulder where the Viridian Warlord sat scowling. The rakkan's ugly face was as grimy as ever, and the thick, rusty stubble across his jaw was broken by a fresh scar. It wouldn't be the only one by the time Darius was through.

He eased his body back out of view but didn't let his gaze leave his mark.

"What's the hour?" Hadrian asked.

One of the guardians looked at the sky. "Still some time until noon."

"I'm starved," another guardian muttered.

Hadrian cursed. "This better not be another wasted day."

Having had more time to study the pocket of the crevice where the Viridians lingered, Darius noted only two paths in or out, both so narrow they would only fit two rakkans through at a time yet would give Darius enough room to swing his sword. One led back to the way he'd come, where Sulla stood waiting at the end, and the other path led presumably to the rest of

497

Hadrian's men. If Darius could get across to their only escape route, they'd stand no chance. He might have only intended to scout, but if circumstances were favourable…

As if the thought of rushing in to attack them weren't inviting enough, none wore armour other than thin iron mail.

Yet, Darius hesitated. The air hung tense and still, and something puzzling about the scene before him piqued his curiosity. What were they waiting for? They didn't look to be readying for a fight. Had they already found the Waif Magician?

He slipped back a little farther behind the rock and turned to Lex.

"Hadrian's there," he whispered.

At first, the words caused no reaction from her. But gradually, a hateful scowl soured her usually striking face. "How many are with him?"

"Not enough to stop me."

"And the Magician?"

Darius shrugged. "I don't see her. And the Staff isn't nearby."

Lex exhaled slowly and slid her sword from its scabbard, muting its ring of death with her finger. She didn't need to say another word; the time he'd awaited for years had finally arrived. Lyra, Brutus and Selene would have justice done in their names this day.

Darius eased himself forwards while Hadrian spat vile curses that echoed from the dark rock on either side of his head. Each of his steps was glacially slow so as not to create too much air disturbance lest the rakkans feel him coming. When he leaned his head back out and caught sight of them again, he had to restrain the ferven wanting to burn in his eyes as his anger swelled. With his off-hand, he reached for the lump of aeternus around his neck. *This is for you, Brutus.* He released it and slowly withdrew the dagger from his belt.

He was ready. But again, he hesitated. His sword arm trembled. Was the mere thought of facing the rakkan who had once bested him so terrifying? The tremor in his hands morphed into a weakness that threatened to steal the weapon from his fingers. The weapons weighed down his arms more heavily than usual, and as he pulled back and turned to gape at Lex, he realised this wasn't fear.

Lowering his sword slowly, he rested it against the rock before it had a chance to clatter from his hand. He barely had time to sheath the dagger before the weakness intensified so much that he had to lean against the side of the ledge to remain standing.

Lex's eyes were now wide with understanding. "I've got you," she whispered, clutching his waist to give him support.

Clanks of metal accompanied curses from the warriors nearby.

Darius hadn't felt such a leeching of his strength for an age. But he hadn't missed the sensation one bit. Slowly, he poked his head out again to see each Viridian dropping their swords and holding the sides of the crevice as Darius now did.

"You're brave," an old voice echoed from above that made Darius's newly trimmed hair stand on end.

He ducked and peered up, but he saw nothing but the thin, bright sky casting shadows below.

"Or foolish," the voice continued. "Rakkans seldom survive encounters with me, and I know you've been hunting me for some time."

Turning back to the Viridians, Darius waited to see them run, close in together defensively, or even move. But none did. Whatever was happening gave him more dread than the old voice that had never faded from his mind, one he'd thought he had the courage to face but now realised he feared more than any other.

51

Darius – Cliffs of Aphatos

"Show yourself," Hadrian growled as the dozen Subdued moved towards him, brandishing their weapons.

When no reply came, Darius wondered whether the Waif Magician was to do the task of slaying for him and couldn't help but regret it wouldn't be his own sword that ended the brute's life. Still, dead was dead. As long as it was as painful as the fates the Warlord had inflicted on others.

"Show yourself!" Hadrian bellowed again.

"I take no orders from rakkans, especially invalids," the Magician replied with an echoing crow that seemed to emanate from multiple directions.

Hadrian grimaced at the insult and continued scanning, his eyes never resting for more than a split second.

The weakness in Darius's limbs intensified. The rakkans groaned, and slowly, a hunched figure emerged from the gap in the rock behind the Viridians.

The Magician's hair sprang from her head, wild with curls, still dyed a dirty red but partially covered by the thin, dark veil hung over her face like that of a horrid widow in mourning. Slung on her back was a familiar blackened staff, whose effect wasn't as intense as when Archimedes had wielded it—by choice on the Magician's part.

Hadrian and the others turned to face the woman.

"You know what I came for," the Viridian Warlord said. His Subdued raised their swords.

Yet the Magician didn't flinch. "That's right. And you are to be disappointed."

"Ah…" Hadrian murmured. "So you invited me here to fight?"

A gasp escaped Lex behind him, and Darius almost mimicked the sound. Why would the Magician invite Hadrian? Perhaps she'd lured them here for a reason and was manipulating them as she had Darius and Lex years ago. Dare he hope?

The Magician stepped forward, now only a few paces from the Viridians. "I invited you because I hadn't the time to waste slaying your algus when you eventually found me."

Darius watched every movement of her hands, willing her to reach for a weapon and begin the same rehearsed dance of slaughter he'd seen her do the last time they'd met. But his disappointment and frustration only grew as she made no move.

"So what?" Hadrian said. "Are you here to bargain for your life? Because I won't stop until I get what I want."

"Ah yes…" The Magician took another step forward and, this time, took the Staff from her back. "The Staff…or rather, the Twin Blades of Trogus."

Hadrian's eyes narrowed. "… How do you—?"

"I know and see many things." The Magician raised a hand and slowly pulled back her veil to reveal her wrinkled face and thin lips curled into a sinister grin. "It strikes me that our goals have much overlap."

"And what might your goals be?"

The amusement slipped from the Magician's face, to be replaced with the same hatred that Darius recalled when he'd asked a similar question of her.

"I want to see Toria burning," she hissed, "with all the algus dead and its king's head rotting on a spike. That's why I'll help you if you help me."

Not a sound left Darius's lips, but his head filled with curses. Surely the Magician wouldn't aid his enemies again... He turned to glance at Lex and saw the same pallid fear on her face that now struck him. Even with Lex's powder trick, he couldn't face the Waif Magician when so far away from her, no matter how much he wanted to gouge out her eyes. Not that he could kill her afterwards, despite the temptation. Selene needed her alive.

And if he risked the chance of revealing himself, then the Magician would know and be ready. He couldn't consider it. Not to mention just eyeing the Staff gave him chills.

"And what do you need help with?" Hadrian asked.

The Magician answered, "Give me as many rakkans as I need, and I will forge a staff to thwart algus like the Staff of Arria thwarts you."

A resounding chuckle from the Viridian Warlord sent shivers through Darius. "Is that why you invited me here?" Hadrian asked. "If you pledge to aid me, I'll give you what you seek, but only once I have the Blades."

His Subdued relaxed a little and lowered their weapons as the Magician pulled back the Staff.

"You will not be unopposed," she said. "Send for more men because a fight looms."

Hadrian frowned and tried to summon the strength to stand but could only manage hunched kneeling, though he still seemed a giant compared to the tiny old woman.

"Who can oppose me?" he asked.

"Many, both humans and rakkans. Without me, you will fail. You can know this to be true because I am a goman. I cannot lie."

Darius ground his teeth together. He'd once believed that witch's lies, and then she'd tried to kill him. But what was her real goal? Hadrian had nothing she needed unless she wanted the Blades too… He could only pray her intentions were malicious but knew she could easily be telling the truth for once. Darius's best option was to slay Hadrian first when the Magician wasn't around.

The Viridian Warlord turned to one of his guardians and had a hushed conversation for a few moments, during which they glared at the Magician several times.

Eventually, Hadrian murmured and broke away. "If you cannot lie, then we have a deal. We'll get word to the Legion, but not all can go where we need to. What do you suggest we do?"

"There isn't time to waste." The Magician paused for a second and looked up at the thin strip of sky visible above.

Darius could only hope Gorgias wasn't peering down too obviously at that moment.

"Well?" Hadrian grunted.

The Waif Magician's gaze darted back to the brute. "Have your commanders muster another army and march to Mount Psilos. We'll travel there at once from here."

If only Darius had listened to the Chief Priest… How had the man known?

"Why not wait for more men?" Hadrian asked. "Why the haste?"

"News of what you've planned has already reached Toria's ears. To wait is to meet impenetrable resistance. Your second army will be for your escape once you have what you want."

"What? How does Toria know? Only a handful of rakkans know where we're heading."

The same question had struck Darius, and he couldn't help but suspect the Chief Priest. Did the man have contacts in Toria?

The Magician's next words were so hushed and slow they appeared carefully chosen. "How they know is a mystery to me. But they know."

Hadrian paused and glanced around at his Subdued. It was clear even to Darius that he was contemplating attacking the old woman now and saving himself worry about the motives she hadn't divulged. Although the Magician's glare was piercing and calm, Darius noted her wide, bent knees, a stance that made her ready to pounce in a heartbeat.

But the Viridian Warlord only sighed and slumped back down. "Very well. It will take us a while to make it to the Mount undetected."

Darius was no expert on maps and charts, but he recalled Mount Psilos was on the southern coast, far to the east. The journey would give him some time to thwart the Viridians' progress and attack, but how would he succeed when the Magician was there? It wasn't like Nasrin could get close to talk to her or distract her with an army around.

While the rakkans again discussed things with each other, the Waif Magician gazed at the sky and squinted as the glare of the noon sun finally reached her with a thin line of rays.

"I must go," she said.

The others stopped with confused frowns.

"Go where?" Hadrian asked.

"There's something I must see to before we travel, and my presence will only hinder your men as they prepare to leave." She pulled down her veil to cloak her face again. "I'll find you tomorrow at dusk. Then we move." Without waiting for any agreement, she turned and disappeared into the gap once again, taking the Staff's cloud of weakness with her.

Every breath came easier and easier over the next few minutes as Darius slipped back to get closer to Lex.

"You heard?" he whispered.

She nodded with a steel determination on her face, one that was very familiar but that he hadn't seen in too long. Her intent was obvious. They had just over a day before his task to kill Hadrian became that much more difficult. The time to strike was now.

He crept back to where he could see the Viridians again, where they still discussed things with one another while the Subdued fanned out as much as they could into a wider perimeter. Now they covered both gaps in the rock that led out of the area, but it wouldn't make Darius's task any more difficult because they stood far lower than the narrow opening he hid within.

His hand still gripped his dagger, ready as ever, and with his other, he picked up his sword again. Then he waited. Mentally, he was ready. His heart throbbed. Muscles were loose and warm. But he wouldn't risk the Magician seeing or hearing the fight to come.

Long he waited, so long that Lex gave him an impatient nudge in the back, which he ignored. When it came to gomans—even half-gomans—it was always best to be safe.

Eventually, the Viridians began pacing restlessly as they talked, and more than one spoke of hunger; Darius doubted the sun outside would be enough to put them off leaving this shadowed area for much longer.

Readying his gladius and dagger again, he began slowly creeping forwards. After a few steps, he was out of the gap, out of its cloak of deep shadow, but still shrouded, nonetheless. Balancing on a ledge above the Viridians, he'd be seen if any of them glanced up. But the closest to him was a Subdued woman, who, despite sweeping her gaze in his direction, didn't spot him in the dark.

By now, the sun's rays had created a crooked line of light across the centre of the crevice, and after a few more steps, he was caught in a shine that would reveal him to the humans if they looked. He crept closer, hands gripping his weapons tightly, his weight carefully shifting from one leg to the next so he could react if anyone saw him.

But none did, and when he was only a few yards from the female Subdued, he leapt down towards her. His sword hacked through the muscles and bone in her neck before she turned to look. He flared ferven across his dagger and ran it across her chest, setting her tunic alight and rings of mail clinking to the ground.

A heartbeat later, the Viridians scrambled to grab their weapons. Arrows began raining down from above, as Gorgias and the other algus must have seen the fire and gore.

The Viridians raised their shields and flared ferven to deflect the missiles while they rushed towards Darius with snarls of rage. The first to arrive parried Darius's initial swipe, but he followed up with a dagger to the neck. The next rakkan wasn't far behind. Darius used the body of the first to block a blow before stabbing through the eye-slit of the rakkan's helmet. His sword screeched against bone and metal. Blood gushed.

Darius peered through the rushing guardians to the back of the space, at the tall warlord as he scarpered to a gap in the rock. The horns of Hadrian's helmet bashed against the stone, too wide to allow him through, and he gazed back while ripping the thing off.

"Stay and face me!" Darius roared as he cut a Subdued's sword arm before an arrow finished the algus off.

"Come get me." Hadrian grimaced before vanishing into the dark crack along with half his Subdued.

A brilliant sword flashed to Darius's right and stabbed into a Viridian's thigh. He turned to see Lex snarling as the rakkan fell, and she pulled back her weapon to parry a blow from a Subdued. Despite it being the first time he'd watched her fight in months, Darius saw no need to worry over her. She was as lethal as ever, which left him to focus on finishing what he'd started.

He barged over a Viridian and charged towards the darkness where Hadrian had disappeared. He cut down another three legionnaires as he met them. Algor-coated arrows struck the shoulders and heads of the two remaining Subdued, but thankfully the aim of Gorgias was true, and Darius had no need to dodge.

After a glance over his shoulder to check Lex was handling the rakkans, he sprinted into the crack after Hadrian. Some parts were so narrow he had to scrape through sideways, but other pockets of space allowed him enough light to see the Viridian Warlord's footprints.

The ground sloped upwards, and the walls of rock at either side of Darius grew shorter. He was swift enough to catch a rakkan but tempered his pace to ensure he didn't catch up with his enemy too tired to fight.

A horn blared. From where, Darius didn't know, though it couldn't be heralding anything good. The last time he'd faced

Hadrian, he'd been outsmarted. Despite the Warlord now having only one good arm, Darius could ill afford to underestimate him.

A breeze of fresh air whistled through the crack as he ran, and he winced at the growing brightness of the sun. The surface would make it easier for him to spot and catch his mark. Revenge neared.

The sound of thudding boots echoed ahead of him. As he took another turn at a fork in the path, the crevice suddenly ceased, and he faced a large dirt ramp back to the hilltop swarming with Viridian warriors and dozens more Subdued like wasps on a nest.

He skidded to a halt as another horn blared and a shield wall quickly formed in front of him.

There were too many to count, even to make a rough guess. And a heartbeat later, they charged forward with cries of war.

At the rear of the mass, Darius spied the Viridian Warlord, but all he could do was curse and turn around. He bolted into the crevice only to be met by Lex sprinting with her glowing blade.

Darius reached out and grabbed her to halt her run. "Turn back!"

She frowned in confusion but obeyed him, nonetheless. A thunder of clashing metal and rock erupted behind them, followed by an ear-piercing scraping of shields and metal through the crevice. He could turn and fight, but the gap in the rocks here was now too thin to swing a sword. If he tried, either one of their spears would end his struggles for good, or they'd simply trample him.

"Is Tiro above us?" Darius cried.

"Yes," Lex called back.

Thank the heavens. "Don't let him lose sight of Hadrian!"

When she didn't respond, he assumed she'd either given the command or else she'd thought of it long before he had.

The rocks on either side of him tore his cloak and sleeves as he ran at a blistering pace in the darkness. Then he spotted an oddly shaped stone that looked familiar, and before he knew it, the crevice opened into the dirty ramp through which they'd entered it.

The ground sloped upward, and cramps seized the muscles in his thighs as they raced towards the figures at the crest. Sulla's men tightened their shield wall and braced their spears while Darius and Lex tore around their flank and headed straight towards the armoured Militia Chief.

"Viridians are coming." Lex panted and pointed back to the crevice they'd just left.

"Advance!" Sulla yelled to his men. "Cut them off at the choke point at the bottom!"

The century ripped free the cloaks that had been sheltering them from the sun and let them fall to the dirt. Ready to fight, they began a thumping charge down towards the narrowing below.

Sulla turned back to Lex and Darius with a stern face. "How many?"

"Far more than we have," Darius said. "But the crevice is thin enough to hold them back. Your spears are longer."

The Margalvians made it down to the narrowest point before the Viridians had arrived and dug in their heels. They didn't have the numbers to face Hadrian's full force in the open, but enough to occupy his troops here.

"We should head for Hadrian above ground," Darius said.

The ring of clashing metal soon filled the noon air, and Gorgias and the other algus had made their way along the top to bombard the Viridians from above. When Darius saw Gorgias this time, a new grit and determination shone in his furious eyes. There was no hesitation in any pull of his bowstring at the sight of the flaming warriors below, and no quivering of his hand as each arrow flew from his bow.

"It's too late." Lex dipped her head. "Tiro sees Hadrian with more centuries. They've disappeared into another ravine where my falcon can't follow. He's lost them."

Darius cursed. What now? They had some algus, but not enough to challenge the Magician once she rejoined the Viridians.

"What happened down there?" Sulla asked. "What happened to 'scouting'?"

"The Viridians and the Magician made a pact," Darius replied before filling in his friend on all the details. "Aran was right. They're heading to Mount Psilos to get the Blades." Why hadn't he just listened to the man?

"The way to the mountain is perilous," Lex said, "crossing the main roads to the Silk City. The easiest path for Hadrian to take would be south and travel through the mountains near Margalvia. But once he learns the Red Militia are here, I doubt he'll risk a forewarned Black Legion cutting him off. He'll go southeast now that he can use the Magician's cogi to take the roads and evade the Xavalan and Torian armies. We can keep up if we take a more direct route. We might be able to stop him from getting the Blades."

Darius tried his best to imagine the map of the lands to understand what she was speaking about and why her tone had contained more than a little hesitation.

Sulla murmured and shook his head. "A direct route will take us far too close to Menara. My men will never go unnoticed."

"There's no need to worry," Lex said. "We can follow the foot of the mountains through the town."

The name Menara sounded familiar, but Darius couldn't recall where he'd heard it.

"*Through* a human settlement?" Sulla's voice was a pitch higher than usual. "That's brash even for me."

"Menara's small," Lex said. "Their garrison has never recovered since their regent was killed." She glanced at Darius for a few moments, but he had no idea why.

Before he could ask, a centurion ran up to them, panting with a blood-stained gladius in his hand. "They're retreating, Chief. Should we chase?"

"No." Sulla raised his hand in a gesture of withdrawal to the warriors down the slope. "We'll follow Lex's plan and try to reach Mount Psilos before them."

"And do what?" Darius asked. "Lay an ambush?"

Sulla nodded. "Hadrian has greater numbers, but with preparation we can give ourselves a chance. Either that or find some way to block off anyone's access to the Blades for good."

But with the Waif Magician, the Viridians would be forewarned of any trap. Darius tried to think of an alternative to the idea, yet nothing better came to mind. They hadn't horses or enough algus to harry the Viridians as they marched, and Darius would be damned before he asked the Silk City or any other humans for help after their antics in the west. And now that Hadrian had the Magician, an assassination was impossible. So, a trap at Mount Psilos was the least bad option they had *if* they could get there before Hadrian.

Darius reached out to Lyra in his mind. *Bring Selene and the others back. We need to make haste.*

"How long until we reach Menara?" Darius asked.

Sulla clicked his fingers a couple of times, and one of his warriors came forward and handed him a map. He unrolled it on the ground as Darius knelt to survey it.

"It's just over a week away if we're fast," Sulla said. "We're travelling light. My algus will race ahead and hunt to have food waiting for us, and we'll camp without fortifications."

Unless an army happened across them, Darius wasn't too worried about the Xavalans taking them unaware at this point. Tiro would give them enough forewarning. From the look of the map, Menara was roughly halfway on their route to Mount Psilos, although the latter half ran closer to the barren, rocky coast where there was far less risk of happening upon humans.

As the two discussed how best to make the journey, Selene, Lyra and the others who had gone with them finally made their way back. Upon seeing the gory spears, shields and armour of the Militia men stomping up the slope, the Chief Priest swallowed and hurried his steps towards Darius. In the downtime, the man had taken the opportunity to alter his disguise by tying up his long hair and wrapping a sheet of green fabric around it.

"What happened?" Selene asked with a far more harsh and bitter voice than usual.

As Darius explained the situation, her grimace only deepened.

"Did the Magician give Hadrian the Staff?" Selene asked.

Of all the questions she could have asked, why had she deemed that the most pressing?

"No," Darius said. "But don't worry. We'll find a way to get her alive." Despite having had years to ponder the goman art of cogi and its weaknesses, he'd had no bright ideas as to exactly how they'd do that, but he was hardly going to admit that to her.

He considered having her shackled to him once again instead of to Sulla's man but decided he'd rather wait until they were safe, until he was sure he wouldn't be needed to fight for a while. The Viridians may have retreated, but that didn't mean they wouldn't try something else.

"I have a friend in Menara," the Chief Priest said, sliding into the conversation. "He can help us. The people there are no more enamoured with the Torian and Xavalan soldiers than the Doltheans were, and my friend says only a few algus are garrisoned there. I'm sure they'll welcome us."

If only Darius had listened to the man before, they'd be halfway there now. He was tired of doubting but wouldn't go so far as to expect to arrive in Menara to applause. Trust was still too much of a stretch, but he'd start listening to Aran at least.

Darius turned to Sulla. "Sounds promising. When should we leave?"

"When you lot have finished wasting time chin-wagging," Sulla said. "We'll head south for a few hours, then set up camp until dusk. My men can't take much more of this sun."

All Darius wanted to do was sprint for their target, but he couldn't begrudge the men a few hours' respite. Their journey would be a tough one, and pushing themselves to exhaustion now would only slow them later on. It was likely Hadrian planned the same unless he wanted his men sunburnt and raw.

Most of the rakkans had now run back up the ramp and pulled their trampled, dirty cloaks from the ground. Gorgias had also returned with Sulla's algus and came to stand beside Darius wearing a boyish grin full of bloodlust.

"Did you see me?" Gorgias asked.

Darius had, and it was the only positive thing his eyes had witnessed recently. He'd let the algus savour the moment.

"I'll tell you what I saw," he said. "I saw the boy I knew die and a *man* take his place."

Pride swelled in Gorgias's chest at the remark. "W-well, my skills with a bow left a lot to be desired—I think I only killed three—but perhaps I can—"

"I wasn't referring to your skills"—which were admittedly lacking—"but you conquering your fear. That's the real battle."

A blare of a rakkan horn stole Darius's attention as Sulla's centurion gave the order to move.

"Double time!" Sulla yelled, then turned and ran onwards. Darius and the rest of them followed, sprinting and leaping across the landscape.

Soon the crevice was far behind them, lost amongst all the other fractured and rocky features blotting the hills. Stomping under heavy armour at a gruelling pace, the Militia warriors' breaths grew harsh and laboured within an hour or two. Darius began scouting ahead with Lyra and searching out a place of respite. Thankfully, the numerous cliffs left plenty of shade for the Margalvians to use along the way, but even so, they wouldn't last much longer. He eventually found a sprawling, overhanging cliff face that cast a shadow so wide it could have covered a dozen centuries from both the sun and rain.

Sulla and Lex liked what they saw too, and soon the century had halted and set up guards and patrols while most warriors collapsed out of the sunlight, snoring within minutes. Darius and Lex found a spot near Selene and Atticus, at one of the farthest ends of the mostly supine century, so they could spring into action if needed.

As soon as he sat beside Lyra, Darius realised that many days and nights of travel with little rest had left every muscle tight and aching. His head pounded, and every time he closed his eyes, the world spun. He hadn't even the energy to check how all the others were faring.

"Sulla will need me," Atticus said without looking at anyone in particular. "One of you has to take the woman now."

When Darius opened his eyes, he saw Selene had already lain beside the man, resting peacefully on her side. Did she really have to be restrained? After having passed up the chance to cut his throat, what more proof did he need that she had no bad intentions?

Lex pulled the key to the shackles from her pocket before tossing it to him and collapsing onto a patch of thick grass.

"I'm spent," she said. "You take first watch."

But despite wanting to free Selene, fatigue made his eyelids leaden, half-closed already. If he passed out, he decided it was best for her to be secured for now.

He carefully unshackled Atticus and attached Selene to himself without disturbing what looked to be a deep, restful slumber. Then he lay beside Lyra while Atticus wandered back to the others.

Usually, he would have obliged with Lex's wishes and forced himself to stay awake, but the tug of fatigue weighed him down more by the minute. It would be safer for them all in the long run if he rested to full strength, or he might not even make it to Mount Psilos. Besides, Sulla's men were already keeping watch.

Darius wrapped an arm around his panther and snuggled up, feeling a calm take hold of them at the intimacy. He'd just rest for a few hours and hopefully awake before Lex.

52

Sulla – Cliffs of Aphatos

Sulla was the first to rouse amongst the men, woken by Atticus to plan that night's march. After splashing his face with water to chase away the deep slumber his body seemed to long for, he grabbed some parchment and a reed pen, then walked to higher ground to get a better look to the west, gazing at the red haze across the cliffs cast by the setting sun. Even the weak sunlight stung his sensitive skin, so he slipped on his helmet and pulled his cloak tight around him. As he did so, Tiro landed on a rock nearby, ready for the mission Sulla had discussed with Lex earlier that day, when Darius hadn't been listening.

"Did you have to walk so far from the others?" Atticus called from behind. Usually, the words of Sulla's most trusted commander were as sarcastic as his, but as their fate became all the more threatened, his tone grew more apprehensive by the day.

Behind Atticus walked a trustworthy warrior they'd handpicked for a long mission. The rakkan had stripped off his armour as instructed and disguised himself with an old human tunic and trousers, then wrapped himself in a cloak until only his chalky face under the hood gave away his rakkan nature.

"It's kind of beautiful here, isn't it?" Atticus said when he reached Sulla. "Some of the tarnflowers are regrowing."

"It's very pretty," Sulla said. "Would you like to go and pick some and perhaps make a necklace to cheer up your men?"

"Already did that yesterday."

Sulla was about to chuckle but instead gaped when the man pulled out a white tarnflower that had been tucked under his belt.

"I should demote him for that," Sulla grunted to the other warrior. "Hadrian must be quaking in his boots at the thought of facing a bunch of flower-pickers."

Atticus snorted a laugh. "Have you written the message yet? I could have walked to Margalvia with it by now."

"Shut it." Writing wasn't one of Sulla's strong points, even by rakkan standards. The humans were far better educated, but he'd never entrust this note to them. Then Darius might find out before it was sent.

It hadn't been difficult for Sulla to make a decision on what to do. An ambush at Mount Psilos would at best delay the Viridians, and probably not for long. Their only real option for preventing Hadrian from becoming overlord was for Varro to take the Blades whether Darius would like that or not. And that meant the Black Legion—or whatever was left of it in Margalvia—needed to set off for Mount Psilos at once. Only after the message had been sent would Sulla and Lex tell Darius about it, when there was no way to stop it.

"Are you sure this will reach the Warlord in time?" Atticus asked.

"It'll reach Margalvia. There's a route along the coast that will allow the Black Legion to march to Mount Psilos while avoiding the steepest terrain we and Hadrian will have to navigate. If Varro's back in Margalvia and not still at the mine, he should get there before us."

Taking his knife, Sulla cut the parchment he had in half and began scribbling down all he wanted to tell the Warlord in two identical messages. Then he rolled up one piece and attached it to Tiro's leg while the warrior took the other.

"Do you know what to do?" Sulla asked him.

The rakkan nodded. "Steal a swift or a horse and ride hard."

"Don't wear the beast out." Atticus patted the man on the back. "Otherwise, it'll never make it through the mountains."

Sulla saw no reason for Lex's escort not to deliver the message to Varro, but the reticent algus had proven too many times before that her true motives were unknowable. He trusted her so far as they both had a common goal—to end this war and slay their enemies. But he'd never trust her on the small things, including delivering vital news to the warlord she hated.

Tiro took off and was soon nothing more than a speck in the crimson sky.

"Get going." Sulla gave the warrior a shove to set him on his long journey. Perhaps he should have sent an algus, but with only half a dozen available, it would be too great a loss to his army.

As he and Atticus watched the man begin jogging through the grass and mud, Atticus turned and said, "Shall I rouse the men?"

Sulla took another look at the red sky. "Give them another hour. The next couple of weeks will be brutal." It would also give him a little time to prepare how to raise the subject of Varro with Darius.

53

Selene – Cliffs of Aphatos

As Selene watched the sun falling over the rocky landscape, old memories replayed in her mind that were not her own. The beauty and warmth the dead Selene had enjoyed in those recollections were now as dead as the city she'd called home. All the others still dozed, but she'd only allowed herself a mindful relaxation of deep breaths and controlled peace. She needed to get free of these chains and was so close to convincing Darius to release her. The fool really believed that she was Selene and only needed one little push to break the restraints. If only she could think of what that might be. Something to do with the bear claw...but what?

She tightened one of the shackles on her wrists then twisted her hand, digging in the metal until it scraped and cut the skin. Hopefully, it would make Darius pity her. Perhaps she should have slit his throat and sawn off his hand when she'd had the chance with the razor. But the King's Orator had been insistent.

Her task was to remain with Darius at all costs until they found the Magician, so she'd been patient and rejected any urge to escape. But she'd still had no orders on what to do *after* they'd found Shirin.

She closed her eyes and tried to relax the tension in her body a little more and did so for a while until disturbed by a light pecking on her neck. The touch brought a rush of excitement that chased away any temptation she'd had to sleep. Wide awake, she opened her eyes to see a tiny wren stood looking at her with a message attached that must have hampered the light creature's flight.

But it was used to such tasks. Despite only seeing the ageing bird a few times before, she knew it was an escort of one of Ophelia's algus.

After a glance around to confirm everyone was still snoozing, she quietly and carefully slipped off the message and let the bird flutter away while she unravelled it. It was short and written in Ophelia's neat and beautiful handwriting, always a stark contrast to the grim mental image of the woman.

> *One will join you at the Mount without our army. Ensure the mark is present; he will tempt her out. Get it first, then terminate.*

Both Selene and the King's Orator had been over vague language enough times in her training that she knew the precise meaning of the message. "One" referred to the King's Sword himself, and it was hardly surprising that the King would send him to take on the Waif Magician. The witch was far beyond Selene's capabilities, and the fact had been drilled into her.

But Jason was unrivalled. And the lack of an army didn't come as a surprise to her. The Torian army would already be camped ready, but the King had always been unsure whether to launch an assault or not. Anything that might spook the Magician was to be avoided.

The second part of the message made sense of why Selene hadn't been allowed to kill Darius up to now. He had to make it to the Mount, and the Magician would show herself to repress him.

But the next part had Selene puzzled. "Get it first" referred to the Staff of Arria, but was she to take the order literally? Was *she* the one meant to retrieve the Staff rather than the King's Sword? Just the thought of Ophelia's fury if she didn't do as instructed sent cold fear that tensed every muscle in Selene's body—although she had no idea why, as the King's Orator had always been nothing but pleasant to her. Yet the image of those split lips smiling brought phantom waves of agony. She had no option but to take the command in its strictest sense. *She* had to get the Staff.

As for the final part, there was no ambiguity. After retrieving the item they sought, she'd finally get to kill the Slayer of Gods.

54

Darius – Silverbark Forest

After a few nights and days of relentless travel, Darius and the rest left the Cliffs and trekked into the flat grasslands to the southeast. *Finally, no hills.* Their progress would now be even swifter.

Darius travelled at the head of the century along with Selene, Lex, Sulla, Gorgias and Aran, constantly scanning the open landscape for men or horses amongst the few herds of wild deer and oxen roaming and grazing. Meanwhile, the rakkans stomped behind with their long cloaks billowing and hoods down in the night.

They made it across the road east after evading another band of raiding algus—thanks to the Chief Priest's pteron forewarning them—and as usual, Sulla's algus had raced ahead and killed a wild ox ready for them to eat. Darius's jaw was already beginning to ache from all the chewing that red meat required, but at least ferven allowed him to cook it just how he liked it—blackened on the outside and juicy pink inside. And Lyra was loving the diet, living like a queen without having to hunt for herself. That one small piece of contentment from her was enough to make the arduous journey tolerable for him.

A couple of nights later, they left the open grass plains and made it into Silverbark Forest. Even in the darkness of night, the trunks of the birch trees seemed to emanate a luminescent glow akin to that of an algus faintly emitting algor, and the colour clashed with the shades of the red leaves in the overhanging canopy, giving the illusion the cold breeze wasn't as stiff as it really was. Not that Darius minded the chills when he could conjure ferven at will, but Selene was shivering beside him even more than she had at the Cliffs.

"Here." Darius released his cloak and draped it across her shoulders.

"Thanks," Selene whispered.

Strangely, Lex and the Chief Priest seemed undaunted by the nighttime temperature, sweating from the exertion of such swift travel, and only Gorgias gave a hint of discomfort, rubbing his arms and cradling his escort tightly at times. Darius had lit ferven to help the man, but Gorgias tensed all the more at the sight of the fire, despite now having the fortitude to stand close and leech some warmth.

Selene made some attempts at conversation with Darius, but she seemed as distracted and tired as he was because her thoughts often trailed off. Lex kept close enough to eavesdrop on their whispers and watch them out of the corner of her eye, but that wasn't what troubled him. All he dwelled on was Hadrian and the Blades. Even if they managed to somehow kill the Viridian Warlord in an ambush, the fact these weapons were now in the minds of many rakkans meant great change lay in the future.

After a lull in the conversation, Sulla shifted position so that he walked alongside him.

"We need to talk," Sulla said, panting.

Those words never preceded a pleasant discussion. "What have you done?" Darius asked.

"You and I both know that our merry band here will struggle against whatever warriors Hadrian has plus the Magician."

"I thought it best that went unsaid." What hope did they have other than groundless optimism?

Sulla grimaced. "My algus' escorts have reported that Hadrian's taking the roads southeast as we suspected. It's a longer route, but *we* have a mountain range to cross."

Ever since seeing the map, Darius had worried over that. Small lines on parchment could translate to rugged or even impassable terrain, but they could always shorten their route through the mountains.

"I've had a thought," Darius said.

"Well, there's a first time for everything." Sulla chuckled.

Despite the worries weighing heavily on him, Darius couldn't prevent a smile. He'd missed the man's terrible insults.

"What if we head south to the coast?" Darius asked. "We'd be over the mountains in a couple of days and could approach Mount Psilos along the southern shore."

Sulla murmured to himself. "It would be a longer route but could be faster. Plus…we might meet Warlord Varro along the way." A slight redness surfaced in Sulla's cheeks, and the man's grin vanished.

Darius frowned. "Why would Varro be east of Margalvia?"

"Fastest way from Margalvia to Mount Psilos." Sulla kept his gaze straight ahead, and it didn't take Darius long to decipher what the man was saying or what it meant.

"So that's what you did…" Darius slowed his steps and looked at the others in the group, who doubtless had all heard this conversation. All of them were acting as if this were nothing new, and he guessed it was a natural reaction to something that wasn't their business. But Lex… If this was news to her, she'd have wheeled and rounded on the Militia Chief in a murderous rage.

After Darius had fallen back a few paces with Selene, Sulla finally turned and looked him in the eye with apologies written all over his face.

"I had to, Dar," Sulla said.

"So what's the plan?" Darius asked. "Let Varro take the Blades before Hadrian has the chance?" In the back of his mind, he'd sensed that was the road down which they were heading, but he'd clung to a delusional hope they could do it alone.

"Better Varro than Hadrian, no?" Sulla said.

Darius wasn't so sure what that would mean for him. Hadrian was at least open about his intentions. "I'd rather neither had them," Darius admitted.

By now, the others had stopped and turned, unable to ignore the discussion.

"Can we not t-trust Varro with the Blades?" Gorgias asked, more to Darius than to Sulla. At least *one* person there valued his opinion enough to discuss these things openly with him rather than scheme behind his back.

Gorgias's question was a hard one to answer given Darius wasn't familiar with the Blades' power and his feelings towards the Black Warlord were biased and bitter.

"Sulla or Lex are best placed to answer that," Darius said. "Clearly, *they* make the decisions without my input." He began walking forward, unwilling to let the century marching behind see

526

too much disagreement at the top; that hardly instilled confidence before heading into a fight against the odds.

The rest of the group again paced with him silently until Sulla broke the quiet. "There are many things I dislike about our warlord, but few are more worthy of the Blades. Once the Staff is close enough, he should attempt to take them."

Darius turned to Lex, who'd tightened her hairband at least three times in the last minute, a tic that betrayed her nerves.

"Do you agree?" he asked.

As Sulla had done, she considered her words carefully before speaking. When she did, her tone was low and resigned, like she had to force the words out. "Varro can be trusted more than the other warlords."

Forgetting his frustrations with her for a moment, he was all the more unnerved by her pronouncement. She wanted the Black Warlord to take the Blades, but would Varro ever forgive Brutus's death? Could Darius ever trust him after being so cruelly treated?

"What about the other warlords?" Darius asked, desperation beginning to take hold.

"Forget it," Sulla murmured. "They aren't even aware we're on the brink of finding the Blades."

The Chief Priest cleared his throat politely. "If I may speak, I'd say that any ally of ours would be a more preferable choice to an unknown—if we had the choice, which it seems we do not. Holding grudges only harms ourselves."

Darius scoffed. "Tell that to Varro."

"I will." The Chief Priest smiled, and Darius could tell he had every intention of doing so. But it wasn't like the stubborn, petty warlord would listen.

"And," the Chief Priest continued, "you have a greater chance of cornering the Waif Magician and helping Selene with a larger force."

… Darius was an arse for not considering Selene. His mind was so clouded with rage and bitterness that he'd lost sight of their goal. Even with Varro and the Black Legion, cornering the Magician and Hadrian was a long shot, and without help, Darius's chances were low.

They marched a while longer until the rising sun shone so strongly through the forest canopy that the rakkans' grunts and curses behind would have made anyone think they'd caught fire.

"We'll stop here and sleep for the day." Sulla held up a hand signal to those behind. But before he could slip away within his men, Darius had one more matter to settle.

He planted his body squarely in front of the Militia Chief and said, "Why didn't you just tell me you were asking for Varro's help?" His glare then shifted to Lex, who came up to him without a shred of the shame Sulla was now showing.

"I didn't want you to change my mind," Sulla said.

The sincerity in his voice made it hard to stay mad at the rakkan, and Darius had to admit his reaction to the proposition might not have been rational and still might not be. It was true that Sulla often paid attention to what Darius said, but that was certainly not Lex's reasoning.

Darius turned to her.

But her only reply was to stare back at him, perhaps trying to melt his frustrations with those piercing blue eyes that captivated him like no others, or perhaps to make him back down like a submissive dog scared of its alpha. Well, he wouldn't let this unveiled distrust of him go, and the uncomfortable silence went on for so long that all the others left them to prepare a place for much-needed sleep, leaving the pair with only Selene, the trees and loose red leaves tussling in the wind about their feet.

However many minutes the lull dragged on for, Darius couldn't say, but Lex eventually broke the stare down and came closer to him, a sadness suddenly slowing her walk in a manner she'd never show in front of others. Maybe the rakkans were the reason she'd remained silent until alone with him.

Lowering her voice, she said, "I know the pain that comes with losing your home, but I can't say I know the pain the rejection of your own home brings. The old Darius would never have forgiven Varro for doing what he did and would have refused to ever stand beside him in battle again. For the old Darius, loyalty was everything."

"It still is," Darius growled, "and *our* loyalty more than anything else. How is keeping this from me being loyal?"

She lowered her head. "It isn't, I know. But I prefer to ask for forgiveness than permission."

Darius scoffed. "Since when do you seek my permission?"

"Believe it or not, I do listen to you." Lex's tone remained soft—nervous, even. "That's why *she* is still attached to you and not on her way to a prison." Without even looking up to gauge his reaction, Lex left to join the century, leaving Darius and Selene to contemplate her words.

"She's always been good with excuses," Selene said, a sting in her voice.

Perhaps Darius was being taken for a fool like all the other men Lex manipulated. But he believed her. When she toyed with others, she did it with a smile and charm, taking advantage of her stunning good looks. Yet with him, unlike anyone else, she allowed her façade to drop to reveal the caring and vulnerable woman beneath.

Sighing, he set off and made his way through the warriors who were collapsing for the day, back towards Gorgias and the Chief Priest. Sulla's men retired as soon as they could while the humans all gathered around a campfire wearing the sullen expressions of people who wondered whether death might not be preferable to their current hell. Darius knew how they felt.

Sleeping in such bright light, even when exhausted, wasn't easy. The nocturnal habits of rakkans were tough to get used to, so instead, Darius used his ferven to cook some rabbits they'd caught earlier and fill their growling bellies.

"Does anyone fancy a game of dice?" the Chief Priest asked.

"No," Darius muttered before handing out cooked meat.

The others also declined the invitation, the mood not one for fun. Although not fond of games, it reminded Darius of his grandfather and the one they'd played. The rules were long since lost from his memory, but he reached to his neck and clutched the aeternus hanging there. The words of his grandfather came back to him: "Even the weakest of lights can break an impenetrable darkness." His thoughts went to his bear claw and the Agathos figurine. Where was the God now? Watching? Would he help them stop the world from burning?

The two sisters who had owned the trinkets in his hand sat opposite him with faces so stern their anxiety was evident. Lex barely blinked as she wolfed down the meat, and Selene's pupils flickered as she watched the flames in the fire.

She looked up at him and smiled when she saw him staring. It only made him feel more guilty at having her chained. But he had to keep telling himself it could all be over soon. If they managed to thwart and kill Hadrian, they'd find the Magician, and Nasrin would convince her to repair whatever she'd done to Selene. Or so he prayed.

"May the Goddess bless the food she provides us," the Chief Priest said before also tucking into some meat.

"I have a question for you, priest," Darius mumbled through a mouthful of rabbit leg.

Aran gave a tired nod and held out a gloved hand in invitation. Perhaps he'd regret that soon.

"When will your God of Justice come down and help us?" Darius asked.

Lex finally stopped munching and turned her attention to him. But whatever her thoughts were on the question, her expression didn't betray them.

The Chief Priest cleared his throat. "That's a question only a mind as powerful as Dianoia can answer. But perhaps the God and Goddess have already given us the power to fight evil ourselves."

Although powerful, even Darius didn't have that kind of potential. "And why do children needlessly die when they've done no wrong to justify punishment?" Such as little boys failing to defend their brothers when circumstances could have easily let a baby live.

The Chief Priest's face grew sombre, grey like his usual hair colour. "Do not think of death as punishment. It is not the end, and Dianoia is the only one that knows when it needs to come; who else but the mind that lay the cornerstone of the world should determine the time?... Did you ever see the fountain of her in Laltos that Regent Theodoros commissioned?"

"The weeping lady with wings of water? Yes."

"Do you know why her face looked so anguished?"

"Because she's created a living hell full of degenerates?" Darius took an angry bite of meat.

The Chief Priest frowned. "No. She feels the same pain as every one of her creations. Every lash to their back, every pain of hunger, is hers to bear as well."

That wasn't really an answer as to why. But it did show the Goddess in a new light that gave Darius pause. Did she share every crack of the whip that had split his back in Laltos? Every fist to Selene's beautiful cheek? It was a good thing Dianoia was a goddess because no human could bear that much woe.

"It all feels so unknowable," Darius said. "Why do you believe all this without seeing, without certainty?"

"… Why would I need certainty to believe in the Duality? I believe all those sitting around me now are real, but I cannot be certain. They could be a figment of my imagination."

Darius had never considered that before and couldn't deny it. He took out his waterskin and began guzzling water, wishing it was firewater instead. The longer he pondered these things, the more it hurt his fatigued mind. After a few more wasted moments silently watching the fire, deciding whether the aroma of roasted rabbit was more tempting than sleep, he stood with a grunt.

"I'm tired," he said. "Pray your gods give me the strength to repay Hadrian the debts of evil he deserves."

"I'll retire with you." Lex stood too, no doubt to make sure Selene did nothing while they slept.

After they found a sheltered patch of grass to lie down on, one woman on either side of Darius, Selene soon dozed, twitching slightly in her sleep. As he watched to make sure she was deep in slumber, Lex rolled over and dug a finger into his back.

"Can I ask you a favour?" she whispered.

Darius grunted his approval, although it was cheeky of her, given recent events.

"If you don't believe in Agathos," she said, "may I have my pendant back?"

And just when he'd rid his mind of that confusing conversation... He rolled over to face her and found her lying so close he brushed his nose against hers.

She let out a subtle gasp, and any annoyance he'd bore made way for his familiar feelings again.

It was only then that he realised he was already clutching the pendant in his hand. "I..."

Did he want to give up the figurine? It was the only piece of her he had, but was there more to it? The Chief Priest's arguments weren't ones he had an answer to. It struck him as unusual to believe in something he'd never seen, but then he supposed he knew the air was real just by its effects, his senses. Was his sense of justice like that?

"I want to keep it," Darius said. "Do you mind?"

"I do," she replied softly. "It was a gift from my father when I first took command in battle. It marks a leader. But I'm happy to let you keep it if it means something to you. Does it?"

The pendant having been hers was more than enough to give it meaning. He nodded, well aware that the movement would rub his nose against hers again.

"Just promise me one thing," Lex said. "If I ever want it enough to ask you again, give it back to me."

That seemed fair enough. "You have my word. Can you promise me something too?"

"Perhaps."

"If I die trying to take down Hadrian and the Magician, and we fail to stop him, give up the fight. Take Selene and go to stay with my grandfather, raise your daughter and live away from Hadrian's crusade."

Lex's gentle stare hardened. "Never."

55

Lex – Menara

The journey to Menara only took another couple of days, but Lex's hip grew more painful by the day despite the Chief Priest's tea. Perhaps it was fatigue. Although as an algus she was quicker than the marching rakkans, the use of those abilities tired her faster too, not to mention her stamina eroding with age.

As the stone walls of Menara became visible through the orange and red haze of leaves, Sulla and his men formed a shield wall and prepared to meet resistance. It had been years since she'd been here, and the wild undergrowth of ivy and vines from the forest had crept and begun climbing and assaulting the stonework.

There was no clue yet as to what she now knew awaited them in the town, a bloody scene that the others were unaware of unless their escorts had scouted ahead like Tiro.

Darius strode with her along with the Chief Priest and a shackled Selene. Every time Lex looked at her sister, all she could think of was her son and where he was in the world. She had no delusions that the boy remembered anything of his past, and she hated her hope that he should be long dead, prevented from becoming the same monster that most of the Numbered grew into. In her mind, her son had died the moment Archimedes had touched him and drained his head. So how could she not assume the worst of her sister? Even Lyra never walked too close to the woman, and the panther always seemed suspicious as far as Lex could see.

But Darius was too wilfully blind to notice.

Yet they'd been with Selene for weeks, and she hadn't done anything to hinder or harm them. Beneath Lex's steadfast decision to expect the worst lurked a growing suspicion that she'd been wrong and had only caused her sister more pain and grief instead of giving her the care she needed.

"I hope you're right about there only being a few algus here," Darius muttered to the Chief Priest, interrupting Lex's pondering.

Aran didn't respond but seemed to walk with a new tension in his legs. Tiro was hovering above the town, having returned from Margalvia within a couple of days after delivering his message. Varro himself had collected it, and Lex knew him well enough to understand that even his hesitant nature wouldn't delay his march to Mount Psilos.

Tiro had no sight of the Chief Priest's escorts in the air and only saw the narrow gaps between the grey-tiled rooftops where the streets ran. Even soaring high, the crimson sheen between the cobblestones caught the peregrine's eye, and the still forms of many soldiers' bodies littered those paths closest to the main gate. Figures in dark clothes scurried around and dragged the dead one by one into nearby buildings while others brought buckets of water to dilute the stains of gore left trailing behind.

There had to have been some sort of battle, which is why she'd expected signs of an assault on the wall. But neither she nor her escort saw any. This battle was most likely fought from inside, a revolt, or someone tunnelling into the town from the surrounding forest.

Gradually, the scene changed as they left the shelter of the maroon canopy and approached the barred gates of the town. Bodies spoiled the muddy earth outside the walls, and most wore the armour and colours of Xavalan and Torian soldiers, but there were no signs of blackened cuts or dead rakkans. Whoever had done this, it wasn't the Viridians or Margalvians.

At the sight, Sulla's men held their shields and spears high and ready while Darius and the other algus drew their swords—all except Lex. Her attention was fixed on the Chief Priest, who seemed pale at the sight of the corpses but remained otherwise the calmest of everyone. It was a stark contrast to the shaken man he'd been in the Cliffs when fighting had erupted. He knew something he hadn't let on.

As they approached shooting distance of the main gate into the town, a man's voice cried out from within. "Stop there!"

The century and algus obliged, but Darius kept going beyond their front line. His reflexes were faster than theirs, and he must have heard the same thing Lex had noticed in the voice that had called out—fear.

"Who are you?" the voice asked, breaking at the last word.

"I'm Darius," he yelled, ferven in his throat giving his voice the deep roar that rakkans used to terrorise. "I don't come here to fight. We only seek supplies and to pass through the town."

After a few moments hearing only the rustle of fallen leaves in reply, he began pacing forwards again. He'd only taken a few steps when a thin dark shape flashed in the air outside the walls. Darius suddenly jerked his body to the side and pulled Selene with him. A heartbeat later, an arrow bounced on the road just behind them and snapped in two.

With another swift movement, Darius brought up his blazing sword and blocked a second incoming arrow with the flat of the blade while Lex ripped the bow from her shoulder.

"It's unwise to anger me," Darius roared with the confidence of a lion.

Lex paused, ready to counter. The arrows hadn't been tipped with algor, so perhaps the Chief Priest was right that there were no algus in the town.

"We had to be sure it was you!" the voice yelled. Soon after, the gates began to clunk and thud as if the braces were being removed.

Darius paced forward, and Sulla and his testudo of warriors stomped after the half-rakkan. Lex followed, arrow nocked. When Darius came within a dozen yards of the gates, they eased open, and a man with ill-fitting Torian scale armour hobbled out. The way he held his shield and sword told Lex he'd had little training with them, and even Darius seemed to relax at the sight.

The Menaran's face shone with sweat that dripped down from his bearded chin, and the hand gripping the sword was thick-fingered and strong with many a scar. "We feared you wouldn't come."

Lex hurried forward to where Darius and Selene now stood. Meanwhile, the man continued approaching until Darius held out a hand.

"You were expecting me?" Darius said.

"Of course," the man said. "Aran sent word."

At that moment, Aran hurried past Sulla's testudo. "What?" the Chief Priest said. "Did you think I wouldn't send *another* message?"

537

Darius grimaced. "That doesn't explain why you'd be so foolish as to announce my whereabouts." He grunted and turned back to the man from Menara as a few others gingerly walked out of the gates. Their armour was several sizes too large for them too, and bore enough fresh scars to show they'd been stolen from the dead. The people's complexions were too tanned for them to be anything other than slaves who worked long hours outdoors.

Had there been a revolt? She'd known such uprisings were brewing for years, as soon as the King had announced an end to the Citizenship Programme whereby slaves enlisting in the Torian army were freed and given citizen status. The move had stemmed the increasingly rapid loss of workers brought about by the programme, but it had a price. And citizens' treatment of slaves had soon become as barbaric and brutal as before.

"What happened here?" Lex asked the Menaran, stepping just beyond Darius.

"We heard what he did in Dolthea," the man said with a cautious glance at Sulla's army. "Only our oppressors weren't rakkan, and they didn't think enough of us to leave any real defence here."

"Are the algus dead?" Lex asked. Even if they had hundreds of slaves, it was impressive that they'd overcome a couple of the supernaturally fast fighters.

"All but one woman," the man said. "She actually helped us. Not all of them forget their former lives as slaves."

Darius turned to the Chief Priest again. "You shouldn't have told them to revolt. They could have been slaughtered."

Aran baulked. "I didn't tell anyone to revolt. I've *never* advocated that. I'd hoped that 'the Slayer's' presence here would quell any resistance like it did in Dolthea."

"It's true," the man said. "It wasn't our intention, but something was about to happen that we couldn't stand by and witness. The Chie—Aran has done much to convince us the algus aren't the gods we once held them to be."

The Chief Priest winced at the near slip of his position at the top of the Order, but it thankfully went unnoticed by Sulla and the rakkans. Although Lex knew Aran's identity wouldn't concern them, she'd respect the man's wish to remain as discreet as possible.

While Darius continued questioning the Menarans, Sulla pushed past his men and joined the interrogation. But Lex instead focused her attention on silent inquiry. She scrutinised every man and woman there, searching for any signs of unusual nervousness, pale noble skin, or the faintest flicker of algor in the eyes that would betray algus in disguise. But she spied nothing other than understandably wary slaves peering at the armoured rakkans.

After a few minutes of questioning, Sulla and Darius seemed satisfied enough and turned to Lex with a silent question for her opinion. She nodded, then Sulla gave the order for his men to relax their testudo and march into the town.

The first streets after the gate now bore only traces of the blood they'd swallowed, still wet with puddles of the water used to wash them clean. But the washing hadn't been enough to take away the stench of death. The air reeked, yet it was hardly new or intolerable to her.

While they walked, many of the former-slaves-turned-soldiers left their homes and places of work to approach Darius with looks of such awe anyone would have thought he sailed down the road on a cloud of lightning.

Lex had never seen anything like it before. The Doltheans had revered Darius, which had been shocking enough, but here were men willing to take up arms they were unskilled and untrained with, all with the confidence instilled by the mere rumours of the so-called Slayer of Gods. Ironically, it had been the Menarans who had given him that name after plaguing the town's algus for years, so if *they* could change their minds, Lex's ambitions for the Empire at large weren't as delusional as she often feared, and with her gold still resting in Laltos, she could find a way to arm and feed armies and rebels.

But Darius's frustrated expression as he strode through the swelling crowd dampened any hopes she had. He clearly hated the attention everyone gave him. He hated the reliance and hope they placed in him. And he hated taking responsibility. Brutus had once said the young Darius had been the same, but with a gruelling education in battle and slaying, he'd become the man he was when she'd met him almost a decade ago. Accepting that Brutus wasn't around to mould the half-rakkan again wasn't easy for her, and it was clear now that she had to be the one to push Darius to reach his potential again.

Lex hurried her steps until she strode alongside the slave soldier who had first greeted them. His awe-filled gaze wouldn't leave Darius for a second, so she grabbed his arm and took his attention by force.

"I need to speak with you." She pulled him to the side of the street, where Darius and Selene wouldn't overhear.

Finally, the man turned and blinked with a captivated surprise she recognised all too well when men locked eyes with her.

"Me…?" he said.

Sometimes Lex's effect on men allowed her to seize what she wanted, but other times—like now—it was nothing but a distraction.

"What's your name?" she asked.

"Cyrus, Algus."

"And who's the new leader here?"

The man frowned, and the movement of his head made his helmet slip down over his brow. He shifted it up and cleared his throat. "No one, really. We were waiting for Aran and the Slayer."

That didn't bode well for their chances when the King decided to retake this place. Although Menara wasn't of much strategic significance, the fertile lands to the northeast of Silverbark Forest were some of the most productive in the Empire, and this town made the defence of those easier.

"And what are your plans now you've slain your enslavers?" Lex asked.

Cyrus stared at the ground blankly for a moment before shrugging. "We'll follow the Slayer. This place holds no fond memories for us."

Because the situation was so similar to Dolthea, Lex knew what Darius's reaction would be. And she wouldn't allow it this time. These slaves might not be able to fight well, but they could at least help take supplies and scout. Plus, they knew the mountains to the southeast well.

"Don't say anything to Darius," Lex said. "I'll speak with him about your fate."

The man's eyebrows rose with trepidation at the words, but he nodded his agreement regardless.

"Is there somewhere our army can stay? And do you have food and water to spare for us?"

Cyrus nodded. "There's an old barn at the south of the city. It should be large enough for you. I'll have people bring you refreshments."

"Thank you." She gave the man an alluring smile that brought a bright blush to his cheeks, then went back to join Darius, Selene and the Chief Priest as they continued through the streets. She directed them south, and they soon found the barn, a huge, old wooden building pressed against the southern wall of

541

the town. Two doors hung open while loose bits of straw limped in the wind across the dirt square in front.

The innards weren't any less decrepit but had at least been cleaned of animal waste, if not the smell. The century all fit inside the single, vast open space, and while they marked out their spots to rest, Lex brought Darius and the rest of their original group to a corner buried under piles of straw.

"I've never seen anything like it," Nasrin said with a shake of her head. "All the people here look up to you so much."

"They needn't," Darius muttered, pulling out some straw bundles to rest on. "I did nothing. They freed themselves."

"But you inspired them," Lex added. "If you say the word, they'll follow you, and we could use them when we march to Mount Psilos."

Darius scoffed. "Those men are no soldiers. They'll be slaughtered."

"They don't have to fight." Yet, at least. Such men could be trained and become fiercely loyal. But not if Darius turned his back on them now. And what message would that send to the rest of the Empire when word spread? People would never join their cause. It was an outcome Lex couldn't allow, however hard that meant pushing Darius.

The man was clearly not the most suitable leader in terms of competence or strategy, possessing nothing close to the genius and fortitude of people like her father or even the King. But the half-rakkan was a symbol, a figure, and any man or woman would find courage fighting beside him. Courage won battles, and battles won wars. A symbol was what the Empire needed if the humans and rakkans were to ever come together.

"Look what happened in Dolthea," Darius said. "I intervened there, and they're probably worse off for it."

Lex smacked him on the arm. "When will you stop avoiding what you need to be?"

He backed up a fraction. "What do I need to be?"

"A leader, one who takes what aid he can get. And don't you dare roll your eyes, or I'll scratch them out."

"And what if I don't want to be a leader?" Darius muttered.

"Too bad, master," Gorgias said with a sullen face. "You are one."

Before Darius could open his mouth to respond, Lex spied Selene taking his hand and giving it a gentle squeeze. Lex's sister had always been more supportive than her and more in tune with people's emotional state, but even Selene would normally have understood how important this decision now was and would have voiced her support. It only deepened Lex's suspicion, and she was tempted to leave her sister chained in Menara. But that was an argument with Darius that would only detract from the most vital one.

Lex straightened her back, tightened her ponytail, then squared up to the half-rakkan. "Do you think I haven't led men to their deaths? Do you think my soldiers were any less outmatched when we fought against the Viridians in a hopeless war? You can't save or protect everyone. No leader can. And we can't win this war alone."

A frown creased Darius's face, one born of frustration, ruminating on the words as he hopefully saw the truth in them. Lex sensed it would only take one more push. And it had to be firm—or even vicious.

She stepped closer to the man and whispered harshly so that only he would hear. "Stop with the self-pity, or people will think you a whining caitiff. Leaders are forged, not born. So step into the furnace and become the warrior you were."

She conjured the faintest hint of algor in her eyes in a way she knew crushed men's resistance to her. But with Darius, it wasn't like with other men. For them, the fervour in her gaze had to be feigned. For Darius, the passion came truly from within.

And then she saw it. His brown eyes hardened with a newfound grit, and at that moment, she had more hope than at any point since the fall of Laltos.

"All right," he said in a low, commanding tone. "We'll take whoever will come, and those who can't fight will wait for us at the foot of the mountain."

56

Rufus – Psilos Bridge

The flowing Toras River ran so broad and wide there was barely a fleck of spume on its surface, but Rufus knew the deceptive strength of those waters. Standing atop the Psilos Bridge, he tossed a discarded leaf onto the current and watched it float away faster than most men could run. Growing up in the mountainous west, far from land flat enough to bear such a large river, he realised how little of the world he'd seen and conquered. One day, he'd follow this water miles downstream to Toria and lay siege to the human capital.

"Does your warlord always leave honoured guests waiting?" the Waif Magician croaked from far away.

Rufus carried on watching the river. "You can forgive him for not wishing to remain close to you." That job had been left to Rufus, given he rarely wore armour, so the Staff's weakness was more tolerable in theory. No one else risked coming close. Still, he daren't even look at her lest she take the weapon from her back and magnify its power again, just like she had on the road when he'd looked at her for a few too many seconds.

"Are we still safe to wait here?" Rufus asked.

"We need to head south within the hour. Torians are coming."

The Magician's foresight had been most useful. Their trek through the Empire had been as undisturbed as an early morning stroll through the rolling hills outside Viridia.

A clunk of metal caught his attention as Hadrian and his centuries of men marched across the bridge towards them. Each had stripped their heaviest armour for their mules to carry, but their steps were still noticeably feebler when they reached Rufus. They pressed their wooden shields together into a wall two-lines thick, behind which the Warlord glared.

"Do we cross the river or not?" Hadrian asked.

Without the Magician, it wouldn't have even been a consideration. Mount Psilos could be approached from either side of the River Toras, but there was no retreat for a rakkan should they cross and get caught on the eastern banks.

"We continue over," the Magician replied flatly, though Rufus suspected she only did it to make the Warlord even more reliant on her.

"Very well," Hadrian growled with a disgruntled glance at his commanders.

Rufus cleared his throat. "I think that's a mistake." He waited for the Warlord to give a nod and indicate he could continue speaking. "We should remain on the western riverbank so that our army is well-positioned to cut off any approaching Margalvian force. If those warriors we ran into at the Cliffs have sent word back home, we cannot allow the Black Legion to amass."

"Even a legion cannot defeat *me*," the Magician said with a crackly, sinister tone that almost stole Rufus's resolve.

But he displayed the courage they all doubted he had and continued. "We should march our army away from Mount Psilos to cut them off."

The Magician ran a hand across her chin pensively. "The weak one may have a point. We could send some centuries west, but we also need men for a rearguard if we're approaching along the eastern bank."

Weak one? "Granted, but would it take many? At worst, sending the bulk of our men to cut off the Margalvians will make it harder for Toria to track where we've headed with you, Warlord."

Hadrian grimaced. "And leave myself less defended? No. All my men come with me. What if the Torians pursue us to the mountain?"

"*All* the men? What about scouts?"

The Magician raised an eyebrow.

"Enough!" The Warlord's yell was so fierce the few warriors in front of him flinched. "With *her*, we don't need scouts. My men will protect me until I retrieve the Blades."

If only the Blades could give a man his spine back. Rufus would never dare say the words aloud, but soon his time would come. He already saw some of the commanders eyeing the Warlord from behind, wondering for the best point to sink the knife in—especially Rufus's older brothers. After such poor leadership of late, Rufus would let fate take its course. The Magician's motives were of far more concern to him, and Viridia's future might depend on Rufus deciphering them.

Ending the debate, the Warlord shoved his men forwards, and they quickly marched across the bridge, leaving just Rufus and the witch alone again.

"Your idea wasn't terrible," she croaked. "Your warlord is making a mistake, but there was no use arguing."

It wasn't like Rufus needed telling. The lunacy of heading towards a foreign mountain without scouts sent more beads of sweat down his temple by the second. The Magician could only see what her eyes would witness, not everything. The Warlord had acted unwisely many times before, but Rufus had never feared it would be the death of him until now.

"Will Hadrian survive?" he asked.

When she didn't answer, he glanced up to see her grinning, wrinkled face. "Would you like him to?"

Rufus wasn't sure. He was many things, but a traitor? "He's my father."

"… That isn't a 'no.'"

"Will *I* survive?"

"Your chances are good if you do as I advise. It's a pity your father's apprehension will have consequences, but fear not. I will intervene in the battle if I must. If I don't, it means I know you'll prevail without my help."

That answer rendered his next question unnecessary. A "battle" meant the Margalvians would be at Mount Psilos. Why the Magician hadn't pressed the point with the Warlord, he didn't know, but he was sure she wouldn't explain even if he asked her.

Rufus straightened his back and turned to face the woman. "I assume you'll need to assist us if the Dreaded One is there, and he'll be after my father again. Will you save him? Don't worry, I won't breathe a word to him if not."

The wind swept through her veil so forcefully it was almost blown free.

"I know you won't," she said. "There's a chance your father will fall. But he's not the only one I foresee leading the Viridian Legion with the Blades in his clutches." The Magician grinned, then began striding towards the other side of the bridge. "Come. We cannot let the Margalvians get there first."

Rufus followed after her with weak strides. Whoever she was alluding to wielding the Blades, he wasn't sure he wanted to ask and find out.

57

King's Orator – Mount Psilos

Under the shadow of the sleeping mountain, Ophelia sat while the King's Sword ran a whetstone down his weapon with regularly timed movements. Each whine of the blade as he scraped sent a shudder through Ophelia's back and made their swifts shake their heads and snort. But she wouldn't say anything of her irritation at the noise. This was his way of calming himself to prepare for battle.

Instead, she peered at the top of the colossal mountain for a distraction. Grey clouds circled above but had yet to release the rain they threatened onto the dry, barren inclines below. Rings of black and grey circled the jagged and crooked heights, running down the desolate slopes for miles. Inside the Mount, there was not solid stone but pits and fractures that made for a chaotic mess of rock.

Songs told of the mountain once spewing clouds of its own from the cratered top, and that its roar had shaken the very earth and reduced great buildings to rubble. But Ophelia had never witnessed anything to suggest there was truth to the tales. Mountains did nothing but sit as the eons passed as far as she'd seen.

Thankfully, the King wasn't so dormant. Ophelia eagerly awaited their final instruction that her algus's escort was yet to bring. Having been away from Toria for so long, she hadn't personally seen the reports her spies around the Empire sent to the capital. Those went directly to the King now, and she felt alone and ignorant because of it. This must have been how normal people experienced life. *What a curse.*

As she continued her pondering, the King's Sword suddenly stopped his sharpening.

Her eyes immediately began scanning the dark sky, looking for the bird she knew drew near. And soon she saw it soar towards them and land with a tiny thump.

Jason held out his hand on the ground and waited for the creature to hop onto his finger. Then he brought it close to him and stroked it a few times in the same rhythmic, mechanical way he had run the stone down his sword. Animals always seemed to love the gentle man. It was only people he slew.

"The message?" Ophelia said when she could take the suspense no longer.

Jason looked to her silently and nodded, then untied the small slip of parchment and handed it to her.

She hurriedly unfurled it and began reading the message. There were only four lines.

> *He must enter at once and hide by the stain of fire.*
> *Wait for him to the north.*
> *He will need you.*
> *His chances are fair, but he must slay her.*

Ophelia gazed up at the ageing King's Sword, at the man the message was about. She still saw that young gentleman when she looked into those now dormant eyes and wished she could see him smile again just once. "Fair" chances were far worse than usual.

He caught her staring and asked her a silent question with only his expression. He wanted to know their orders.

"You must enter now," Ophelia said. "Wait by the Blades." The weapons' fire would be what had stained the surrounding ground.

"Staff?" Jason asked flatly as if retrieving it would be as simple as picking a flower.

Ophelia scratched her scalp, suddenly getting an unrelenting itch that she couldn't ease even by scraping the loose skin away. Another reason she hated being away from the capital was that she couldn't take her regular milk baths.

"You must kill the Magician if you're to take the Staff," Ophelia said without betraying a hint of the significance of such an act. She studied Jason's expression as her command registered, but as he nodded, there was no trace of reluctance to carry it out. Her friend had no idea that he'd be killing his sister, and she would have felt guilty for concealing it if she'd had any choice in the matter, or if his sister wasn't such a deplorable malefactor.

"She'll see your attacks coming," Ophelia added. "She has similar powers to you. So catch her blind." Although this wasn't something new to Jason, given the King's assessment of the odds, she thought it worth a reminder, and experience had taught her that the mental blocks in his mind had such strength that he'd never connect the clues of his familial bond with the Magician and retain such an inference.

Jason bolted up like a puppet yanked up by his master and readied his whetted blade.

"Be careful." Ophelia stood with a lot less flair than her friend and placed a hand on his shoulder.

The man froze for a moment as if savouring her farewell. Then he gave a grunt of appreciation and stalked off towards the mountain.

58

Lex – Mount Psilos

The march from Menara to Mount Psilos took longer than Lex had feared, losing them too many men in the rocky mountains. Thankfully, Cyrus had stepped up to lead the Menaran slaves on a path a lot of them knew well. But most of the time, they hiked through the night with thick clouds covering any light the moon might have given. Several Menarans lost their footing in the dark and twisted ankles or tore ligaments, and so had to return home, but the rakkan warriors trudged on, only frustrated by the gruelling pace.

And it carried on for many nights and evenings, which Lex endured in further discussion with the Chief Priest and Cyrus. The latter relayed the stories of when his forefathers had last trekked to Mount Psilos. No one had ventured close since the Battle on the Mount, one and a half centuries ago, but the location of the entrance to the mountain had been passed down with a significance impressed on all Menarans but never explained. Those ancestors must have known that the Blades of Trogus would become vital at some point in the future but had tried to lose any recollection of them into history. It had worked up to now.

But finally, they reached the base of the towering Mount Psilos, which rose from the ground like an ancient black spearhead long since battered and worn by the elements. The top was hollow and splintered as if it had been blown off by a force from inside, and the entire structure had deep cracks and fissures running down it.

Dark rock crumbled to ash under her boots as Lex trudged at the head of their army and noted another trail of footprints treading up to the mountain. *Tiro. Find whoever made those.*

Her falcon obliged and struggled against the coastal winds that whipped up the dust, nettling her throat. And the constant coughs of the rakkans and humans behind told her they were as irritated as she was. At least, she hoped it was the ash and not fatigue.

It didn't take long for Tiro to spot the army that had made the tracks beneath her feet, and as they came from the west, her falcon confirmed who had made them—the Black Legion. Her escort dove, battling against the turbulent winds that almost spun his light wings a few times, but eventually, he sank low enough to glide over the top of the resting Black Legionnaires, right up to the rakkan wearing the horned helmet.

Tiro landed in front of Varro and gave two nods to indicate they were close. The Black Warlord raised a bare, white fist in reply. They were ready to march to battle.

"Darius," Lex called, leaving her escort's senses and pacing towards the man and Selene as they walked.

"Damn…" Darius gaped up at the mountain before them. "That thing's massive. Don't tell me we have to climb to the top."

"Thankfully, we don't," Lex said. Cyrus had sung an old song telling of the mountain and the chaos that had birthed inside. "The Black Legion are up ahead."

The news made Darius's face twist with a sour rage. "I take it *he's* with them."

"Of course. And we're better off for it." As much as Lex resented her former partner for breaking her heart, for declaring he'd lied when he said he was in love with her, she had to admit he was the most feared rakkan in the land. She'd never have thought anyone could rival Darius on the battlefield, but the Black Warlord had, on many occasions—never fairly, but instead taking advantage of the weaknesses he knew of the half-rakkan. She did wonder how a fight would end now, though, seeing Darius's aversion to blood improve over the last few months.

But that was a scenario she couldn't let play out now. They had to be forced to work together, regardless of history.

Darius strode out a few steps ahead of his army with Lyra prowling at his heel as they neared the black mass of armour. The metal sea of legionnaires stood and parted for them, watching silently while leaving an open trail of ash right up to the waiting figure of the Black Warlord. The winds sprayed dust across the kuraminium coats of the warriors, sending a faint sound into the air like tiny ringing bells, and the black sand cloaked Lyra entirely except for her bright, narrowed eyes.

While they approached, Lex noticed the muscles on Darius's neck tense with every step, and Selene scanned around them as if fearful any of the rakkans there might try something.

Another musclebound warrior with thick black tufts of hair stood beside Varro—Julius, his most celebrated commander. The rakkan leaned and whispered to Varro before folding his arms and facing ahead.

Before Darius and Lex reached the pair, Sulla sprinted from behind, right up to Varro, and the two rakkans exchanged a firm clasping of hands.

"You're alive, then!" Sulla grinned. "Does that mean we have the mine back?"

"We do. But it came at a cost." Varro's gaze slipped to Darius, who had stopped a few yards behind Sulla with a bitter grimace.

Sulla shifted until he blocked their sight of each other. "Don't start."

The Warlord pushed past his Militia Chief as if he hadn't spoken and approached Darius.

Lyra spat a deep, hateful growl while Lex watched intently and waited for her time to intervene. She'd let them vent their anger a little first.

"Warlord," Darius grunted with a half-hearted rakkan gesture of greeting. "Or are you just plain 'Varro' to me now?"

"You'll address me with the respect I deserve," Varro said.

"I see… So what address does a resentful bastard deserve?"

The Black Warlord's voice became as biting as the wind. "You may be an exile of my city, but I will not tolerate such contempt of the position I hold, of the position your *grandfather* held."

"Sorry, I'll rephrase: What address does a resentful bastard deserve, *Warlord?*"

"Hey!" Sulla yelled and stepped between the pair of red-faced rakkans again. "If you two are finished comparing the size of your swords, we have a real enemy to face."

"And what else?" Darius growled. "Let's answer the important question. If we march up this mountain together and beat Hadrian, what becomes of the Blades?"

Varro let a lull follow the question when more than one set of eyes shifted to him expectantly. When he decided to speak, it was with a calm yet authoritative voice. "We all know what needs to be done. If you have an issue with that, let's settle it now."

"Don't tempt me."

Varro stood still, his hand ready by the hilt of his spatha. Lex knew it wasn't his preferred weapon in battle, but it was in one-on-one combat. Tempted to step in, she caught Sulla's gaze and saw he was as alert to the situation as she was. So she let them continue, praying for a resolution.

"You didn't even let me go to Brutus's burial," Darius muttered in a sombre tone.

"It was best you didn't."

"He would have wanted me there!"

"Don't tell me what my brother would have wanted. It's your fault I no longer have anyone to call 'brother.'"

It was Varro's hand that went to his sword first. His spatha was halfway out of its sheath when Sulla clamped a hand on his wrist, and Lex ripped her sword from its scabbard.

The Warlord pushed away his Militia Chief and went for the sword again but instead dodged as Julius's hand came from behind to seize him. Lex had never seen Varro so emotional, so unable to control the anger he usually buried deep. *Please, don't let this come to a fight.* But her sword was brilliant with algor and ready.

Darius drew his gladius and sent flames whirling down the blade. Lyra bared her fangs and roared while ranks of Menarans pulled out their own weapons and raised their shields, though they held back with a sensible dread of the unthinkably strong warriors everywhere.

And surrounding the men bracing for a fight, the Black Legionnaires drew their swords with a single ominous ring of metal, throats rumbling with the same growls that should have been terrifying the Viridians, not Lex and the other humans.

"Come at me, Warlord," Darius sneered. "Make your brother more ashamed of you."

As Varro lunged forward to score a piece of the man, Sulla pushed him back again.

"Stop this madness!" Sulla cried. "The real enemies are in there!" He pointed to the mountain.

"Do you forget," Darius yelled, "that Brutus died protecting me? What would he think of you now?"

Varro froze, breathing heavily, with a hint of awareness in his glare that he'd lost control.

Across from him, Darius's face contorted with a hatred that only a man with a deep wound bore. But *he* didn't rush forward; instead, he held his composure in a way Lex had yearned for him to do for so long.

With a deep breath, the Warlord sheathed his sword and turned to the mountain while everyone else waited and breathed again. Darius took a moment to peer behind at the Menarans and even at the Red Militia with weapons ready to fight for him. The puzzlement the sight brought to his face was innocent yet frustrating.

Uttering a quiet curse, Varro flicked open the clasp of his sword belt, letting it fall to the ground, and stepped towards Darius slowly, his palms held out.

This time, Sulla let him pass as Darius and Lex watched him suspiciously.

Varro stopped a yard away and surveyed Darius's figure properly for the first time, across the recently trimmed beard and loose-fitting clothing.

"You look strong," the Warlord said.

Darius frowned and paused as if taken aback before he seemed to remember he was angry. "I feel it." The man's eyes narrowed. His fingers still twitched by his sword's hilt.

"Sulla's right. This is no time to quarrel. There's a warlord close by that has wronged us both in many ways. I should lay the blame for Brutus's death at his feet, not yours."

Still with a look of suspicion, Darius said, "It took you long enough to realise that. So…truce?"

Varro paused for a moment. "Are we united in our goal? Are you willing to help me do what's necessary?"

Darius scoffed. "Kill Hadrian? Believe me, I'll only rest easily when he's in hell."

"That wasn't what I was referring to." Varro took a step closer. "We know which warlord needs to wield the Blades."

A low murmur escaped Darius's throat, and after a long pause that stretched out across all the men and women there, Darius lifted his chin. "Are you confident you're worthy?"

"A damn sight more than Hadrian."

Darius snorted a laugh. "That isn't saying much, but…" The man looked around restlessly and said no more.

"It's not only the Viridians we face. Branz have declared war."

"Sulla mentioned."

"This isn't a war we can win," Varro said, "unless I take the Blades and all legions submit to me."

Darius stared at him intently for a while before sighing loudly and fumbling his next words, as if it pained him to utter them. "Then I'll…fight to my end to get the Blades in your hands."

Sulla groaned a sigh of relief. "That's settled, then. We need to—"

"And will you allow me back into Margalvia afterwards?" Darius asked, a rare hint of nervousness in his voice.

"I don't know," Varro answered. "If we both survive, we'll discuss it. If I fall…the next warlord can end your exile, should he so wish."

Darius lowered his head but gave no further argument.

"Julius!" Varro said.

"Yes, Warlord?" the commander answered.

"Ready the Legion. We march on the mountain."

59

Darius – Mount Psilos

Darius trudged alongside Lex, Selene, Gorgias, and the brave Menarans who had decided to come, prepared to fight—or was that die?—with him. Why? Surely they wouldn't have been foolish enough to stand against Black Legionnaires? But he'd resolved to not let them have the chance to throw their lives away on this mountain.

While the Black Legion began marching towards their target, he held the Menarans back while pulling the Chief Priest quietly aside. Just by Aran's deflated shoulders, he sensed the man knew what he'd say.

"You're not coming," Darius said plainly.

The Chief Priest nodded, though with a regretful bite of his lip. "May I ask why? Haven't I proven my usefulness and trustworthiness?"

As far as Darius was concerned, he wouldn't trust anyone outside his closest circle of friends, and even that was hard after

Selene's betrayal a year ago. But the Chief Priest had done enough for Darius to keep him around when it suited.

"It has nothing to do with your usefulness," Darius said. "But this will be no place for you. I don't want holy blood on my hands."

"I sense your mind is made up, so I won't argue. I'll only offer you my prayers that you triumph, and one word of advice."

Darius raised an eyebrow, waiting for the word.

"Have faith in yourself," the Chief Priest said with a smile.

"That's four words. But thank you." However, Darius couldn't see how that was relevant to the fight at hand. "I hope you'll help me persuade the Menarans to stay here with you."

"Leave it to me. I doubt they can be of much use to you in such a battle. And I'll speak with Nasrin as well. I presume you wish her to stay too?"

Darius hesitated before answering, looking at Selene with his familiar desperate longing to see her restored. Convincing the Magician would be impossible without Nasrin, so they'd have to somehow capture the old witch amidst a battle if it came to it. The risk for Selene was so great he almost rebuked the Chief Priest there and then, almost consigned Nasrin to enter a dangerous and probably fatal place for her. The carer didn't deserve that, but Selene didn't deserve to be left with a manipulated mind either.

"Well?" Aran asked.

Darius twisted his head until Selene was out of sight when he answered. "Nasrin will stay with you." However difficult it was, the Magician would be left alive—chained, writhing and blind, but alive.

As the Chief Priest walked to address the Menarans, Cyrus then broke away from speaking with Lex and Gorgias and approached.

"Master Darius?" he said.

"What's wrong?"

"Am I right in thinking that you're not taking us with you?" The man's tone was almost relieved rather than frustrated, as it should have been.

At least one of them has sense. "That's right," Darius said. "Wait for us here for a few days with the supplies we brought. If we don't return by then, assume the worst."

"Very well. I have no doubts the *Slayer of Gods* will be victorious, but I'd best tell you what I know about the mountain first. Before the Battle of the Mount, the humans found a way through the fissures that links to the rakkan paths inside. It's how we caught them unawares. The location was passed down, in case we ever needed those routes again." The man pointed to a particular crack several hundred feet high that forked into a black opening at the bottom. "I can explain where to go from there to get to the main crater on top." Cyrus went on to describe the route in detail, with many sentence arrangements of what rhythmically appeared to originate from a song.

"I'm not sure I'll remember all that," Darius said nervously when the man had finished.

"I will," Selene said.

It looked like he'd have to trust her on that, but he had his doubts about this path even if she'd memorised it. From what Lex had told him, the Battle of the Mount had been a long time ago, so there were no guarantees this route was still viable or that this unknown stranger was telling the truth. Yet getting inside the mountain and somehow surviving would be of no use if he couldn't find the right place. If the plethora of cracks outside the steep slopes were any indication, the passages and holes within must have formed a labyrinth larger than any manmade structure Darius had ever seen.

Cyrus gave a salute, then left to rejoin the other Menarans to make a camp. Meanwhile, Darius stepped to rejoin Lex and Gorgias, but Selene held him back with the chain.

"Wait," she said, sheepishly tilting her head. "I have something to ask of you."

If she was going to request he release her, he was already tempted to do so without her asking; they'd need every fighter they could get. But he also realised that if Nasrin wasn't coming with them, there wasn't much point in Selene going at all.

"Can I have my bear claw back?" she asked.

The question caught Darius by surprise. At first, he didn't know what to say. He'd never shown her that he wore the claw around his neck because it made him seem like a sentimental fool. Yet she knew he'd kept it? And why would she want it back if she'd lost all emotional attachment to it like Lex had claimed?

"What for?" he asked.

"Isn't it obvious? It's unlikely I'll make it out of this mountain if I have no weapon and I'm chained to you or anyone else. I'd rather die with at least one thing I love."

How could he refuse her that? He reached up and untied the necklace from which his three keepsakes hung.

Her mouth fell ajar when she saw where he'd kept it, and a little flush came to her cheeks. She was clearly touched by how special he considered both the claw and their relationship. And how could he not treasure such a cherished item? She was the first woman who had shown him truly selfless love.

The stone of aeternus was the first thing he touched, and how he wished Brutus were here now, not just to rebuke Varro but to offer some words of wisdom.

Darius let go of the stone, then removed the bear claw and gave it to Selene, watching the joy light in her eyes when she took it and breathed deeply as if reunited with the bear itself.

And at that moment, he saw how wrong Lex was. Emotions as strong as a person's bond with their escort could be tampered with, but they could never be detached. Even when Archimedes had used far greater powers on Darius's mind, his care for Lyra had broken through the obstacles put in its way, his care of Lex had been there underneath it all, and he'd never hurt either of them despite having no qualms about slaying any woman, man or beast.

The connection he'd had with Selene was the same—a love too strong to pervert, and that left a bond damaged but unbroken even by the most bitter of betrayals. What hope would the Waif Magician have of impairing that enough to cause him harm?

Given that realisation, should he even allow Selene to go into the mountain with them?

"You should stay here with the others," Darius said. One of the rakkans would be capable of making sure she didn't leave, although perhaps such a precaution wasn't even needed.

But Selene's eyes became as fierce as her sister's. "I don't run from a fight. I'll go to face this magician myself."

"There's no need. It's much safer to—"

"Do not treat me like a child!" Her voice rang out into the coastal winds, just like the commanding leader she'd been when fighting the Viridians with him.

"But Lex will never allow you to have a weapon."

"Then I'll fight with my bare hands." Selene raised her fists, knuckles white, with a familiar determination. The woman he'd fallen in love with.

Her anger reminded him of his own towards Lex when he'd been in a much worse state than Selene. Lex had treated him like a child and far worse. There was nothing more enraging than knowing who you really were but everyone else seeing you for something you were not, a traitor or an implanted spy. And now

566

Darius had been treating Selene the same way, when he'd suspected all along she posed little threat.

Based on what? Nothing more than Lex's stubbornness, born of her own tortured past.

It had to end. Selene's life was on the line now, and if she wanted to fight, how could he deny her the right? And there was no way he'd allow her to carry on without a weapon.

He stepped closer and whispered, "Fine. When we get in, I'll make sure you have more than fists to kill with." In the chaos of battle, there would be an opportunity to let her fight for the first time, to let her prove to Lex how much of her old self was still in there.

At his waist was both a kuraminium gladius and a steel sword for when the Staff of Arria was near. Selene would be far more effective with the sword in that eventuality.

She finally bore a look of deep satisfaction that he'd seen her for what she was, eager for what lay ahead.

They rejoined Lex and Gorgias before hurrying to the front of the marching army, where Sulla and Varro strode with a tense thunder of boots behind them. Darius took the opportunity to wrap his clothes tighter around him, ensuring his sleeves left as little of his flesh exposed as possible in case the Magician tried to touch him again.

"Do you need a rakkan to take Selene?" Sulla asked Darius.

Ordinarily, Darius would have said yes, whatever his intentions with her, but then he and Selene would no doubt end up separated in the fight, and he'd no longer be able to protect her.

"No," he said.

Sulla frowned, and even Lex seemed confused.

She paced closer to him and said, "But we need you free—"

"No," Darius repeated in the same forceful tone she used when her mind was made up, also relying on the hundreds of warrior eyes and ears in front of whom she wouldn't want to have an argument.

She fell silent when she realised his stubbornness and what he intended to do. Perhaps Lex's lack of resistance afterwards was an admission that Darius was right in planning to free Selene. That's how he'd take it anyway.

Lex cleared her throat. "Darius, can you—"

"I'm not shackling her to anyone else," he said.

"… I wasn't going to ask that. I was going to ask for your aeternus. I'll need it to light the powder if I'm in a position to blind the Magician."

That was a better idea than relying on his strength to conjure ferven, though he was loath to let go of Brutus's gift. Hesitantly, he untied his necklace a second time and slipped the Agathos pendant off and into his pocket. Then he lit the aeternus with ferven in his hand.

"Will it be hot enough?" he asked. It would almost burn forever but barely warmed his palm once the ferven was banished.

"I'll have to pray it is." Lex took the necklace from him and tied the now glowing stone around her neck. It rested behind her tunic and mail, giving off a soft shine where she conjured algor to protect her clothes.

"Keep it safe," he said, worry seeping into his voice.

"I will," she said, and focused on their target once again.

At each mile they got nearer to the fissure, the mountain's size swelled to more unthinkable heights. He'd underestimated the size of that great crack, and when they neared it, he saw it was tall and wide enough to fit an entire building within. At the top, the fissure narrowed to form the upper jaw of the mouth. Shards of rock hung down like shattered teeth and threatened to fall and crush them as they walked through the deep gloom underneath.

As soon as they entered the darkness, the air became thick and foul with a sulphurous malodour that gave him the impression that not only death lingered here but something far worse. Lyra suffered the most from the stench and shared her revulsion with him, but he did his best to distance himself from her mind, somewhat unsuccessfully.

Fractures in the rock at his feet ran deep, with abysses threatening to swallow their warriors should they place a foot wrong. It was even fouler than Cyrus had described.

"Order the algus to scout ahead. Quietly," Varro said, his voice breaking the thumps and clanks of metal.

Julius relayed the order to some scouts, and a few algus ran into the darkness with a little algor lighting their way.

"We'll go with them." Darius turned to the Warlord and Lex as he spoke. None of those algus would see in the dark as well as he, and he wouldn't risk Hadrian finding the Blades first.

Varro and Lex gave a silent nod, and Darius looked down at his panther.

Stay with Sulla. Help them follow us if we find something.

Lyra gave him a growl and fell back until prowling by Sulla's heel.

Don't worry. You'll be fighting beside me soon enough. There was no other place he'd rather have her in a battle.

He took off and was soon racing into the darkness with Selene, Lex and Gorgias behind, following what he recalled of Cyrus's route. The cracks in the rock were almost impenetrable to his eyes, but he was able to guide them around the gaping holes in the ground and see that no one had set foot on this path recently.

The anticipation of battle gripped him like a looming prospect both unnerving and welcome. Soon his sword would taste the blood he no longer feared it spilling.

60

Sulla – Mount Psilos

A few hours passed after Darius and the other scouts left, and none sent word back, so Sulla hurried and risked that the padding of his boots might give not only him but all their men away if an enemy was nearby. But it was too bad. They'd wasted far too long having petty arguments amongst themselves and getting everyone inside the mountain.

Warlord Varro stalked silently beside him. Only the pair of them marched in the vanguard. Greater numbers would hinder them in sensing movement in the air ahead.

"How much farther?" Sulla whispered.

The Warlord shrugged. "We're on the path Eugenius described. All he said was that we'd know when we arrived." That was the same answer he'd given an hour ago, yet they ascended in total darkness. Even his rakkan eyes would have been unable to see if not for the trace of ferven he conjured.

A brief flicker of light in the pocked stone overhead drew Sulla's gaze, but no sooner had it appeared than it vanished.

"Did you see that?" Sulla asked.

The Warlord hadn't looked up but nodded. "The stars. The gaps in the rock lead out to the air."

We're that high? Sulla's aching thighs could believe it after yet another steep slope of dusty stone. As he was about to ask more questions, the fissure they'd been walking through suddenly ended and led into a vast, sprawling crater. Above, his eyes were greeted with not just a lone star but an entire cluster of sparkling lights between a break in the clouds of the night sky.

Before them, the top of the mountain stretched into a basin of black rock that was as erratic as anything Sulla had ever seen. The floor of the crater was broken by holes that looked so deep he believed the rumours—that they descended all the way to the underworld. Spirals of chaotic, sulphurous air rose and made it almost impossible for him to sense the movement of the army behind him as he had done only moments before.

And above the ground, a jungle of dense vines spiralled all over in an interlocked mess. Only these weren't the vines of a plant but of black rock, as if a giant creeper had spread throughout the place aeons ago, then turned to stone. Each vine was as thick as a barrel of beer, and the tangle curled to reach a height of at least thirty feet.

"I never thought hell would be uphill," Sulla muttered as he went to one of the rock vines jutting out of the basin floor at an angle. It was so steep they would have to climb, not walk to the top of the natural structure.

While he scanned the landscape, something grazed his leg, so bulky it could only have been Lyra. When he ignored her, she nipped his calf.

"What's wrong?" he asked. The panther's gaze fixed ahead for a second, ears standing to attention, before she leapt and began clawing her way up the rock vine.

"Does she want us to follow?" the Warlord asked.

"I guess."

"But Eugenius said nothing of climbing these. We should stay to the basin floor as he set out."

Loose, black stone rattled down the column as Lyra's claws dug in, still climbing. Their whole army couldn't follow, but some could.

"Darius spoke with the Menarans," Sulla said. "They told him the way."

Varro shook his head, the horns of his helmet swaying as he began marching forward again. "I'll trust our former warlord."

Whatever Sulla thought, there wasn't time for arguments. With battle looming, the chain of command mattered more than anything.

"Get down, Lyra," Sulla called as quietly as possible but so that the panther could hear.

Lyra froze, claws sunk in the stone, and peered back at him.

"Don't give me that look. Down."

After a few moments of hesitation, the cat relented and scratched her way down, almost landing on top of him when she jumped the last few yards. With a quiet curse, Sulla started after her and Varro.

61

Darius – Mount Psilos

Darius crouched behind a vine of rock that split the thin ribbon along which they'd been walking. Although he was only halfway to the top of the sprawling tangle, with twisting columns surrounding him on every side, the wind still howled and tossed his hair, one moment to the left, the next to the right. It was a good thing he'd cut his hair short, otherwise it would have constantly raked across his eyes as Selene's now did.

Lex paused beside him and tightened her hairband while Gorgias hid farther behind. Meanwhile, Tiro surveyed from such a height that Darius couldn't see him, and Lex hadn't let them so much as whisper for half an hour. There had been no sign of anyone below them on the pitted basin floor, but Darius inferred Viridians were around. They hadn't beaten them here. They hadn't been swift enough.

He tapped Lex on the shoulder and raised his eyebrows when she looked. In reply, she held up two fingers and pointed to the other side of the rock they were crouching behind. Whether that meant there were two warriors or that the entire Viridian Legion was two yards away, he couldn't be sure. But with both swords in his hands, he was ready for anything.

Lex slowly eased herself around the rock, toes hanging over the edge of a small lip supporting her.

Darius swallowed. *Hope we don't have to fight up here.* Once around the vine, he scanned across the web of thinner rocks stretching throughout the crater, but there were no rakkans or half-gomans in sight.

Just as he was about to give Lex a nudge again, to ask what had spooked her, movement below caught his eye.

Lex froze before he did and slowly lowered herself to her knees, an act he soon mimicked to lessen his chances of falling while he took in the sight below. Appearing between a gap in the rock vines, a group of Viridian Legionnaires roamed quietly along the edge of a gaping hole in the crater. Two warriors at the front scanned the ground beneath them and avoided the black pits dotted around while the others constantly looked to their flanks in wide-ranging scans of the landscape.

And then Darius saw him. From above, the horns weren't obvious, but those brutish shoulders could belong to no other. With Darius and the others frozen above, the Viridian Warlord kept striding until almost directly beneath them. If only the gap in the rocky tangle were large enough for Darius to drop down, the erratic wind would mask his approach until it was too late, until his blade bit down into the Warlord's spine.

Lex stealthily slid an arrow out of her quiver and nocked it. From this angle, all Darius saw of Hadrian was black armour. Although algor could penetrate steel, it took so much force to puncture kuraminium that Darius usually had to throw weight behind his sword. An arrow stood little chance, and that's if it hit its mark. Given the erratic wind, even Selene would struggle to find the narrow gaps between the pieces of metal armour.

Darius looked over his shoulder, and he saw the hate in Selene's eyes that he'd expected. The sooner he could give her a sword, the better.

Gorgias now knelt behind her and gaped down at the Viridians, sword drawn but chest rising and falling rapidly.

But as Darius plotted to deliver justice upon Hadrian, some of the Viridians suddenly broke into a run with a roar of triumph.

Darius's stomach sank as even Hadrian hurried his pace. No longer caring about stealth, Darius stood, then bolted forward, leapt over Lex and followed as best he could through the criss-cross of rocks. His algus agility made it easier to keep his balance, and Selene had more than enough dexterity to keep up close behind.

After a few leaps and bounds, he saw the Viridians slow and begin fanning out in front of something where the jutting columns ended. As Darius approached, the rocks he traversed all ceased so abruptly it was as if a giant had cleaved the ends with a scythe and reaped the rest of the stone away.

Only when he got closer did he see it wasn't just the walkways he was on; all the rocky vines, both directly ahead and spreading outwards, stopped with sharp, clean ends to the stone, creating a perfect sphere of empty air above a short, glossy basalt platform onto which the Viridians seemed not to dare step. And in the centre of the obsidian rings, two sharp weapons protruded, so dark they barely stood out.

Darius slowed his pace and began making his way to the lower vines of rock whenever he saw the chance. Soon he heard Lex and the others gently stepping behind him, but he still crept closer until he risked being seen, one sword arm ready to cut the chain attaching him to Selene, the other ready for the Viridians ahead.

One of the warriors took a step towards the basalt. His toes couldn't have touched the black rock more than a fraction, but a faint glow rose in the protruding objects to give them the outline of two half-buried swords. Each weapon had two cross guards, one straight and wide, the other curved and pointed like fangs. While one edge of the blades ran straight and sharp, the other was jagged and serrated, made to rip and rend flesh beyond repair. As Darius watched, a violent red ignited to trace symbols on the dark blades, threatening anyone daring to look upon them with their hidden power.

Darius reached out to Lyra in his mind. She confirmed what he feared—Varro and Sulla were on their way, but they might as well have been a mile away. *Let them know to hasten.*

"Move closer!" Hadrian barked at one of the legionnaires.

The rakkan that had stepped forward looked at either side of him as if to shift the order onto one of the others. But they all backed away from him. With a grunt, the rakkan took a few moments to stare at the Blades before stepping forward. No sooner had his foot hit the obsidian than a blinding flash erupted. Ferven spiralled from the weapons, two swirling columns of flame that spit up smoke and ash in a constant stream. The torrents swelled to thrice their size within a heartbeat, and soon their brightness pained Darius's eyes so much he had to squeeze them shut.

A scream of pain came from the Viridians below. Selene buried her head behind him, and the coldness of her algor bit his neck. Without it, the heat that now singed his eyebrows would have burnt her too.

A flash later, all went dark again, leaving white spots underneath his eyelids. When he opened them, only the smoky ground and an ashen hue where the rakkan had stood remained of the fire. The other Viridians who turned around had sooty faces with deep white lines at the corner of their eyes.

Darius's first reaction was to grin. At least the Viridian Warlord couldn't simply walk up and take the things. But that relief soon twisted into horror when he imagined Hadrian taking those weapons with the Staff and how terrible his wrath would be if he wielded such power.

"Damn it!" Hadrian kicked a rock, and it shattered to dust on impact. "Where is she?"

Darius looked over at Lex as she crouched behind a stone. The shrug she gave him wasn't what he'd hoped. Something was off. Where were the Subdued or the rest of Hadrian's army?

But every second he wasted worrying about that was a second longer for the Waif Magician to arrive. They didn't have time to wait for the Black Legion.

The Viridians began arguing amongst themselves over what the Blades were capable of, which gave Darius enough cover to risk speaking.

"Ready?" he whispered to Selene.

She stared at him, hand trembling from what must have been fear of facing her torturers.

"Stay by me," he whispered. "I'll die before I let them hurt you."

The words only caused her expression to become more pained. But he couldn't let her delay him any longer.

Lex waved a hand and caught his attention, then tossed him a key and pointed to Gorgias.

Darius caught it and squeezed it into his palm, knowing what she wanted him to do. But when Lex turned away and began stalking across the rock vines again, Darius hesitated.

Gorgias came closer and whispered, "I'll keep her safe and await the Margalvians."

But four fighters were better than two, and the woman Darius loved would be a prisoner no longer. He took hold of the chain that had connected them for far too long and conjured ferven on his palm, melting the metal in seconds under the gaping eyes of Gorgias. Then he held out the hilt of his steel sword to her.

Selene took it with the grin of a woman finally unleashed, a woman finally able to exact revenge for what had been done to her.

Despite a horrified look of protest on Gorgias's face, the algus remained silent, obedient, understanding.

Darius gave him a nod. Then, gripping his gladius tightly, feeling the heavy weight like a cathartic pull on his arm, he began making his way down the stone vines to the ground.

When he looked back, Lex was almost at the edge where the structure ended above the obsidian rings, and she held her bow with an arrow nocked. Gorgias and Selene followed him, Selene with ferocity in her eyes more intense than in any battle before, and it was a damned sight better than the beleaguered expression of a captive.

At first, the three used the web of rock to hide as they climbed down to the basin floor, but once on the same level as the Viridians, there was little cover but the night's darkness and the odd stone vine stemming from the ground.

The Viridians still argued amongst themselves, so Darius took advantage and stalked forwards, around the chasms, one quiet step at a time but always ready to bolt.

A dozen yards away, it was a Viridian Legionnaire who turned his gaze to them first.

"They're here!" the rakkan yelled as he readied his spear.

A second later, one of Lex's arrows tore through his eye socket.

Darius's focus didn't leave Hadrian. The Viridian Warlord's helmet turned as Darius sprinted forward and raised his sword. Blood wouldn't save Hadrian this time; no tricks would prevent the inevitable.

Two of the Warlord's tattooed guardians stepped in front of him as Darius took his first swing. They parried his blow with their shields before stabbing and slashing at his body. He dodged out of the path of one blade only to narrowly miss another an inch from his stomach. To his side, another legionnaire lunged forward with a spear, but Gorgias bolted in and knocked the weapon just in time for it to glance past Darius's shoulder.

Meanwhile, the other dozens of legionnaires rushed towards him with Lex's arrows darting between them and catching a couple in the neck.

Darius took a step back to avoid getting surrounded and flared algor across his sword. Hadrian stood growling within his helmet, wedged between the warriors in front of him and the ring of obsidian behind. If Darius could scare the Viridians enough to back up just a couple of steps, they'd shove their leader in the Blades' range of death.

The Viridians pressed together into a shield wall in much the same way they had in Dolthea, and set their shields and spears ablaze with ferven. Although Rufus wasn't among them, Darius feared some of these men were the same he'd faced. He should have brought a shield so he could charge at them.

Gorgias backed up to Darius, his sword trembling.

"Hold it together," Darius growled to the man while Selene came to his other side. "Aim low."

Then he charged. He leapt and soared towards the formation as the defenders raised their spears and shields a fraction. Drawing upon both his algus agility and rakkan senses, he tracked the moving weapons and used his armguard to bat away the only spear threatening his body. He aimed a kick at the raised shield of the warrior in front as gravity brought him down.

The testudo stood firm and took the brunt of his fall without budging. But moving them hadn't been his aim. They'd lifted their shields.

Gorgias and Selene followed up with two low, rapid swipes of their swords that left brilliant blue arcs in the air. Both scored the greaves of two guardians who roared with fury but didn't budge an inch.

Lex loosed more arrows, this time arcing high and over the top of the front rank towards the Viridian Warlord, but Hadrian grabbed a shield from one of his guardians and blocked every arrow. Some of the legionnaires in front raised their shields to help block too.

Hadrian barked at them. "Keep your formation!"

Darius's idea wasn't going to work. These Viridians had more fear of their warlord than him, and most would be willingly hacked to pieces before backing up into the brute. And something else unsettled him, like a lead ball in his stomach. Where was the rest of Hadrian's army? And why weren't these warriors attacking?

"What's the matter?" Darius yelled at Hadrian. "Too afraid to test your worth? Only willing to cheat your way to the Blades?"

The Viridian Warlord snarled and made no movement to get closer to the weapons he craved, but a couple of the guardians reacted. If Hadrian couldn't be moved, perhaps they could.

"Are you going to hide away?" Darius yelled to the Warlord. "You craven. Would Hadrianus the Great have shrunk away from a challenge?"

One of the guardians roared with fury and lunged forward, stabbing with his spear. Darius was ready and dodged to the side, slicing through the elbow of the man's extended arm as easily as cutting a reed. A cry had barely escaped the warrior's mouth when Selene's bright sword stabbed into the eye socket and ended the man's life.

The other warriors shifted until their testudo was tight again while Darius picked up the shield of the fallen warrior and stepped back out of their range.

"Nice of him to give me a scutum," Darius said. But no sooner had he taken the heavy kuraminium in his hand, the weight seemed to triple.

The Viridian Warlord released a guttural chuckle that chilled Darius's spine as if algor had coated him.

"If you'd spent less time jeering," Hadrian said, "you might have got me before she arrived."

Darius's gladius suddenly became too heavy as well, and both shield and sword slipped from his fingers and clattered to the black ground. If he'd been wearing any armour, he'd have collapsed under it, but thankfully he'd had enough sense to wear only steel mail. Stepping back, he almost tripped into Gorgias, but the algus held him up.

"Lex!" Gorgias called, courage finally in his voice.

Darius turned to see the plea came too late. Walking atop the web of stone vines, her black veil swirling around her head, the Waif Magician approached with the charred Staff of Arria pointed at the spot between his eyes.

Every step closer she took brought greater weakness. A Viridian was the first to collapse with a grunt, soon followed by any wearing even a single item of kuraminium. Eventually, Darius's knee gave out, and he would have collapsed to the ground if Gorgias hadn't grabbed his waist.

"You can't quit that easily, master," the algus said.

The Magician stopped at the edge of the vines, just before the hot, empty air above the obsidian platform, and her eyes flared with algor to reveal her grin.

Hadrian let out a cross between a growl and another laugh, then dropped to his hands and knees.

Lex loosed a few more arrows at the struggling Viridian Warlord, but the brute still had the strength to dodge or block each one with his armguard. Seeming to admit defeat for now, Lex ignored the quivering rakkans around them and instead aimed for the Magician.

Darius cursed. Would Lex risk killing her and losing Selene's chance at recovery? The Magician was too far away to maim with any precision, even for someone as skilled as Lex.

"Forward!" the Magician croaked, dodging one of Lex's arrows. Her voice was almost too weak to be heard above the chaotic winds, but the shadows that began moving between the rocky vines surrounding them on the basin floor meant it had been loud enough to doom them all.

With swords drawn, pulsing with algor, the Subdued raced forwards.

Darius didn't need to survey or count the new arrivals to know how quickly he and the others would be slashed to pieces. He grabbed Gorgias's collar and growled in his ear. "Get Lex and Selene out of here."

Gorgias grimaced with a shake of his head. "I'm not leaving you."

"Then you're a fool." As Darius opened his mouth to say more, Selene came up right beside him, eyes trained on the Magician as if no one else existed.

"There's too many." Selene gasped.

Darius couldn't even summon ferven to scare any Subdued that might fear the fire like Gorgias. The Staff sapped so much power that his grip was as weak as a child's, yet the Magician had stopped moving, not bothering to circle around and come directly above him. For whatever reason, she spared him the worst of the Staff's debilitation.

"She's afraid," Darius said. "There's still a chance for you all to get away."

"Don't even think it." Selene gave him a kick in the shin, which hurt far more than usual.

Darius cursed under his breath because he knew they wouldn't listen no matter how much he laboured the point. "Then kill Hadrian."

Gorgias's eyes narrowed at the fallen Warlord, still with a trace of fear that would likely never leave him, but the man gripped his sword tight and stepped forwards anyway.

As he did, Selene grabbed his arm and held him in place.

"Forget Hadrian," she said, her fixation never leaving the Magician. "We need to focus on her."

Darius was tempted to argue the point but held his tongue. He knew why Selene was so focused on that woman. She wanted this ordeal to be over and her mind to be made whole again. Revenge was secondary, and what kind of friend would try to convince her otherwise?

Lex loosed an arrow, this time without algor coating its head, almost invisible in the night. But the Magician still casually stepped out of its path. Giving up after a couple more attempts, Lex again turned to Hadrian and loosed.

The Viridian Warlord was down but curled under his armour. Most arrows bounced off his strong cuirass and helmet, and those that would have stung flesh he batted away with his armguard. It must have only been steel, but still, the Viridian

Warlord was even stronger than Darius remembered to lift that under the Staff's curse of fragility.

The attack on the Subdued's master spurred them on. They rushed forwards, seconds away, while Darius looked desperately at the lines of rock crisscrossing above him in search of a way of escape, as if he might suddenly see a rope hanging from one. Unsurprisingly, there wasn't one, but something else caught his eye.

A figure crept along the walkway behind the Magician, hooded and moving like a shadow. Was it one of Varro's algus?

Before he could fathom its identity, a horn blared in the distance. Margalvia's low tone rang out as a herald of salvation in the crater. The Subdued all skidded to a halt, and even Gorgias flinched with a nervous glance in the direction of the rakkan call.

Lyra's relief suddenly eased Darius's fear, and some of the strength that had been sapped now seeped back into his muscles. "It's Varro," Darius said to Gorgias.

No sooner had the triumphant words left his mouth than he caught sight of more dark figures charging through the basin from the opposite direction.

He gaped up at the Magician again. She'd turned around and slung the Staff to her back, withdrawing its influence enough for the full might of Hadrian's rakkan army to approach.

But the Magician was no longer watching anything of the roaring rakkans and the thunder of charging men. She'd turned to face the now motionless figure that had crept within yards of her, and the pair silently glared at one another. Or perhaps they were speaking and were too far away for Darius to hear.

Then, in a sudden movement that was almost impossible to track, the mysterious figure lunged forward with an arcing attack of his algor-pulsing sword. His first stroke was so swift and fluid that the Magician's artful dodge looked wooden in comparison, but she managed to duck and stab her sword for her enemy's belly in a move that Darius had seen disembowel many algus before.

The figure had moved a second earlier, seeming to anticipate the strike, and instead launched another counter of his own towards her nose.

Within a few more heartbeats, the two were nothing but icy blurs, locked in a fierce combat that saw them dart across the stone vines until they were far enough that Darius's eyes could burn with ferven once again.

"Get them, you cowards!" Hadrian bellowed at his algus while the Viridians guarding him got back to their feet like risen corpses. "Stick to the plan!"

But the Subdued didn't renew their charge. They gaped fearfully as the Black Legion's rectangular shields burst with ferven and advanced between the narrow rock stems, taking chunks with them and trampling everything beneath to dust while avoiding the chasms. Opposite them, a Viridian swarm charged with a similar relentless fervour.

Gorgias's whole body tensed, but Darius couldn't calm the man any longer. He pushed away Gorgias's supporting arm and went to pick up his gladius while Selene continued staring at the Magician and her mysterious opponent.

"Jason…" Selene suddenly darted for the nearest rocky outgrowth and began climbing.

"Selene!" Darius cried, but she paid no heed. Could the figure really be Jason, the algus who had killed her escort? When Darius looked up again, he recognised the slick and precise strokes as those of the King's Sword. He was a fool for not seeing it before. And now Lex's arrows whizzed past the algus's head as she focused every shot on him.

"Go and protect Selene." Darius shoved Gorgias, but the man skidded and turned back.

"No," he said. "I'll help you—"

"Now!" Darius ordered in a fiery roar. Selene had been no match for the King's Sword in Laltos and would be no match now.

The man finally relented and sprinted after Selene, leaving Darius to weakly pick up his gladius. If only he could approach the Magician and help Selene… What could he do for her when so weak in the presence of the Staff?

As he retrieved his weapon, Hadrian unleashed a ferocious howl that pained Darius's ears, expressing no less hate than at Laltos.

Darius turned to see his foe once again braced behind a row of guardians. The Black Legionnaires' charge and the algus sprinting ahead had almost reached them, as had the incoming Viridian Legionnaires.

But Darius was damned if he'd let anyone but him take the life of the Viridian Warlord.

He rushed forward and pulled back his sword to sever the head of the closest guardian. But before he reached the man, the gladius slipped from his fingers, and all strength left his legs as if every strand of muscle had snapped. He tripped, skidding face-first along the ground, tasting dirt and ash.

A thunderous crash echoed throughout the crater, followed by roars and groans, and even Hadrian and the Viridians fell to their knees with deep, laboured breaths.

Darius gazed up. The Magician was directly overhead once again. One arm wielded her blade and parried every blow from the King's Sword, whose strokes came within an inch of severing her neck. Her other arm wielded the Staff and pointed it down at all those below.

But holding the weapon came at a price. The King's Sword chopped with a two-handed blow that the Magician barely parried with one arm, and her own blade bit her shoulder.

Then Darius realised she was only using the Staff because she must, because he and the Black Legion posed too great a threat. Only the Staff stood between them and victory.

As the Magician and the King's Sword fought, Lex continued unleashing arrow after arrow while Selene and Gorgias raced up the vines of rock, only moments from reaching the two fighters.

Meanwhile, Hadrian's Subdued had now found their grit and were locked in combat with Laltos's finest algus, outnumbering them two to one. Others tore through the downed Margalvian warriors and sliced until the ground ran red.

All Darius had the strength to do was yell. What was Selene's plan? Surely she hadn't been overcome by rage… Of course she loathed the King's Sword, but did she really believe she could defeat him? Perhaps her desperation was from fear of the Magician dying or her mind being left altered forever, just as Darius's was. Would that be such a bad thing, though? So much of Selene was still left, and whatever the Magician had done wasn't worth her throwing her life away.

As his mind went round in frantic circles, Lex tossed her bow and empty quiver, then unsheathed her sword, staring at the fighting Magician upon the vines. Without a pause, she started towards the duel.

Darius's heart pounded in his throat. His desperate panting brought ash and dust into his lungs. He scanned around for a sign that Laltos's algus were rushing up the web of stone to join the clash, but most were in fights for their lives against Hadrian's Subdued. One algus had his head cleaved off in two savage blows from an enemy, while another algus tripped as three Subdued hacked at his back like they were chopping a thick, bleeding log.

No one else could help, and Darius couldn't watch those he cared for die again, whether the Staff was there or not. What hope had three algus against the Waif Magician and the King's greatest warrior? He'd bet whoever walked away alive from that fight would be one of his enemies.

He had to do something. He pressed his palms into the rock and pushed with all his might, getting his chest high enough to slide his knee under his hips and keep himself up. Scanning the stone jungle desperately, he searched as if a hidden saviour or god lay in waiting to help. But his eyes latched on to nothing but the dim, red glow of the Blades in the centre of the platform as they pulsed. *The only weapons that have ever damaged the Staff.* Were they the answer?

His agreement with Varro lingered on his mind, and he reached out to Lyra. She defended the downed Black Warlord and Sulla while algus fought around them, and Darius tasted coppery blood when Lyra pounced and sank her jaws into the neck of a Subdued.

He retreated until his own sensations were dominant once again. Varro was nowhere close and didn't have the Staff. Every moment wasted could be the death of Selene or Lex.

Darius stared harder at the Blades. If those weapons had the power to burn the Staff, then they'd do a damn sight worse to the Magician, the King's Sword and Hadrian.

And what was stopping Darius? Fear of death? His emotions were barely sane, and fearing death wasn't one of them. Death would have made it all easier. No, his real fear was what would happen if he took the Blades. Lex and others were so intent on him being a leader, being a man that could influence fate rather than watch it steal everyone he cared for. He had little interest in that, but if the swords gave him the power to protect those he loved, then to hell with what he wanted. He'd take them or die trying.

With his anger rising once again, Darius struggled up farther until he was kneeling in front of the collapsed Viridian shield wall. If only he had the energy to leap.

62

Lex – Mount Psilos

Lex sprinted along the narrow stone vine while Selene and Gorgias leapt from below to join her. The sword in Selene's hand sent a nervous shudder down Lex's body, but her sister's entire focus was on the Magician. Darius had been right. They should have freed Selene before. Although the King's Sword was a great threat, the Magician was the greatest, and all their efforts had to go into disabling her and getting the Staff. Selene clearly had enough of her mind to realise that too.

The three algus separated into different pathways, and Lex soon realised why the Magician was up here. On flat ground against four opponents, even she didn't stand a chance. But the Magician's chosen spot atop the stone vines didn't allow her to be attacked from all sides.

But that wouldn't stop Lex trying. She and Gorgias darted towards the Magician's back while Selene circled around. They both swung for the Magician's neck as the King's Sword continued his relentless assault, but Shirin leapt to a parallel vine out of the path of all their blades.

Jason pre-empted the move, and by the time she landed, he had a solid footing and used it to lunge with a far-reaching stab of his sword.

The Magician deflected the attack before glancing over her shoulder for the briefest of moments at Lex. As soon as the Magician's gaze went back to her foe, Lex leapt to the other vine and sprinted towards the pair. It wasn't a stretch to know what the King's Sword was after. Lex would die before she'd let the King have the Staff again, but that was still preferable to letting Hadrian get the Blades.

The King's Sword parried every one of the Magician's strikes, sending a haze of sparks twinkling down below them. Even if he was the most feared algus in the Empire, how could he stand toe to toe with a half-goman? How could he consume the witch's energy so much that she wouldn't have a chance to do anything other than dodge and parry the attacks of the other algus there?

Those were questions for later. Lex jumped onto the same vine as the Magician and rushed towards the woman's back. She swiped her sword at the Magician's legs, but the old hermit leapt over the blade while parrying another one of Jason's strikes.

The King's Sword feinted and changed the direction of his slash, scoring a cut on the Magician's arm that splatted blood onto the stone beneath.

She gasped.

Lex sensed her chance. "Undo what you did to Selene!" Lex yelled as she launched two attacks that were met by swift dodges, but a third forced the Magician to leap onto another vine.

The jump was almost too far for her, and after landing, she wobbled for a couple of heartbeats before regaining her balance.

"What?" she croaked at Lex with a grimace.

When the King's Sword jumped to meet the Magician once again, she retracted the Staff and slipped it through a sling on her back. Warriors groaned below, released from the worst of the Staff's grip, but Lex didn't look. She burst forward again as Selene joined her across another vine and took a leaping stab for the Magician's head.

Lex faltered. Why would Selene go for a lethal strike?

The Magician turned in time to evade the attack, but Gorgias jumped from a lower vine behind her and aimed a stab through her thigh. With a graceful leap and kick, she left his blade sweeping through the air below her while her foot connected with Gorgias's chest.

The man yelled, his jump suddenly cut off, leaving his centre of mass over nothing but sulphurous air. He fell, suddenly silent and with horror in his eyes, flailing and grasping at the Magician's tattered veil as it fluttered in the wind. He caught hold of it, but twisting her head, the Magician let the veil tear free and plummet with Gorgias towards the bloodstained ground and chasms below.

Lex couldn't afford to take her eyes from the Magician's face and the fatigued smugness she wanted to cleave from it. From this height, Gorgias might survive, albeit broken. But if he did, chances were he'd meet an enemy's sword soon after.

"Undo what you did to Selene!" Lex yelled again as she unleashed another flurry of swipes at the Magician.

Shirin's only reply was a confused scowl as Selene and Jason joined the fray with such rapid attacks they left a brightness of the algor streaming in the wind that had Lex squinting.

The Magician shrieked and took a wild upwards slash that skimmed Jason's nose and cut through his hood at the top, ripping it off to reveal his weathered, tanned face. The King's

Sword staggered back a couple of steps, eyes wide and shaken as he lightly touched his unmarked nose.

Lex stared for a moment, never having seen the man properly before. Was he really as old as he looked?

The Magician seized the chance to leap to an adjacent stone vine, her own breaths now leaden and showing her age.

But Lex wouldn't give the Magician respite. She ran, leapt, and chopped her sword only to meet the witch's stiff weapon. As they clashed, Selene rushed in again with a stab that forced the Magician to duck.

As she did, the witch slashed Lex across the thigh with her sword, and with her free hand, reached out to catch the wrist of Selene's sword arm and prevent a follow-up slash.

Lex's heart stopped as she watched the Magician's hand touch her sister's skin, then a searing pain grew in her leg. She staggered back and fell to one knee, warm blood quickly soaking her trousers and dripping down her shin while the Magician froze and gasped, a sudden terror stealing the flush of exertion from her face.

She held Selene's wrist for a few more moments, then turned and sprinted back a few vines until yards away from them all. She gaped at Selene, then at the King's Sword as the two slowly came forward and circled around her.

"The King…" the Magician croaked. "It can't be…" She suddenly fixated on Lex. "Why would you help her?"

"She's my sister!" Lex yelled with fury. "Now undo what you did to her!"

The Magician grimaced. "What *I* did? You fool. The *King* has done this to her."

The accusation struck a low blow to Lex, breaking open the old fear that she'd been right all along about her sister. But of course that's what the witch would say. There were only so many lies Lex would put up with before giving up on maiming the woman instead of seeking to kill. As painful as it was, Selene's plight was nothing compared to the plague that allowing Hadrian to take the Blades would inflict.

Selene stared at the Magician flatly, her sword arm rising and falling with her deep breaths while the King's Sword continued creeping behind the Magician, not unnoticed by her. The witch spun to face him with a harsh movement, almost completely turning her back on the injured, kneeling Lex.

"Do you even know you serve a goman king?" the Magician spat at Jason.

The King's Sword grimaced and clasped his head, and Lex watched as the pain of her injuries suddenly faded into nothing because of the sight before her. Could Jason's mind block be a new one? Or was it an old one from Archimedes's time?

"I see not." The Magician then turned her hysterical gaze on Selene. "And you! Do you know you've been manipulated? Do you know that your mind is not your own?"

Clambering back to her feet, Lex watched the three fighters pause. Jason's torn cloak flapped erratically in the wind while Selene continued her flat, hateful stare. There were no signs of mind blocks in her, no signs of the Magician's words causing any resistance.

What was Shirin playing at? Unsure what to believe now, all Lex could do was stay true to their original goal. Disable the Magician, get the Staff, and end the threat of Overlord Hadrian.

She reached into her pocket and cupped the pouch of flash powder, then banished the thin layer of algor she'd continually conjured on her chest and felt the warm stone hanging there. Its fire was uncomfortable but not searing. *Please let it be enough.*

Clutching her sword tightly, Lex shifted her weight onto her one good leg, then began creeping along the vine towards the

Magician as quietly as she could. The Magician still had her back turned, and only Selene and Jason could see Lex approach. Neither so much as looked at her to give her away. With her free hand, she pulled the powder from her pocket, then took the burning necklace off. Carefully, she shifted the aeternus to the end of her fingers and held the pouch in her palm. The material had been the most flammable she could find whilst remaining sturdy.

All she needed was a few more yards. All it would take was one swift strike through the back of the thighs, then a powder ignition when she turned. The witch would never see it coming.

The King's Sword still clutched his head but pulled the slashed hood over it once again.

Lex was only a few steps away. As she drew back her sword and flared the algor that would cut through muscle, the Magician swivelled and tossed a dagger.

The algor on the blade flashed before it lodged into Lex's belly, tearing through her chain mail, stopped only by the flat of her sword as she brought it up and caught the hilt.

Too late. It was already inches deep. Lex squeezed her fist, mashing the aeternus into the pouch. But nothing happened, and seconds later, she backed up, gasping not from pain but from the red staining her tunic and mail. *Ignite, damn you!*

The Magician advanced. "Thought I'd forgotten you?" Her face twisted into a grin as renewed tentacles of algor stretched down her sword.

Lex backed up in such a rush that it began—the pain. This wasn't the first time she'd been stabbed. Shock only saved her from agony for so long. Eventually, every movement intensified the hot, piercing sting until even the threat of death wasn't enough to make her power through. She gasped and fell to one knee, still clutching the aeternus as if it would suddenly save her.

The Magician pounced, raised her sword.

Agathos, save me.

As Lex glowered up at her enemy, an arcing light flashed behind the witch's head. A heartbeat later, a flaring blade sliced through the Magician's skull from the back with such vicious precision that it cut through both her eyes and sent icy blood splattering across Lex's face.

She gasped and stumbled backwards as if slapped by the touch of death.

When the Magician's body dropped, the King's Sword was left standing behind with his dripping weapon calmly held out. His eyes glowed with a cold indifference at the feat of having killed the most formidable woman who had ever lived, as if this were nothing but another day of slaying for him.

He reached and grabbed the Staff from Shirin's back, slicing his bloody sword through the sash that tied it and left the small, frail body dangling from the rocky vine, ready to plummet into the shadows below.

Jason held up the Staff, algor still pulsing from his hand and shining across his stony face.

Lex dared not even breathe while the algus didn't pay her attention. She prayed to Agathos that what the Magician had said of the King was a lie. How would he ever be defeated if it wasn't? She'd prayed for so long that the Magician would meet her end that she'd barely thought of what would follow, of how fearsome the one that defeated her would have to be. She'd always assumed it would be Darius.

The King's Sword looked up and finally met Lex's gaze.

"Jason! Give me the Staff!" Selene rushed up to the man and tried to grab his arm, but he'd already slipped out of reach and towards Lex.

Did her sister really think he'd just hand it over if she asked?

"Jason!" Selene cried again. "Ophelia said it was I who had to take the Staff!"

The King's Sword stopped. His eyes narrowed slightly.

But all Lex saw was her sister's expression, so foreign it was like that of a stranger—impatient and petulant as she reached for the Staff again and Jason turned to face her.

The Magician had been telling the truth? Lex clenched her jaw until her teeth ached. Hot tears threatened to fall from her eyes, so she flared algor to seal them in. She'd seen enough Numbered to know her sister was dead, and whoever Selene was now was twisted and warped beyond hope. Lex should have trusted her gut, should have imprisoned Selene when they'd had the chance. And now what? What was this woman's real aim?

It wasn't like Lex would live long enough to find out. She grimaced at the pain from her wound and lowered her head. She couldn't stand. She couldn't fight.

63

Darius – Mount Psilos

Darius dug his elbows into the ground and crawled forward another few inches, still weakened by the Staff's aura but not as much as before. It had taken almost all his strength to drag himself around Hadrian's men—who still lay pinned under heavy armour—and to the edge of the obsidian platform.

His exhausted body begged to collapse. But he'd never give in.

The Viridians all watched with a twisted mix of hate and horror as he moved just out of their reach. Some thrust their spears at him, but their blows were too weak to breach his mail.

He paid them little heed. Instead, all his focus was on the basalt rings that could soon be his death or salvation. The odd glint of orange light glowed from the Blades as if they knew a test was soon to come and prepared to unleash their fury.

At the back of his mind, Lyra's ever-increasing panic threatened to steal his nerve. She knew what he was crawling to do, and was unsure whether to obey his command for her to stay and defend Sulla or race towards him as she longed to do. But he'd never let her near the fires about to spring from the weapons.

His hands reached the edge of the obsidian rings, and all it would take now was for him to extend his fingers and touch the gleaming black stone. But he dared not yet. Glancing up one last time, a new panic gripped him when he spotted the Magician's body hanging over a stone vine, with Lex kneeling nearby. Heavy blood spilled from the rock, and he prayed it wasn't Lex's. Selene was standing without an evident injury, but a new threat towered over her. The King's Sword stood ready, Staff of Arria in one hand and his lethal blade in the other.

Darius was out of time to hesitate or fear. This was for Lex and Selene. Nothing else would save them.

With a cry of desperate anger, he conjured algor over his whole body, then reached out and pressed his fingers to the obsidian.

Fire erupted in front of him until all he saw were swirling flames, as blinding as the sun, as if the mountain itself spat bile at him. The heat swirled and writhed until forming a molten ball that ended at the exact point the obsidian rings rose from the ground. Only his fingers were caught in the torrent, pained by the flames but withstanding the damage of the heat.

He pushed forward and thrust his hand and arm deeper into the fire. And something happened. It burned, but at the same time, the fibres of the muscles in his arm tensed with some of their old strength, as if the Staff's weakness were dulled. The arm hadn't its full rakkan might, but it had more than enough to claw at the basalt ground and drag the rest of his body into the thick, searing air.

Blinding light engulfed him. But he finally had the strength to stand and trudge forwards. The only things he saw now were the two black objects he sought. Their ferven burned, despite his algor, as if the inferno were only stopped by the thinnest of sheets from consuming him. His algor slowed him. Every stride was like trekking through a hurricane. But that only meant he strode at a normal human's pace. Each step closer intensified the heat and consumed his algor until only a hint of blue was left visible in his eyes.

The algor on his arm failed first and let the heat burn his sleeve to ash in an instant. Ferven seared his skin to blisters, but he carried on and flared algor again with every ounce of energy he had until the glowing runes of the Blades could be made out amidst the swirling, raging tongues of ferven they spat.

They were buried into obsidian that somehow withstood the heat, and Darius prayed he had the strength to take them.

"Darius!" Sulla's yell filled his mind. It must have been via Lyra because he only heard the roar and crackle of fire.

The distraction was enough for his algor to fail again on his head. A patch of his hair smoked and burned away before he could renew his algor. But all he could do was press on.

Once within a yard, he saw the hilts of the Blades, the only part of them that wasn't coated in flame. They called to him, inviting. And he answered.

With a last push of algor to his palms, he reached out and grabbed the hilts just above the two cross guards. He'd expected red-hot pain, but instead, iciness bit his hands. Suddenly the spiralling fires reversed. The runic symbols that had spewed now sucked as if the mountain inhaled its hate through the gaps.

A few seconds later, only bright spots filled Darius's vision, a ghost of the torrent that had tested him. His algor soothed the searing pain covering him, and after a few breaths to verify he still lived, he realised the Blades remained buried in the rock. He tugged gently, and they slid out as if gliding through water. The symbols of fire pulsed, then dimmed.

Left with only hot, ash-filled air to breathe, Darius coughed up the stink of his seared hair. Half of his mail armour hung loose and melted where the Blades' power had breached his algor.

Although the ferven of the Blades was gone, he was still standing while Hadrian and all the rakkans around continued weakly shifting on the ground. He squeezed the hilts of the heavy weapons with some of his usual strength. If he had to guess, he'd say he was a little stronger than a human, but then why could he bear the weight of the kuraminium swords in his hands? Could it be they allowed him to?

As he gripped the Blades, he felt a warmth emanating from them, moving with a force of its own as if energy flowed out of the metal and towards something above, towards the Staff of Arria.

When the spots in his vision had faded enough, he saw the King's Sword and Selene up high, still facing off against each other in some sort of heated argument that hadn't yet become violent. But it was only a matter of time.

With the speed of an algus, he sprinted towards the vines stemming from the basin floor, soon approaching the edge of the smoking obsidian rings.

The downed Viridian Warlord and his guardians were the first in his path, too weak to stave off any attack he could launch. But he hadn't the time, and he wouldn't give Hadrian the mercy of a quick death.

As he ran, the Viridian Warlord's horned helmet rose until the pair exchanged a glower of loathing. There were no guardians between them this time. No magic to stop him. Darius raised his new weapons, and without any intention or effort on his part, the

Blades burst with fire, the runes hissing with ferven until white-hot.

Darius neared. Hadrian roared and began bringing up his armguard to block Darius as he swung both swords towards the brute. Although weakened, the Viridian Warlord bore enough strength to twist his body until Darius's weapons hit the rakkan's solid armour rather than the exposed flesh he'd intended.

Darius hadn't the time to adjust. His first sword struck the Viridian Warlord square on his armguard, but he barely felt the blow. The blade cut through the kuraminium as if it were straw and cleaved through the rakkan's arm and bone. Hadrian hadn't the time to roar in pain before Darius's second blade followed his first, through the open space and straight across Hadrian's cuirass. Again, the fire of the blade sliced the armour as if it weren't there, and the deep slash tore through the Viridian Warlord's innards and bowels with a burst of blood and filth.

What the…? Although reeling with shock and disbelief at the power in his hands, Darius didn't slow his sprint a fraction. The wound he'd just inflicted was fatal, but it wouldn't kill quickly. Hadrian could wait. Lex and Selene couldn't.

He leapt between the Viridians, his feet finding any free bit of ground he could. Readying the Blades, he waited for the warriors to reach out and grab his legs as he ran, but only a few Viridian Guardians tried, too slow to catch him. The rest of the Viridian Legionnaires merely gaped and froze as he passed, and even the Subdued only took a glance at him, then ran. Did they fear him or the ferven spitting from his weapons?

He reached a rock vine stemming from the ground and tore up it. Each stride took him closer to the Staff and weakened his muscles until the Blades became even heavier. But this time, it wasn't enough to bring him down.

When he tried to summon ferven of his own, it only sparked for a moment, then fizzled out. It was more than before, but not enough. So all he had left were his algus abilities—no advantage over the most celebrated algus in the Empire.

Now higher, hellish winds buffeted him harder. With a last leap, he reached the top and only slowed when a few yards from Lex's kneeling figure. She'd dropped her sword, and her hands were thick and red, one permanently clenched into a fist with his necklace hanging between her fingers.

How badly was she injured? He'd been too slow, too weak.

As he approached her, the King's Sword suddenly turned his attention from Selene to him.

"She said I should take it!" Selene cried desperately at the algus's back.

Once in front of Lex, Darius halted and raised his swords, and the flames from each fizzed and waned into only ghosts of fire, sighing in the air and flowing towards the Staff in thin orange wisps of smoke.

"How hurt are you?" Darius asked, not taking his eyes from the King's Sword. The man's sole movement came from his tattered cloak.

"I'm fine." But Lex's voice was forced and laden with pain. "Selene's gone. That isn't her."

Was Lex saying that because the Magician was dead and hadn't fixed Selene's mind? But the moment Selene's glare shifted from Jason to Darius, he saw the ugly baring of her teeth as she slowly walked to stand beside the King's Sword.

"What is this…?" Darius's words were so quiet he didn't expect anyone to answer. Selene's glower hurt more than a spear through his side would have. After all this time with her…

"Kill them both." Lex's voice bore vicious hate as she struggled up to one knee, one hand now clutching her sword, the other gripping her abdomen as she hunched over. At her feet lay his necklace, the glowing aeternus still pressed into the powder pouch where she'd clasped it.

Any heat from the Blades that had warmed Darius's skin disappeared as his whole body went numb, as if it were no longer his own. This couldn't be happening. The Chief Priest had assured them the Magician couldn't change someone so drastically…

Lex clambered back to her feet, all her weight on the leg that wasn't stained a deep red.

"Stay back." Darius planted his body firmly on the stone vine between her and the others. There was no way he'd let her fight in this state.

Before he had time to collect his thoughts, the King's Sword rushed forward with his weapon drawn back and flaring algor. Darius crossed the heavy blades and caught Jason's first strike between them. But when he pushed forwards and tried to throw the algus off-balance with his usual rakkan strength, all he managed was to shove back the sword.

In one swift motion, Jason withdrew his weapon and spun, lighting a ring of algor around himself as he brought the sword over to slice with such speed Darius barely felt the air shift at the incoming attack.

Darius brought one blade up above his head, and the swords clashed, sending sparks over his hair and tattered tunic as the strike stopped dead.

Jason let out a short gasp at the block, as if surprised Darius had the reflexes to defend against the rapid attack. Without his rakkan senses, Darius wouldn't have survived it.

Unable to budge Jason's raised sword, Darius stabbed his other blade towards the algus's stomach, an unstoppable strike against most foes in that position without a shield. But Jason began moving before Darius had even thrust his blade.

Left lunging and stabbing nothing but air, Darius stopped the stroke as quickly as he could and began retracting his extended weapons to defend his exposed torso.

But Selene flew from behind the King's Sword in a furious blur. Her weapon arced towards Darius's still stretched arm. Darius sensed the air shifting but was already moving as fast as he could.

So he twisted the extended arm, flared algor across his steel armguard and braced himself. When Selene's chop hit, it slammed Darius's arm down, stabbing his fiery blade into the rocky vine they stood upon. Selene's strike failed to pierce his armour, but the force cracked a bone in his forearm and almost stole the weapon from his grasp.

Somehow, he held on, hand trembling with a new weakness that was yet to register pain over his fear.

What had they done to Selene? How much of her was left? Whatever the answers, he'd never know them. He had his weapons, but it was too late. His weight was no longer over his feet, and the only thing holding him upright was the blade digging into the stone and the faltering strength of a partially fractured arm that threatened to snap at any moment

He swung across his other blade to defend against the inevitable follow-up attack, but in this position, there was little he could parry without rakkan strength.

As if smelling the weakness, Jason brought up his sword again with a silent, vicious flash that shone algor across his face. There was an unrelenting intensity in his glare but no malice, no anger—only cold death.

But as his sword flew down, Selene suddenly brought hers and parried the attack.

"She told *me* to do it!" Selene cried while Darius seized his chance, regained his balance, and backed up a couple of yards until he stood just in front of Lex. Pain finally registered in his left arm, and it surrendered to its injury, dropping one of the Blades to clatter onto the stone vine. Slowly, the trace of ferven dimmed in the dark metal, and the sword's twin spat all the more wildly because of it.

When Darius looked up, Selene and the King's Sword were glaring at one another. Suddenly, Jason's cold gaze fixated on him again. Except this time, his eyes bore emotion. The algus frowned, gaze darting all about the area as if expecting an arrow from somewhere that never arrived.

And then it came. A pulse burst from behind Darius, first sending a light so brilliant it consumed his sight with a curtain of pure white, and next a force that pushed him forwards until he almost tumbled off the edge. Apart from causing shock and blindness, the flash hadn't harmed him, and it took him a second to realise what it had been—Lex's powder. This was his chance.

He flared ferven in his eyes to see if it would aid him, but it did nothing to break the white film still cloaking his sight. So instead, he sensed the air, trying to block out the swirling mountain winds and discern movement from any figures ahead. Moving forward with each foot carefully finding the centre of the rocky vine, he stretched out his sword arm but with the blade turned away. Whatever had happened to Selene, he wasn't ready to accidentally kill her. He wanted answers.

Something moved ahead of him, like an arm reaching out, and when he got closer, he suddenly struck a hand and felt it ball into a fist and pull back. Whoever it belonged to shifted their head.

He felt it move at too great a height for it to belong to Selene. Before he'd decided to react, he sensed a sharp sword screaming through the whiteness in front of him. He brought up his blade to parry and kicked low, praying he connected with Jason's legs with the blind swing.

His foot hit a knee, and he heard the man's grunt as the leg buckled and the body above fell, air streaming out. Stepping back, Darius kicked again, this time landing a blow on the figure's head and sending it toppling over the edge.

Darius stepped back as the darkness of the mountain began to break into his vision at last. He waited for the weakness in his limbs to dull as the Staff plummeted below, but it didn't. His left arm throbbed with a deep pain that battled to steal his attention. But he wouldn't take it from the woman's figure now coming back into focus.

Selene stood alone with the Staff of Arria in one hand and her sword shaking in the other. She blinked and gaped at no one and nothing in particular, paralysed and still blind.

He should have sprinted up to her, knocked the sword or the Staff from her hand. But all he could do was gape at the woman he'd loved. He knew a part of her was still inside, but what had made her do this?

Although his hesitation lasted only a few heartbeats, his chance to disarm her passed, and her gaze finally rested upon him with the same ugliness that had twisted it before.

"Do you know who you are?" Darius's voice was powerless and dry.

"I'm the woman you forced yourself on," she snarled.

Her accusation almost made him forget the pain in his arm. "I've never—"

"You know what you did." She thrust out the Staff and pointed it between his eyes.

The move had no effect on him, but the blade in his hand faltered and hissed even more.

"Kill her!" Lex cried as she hobbled right up behind him. "It's not Selene anymore."

His sword arm trembled. That was Lex's solution to everything. She'd killed Omid in Laltos without hesitation, but the act had left a wound in Darius that he didn't want to repeat.

"Who fed you these lies?" he asked.

"Lies?" Selene scoffed. "I have the scars on my back to prove it."

"What? You think *I* made those?"

Selene faltered. "If not you, then who?"

"Whoever you've been with for the past year!" he said.

She frowned. Her eyes danced as if he'd finally caused her warped mind to have a rational thought. For the first time, he saw a break in her angry mask.

Lex tried to push past him, but he braced himself and blocked her way. Was he getting through to his former lover?

"Who were you with?" Darius battled to contain his rage at the thought of someone doing this to her. "This was no Viridian or the Magician. Whoever it was, I'll burn every inch of flesh from their bones before I let them die."

The expression now on Selene's face was that of a woman wrestling against an almost overwhelming force. "He helped me."

"Who?" Darius carefully stepped towards her, so slowly she'd know he wasn't threatening her.

"The Magician has nothing compared to his power," Selene whispered.

"Who?" Darius took another step when he saw she hadn't reacted to his first move.

She hesitated and pulled back the Staff. For a few moments, her silent stare lingered on him, weighing him up, testing his words against whatever went on in her mind. Then, she began walking towards him.

"She'll kill us." Lex tried to get past him again, but he held her hunched figure behind him on the vine.

When Selene came close enough to strike him, she made no move to. Her sword hung loose in her grasp as he looked at her as he once had, studied the faint freckles on her face with love.

"Darius…" Her eyes softened, and she leaned in as if to embrace him.

For a moment, a wave of relief took away his hurt and sorrow, took away the fear he bore over losing the two women with him now.

But then he sensed her sword move.

Suddenly rigid and strong, her sword arm swung upwards from her side and burst with algor.

Darius hadn't the time or space to block, but he brought up his blade reflexively, felt the bite of Selene's sword as it cut into his hand and stole his last weapon away from him.

The blade hissed as it spun into the air and plummeted to the dark ground far below, taking most of the strength he'd had with it.

Suddenly his legs gave out, the Staff's vines of weakness gripping his body. He dropped to one knee as Lex's sword erupted with blue fire and swung above him, clashing with Selene's weapon with a shriek of steel on steel.

Darius pressed his arms into the rock and battled to keep himself upright. His muscles still had a little energy, and the whispers of a blade caught his ear. A few feet behind Selene, the other twin blade lay on the stone vine with a new glow emanating from its runes. It stole some of the Staff's power, but not enough for him to fight.

Lex stepped over him with a cry of pain, sending blood splattering from her belly with the move. The warm fluid caught his neck and felt worse than anything else that could have touched him. He couldn't watch her die, but what *could* he do?

The two sisters clashed with a flurry of strikes that lit up the night sky. Despite Lex's infirmities, she pressed forward and pushed her sister back through a relentless onslaught that took the pair beyond Darius's second blade.

He forced himself to his hands and knees and crawled towards the sword, biting down at the agony the movement brought to his injured arm. All he imagined was Lex pierced by Selene's weapon. The anguish the thought aroused rivalled seeing Selene lost in Laltos. While there was still breath left in him, he'd never let it happen again.

Each swing Lex took left her with visibly less strength, more laboured, more exhausted.

But every foot closer to the Blade he got, strength returned to his legs, and when he finally grasped the hilt with his fingers, it burst in scarlet flame and gave him the power to stand again. He picked up the dreaded weapon and rose to see Selene lunge forward with a stab that cut Lex's good thigh.

A follow-up attack smacked Lex's sword from her grasp and brought the injured algus to her knees.

Lex shrieked in pain, clutching her bleeding stomach while her sword tumbled down and bounced off the stone vine, ringing in the night.

For a heartbeat, Darius gaped. He'd never seen Selene so full of hate, so intent on slaying the one before her. It was a hideous face that wasn't Selene's.

Lex was right. And Gorgias had said the Numbered could never come back from what had been done to them. Darius only had one option.

Selene towered over her fallen sister, then roared as she chopped with her sword and flared algor to the point.

Darius rushed forward, a sudden burst of speed that Selene didn't see until too late. As her sword came down, Darius's came up with a parry that launched Selene's weapon up and over her head.

She managed to keep hold of the hilt, but it didn't matter.

Darius looped his swing around, then stabbed with a yell of anguish and regret. Ferven blazed from the runes etched onto his sword with a rage that made him wince.

And despite its lethal sharpness, he felt the moment the point met Selene's chest.

He carried on the thrust, closing his eyes when the blade scraped across bone and the serrated edge shred her flesh, then burst through the back of her torso.

Selene screeched so vehemently it set a buzz in his ears, and when he finally opened his eyes, tears burning them, he saw the pain in her grimace. He couldn't bear it for more than a second. He ripped out his sword, tearing at flesh and lung and bringing the blood of yet another he loved to splatter over him.

She stumbled back, a red hole in her chest, gaping at him with hate and agony.

He opened his mouth to say something to her, but only a silent breath came out.

When she stepped back again, her heel slipped off the edge, and she tipped over. The look she gave him only darkened and twisted further, and it was the last thing he saw as she fell, a haunting image that remained engraved in his mind long after she plunged into one of the chasms below.

He kept staring, longing for those eyes to have looked at him as they once had, the first pair of eyes that had ever seen him as something other than a warrior, that had ever wanted him for something other than slaying. And he'd stolen the light from them.

The Staff's grip on him released entirely, only to be replaced by another pain, like a band crushing his chest. Whatever happened next, all Darius knew was that at some point he choked, realising he hadn't been breathing. His vision blurred with tears, but his mind resisted believing anything that had just happened. He'd never known real love before he met Selene, never known what it was to be loved. Even though the woman he'd loved had probably been erased long ago, the feeling of his blade tearing through her was one he'd never forget, one that would never leave his conscience.

He dropped the blade on the vine and knelt beside Lex, taking her into his trembling arms. The blood and gore from her wounds sent a fierce stench to his nose, and even though he was now desensitised, he had to bury the urge to retch by force of will.

"Lex?" he said, running a bloody hand through her soft hair.

"I'll live," she grunted. He felt the tension in her jaw from the back of her head.

Tiro dove from the dark sky and landed by her legs, worry plain in the falcon's twitches.

"It'll be all right," Darius whispered, although the words were more for his own comfort. Selene was dead. If Lex died too... "It'll be all right," he repeated.

His hands shook, remembering the blade cutting through Selene's body. He pressed his eyes shut and tried to block out the thought, but it only plagued him more.

"The Blades..." Lex croaked.

"Don't worry about that," Darius said, cradling her more tightly in his arms. "Hadrian's as good as dead."

"No... I mean you need to get them down there."

The basin below thundered with the metallic sound of centuries of warriors roaring and clambering to their feet, readying their shields and weapons. The Staff was gone. The Black and Viridian Legions had awoken.

64

Lex – Mount Psilos

Fiery orange lights erupted once again in the basin below as Lex gaped over the edge of the high rock vine, wondering which dark pit or crevice her sister had fallen into. Had that just happened? Had Darius killed Selene to save her? Even though it hadn't been the Selene they knew inside, it had pained Lex to swing a sword at her, to try to spill her blood, to watch her die…

Lex had doubted Darius could ever lay a hand on her sister, warped or not. The shock at seeing him wielding the Twin Blades had been nothing compared to the shock of seeing him stab Selene with such a savage blow. It was almost enough to distract her from her wounds. Almost.

His strong arms wrapped around her and brought a relief that nothing else in the Empire would have. But that relief came tainted with something she'd never imagined before—blood. Her sister's blood. That's all Lex now felt as his hands ran over her shoulder.

On any other day before then, she could have stayed in Darius's arms for hours to distract from the blinding pain of her wounds. But her sister's dying face was too fresh for her to bear the feel of the man yet.

And his task wasn't over. The fight below threatened to rage again while blood seeped between the fingers pressed to her stomach. She needed bandaging, but she dared not begin before Darius steadied his shaking body and went below.

"Darius," she whispered. "You need to go."

He broke his tight embrace and leaned back, his irises glistening with algor. But the streaks down his cheeks betrayed the tears he'd already shed.

"Show me your wounds," he said.

She shook her head and wrapped her arm further around her abdomen. "It's nothing a bandage won't fix." She prayed. But she'd never taken a stab this deep.

Without another word, he reached down and forced his hands under hers. Then, gripping her chain mail and tunic with his rakkan fingers, he tore it all open and winced with fresh tears at the sight of the oozing wound.

"It's too deep to cauterise," he said quietly, as if to himself. He dug around in his pocket and removed one of his bandages before bundling it and pressing hard into her stomach.

The cloth was dry and hot on her skin like it burned. Lex cursed but knew asking the man to stop would be pointless. The truth was, she couldn't have bandaged her belly properly herself given the pain simply moving caused.

This was the part she feared. She needed a distraction, and focusing Darius on what lay next was more than enough. As stunned as she'd been to see him grab the Twin Blades, her heart had leapt when he had. Her chance to see him as what she'd always known him capable of being approached. She knew without asking that he hadn't taken the Blades to ascend as a leader but to save her or Selene. But whatever the reason, a leader he had to be.

"Get both the Blades before you go down there," she said.

"I'll only need one," Darius replied. "These things tear through kuraminium and steel alike."

"Not to fight. You need to stop the fighting. The leader of all rakkans must wield both and command all."

Darius froze, the weight of his thoughts darkening his seared face.

"It was the King who turned Selene," Lex said. "The Magician said it after touching her and seeing her mind. He must have another goman."

Darius let out a low breath, hands trembling all the more but this time clenched into fists.

"Unite the legions," Lex continued. "It's the only way we can bring down his empire."

Darius's response was only a belated, sullen nod. But at least he wasn't arguing against his fate now. She didn't have the heart to ask the full extent of the horror going on in his mind or any other question.

Eventually, Lex got used to the pressure on her belly and the agony. Pain was something she'd known for so long that it was almost natural for it to be back.

As the chimes of clashing swords and shields began filling the night air below once again, Darius finished wrapping the tight bandage around her, and it seemed to have stemmed her bleeding. When she reached into her pocket for her vial of the weeping plant's tears, he went to get another bandage.

"I can wrap my legs myself," she said, grabbing his wrist. "You must go."

He gave her a nervous look for a moment, like a gladiator before entering the arena for the first time, but soon a furious scowl took over, and he turned to the blade on the vine nearby.

He growled, "The Viridian war finishes tonight."

65

Darius – Mount Psilos

Darius picked up one of the Twin Blades lying nearby. This time, the fire that came to life was a controlled yet intense flare that not only lit up the sword in his hand but another that caught his eye. Resting on a stone vine below, the blade's brother called out to be wielded again.

Leaving Lex wasn't easy, but many below could die if this battle didn't end now. He'd known this moment would come as soon as he'd decided to take the weapons yet still didn't feel ready for it. Fate rarely waited for him to be ready, though.

Lyra. Nudge one of the field surgeons and bring them to Lex.

Once sure his escort had received the message, he set off at a sprint with his tired limbs fuelled only by rage. His chaotic mind couldn't deal with the King and what that might mean at the moment. The Viridians were all he could focus on while keeping his sanity. They might not have tortured Selene, but that did nothing to dampen his hate. They'd killed Brutus and slaughtered tens of thousands. The God of Justice needed appeasing.

His leap to the second blade was longer than it had looked, and his foot almost smashed completely through the vine when he landed, but he eventually reached and picked up the sword. His injured arm hated him for the effort it took as he scanned the basin below him. Armoured bodies moved unencumbered once again, but apart from the odd Viridian Guardian charging into the Black Legion's shield wall, most stood and gaped up at him.

They'd all seen him take the Twin Blades, but most wouldn't have seen his mortal blow to the Viridian Warlord. His eyes swept the area until he found the rings of obsidian again, and Hadrian lying beside them with a cluster of Viridian Guardians kneeling nearby.

He ran across the stone vines towards the brute, the Blades now a brilliant white in a display that lit up the armour of those below. When he neared the huddle of guardians, he leapt from the vines and onto the basin floor, landing with a thump that shook the ash on the ground.

His fists tightened around the hilts of the Blades, ready to fight once again and slay anyone that dared stand against him. But none so much as breathed. For the last few yards he walked, Margalvians, Subdued and Viridians alike parted for him and winced at the brightness of his weapons' aura.

The guardians turned as he neared, the sight and stink of fear obvious as they backed away and revealed their bloody and rotten ruler lying in the dirt.

Darius had waited too long for this moment. The fiend had better not be dead already.

But to his sinister relief, Hadrian coughed a spray of blood onto the rakkan closest to him—a burly commander with hair as rusty as the Viridian Warlord's. Darius guessed it was one of

Hadrian's sons, and the sight gave him an idea of how to humiliate the Warlord even more than making him die accompanied by the stench of his own entrails.

Darius stopped a yard short of Hadrian and glared into the commander's black and defeated eyes.

"You…" Darius pointed a blade at the commander.

The rakkan slowly rose, hands empty of weapons and raised to show it.

"Come to me," Darius ordered.

The commander looked down at his warlord, whose furious face said so much that words weren't necessary. But the commander stepped over Hadrian and obeyed Darius nonetheless until he stood in front of him with a lifted chin that showed a readiness to cross into hell.

It took all Darius's restraint not to send him there. As far as he'd seen, each Viridian was as depraved as the last, and the world would be a better place if he put them all to the sword. Then he really would have earned the title of "Slayer."

But death was too kind a punishment to mete out to some.

"Kneel," he growled.

The commander's expression hardened as if he'd rather die, but then the rakkan's gaze fell to the Twin Blades, and he froze.

Darius readied himself to strike in a fraction of a heartbeat, ready to mercilessly punish disobedience in front of every rakkan there. But to his surprise, the commander wilted and slowly lowered himself.

Hadrian spat filth and blood at his kneeling subordinate's back, but he was the only one to do so.

Darius had assumed it would take at least a dozen executions to get even a single Viridian to surrender.

He turned his attention to the hundreds of them still watching and summoned ferven in his throat to add to his roar.

"All of you too! Kneel before your overlord!" His voice thundered in his ears as if it weren't his own, as if it belonged to a glorious warlord such as his grandfather or Trogus himself.

The warriors around began falling to their knees, and he turned to bask in their humiliating submission. But in the sight of so many defeated foes, he found no pleasure, no pride, no relief—only a hollow emptiness worsened by Selene's and Lex's blood still staining his body.

Eventually, the Margalvians mirrored the Viridians in kneeling without having to be prompted. Including, as Lyra saw, the Black Warlord himself.

The Subdued remained standing, all nervously looking from Darius to the Viridian Warlord and back. Darius roared and ignited ferven on his hands that set off the Blades into a column of fire soaring from him towards the clouds above. His yell soon became lost in the rumble of flames that whirled tightly around his body, and every Subdued backed away with horror before dropping to their knees too.

After terrifying Hadrian's algus into submission, Darius let the rage of his ferven fade away, struck with a fresh fear. What now? Usually, he had Lex or Brutus to help him in moments like this, to guide him on the best course of action. They'd both want these Viridians humiliated and dead. He'd achieved the first under their dying warlord's nose, but what kind of message would it send to the other legions if he slaughtered everyone there? And would Brutus have been proud of a man who did that?

No. The rakkan would have cursed his name and quite rightly. Whatever the Viridians' punishment should be, a massacre of surrendered warriors wasn't just. But that decision didn't help him determine what to do next.

Darius scanned the Viridians, searching for inspiration. And surprising himself, he found it in the form of a small-framed commander behind the lines of Viridian Legionnaires, kneeling but staring at him without a trace of fear, just like the rakkan had in Dolthea.

"Rufus!" Darius called, and waved the man over.

The commander stood as a gust of wind tossed hot ash into the air. Although wearing armour and a scabbard, Rufus clearly hadn't fought or even bothered to pull his weapon from its sheath. The faults of the Viridian Legion were many, but this commander was the least objectionable Darius had met, and the only one who uttered a word of truth or rational thought.

Rufus walked forwards with a quiet confidence in his steps, and when he reached the kneeling commander, Rufus instead remained standing proudly.

"Unsheathe your sword," Darius growled.

With a curious frown, Rufus did as instructed and held out the clean, polished kuraminium spatha as if for inspection.

Darius let the man stand in silence for a moment before speaking. "Now…go and challenge your warlord. Succeed him."

Many of the Viridians grunted their objection to the command and cursed beneath their bowed heads, but Rufus's reaction was as measured as ever. The only insight into his thoughts was when he glanced at Hadrian hungrily out of the corner of his eye.

Before the commander could respond to the order, one of the Viridian Guardians behind Hadrian rose to his feet. The rakkan's tattooed arms bore many symbols whose true meaning Darius had come to know, as he knew the butchery and barbarism behind each one.

"I'll die before I allow such a cowardly challenge," the guardian spat. "I fight in my warlord's stead."

His was a reaction Darius had expected and wouldn't allow. He turned and squared up to the guardian, prepared to give him one chance, despite him probably not deserving it.

"If you wish to be Hadrian's substitute," Darius said, "then I shall be Rufus's."

The guardian's arms tensed and shivered at the threat.

"Or you can stand aside," Darius said, "and allow the challenge to be resolved by the men themselves."

After a few moments of hesitation, the guardian picked up a shield lying nearby. "Never."

A hiss came from the Twin Blades as Darius turned back to Rufus. "Issue the challenge."

The commander eyed the dying Viridian Warlord. "You know they will all challenge me soon after. My brothers won't respect my authority."

"And I will fight in your stead at every contest," Darius said, "so long as you clean up your legion and city from the depraved cluster of waste it is."

Rufus nodded absently as if he'd barely paid attention, then shouted, "Father, I hereby challenge your leadership!"

The guardian roared and rushed forward, drowning Rufus's last words. Ferven ignited on his sword and shield until the rakkan became a charging ball of fire.

But the display would do nothing to protect him from Darius's fury, only sap his strength as the extent of his ferven drained his rakkan power. Darius knew this wasn't a practical exercise of force or might but one of rage. The guardian knew what was coming.

Summoning the true ire of the Blades, Darius rushed forward and swung his good arm towards the rakkan's shield and head behind it. The weapon clashed and sliced through the metal scutum, taking most of Darius's strength to do so. But once through, the Blade cut and tasted flesh, ripped through the guardian's gullet and spine, then sent the once flaring body into the dirt with a hiss of defeated ferven.

The rakkan's head spun and thumped on the ground soon after, but Darius still moved forward and only stopped once he reached the fallen Viridian Warlord.

Hadrian glowered up at him, blood spilling from his lips and staining his beard. As if the sight wasn't off-putting enough, the stench became as foul as any sewer, tolerable only due to the winds delivering a stream of less stifling sulphurous air.

"He'll never last," Hadrian growled with a forced smile.

Darius took in the sight of the rakkan who had killed Brutus, wondering what spot would cause Hadrian the most pain. Judging by the tension in the brute's jaw, the current wound was as excruciating as a crucifixion.

As he pondered, a familiar feline presence approached, and he saw himself through Lyra's eyes—a glowing beacon in the otherwise shadowed crater. His rivalry with the Viridian Warlord had begun because of the brute's attack on his panther. He decided it was only fitting that she should end it.

With a stab of his sword, Darius cut through the meat of Hadrian's good forearm and pinned it to the ground. The rakkan roared and reached across with his handless arm to try to free himself, but Darius was too fast. He swung his other blade, gritting his teeth at the pain of his injury, and cleaved the Warlord's arm again, this time at the elbow.

Hadrian roared and writhed in pain as Darius turned to his escort, seeing the thirst for vengeance in her eyes.

End him.

Lyra snarled and bared her teeth before pouncing at Hadrian's screaming head. When she hit, a crack of bone echoed in the crater, and her canines sank into the Warlord's neck. She tasted blood so foul that Darius spat as if it would rid him of the sensation of the taste.

Usually, Lyra clamped her mouth around the neck of her prey, cutting off their air, subduing them to a quiet death.

But not this time.

She clenched her jaw with a fierce might and threw her head from side to side, letting her fangs rip through the brute's flesh, veins and throat in such a vicious display that, for those moments, she wasn't feline at all; she bore the feral savagery of a wolf, killing her prey through pain and shock and blood loss.

This was for Brutus.

She clamped down harder on Hadrian's ravaged neck while he tried to bat her away with half an arm and ever more feeble strokes. But he hadn't the reach and only sprayed her fur with gore. He squirmed, as helpless as all the souls in the west of the Empire when his legion had scourged the land and people. Lyra showed him the same mercy and pity Darius would have, the same mercy Hadrian had shown others in his life—none at all.

Darius knelt beside the dying Warlord and yelled above his panther's ferocious snarls, "I will tear down everything you have built, melt every stone your name is engraved upon. Your sons and daughters will never utter your name again. You will be forgotten, lost to the passage of time, with no memories lasting other than your death now—cowering and weak, slain by a beast."

Pain and anguish raged in the Warlord's bloodshot eyes while, slowly, his splutters quietened as the underworld ensnared him to hopefully meet justice.

Finally, he fell still, never to plague the world again.

Just as Darius had found in the past, his enemy's death brought no satisfaction or any release of the hate that had burned within him for so long.

Lyra spat out the dead Warlord and stalked back to Darius's side with fangs dripping blood while the rest of the crowd still knelt in silence. Only Rufus remained standing, watching with a pitiless indifference, waiting for the crown he clearly cared for more than for his own father.

Darius reached down and picked up the Viridian Warlord's horned helmet that lay to the side. Then he strode to Rufus and handed him the soiled item.

"This rakkan," Darius shouted, "is the new Warlord of Viridia. Some of you once worshipped that stain of blood over there as if he were a god, but no more! Gods do not fall to a hammer, or a sword or the jaws of a panther. That rakkan was as mortal as any other I've slain.

"Many of you fear me, call me the Dreaded One... You are right to. You're fortunate I don't slay every man here after what you've done. But I'm giving you a chance. Rufus is your new warlord because he's the only one I have even a smidgen of faith in. If anyone challenges him, they'll face me and die as that headless guardian did."

He paused, letting his revenge on the Viridian Warlord sink in. Hadrian was nothing more than a torn pile of flesh and bone. For a long time, his anger had been so focused on one rakkan that it now left a void. But soon, a fresh rage arose when he looked down at his hands still coated in Selene's blood. The King had turned her into a woman she'd have loathed, and had left Darius no choice but to curse himself with the memory of slaying her.

Now he understood Lex's drive, her fury, her relentless pursuit of those who ruled this world. Together, their vengeance would be vicious. He'd crush the King who threatened the few people he cared most for.

It was time for unity, and what better way to bring the rakkans together than to give them a common enemy? Rage threatened to overwhelm him, stoked by a new energy from the Blades in his hands. Now the thought of leading thousands didn't bring fear but a newfound sense of strength.

"There will be no more bloodshed between the rakkan legions," Darius roared. "We face a greater threat that we cannot ignore any longer. Archimedes plagued your lands, drove you back into the mountains that birthed you. Do you really believe you've avenged that by destroying Laltos? Tell me, was it Regent Theodoros who commanded Archimedes? Or was it the *King of Toria*?"

An angry rumble spread throughout the Viridians, his words tapping into the hatred among them.

"Withdraw now! Go back to your home and leave the places you've invaded. Wait within your city until you're called upon. Because the day will come when I muster every rakkan who can wield a sword. The day will come for revenge. The day will come when Toria burns in rakkan fire." His last rallying cry left his mouth in a roar of hate, a sound soon eclipsed by the avid clamour of the legions.

66

Darius – Mount Psilos

Watching the Viridian Legion leaving the mountain stirred a bitter resentment inside Darius. The urge to slay them still lingered but was soon overwhelmed by a new hatred that turned itself inward. He'd been the one to kill Selene or whoever it was that she'd been warped into. If he'd been in her place, he'd want her or anyone else to give him the same relief of death. But that didn't make him loathe himself any less for what he'd done.

He hid his struggle well from the rakkans withdrawing around him, instead standing like the leader he now was. But the urge to collapse soon left little strength in his legs. Tears threatened to flow and had to be quelled by conjuring ferven in his eyes. Only when most had their backs turned did the fight within him cease. Composing himself as much as he could, he walked away, as if with a purpose, and found a quiet place behind one of the rocky stems protruding from the crater.

Once he was sure no one could see him, he dropped to his knees and took the Agathos figurine from where he'd stashed it in his pocket. The lump of aeternus he'd recovered pressed into his palm too, but it was impossible to see the light it symbolised, however weak. All that remained was darkness. *Brutus, how do I bear this?* But as the weight of Selene's death crushed him, he felt someone reach out.

Lyra's presence squeezed itself into his troubled mind, and soon after, her fur physically pressed against him too. He took her in his arms, and the tears flowed again. Even if he'd wanted to appear strong for her, he couldn't have. He'd never borne pain like this before. More than anything, he wanted it to be gone.

But he didn't have any more time for this at the moment. He wiped away the tears and took strength from his panther's presence. Lex needed him. And he had many more difficult trials ahead.

***

The first friendly face Darius found among the Margalvians was Sulla's.

"Where's Lex?" he asked the man.

The grim expression that overtook Sulla's face made Darius's heart stop.

"No…" Darius whispered. "She can't be—"

"She's not dead, Dar." Sulla tried to force a smile but failed. "But her scrape is bad."

"Where is she?" Darius asked.

Sulla signalled behind him to two dark-haired algus lying among many other wounded. "One of the field surgeons tended to her wounds and brought her down while you were toying with the Viridians, but she's cut deep; there's nothing more we can do for her but wait and see if she can avoid infection. Your other friend was found sprawled on the ground. He's broken, but he'll live."

Darius grabbed the rakkan's arm and began pulling him towards where Lex and Gorgias lay.

"We've much to discuss," Darius said. "What happened here will change everything."

"That's putting it mildly," Sulla muttered.

When they reached Lex, she lay on her side with her head resting on one hand, the other still gripping her stomach. Gorgias kept his eyes closed but was breathing deeply and smoothly.

Darius crouched in front of Lex, relieved to see her smile when she saw him, even if the expression was feeble. Her eyes were dilated and slightly closed, hopefully the effects of the weeping plant's tears and not her injuries.

"How's the wound?" he asked.

"Time will tell." She exhaled slowly, but her demeanour changed when she spied the Blades. "I heard you with the Viridians… Did you mean what you said about the King?"

He didn't need to ask what her thoughts were on leading the legions against Toria. Her hatred of the King had laced most of her life, and for years she'd borne the awful emotions now ravaging *his* insides.

"How do you deal with it?" he asked.

"What?"

"The anger. The overwhelming urge to kill."

Her eyes were the only sight so far that calmed his murderous impulses.

"You unleash it," she said. "You channel it. You slay every wretch that took away the ones we love. Justice must be done."

He was under no illusions that this was a thirst for justice anymore. This was revenge. A voice inside spoke to him, told him to resist these feral urges, taking on his grandfather's, then Aran's tone. But rage and fear drowned it out.

"If I'm to lead," Darius said, "I'll need you. Don't let this wound take you." He hadn't the brains for leadership, as he'd displayed in Dolthea. The last thing he needed was more innocent people dying because he'd led them into danger, like that poor freckled girl in the west of the Empire.

"I've always stood by you," Lex said. "And I always will."

The devoted words sent gooseflesh over his body, and something told him that she was loyal to him not just as a leader. There was so much he wanted to say to her in reply, but not in front of Sulla or others. So he simply dropped one of his swords and took her hand gently, feeling her squeeze back but concerned by how hot it was.

Darius then turned to Sulla. "And you. I need those I trust beside me."

Sulla grinned. "If I profess my undying loyalty, will you hold my hand too?"

Although Darius was tempted to scoff at the man for not answering seriously, he realised he needn't have asked the question. When had Sulla ever not stood by him?

"I hope one of you has an idea of what to do next," Darius muttered, already feeling the weight of the Blades. But any temptation to avoid his fate was gone.

"I have plans," Lex said.

"I'll bet you do." The voice behind Darius was cold and tense.

Varro. Darius's first move was to pick up the second Blade again. Then he rose and turned to face the Black Warlord, noting that the rakkan still wore his horned helmet.

"Darius…" Varro growled, hand hovering near his sheathed sword.

"I guess we have a feud to settle," Darius said, unsure where to begin but clutching the Blades tightly.

"No, we don't." Varro paused for a moment as if measuring up Darius before he continued. "Our rakkan lands were once united, much like the humans are today. They called that land Rakka, and I believe it should be known as such again. I am Warlord of the Black Legion, but you are now Overlord of Rakka. Whatever our differences, duty comes first. I hope you remember that."

Darius hadn't any words of response. Despite their past hostility, any bitterness now paled in comparison to his hatred of the King.

"You'll follow me in whatever comes next?" Darius asked.

Varro didn't hesitate before nodding. "I'll do as commanded by my overlord, but will voice my concerns where I have them."

As the only leader of a city that Darius knew, any insights the rakkan had would be useful. He needed not only his friends but dissenters.

He dropped his voice so that only Varro, Lex and Sulla would hear. "If I'm honest, I don't know where to begin."

"Xavala." Lex's face turned marble white. "We'll pay back the blood debt of Laltos."

But Varro shook his head. "First, you must cultivate a bond with all the rakkan warlords. Many resent you, both in the highest and lowest ranks, and warriors that don't believe in a cause won't fight with the vigour we'll need."

What the Black Warlord said made sense, but so was the pressing need to do something about the Xavalan and Torian raids into the west.

"If the Viridians withdraw as I instructed," Darius said, "another legion needs to step in and fill the power vacuum—one that can be trusted."

The three mulled over his words for a while before nodding. They knew it needed to be the Black Legion, which still held a strong position in the south in Denehill.

After a short wince of pain, Lex said, "If we establish a new fortress to guard the gap between the Cliffs of Aphatos and the mountains to the south, it would help protect the entire west from raiders." The confidence with which she spoke suggested this wasn't a plan she'd just devised. "We won't need a rakkan presence farther west."

"We'll have to discuss specifics," Varro said.

When it came to strategy, Darius would defer to those with experience. For now, his task was to win over the rakkans to his cause just as he had inadvertently done in Dolthea and Menara.

"I'll meet with all the warlords," Darius said. "And we'll prepare for the real war to come."

67

Ipu – Toria

Ipu scribbled frantically on the parchment in front of her, collecting the key pieces of information from the mess of notes by spies on her commanding desk. Despite the vast wooden tabletop being so large she couldn't reach the far side standing, not an inch of the mahogany was visible beneath reams of parchments that piled up in small towers and spilled onto the floor. Sweat dripped down the smooth skin below her nose, her mask reflecting her own warmth. But that was purposeful. The roaring fire beside her was stacked twice as high as usual, and the orange and sandy colours on the artistic walls of the small room intensified the heat she missed so much. It reminded her of Goma's humid summer, the home she'd never see again. And of her fallen husband.

Waiting to hear the full details of which future had played out was the worst part of being Toria's king. Ophelia would walk through the concealed door any minute, but Ipu had other work to do. She lost herself in the One Mind again to see her future memories and began scribbling. One fiery image caught her attention, and she dove deeper into it, seeing a picture she'd drawn in a fit of red ink—the Silk City burned to ash and dust.

She withdrew from that memory and viewed another she saw. She stood at the back of an army in the gap south of the Cliffs. Her victory was near as she watched the charging swifts of the Alogos army harry retreating rakkan legionnaires with algor-coated spears and arrows. This memory mirrored others she'd seen of triumph. The rakkans had never ventured far enough east to feel the true might of a cavalry. They thought the Silk City was strong, but Aristippus only bought the second class of the Alogos breeding program. That was one of her key advantages, but still… All depended on Ophelia and Jason having succeeded.

As she withdrew from that memory and scanned the others, some began to fall away, vanishing into the darkness of her mind as events in the world happened and those memories became impossible.

Coming back to her senses, Ipu heard the door swinging open on its oiled hinges, and Ophelia slowly stepped inside. Her harrowed expression was one beleaguered after a long and fast journey, but there was a twinkle of something in the woman's eyes.

"*Report*," Ipu commanded, unable to wait a moment longer.

"Hadrian and the Waif Magician are dead, my king," Ophelia said. "But Selene failed. Darius still lives, and he has the Blades."

Ipu cursed and began scribbling at once on a fresh sheet of parchment. The gamble she'd taken hadn't paid off in full. The chances Darius would take the Blades hadn't been high, but enough to be a worry. Still, it had been worth the risk of letting him live until the Mount because it had been their best chance of retrieving the Staff. The coming war would be fierce, but the combined might of Shirin and a Viridian overlord would have been unstoppable.

"What about the Staff? Don't tell me they have it…"

When Ophelia didn't answer, Ipu took her eyes from the parchment and saw a smirk on the Orator's face, just as she had in some visions of the future. The relief passing over her seemed to make the orange hue in the room all the more vibrant. Ophelia stepped aside to reveal a man hobbling behind her, the one Ipu had sculpted and moulded into the finest algus alive.

Ipu wiped the sweat dripping from her chin as Jason limped one step at a time, left arm and leg broken and bleeding into his grey tunic. But it was his other arm that arrested Ipu's gaze.

A triumphant flutter went through her stomach.

Clasped tightly in Jason's grasp was a staff as black as shadow. The Staff of Arria.

Other books in the series:

A Mark Of Gods

Prequel to the Rakkan Conquest series

Available for FREE at AndyBlinston.com

The Slayer of Gods is coming

Javad dreams of the eastern sands, of a life where he and his family are free from slavery to the Empire's gods. But those dreams are fading.

When a panther is attacked outside his town, the blame is wrongfully laid on his brother. He tries to convince the people of the truth, but they aren't interested; they only want someone to take the wrath of the panther's master...

The Slayer of Gods is bent on revenge.

Javad's brother will be offered in appeasement, but Javad won't stand by and watch them condemn an innocent boy.

Even if it kills him, Javad will save his brother from meeting the merciless Slayer.

Printed in Great Britain
by Amazon

13240508R00369